F

by

Copyright © 2019 by Jim Mather
All Rights Reserved

No parts of this publication may be reproduced, stored in a retrieval system, or transmitted in any form or by any means, electronic, mechanical, photocopying, recording, or otherwise, without the prior written permission of the copyright owner.

This book is sold subject to the condition that it shall not, by way of trade or otherwise, be lent, resold, hired out, or otherwise circulated without the publisher's prior consent in any form of binding or cover other than that in which it is published and without a similar condition including this condition being imposed on the subsequent purchaser. Under no circumstances may any part of this book be photocopied for resale.

This is a work of fiction. Any similarity between the characters and situations within its pages and places or persons, living or dead, is unintentional and co-incidental.

Dedication

This book is dedicated to my dear wife Caroline, my daughter Lauren (the inspiration to finish this novel and a fellow author), my mom (always told us we could achieve anything we strived for) and my sister, Cindy (the best writer in the family). Thank you for all the time, love and support you provided during this process. Also, Del, Andre, Ritch and Cory, my close friends who test read the first drafts and provided input that helped shape the final version. And, to my editor, Tim who guided me through the more technical aspects of writing my first novel. Special thanks to each of you.

Preface

I love sports and the athletes who play them. I also love the intrigue, drama and excitement of suspense novels–all things geo-political, criminal, international and financial. Finally, I love a great story. An interesting literary journey that lets me escape to an exciting other-worldly dimension with great characters I can identify and connect with. I want to immerse myself in their world and accompany them through the highs and lows of their adventures to an emotional climax that leaves me on the edge of my seat right to the very end.

Big League is a sports action adventure novel that follows two very different NHL rookies as they move through their first pro hockey experiences. Their fledgling sports careers are quickly turned up-side down by dramatic events and unseemly characters that exist on the dark outside fringes of pro sports. You'll laugh and empathize with David Stone and Riley Sawyer as they compete against each other, get to know one another, and share a life altering, death defying saga that makes the game they play seem very minor league. Who ever thought hockey could be a game of life and death?

Testimonials

"A true to life sports adventure novel. Loved it. Jim gets the world of professional hockey and turns an exciting hockey story into a real thriller. A great read for anyone who loves sports and international intrigue."

John J.

"Wow. This is fun. My favourite things in one novel, sports with an adventure twist. Loved it."

Del R.

Chapter 1

The hot sun of August had turned David's skin a bright shade of crimson as he laboured diligently on the family farm. With every muscular contortion, a contradictory combination of pain and self-satisfaction flowed through him. After another few hours of hoisting 60-pound hay bales onto a flatbed trailer it would be time for him to hit the local high school gym for his daily training. David stared into the distance at his father, Paul Stone, who was propped high in his tractor seat, focused intently on completing yet another monotonous lap around the slowly transforming field. Every half minute or so the automated baler he was piloting through the deep swaths would spit out a perfectly bound golden cube like so many rabbit droppings.

What a life, thought David, raising a grease stained forearm to wipe the sweat and dust from his brow. *This farming thing is definitely not for me.*

Since sunrise, David, his father and older brother, Luke, had been working the fields of their family farm, 60 km southeast of Swift Current, Saskatchewan. Hard work was nothing new at this time of year for everyone in the region with the onset of harvest, preparing livestock for market and trying to keep rickety old combines, grain trucks and other equipment operational until early November when the cash started to roll in. There always seemed to be way too many things to do, but really never enough time or enough hands to get all the work done.

This saga had been much of David's life for 20 years. But, this summer was different. That's because David Stone had quite unexpectedly received an invite to the Detroit Red Wings' rookie training camp as an undrafted and unsigned walk on. In early September, he would fly to Auburn Hills, Michigan, to participate in his first professional tryout. Emotionally consumed by this incredible, long-shot opportunity, David had found it almost impossible to adequately prepare his body and mind for training camp while still holding up his end of the farm chores.

"Hey, superstar!"

David turned at the sound of Luke's sarcastic comment and grinned as his brother tossed not one, but two hay bales at a time onto the trailer.

"Stop day-dreaming and get lifting. We don't have all day. If you want to take off early again, you better bust your butt now," Luke scoffed at his younger sibling.

David idolized his brother, a tall, chiselled farm boy with a big mouth and the bulging biceps, forearms and tough-as-nails disposition to back it up. For years, David had grown up in his brother's shadow and loved every minute of it. Around Vanguard, the closest hamlet to the Stone's farm, Luke was a hockey icon. He was captain of the Screaming Eagles, a South Saskatchewan Senior Men's hockey club, the league's leading scorer and by far the biggest badass around.

Luke had never pursued a professional hockey career, despite his notoriety and lots of junior and minor pro-interest over the years. His future was squarely set on taking over the farm to ensure the Stone family legacy in these parts would be perpetuated for at least one more generation, just as it had been with his father and grandfather before him.

Good for him, if that's what he wants, thought David, *but it's not the life for me.* He answered his brother derisively. "Yeah, I'm on it hayseed! Don't get your panties in a bunch!" The words had barely passed his lips when David felt a stinging blast of hot straw hit his face. It was a non-too-subtle reminder from Luke as to who was boss around here. But David didn't care.

This was going to be the summer of his destiny.

* * *

A convertible Corvette, sleek and cherry red, raced into the shopping centre parking lot and lurched to a stop. Riley Sawyer lowered his shades and glanced into the rear-view mirror. Yep, everything looked pretty good—great actually. Hair was appropriately coiffed. Skin was clear and perfectly darkened with the hues of a summer tan perfected up in Muskoka lake country. Teeth were nice, straight and, most importantly, sparkling white. He ran his tongue over their pearly surface, across his gums and finally over his smiling lips.

Within seconds the air filled with squeals and shrieks of delirium from adoring female fans, and excited exclamations from a few local reporters. Riley rushed from his vehicle towards the staff entry doors at Toronto Eaton Centre, the city's premier downtown mall.

Fame was nothing new to Riley, even though he had just turned 19 years old. The son of a prominent Toronto lawyer, Riley had been born into a life of privilege and groomed since childhood for his inevitable rise to NHL superstar. He had received the finest coaching available through his formative years at private sports academies and professional hockey development programs. His summers had been spent learning the game and getting instruction from the best national level trainers and coaches at private hockey and skating schools, which also featured advanced fitness and skills regimens. Since the age of seven, Riley's father had even leveraged the family's high-profile civic reputation, season ticket legacy and blue-blood pedigree into some unique opportunities for the young protégé including practice time with the Toronto Maple Leafs during pre-season and some optional scrimmages.

To his credit, Riley had not squandered his father's investment or the advantages provided to him. He had parlayed his natural athleticism and innate hockey acumen into a meteoric rise through the tough ranks of Ontario's cult-like minor leagues, often having to overcome the bias and bigotry of being labelled a spoiled rich kid who was only riding on daddy's coat tails. Sometimes he had to deal with that jealousy using his fists. However, more often those sorts of malevolent actions were delegated by a coach or team official to other, less gifted teammates with more advanced pugilistic skills than Riley possessed.

Riley had been the Most Valuable Player and leading scorer on almost every team he'd played for as long as anyone could remember: MVP of the Quebec Pee Wee Tournament, the world's most famous showcase for 10- to 12-year olds; leading scorer and MVP at the Royal Bank Midget Championship, Canada's final curtain call for the next generation of NHL draft aged kids; and, against all odds as a second-year captain, he had actually broken the Ontario Hockey League junior scoring records of The Great One— Wayne Gretzky—making him the undisputed alpha dog of the Soo Greyhounds, a delicious irony as that was Gretzky's alma mater.

Put it all together and there had been little doubt at June's NHL Entry Draft who the consensus number one draft pick would be for the Detroit Red Wings. After a week of media sensationalism and celebrity hysteria bordering on the insane in star-driven Los Angeles, Detroit's team owner, Mike Layton, and General Manager, Dave Hellan, had stepped up to the microphone and announced to the world, "With its first overall pick in 27 years, the Detroit Red Wings are pleased to welcome to our proud and storied hockey family, the NHL's next generational superstar, Riley Sawyer of the OHL's Sault Ste. Marie Greyhounds."

The building had erupted in thunderous applause as hundreds of newspaper and TV cameras captured the young Adonis embracing his tiny mother and then shaking his father's hand before confidently striding to the podium as he prepared for the honour of donning the team's jersey for the first time. As he went Riley had nodded smugly at his peers, well aware that many players and hockey experts in the crowd considered him an arrogant, self-serving prima donna with a history of caring little about teammates or team success. He didn't care. It was tough to argue with skill like his. This would be the start of a career that would bring Riley untold fame, fortune and a future far beyond even his own elevated expectations.

This and a lifetime of other memories raced through Riley's mind as he pushed toward the shopping mall. He was quickly surrounded by security and, for the first time, he realized from the size of the crowd and the intensity of their attention, that his celebrity had reached global proportions. Two weeks ago, this kind of minor mall promotion on a nothing Saturday afternoon might have pulled a hundred young boys and teenage girls enthralled by his achievements and rugged good looks, and with the hopes of meeting a local celebrity. But today, thousands of screaming hockey fans from the age of five to 70, clamoured for a glimpse of the next "one", desperate to bask in his awesome glory.

It was an excitement that Riley would never forget and a responsibility he had begun to wonder if he could live up to. A flicker of uncertainty raced through Riley, but he bunched his shoulders, put his head down, and pushed through the doors to the mall.

Chapter 2

Autumn's first golden leaves, clinging to the motley willow trees around the watering hole, let David know his summer of destiny was winding down. The once-a-day workouts had evolved into two and sometimes even three-a-day torture sessions that had pushed his young body to its limits. Who could have imagined that such simple, everyday implements easily found on every farm could be transformed into the most hellish instruments of strain and suffering, all in pursuit of a career in hockey's most hallowed institution—the NHL.

Lifting heavy bales of straw was the equivalent of doing excruciating 100-pound upright lifts, repeated until his shoulders ached from exhaustion. Hauling oats for the animals was akin to arm curls that ripped every muscle, vein and tendon in his biceps and chest. The endless repetitions eventually gave David the appearance of a human anatomy poster in a high school biology class rather than Saskatchewan's next NHL hope.

And the running! So much running. He covered endless stretches of prairie terrain each day, comforted only by the inspired anthems of Axel Rose, Garth Brooks, Blake Shelton and a few Mick Jagger tunes which pulsed through his earbuds. David followed up his runs with leg-thrashing, lung-busting wind sprints, made more intense by a resistance chute strapped on his back. His chest exploded with sharp pains toward the end of these gruelling dashes over the football field's parched earth, witnessed only by a few gophers, crows and some curious kids enjoying the last days of summer, playing football before heading back to class.

Just when it all seemed too much and agony screamed from every pore, he would finish with the dreaded tire flips. This particular bit of hell was simple enough. You lifted an oversized tractor tire and flipped it forward for 40 yards or so as fast as possible. The first three flips were usually a little respite from the high-stress cardio exercises and wind sprints. However, after those, each flip became exponentially harder on the body, mind, back and especially the hands. There would be about 15 flips per set and then you'd do it again – and then again.

Sometimes he did it under the hot sun. Sometimes there was rain, cold winds, or stinging dust, but still he trained. It was the last two weeks of cross-training and the intensity was far beyond anything David would have believed himself capable of had he not actually done it.

His trainer for these sessions was Mel Simms, David's high school physical education teacher, and the region's most prominent conditioning guru. When David had begged for his help, Mel had readily agreed to train him over the summer. Mel's claim to fame was a brief two season stint in the Canadian Football League as an offensive lineman and special teams "wedge buster" with the Saskatchewan Roughriders. Like so many others before him who had achieved the supposed dream life of a professional athlete, his career had been brief, ripped away before amounting to much. Still, Mel had a great deal to offer David, not only in training discipline, but also in wisdom, experience and perspective on a pro-sports lifestyle.

After each gruelling two-hour work-out, they would often talk for another hour into the evening. Mel was always happy to share his memories of the big leagues with his prized pupil, while David listened with rapt attention, physically drained from his long day, but eager to take-in every story.

About 9 PM each night, Luke would roll up in his beat-up pick-up and join in the jock talk for a few minutes before the brothers would say their good-byes and leave, promising Mel that they would pass on his best wishes to their mom and dad.

It's been a good summer, thought David on this particularly idyllic night as they travelled home in Luke's truck. He peered over at his brother. Luke was equally tired from a 14-hour day in the fields, pulling double duty now so his sibling could get in his workouts. David turned away and looked out the window. He felt a twinge in his gut, but ignored it and just spoke openly. "Thanks, man. I know it's tough on you, having to take care of everything on the farm while I'm screwing around with all this hockey stuff. You're a great brother and the best role model I could have ever had. I feel really lucky to be your brother and I just thought you should know that." David finished abruptly, unsure of how Luke would respond to his moment of honest emotion.

There was an awkward silence of almost 30 seconds.

"What? Are you delirious or something?" Luke shot back in a gruff tone that was pure drill sergeant in cadence. "Christ, just go make the fucking team and spare the rest of us all your touchy-feely bullshit. If you don't make it, trust me, I'll work your sorry ass to death when you come crawling back home, you lucky little bastard."

Another moment of silence filled the truck.

Luke broke the silence first. "The Detroit Red Wings!" he exclaimed. Luke smirked and looked at his young brother. "My God. Steve Yzerman! Gordie Howe! And now, David fucking Stone. That's just bat-shit crazy. What's the world coming too?"

The brothers started laughing at the sheer absurdity of Luke's comparisons and soon both had tears of happiness welling up in their eyes from the unexpected euphoria.

This is why David loved his brother. Whenever his own doubts or insecurities crept in, Luke would slam everything back into perspective, doing so very succinctly with a well-turned profanity and some good, old "Stone Cold" common sense as he called it.

They turned off the road and onto a bumpy driveway leading to their house. The sight of his childhood home, cloaked in dusk and emanating warmth through its soft porch light and windows, choked David up for a moment as he realized his farm life would soon be a distant memory and his future was now hopefully in Detroit.

As the truck pulled to a stop, Luke grunted. "Oh, and if you get the chance, pop that irritating Riley Sawyer. What a jerk he is."

"If I can catch him, Luke, for sure. If I can catch him."

* * *

David felt a sense of anxiety as he hurriedly added a few final items into his carry bag. He knew the odds of a guy like him making Detroit were excruciatingly small if they even existed at all.

As a rookie camp walk-on there were no guarantees. They usually got airfare and a week of hotel accommodation provided by the club once they signed a camp contract, but other than that they paid their own way physically, mentally and financially. Many relied on summer jobs, family and friends and, in David's case, a town-sponsored bingo fundraiser, to earn money, all in pursuit of the dream they would be that one exception who overcame the odds and earned an invite to the main training camp.

In reality, walk-ons like him were usually camp fodder for the drafted players to hone their skills on prior to attending their first pro camp. Rookie camps were also a sort of insurance policy for the sophisticated scouting systems now employed by NHL teams that gave them confidence no-stone was left unturned in their pursuit of young up-and-coming talent. There were stories of walk-ons who had gone on to become everyday pros, even superstars in the league, each a testament to hard work and perseverance. Adam Oates had been one; Marty St. Louis was another. However, there were far, far more who never made it and were promptly shipped back home. The NHL's formulaic, centralized, talent identification processes and personnel were extremely efficient at finding, evaluating and selecting a few dozen new pros every year from the thousands of junior, college and minor league players all over the world.

David sighed and his thoughts returned to family. Luke and his father were already in the fields, had been since 5:00 AM. It was harvest time and every minute of daylight and dry weather counted, so there was no time for them to say goodbye this morning; they'd bidden him farewell the evening before instead.

David's mother, Anne, would drive him the four hours or so to Regina, where he would catch West Jet flight #4901 to Toronto. Then he'd take a short connector on to Detroit. Upon his arrival, David would settle in Auburn Hills' most non-descript Motel 6, about 14 blocks from where Detroit's rookie camp was to be held.

As he stared at the open suitcase, his mother appeared next to him and gently gripped his shoulder. It triggered a surge of emotion and he turned to look into her moistened eyes.

"Are you okay, David?" she asked with a mother's concern.

"I'm fine, Mom. I feel a bit guilty because of Dad and Luke and well, all the work they have to-"

She gently shushed him and held up a finger to signal his silence. "They're fine, David. And both are so proud of you. But, you know them; they'll never say it out loud. You've worked so hard these last few years and done well. I even heard Luke tell your dad that he really believes you can make it if you don't let your own fear and insecurities get in the way."

"It's just...now that it's time to go, I'm feeling pretty nervous," David spoke softly. "I'm used to our life here and after not getting drafted I had kind of put hockey out of my mind. It's a long way away and I'm totally on my own." His words trailed off.

"Yes, it'll be a challenge that's for sure, but life is full of uncertainty regardless of where you are. You're right, there's a certain predictable comfort being at home. We have a pretty darn good life, but what we don't have here are any really big opportunities. It's good to do new things, push yourself out of the comfort zone and have adventures. We'll always be here. This is your home and there will always be wheat to grow and cattle to feed, God willing. But, you need to go and do this. Challenges are what help us grow. Just do your best, David. I've always hated you and Luke playing this stupid game, what with all the cuts and bruises to your beautiful faces and then all the injuries. It just seems so stupid to me. And then there's the money they pay those guys—it's nuts. But, if it's your dream, well, I'm behind you 100 percent and I can assure you that dad and Luke are too."

"Thanks, Mom." David felt a surge of affection as he wrapped his arms around her and both remained still for a moment. Anne was a strong, farming mother who had held the Stone family together through every type of calamity including storms, droughts, cash crunches and countless sports and work injuries.

"You only get one shot, so try to enjoy it and be thankful you got the chance to try out. Not many kids from these parts get that opportunity. Show up and do your best, that's all you can give. The rest is in God's hands. We know you'll do your best. You always have."

"I will, mom. Promise."

With that, Anne delicately placed two shirts and a few extra pairs of socks in his beat-up suitcase and pulled the zipper tight.

"Now, David, do you have your passport?" his mom probed abruptly, transforming from psychologist to logistics coordinator.

"You know they won't let you into the United States without it. Evelyn told me that Allan Thompson missed his whole trip to Mexico because he forgot his passport. You don't want to—"

David cut her off in mid-sentence. "Yes mom, I have my passport."

"And, you've got the money Uncle Ernie sent you, right? I think he sent you 200 dollars or something. Do you have that?"

David chuckled. "You bet, Mom. I've got it and God bless

Uncle Ernie because it was actually 500 dollars."

"What? 500 dollars! Good heavens, what's he doing giving you that kind of money? I'm going to have to send him a card for that and it wouldn't hurt you to—"

"Already done, Mom. I sent him an email and thanked him, even put a smiley face emoji on it."

"Email! That's not a proper way to thank someone. Why don't you send him a card or call him?"

"You know what? As soon as I get to Detroit, first night, I'll call Ernie and tell him thanks. Then I'll get him some famous player's autograph. How does that sound?"

"Now that's a proper thank you." Her attention drifted off as she headed towards the door, looking for her keys. "Let's go David, we've got a long drive ahead of us."

David felt a lump form in his throat and it went straight to his eyes, transforming into a few more tears as he watched his mom reach for her coat by the front door.

The final workout of David's excruciating summer would be dead lifting his overstuffed suitcase across the linoleum floor and out the front door. Standing by the car, he took a final look across the fields and firmly committed himself to never returning, unless of course it was to visit the family.

* * *

The trip to Regina began with lots of banter and laughter as David and his mother discussed how good the harvest appeared to be and the funny things they experienced each day as a farming family. Soon, they turned onto the TransCanada Highway, the main travel artery that connected the beating hearts of every small Saskatchewan town to the rest of the world. David recalled driving this road so many times: to Moose Jaw for hockey tournaments; to Medicine Hat for baseball games; school trips to Prince Albert for provincial basketball championships; and, of course, going to Saskatoon for his first junior training camp after a stellar Midget AAA career as an elite forward in Swift Current.

David had made the Saskatoon Blades on his first try. He'd toiled as a first line forward for three years and, though he was a minor celebrity about town as a member of the Junior A club, his on ice performance had only been considered average by the tough standards of the Western Hockey League. But, David could skate. He was faster than almost anyone and had a grace that seemed to belie physics and the natural laws of motion. His effortlessly efficient stride when combined with decent puck sense, a talent honed from being too slight to out-muscle larger players, made him one of the best pure passers in the league.

Unfortunately, he'd been on a woeful team that really needed scorers to properly profile David's prolific skills. A lack of team success had meant pretty average stats for David and his performance had been further hindered by reoccurring shoulder problems compliments of an old football injury. Despite all that, his pure speed and seeing-eye passes had caught the attention of Del Jackson, Detroit's sage-like Western Canadian minor league scout. Gifted play makers were tough to find for sure, but even harder to find were great character guys like David. There was always a need for hard-working, natural born leaders with a will strong enough to persevere through every challenge and eventually rise to the top in every situation, both good and bad.

While the opportunity to showcase his skills had not presented itself to David very often, Jackson had seen enough during his two years covering the WHL that he had pleaded with Detroit to draft the young centerman. But, on a team full of veteran centres, and with Riley Sawyer sure to be the Red Wings' first round pick, that was never going to happen. However, Del's relentless determination and the trust that Detroit's General Manager had in his judgement had gotten David an invite to the team's rookie camp. They'd give him a look and, if he performed well, maybe offer him a minor league contract and keep him in the system as insurance in case of injuries down the road. Still, David couldn't help but hope for more, like a real shot at the NHL itself.

Only half paying attention to his mother's talking from the driver's seat, David's last conversation with Del replayed like a loop in his mind as nondescript terrain and tranquil summer sky rolled past the window.

"Detroit needs a playmaking centre. Everyone there now is a shooter, which is great, but it's hurting overall goal production. No one wants to pass the puck. We need more balance up front." Del had told him directly.

Goal scorers were great. But with no one regularly feeding the wingers, it meant that scoring chances were falling fast and exposing an ugly weakness other teams were becoming well aware of and beginning to exploit.

The final hour of the drive passed in virtual silence. Then Regina's squat skyline peaked above the prairie horizon. *Thank God*, thought David.

A few turns and a bad parking job later and David, boarding pass in hand, was wading through a long security line. He moved through the metal detector, then waved goodbye to his mother as she vanished from sight.

As he walked down the corridor to his gate, David took a deep breath to steady himself. In about six-and-a-half hours, he would arrive at Metro Wayne County Airport and be totally on his own for the first time ready to take on the biggest challenge of his life.

Chapter 3

The terrified youth, helplessly kneeling on the floor with his hands bound behind him, hung his head in submission after the beating he'd endured for over an hour. Though Clarence Reyes couldn't see his captors through the smelly, oily, canvas sack that covered his head, he could feel them within striking distance. His body ached from the blows and he could feel warm blood oozing down his throat from lacerations to his tongue and lips and the loosened teeth in his mouth.

    His quiet weeping contradicted the tough guy persona that, earlier in the day, had terrified residents of the Beltway projects. Reyes was a notable player on the brutal gang-infested streets of Brooklyn. A mid-level street dealer and thug, who'd terrorized Beltway residents for over a year. Drug dealing, extortion, muggings, prostitution of minors, and protection rackets, nothing was outside his purview and he had been rewarded well. His success had been tied directly to the rise in power of a Russian mob syndicate called Odessa, now a major criminal enterprise along the east coast. They'd taken root in the United States during the late nineties when the collapse of the old Soviet Union had caused rapid exportation of organized crime to the America's, with a special focus on Columbia, Mexico and, of course, their largest market, the United States.

    The Russian mobsters loved street punks like Reyes, kids who felt bullet proof, would do anything to prove themselves and, best of all, they were completely disposable. These kids would do any type of dirty work for basically pennies, girls and a bit of street cred. Violence was how you controlled them, with death the commonly paid price for acts of disobedience, bad intentions or thoughts of disloyalty.

    As Reyes awaited his fate, he knew that the situation was dire. He prayed softly between sobs to St. Francis, the only name he could recall from the Sunday school classes that his hard-working mom had made him attend as a child. He prayed for a miracle that would get him home to his mother and sister, just one more time. A sliding metal door clattered in the distance, breaking the room's temporary silence while the hurried sound of patent leather shoes moved ever closer to the bent and broken captive.

Reyes desperately whispered into the folds of the cloth over his face. "Dear, St. Francis, please forgive me. I am so sorry for my sins. Please help me now and protect me from—"

"So, Mr. Reyes wants to have business for himself, da?" The voice was immediately recognizable as the halting, broken English of Alexi Tsarnov, the undisputed boss of Odessa in New York. "What? We don't pay you enough? You don't have enough girls or power, you pitiful pig? So, you steal from me. That is so very stupid. But then, you wetbacks all stupid, aren't you?"

Tsarnov circled the broken youth slumped on his knees and sensed the fear coursing through him which only heightened Alexi's sadistic enjoyment. The crime boss reached back and with all his might hammered his fist into the back of Reyes head, propelling him forward and eliciting a shriek of pain.

For Tsarnov this was entertainment. Inflicting pain was like an aphrodisiac for him. He became almost gleeful when those working for Odessa let him down because it provided the opportunity to deal with them in the most sadistic ways imaginable. He loved to cause fear and craved the power that came from controlling someone's life or death. It was the same, sick pleasure that serial killers get with each kill and trophy taken. His first blow was immediately followed by savage kicks to Reyes's stomach and back, then a vicious stomp to the side of his head.

The traumatized juvenile now cried openly. "Please! Please, Mr. Tsarnov! Forgive me. Have mercy. Please!" He knew that he was pleading for his life, well aware of Odessa's grisly punishments for disloyalty.

The two soldiers who had captured Reyes grabbed his bruised body from the filthy concrete floor where he'd fallen and slammed him back up onto his knees.

Blood spit from Reyes's lips as words tumbled from his mouth. "Please, Mr. Tsarnov! I didn't take your drugs. I sold only what I got and that's the money I gave you. You have to believe me! I would never, ever steal from you. I love this job and I love working for you. Please, you have to believe me. I would never steal. Never! Please, please, please! Let me work. I'll work even harder. For less. I'll do anything!"

Tsarnov whipped the canvas bag off Reyes's head and looked straight into his battered and bloody face. "See me now, Clarence. See my eyes. I've killed dozens of mongrels like you for much less than ripping me off. You were given 125 ounces of cocaine, but you only paid me for 110. What, you think I'm fucking stupid, like you? I can't count? Don't know what's going on in my own operation? You think I'm some dumb immigrant who doesn't pay attention? I know everything, you little shit. And I know a stinking thief that I can't trust when I see one. So, here we are. Me wanting my money and you on your knees, begging for life. What a predicament."

"Mr. Tsarnov, please. I got 110 ounces and that's what I paid for. Please, that's all I got, honest. Someone is setting me up. But I'll pay the difference. Whatever you want. Just give me a chance. I won't let you down."

"Really?" Tsarnov snorted in mocked amazement. "Someone is wasting their precious time to set up a small-time piece of shit like you. Who would waste their time to do such a thing? Who?"

"I don't know. But that must be it." Reyes gurgled through his bloodied lips as he sensed vaguely this might be a way out of his current plight?

"Where's the rest of the money, Clarence?" Tsarnov thundered. "Just tell me where the money is and you can live. Then, maybe we find this despicable cockroach that's out to frame you."

"Like I said, Mr. Tsarnov, I only got 110 ounces. But, I will pay for the missing amount with my own money. I keep a money stash at home, at my mom's. Under the floor boards at the head of my bed. It's yours. Everything. There's probably 15 grand there. That should be more than enough to cover any short falls. And I'll work harder, Mr. Tsarnov. I'll work so hard you'll never have anyone better, I promise. I'll go with you to get it. And I'll be the best worker ever, Mr.—"

A bullet pierced the skull just behind Clarence's ear and blood splattered violently against the wall as his limp, beaten corpse collapsed to the floor. Tsarnov stared at the mess and then shot again into the lifeless body, then again just because it gave him a rush. He smiled.

"Get me my money," he growled to his men as he stared at the rumpled mass of Clarence Reyes laying at his feet. "And kill everyone there. If one of the family stole from me, they all stole from me. Lessons must be learned. Make it big and messy so no one else gets ideas like his."

The soldiers nodded their approval and strode toward the exit, leaving Tsarnov towering over his kill.

"Oh, Clarence. Tell me where my money is and you can live?" mused Tsarnov as he stared into the dead eyes, frozen forever in fear. "Well, live in hell." He spat and then calmly booted the dead man's face toward the concrete which was slowly getting covered in blood.

The killer turned and eased his shiny, silver Glock and its extended silencer into an extremely expensive, gold-encrusted shoulder holster beneath his coat. As he moved toward the door, a sense of happiness filled his soul and he whistled a Russian folk tune that he remembered from his childhood.

* * *

The modest Reyes home was lovingly headed by mother Ruth, a seamstress and hard-working illegal immigrant from Panama. Her two greatest treasures were her children, Clarence and Janie. Tonight, Ruth had made Janie's favourite dish to celebrate the last day of her summer job and the start of her final year in high school. Janie hoped to be a doctor and had dreams of one day returning home to Central America to help others via the Doctors Without Borders initiative.

"Janie!" Ruth called from the kitchen where she was just finishing setting the table. "Dinner is just about ready. Now all we need is Clarence. I swear, that boy would be late for his own funeral." She laughed. She felt so good and was so proud of all that her children had accomplished.

The crash of their thin wooden door and the pops of muffled gunfire would be the last sounds Ruth and Janie would ever hear, as Odessa's assassins burst in.

The slaughter was over in seconds. A perfectly prepared dinner table sat in surreal contrast to the bloody carnage that lay around it. In the background the haunting whistling of an obscure melody was really all any witnesses could recall of the atrocity when questioned by detectives later in the evening.

Chapter 4

"Well, of course I'm honoured to be a Detroit Red Wing," proclaimed the six foot three inch scoring sensation from the Soo as he stood before the assembled media horde in Detroit's Metro Wayne County Airport VIP lounge. "As a Toronto boy, I've always loved the rivalry between the Wings and Leafs. And if the Leafs couldn't win, which was often, then I was a big Wings fan. So, you could say I've always been a Wings fan!"

The partisan gathering of reporters laughed loudly at the well-timed shot at Detroit's cross-border rivals. They strained to get into better position for the young superstar's next witty snippet, hoping for just the right quote before they scurried off to their offices and blogs to hammer out some insights and commentary on the arrival of Riley Sawyer. Hype for a first-year player hadn't been this frenetic since Sidney Crosby, maybe even Mario Lemieux or the great Gretzky, had entered the league.

Detroit had earned the first overall pick through a combination of shrewd management acumen and plain dumb luck. Three years ago, General Manager Dave Hellan had traded an aging, though competent, veteran defenseman to a desperate, rival team anxious to make a play-off run in exchange for a future first-round draft pick. As fate would have it, the trade had not worked out well for the other team. They hadn't gone all the way in the playoffs that year and had subsequently fallen on hard times and plummeted in the standings.

The demise of the other team had given Detroit an incredibly favourable position in the latest draft lottery, where by sheer luck, they had won the honour of drafting first overall that year. Never before had a team performing as competitively as Detroit enjoyed such an enviable draft position. Today, they had the opportunity to show off their highly touted winnings to Detroit's media and fans. The excitement was infectious. Dave Hellan could not help but shake his head as he processed in his mind the team's good fortune.

Riley Sawyer was a magnificent physical specimen to be sure. He was tall, muscled, powerful and handsome in a pop star kind of way. His jet-blue eyes pierced the cameras and took command of anyone watching from home.

Riley's agent, Alex Moore, flanked the youngster during his opening comments. Alex was president of ISM, the world's largest talent management company and a highly respected professional in the world of sports and entertainment representation. Despite hockey languishing behind other major United States team sports in audience awareness and television ratings, a phenom like Riley in a major American market, on a cup-contending team, could change all that in a few short years. He made no secret that he wanted that to happen. ISM had staked a great deal on Riley's success as an athlete, celebrity, endorsement darling, sports superstar, and role model and the NHL's marketing machine was following suit in many major ways. Both were extremely vested in every aspect of his public profile and packaging.

Alex stepped up to the microphone to begin the presser and introduce his agency's newest star. "Welcome to the beginning of Detroit's greatest hockey era— ever!" the over-the-top agent bellowed, startling everyone and eliciting a shrill squeal of feedback from the speakers that cut through the gathered scribes.

It was a pretty outrageous comment considering the storied history of Detroit's hockey club, an original-six franchise. Over the decades, a legion of legendary names had laced up for the revered red-and-white winged wheel. Even the team's owner, Mike Layton shot a sideways glance toward the podium at the outrageous statement. Then he shrugged. Oh well, the circus was in town, so a little hyperbole was to be expected.

Alex continued. "We believe Riley Sawyer is the league's next marquis superstar and will help restore the Red Wings to heights not seen since Stevie Y's days. Riley has the talent, skill and character this team needs to bring Lord Stanley's hallowed mug back to this incredible city and its fans, and we are excited all of Michigan can share in this incredible journey."

A polite round of applause followed. The comments, and the extra effort being put into the event, were designed to infuse fresh hope into everyone watching. This climate of renewal was much needed by the general populace after the terrible beating that Detroit, and indeed the whole state, had suffered during and after the great 2008 recession. During that period the city had been one of America's first municipalities to declare bankruptcy amidst an embarrassing backdrop of political mismanagement and corruption. Almost overnight, 25 percent of the city's population had disappeared, a mass exodus caused by tens of thousands being thrown out of work. Detroit would go on to become the nation's capital of foreclosure and crime.

During the truly lowest points of this difficult period, vulture investors and others looking to line their pockets had been able to purchase one of the city's thousands of repossessed homes for only 1 dollar from designated sheriffs standing on the steps of City Hall during daily liquidations. All you had to do was pay the back taxes on it. Even then, on most days, there had been very few takers.

Prior to the recession, dozens of new suburbs had sprouted around the city like spring flowers, all thanks to a fraudulent, mortgage-fuelled real estate boom. Now, they were completely empty or dotted with half-finished and abandoned buildings. The city, with no money to service or maintain these neighbourhoods, and fearing they would become crime- and drug-infested ghettos, had bulldozed entire communities into the ground, shrinking the city's civic limits by almost 20 percent.

The auto industry, which had been slowly creeping back to life during the early 2000s, had once again been hurled back into chaos and placed on life support. Without a trillion dollars of emergency government-backed loan guarantees, Ford, Chrysler, and even vaunted General Motors, bastions of America's manufacturing might, would have passed into oblivion, relics of the country's great industrial past.

Hockey Town needed something big to restore its faith and hope, and the beloved Red Wings were offering up Riley as the saviour, a harbinger of better times ahead and a brighter future, one unfettered by the stench of past failures. Today, at this press conference, the future looked like Riley Sawyer.

Yes, promoting a rookie hockey player so much was a big gamble to be sure, but professional sports was all about playing the odds. And the payoffs could be huge, if you bet right. There would be no turning back now. The table had been set and nothing less than a Stanley Cup, earned quickly, would satisfy the heightened expectations of the populace.

* * *

It was Danielle Wright's first hockey presser and she could not believe what a battle she was having to get a good viewing position for photographs and sound bites from this guy. She glanced up at the stage. *Wow, he's pretty good looking,* she thought. *Maybe he'll notice me more if I just step back and let my assets work their magic. It had always worked in college. Why should the pros be any different?*

Danielle was a journalism graduate from Illinois State University. Her father was a huge Black Hawks fan and alumni. She'd picked up a lot from him and could work her way around a hockey story pretty easily. She had also been an NCAA All-American volleyball star, so she herself was familiar with the self-obsessed personalities and egos of high-performance jocks. She also possessed a competitive zeal that allowed her to size up and overcome tough situations.

Tall and blond with dark rimmed glasses, she knew that her shapely body and model good looks naturally attracted attention. She moved back from the scrum and stared above the raised arms and shouting heads before her, directly at Riley, who was elevated slightly above the crowd.

Riley finished answering some banal question about his favourite local eating spot, then glanced up, as if looking for a respite from the verbal barrage assaulting him. Almost instinctively, his gaze came down and settled on Danielle and her recorder, standing just beyond the bedlam, waiting patiently. The sight seemed to stun him for a moment. Then he raised his hands to minimize the frenzy of shouts.

"Did you have a question for me, Miss?" Riley asked her with raised brows and hands.

The scrum went silent. Heads craned as if they were on swivels to see who Riley had addressed, seeking out the Miss that he was referring to.

"Yes." Danielle began in her most earnest reporter character. "It seems to me that it's pretty pretentious for a very young rookie who's yet to play a single game in the league to think he can dominate on an already pretty good team and improve on the legacy of this iconic franchise. How are you planning on doing that?

What's the missing magic you bring to Detroit that we don't have now?"

Riley's steely blue eyes locked onto Danielle and with an arrogant grin he answered. "Well, I guess I'm just a winner. Always have been. I plan to win here too. There's lots of great players out there and Detroit has a few of them, but they haven't won the big prize for a while. I like to think that winning's my thing. My strength."

Danielle clicked off her recorder and smiled knowingly. "Thank you, Mr. Sawyer." Poor kid. He'd taken the bait and now she had her story: how this arrogant newbie had looked past all the key dynamics for building a better team and insulted a veteran laden line-up by thinking he was better than everyone else.

The media scrum went silent for a few seconds as the press jackals contemplated Riley's response.

Alex Moore clenched his eyes shut and shook his head in frustration. It had all been going so well and then the question. With it, Detroit had been given a first look into the self-absorbed soul and conceit that was Riley Sawyer.

A reporter raised his hand. "So, Riley, does that mean Detroit is full of losers now? Except for you, of course."

Riley's confident smile vanished. He blinked. "Well no, what I meant was I've always won, so—"

Danielle bit back a laugh as she watched the rookie frantically try to regain control of the session. It was no use; the genie was out of the bottle and you could not stuff it back in no matter how hard you tried. It would be interesting to see how the Red Wings' talented veterans would welcome their young pretentious superstar after such a comment. Getting body checked on the ice could hurt you, but in professional sports, with its massive egos, primal rituals, million-dollar salaries and hierarchies of power, media hits could hurt twice as much and could damage a player far more. How would his new teammates respond? How would Riley's introduction affect his public persona from now on? Only time would tell.

* * *

Alone outside his boarding gate in Regina, a sturdy bronzed farm-boy sat in a small sports lounge eating chicken wings, drinking his Diet Coke and watching the Detroit press conference on TSN. His jaw dropped and he laughed in shock at Riley's comments.

Wow, what an asshole. Won't make any friends with comments like that, thought David, chucking to himself as he put another chicken wing in his mouth. Then he caught sight of the female reporter who had asked the loaded question. *Man, is she hot!*

Chapter 5

Ted Arnold had worked at the Auburn Sports and Recreation Complex for 37 years, but he'd never seen or experienced such chaos for the first morning of rookie training camp and the arrival of this year's participants. As he pulled into the facility parking lot at 6 AM, he was stunned to see thousands of people milling around the front concourse entry doors. And, based on the signs they were holding and the demographics of the crowd, most were waiting for Riley Sawyer. *Mercy me*, he thought. *It's amazing to see the massive power of television and America's star culture at work.* He shook his head and entered the arena.

Over the years, Ted had seen and met all the greats. As a kid, he'd watched Gordie Howe and idolized Mr. Hockey's singular combination of skill, leadership and toughness. He personally remembered Steve Yzerman's first day of rookie camp. He'd only been two years into his arena maintenance job and had very much been star struck as the class of 1983 showed up in much the same fashion that today's young men would. The lean, quiet, good-looking kid had walked into camp and hoisted the Red Wing franchise squarely on his shoulders before guiding them to hockey's promise land. He was a born leader and Ted's favourite player.

Ted doubted there would ever again be anyone like Stevie Y walk through these doors. Yzerman had carried the Wings to four Stanley Cup championships and given the city so many inspiring memories that it was tough to get worked up over this new kid, Sawyer. But, times change and Ted would have to wait and see if the kid was worth all the hype.

With that, he climbed onto his dated black Zamboni, with the bright red and white wing emblazoned on its side, and drove onto the ice surface.

Looks like it's gonna be a weird day, he thought.

* * *

From the cab's back seat, David nervously peered out the window at the huge sports complex coming into view on the horizon.

It would be in its large, concrete and steel arenas that he would need to make his biggest impression. *Those rinks look really ugly* he thought to himself, perhaps as a defensive posture to the terrible butterflies churning in his stomach. They were impersonal structures of massive metal roofs and elongated structural beams that gave them all the humanity of a Transformer from the hit movie franchise. They were purposeful but lacked personality. A far cry from the bustling, small town arenas where he had played growing up. Those rinks had been wonderful community gathering places that brought life, happiness and love to isolated prairie towns every winter and inspired the citizenry onto bigger dreams. Like his.

Well, it really didn't matter, he thought. *I'm here on business, so perhaps the look and feel of the rinks was entirely appropriate.* This was no time to get emotional. He needed to focus on the task at hand.

The driver pulled into the parking lot then unexpectedly swerved sideways, causing his wheels to hit a curb, abruptly hurling David hard against the ceiling and door handle, before coming to a abrupt stop. Frowning, David looked up to see a speeding red Corvette had cut them off in an aggressive move to steal the final open parking stall at the front of the lot.

The 'Vette screeched to a halt. Its window slowly descended and Riley Sawyer made a rude, middle-finger gesture toward the shaken cabbie. "Learn how to drive, asshole!" he screamed. Then after turning off his engine, Riley jumped out of his car and carried on as if nothing particularly notable had occurred.

The stunned and embarrassed cab driver apologized profusely to David as he proceeded to pull up near the front doors amidst throngs of people.

David watched as the crowd finally noticed who was driving the bright red car that dangerously entered the parking lot.

"He's here! He's here!" shrieked a pretty, blonde, teen girl.

The massive cluster of humanity in almost perfect uniformity surged towards its high-profile target. Harried security guys rushed to Riley's aid trying to keep the crowd at a distance, but there was little chance of that. Hats, programs, player pictures, flailing hands and anything else that could possibly be signed was thrust into his path as the young superstar fought his way toward the entrance. He scribbled a few autographs, smiled a bit, took a selfie or two and finally disappeared behind the oversized glass doors.

David quietly exited the cab and grabbed his duffle bag.

As they stared at the mayhem, the cab driver muttered quietly to no one in particular. "So, that's the great Riley Sawyer. Seems like a real dick to me."

David chuckled at the adroit observation, then began his own journey through the crowd. As he moved and bumped his way past people, a number of questions were directed at him.

"Hey, buddy, you a Wing?"

"Who are you, sweetness?"

David just kept his eyes focused on the entry doors and, once in the arena, was directed to a registration area by uniformed ushers wearing bright Red Wing track suits.

"Welcome to Detroit. Well, to Auburn Hills actually," said a matronly looking Red Wings Ambassador whose nametag read, Margie. Her job was to escort David to the auditorium where he would be signed in and assigned a jersey colour that would designate his training camp team. Then he'd participate in an orientation class. She gave him a warm smile. "And you would be?"

"Uh, David Stone. I'm from Saskatchewan."

"Oh my, you're a long way from home. Well, don't you worry, we'll take very good care of you. And if there's anything you need, my name is Margie and I'll be happy to help out. Where are you staying, David?"

"Uh, at the Motel 6, ma'am," answered David with a slight grin. He could not help but sense a bit of his own mom's nurturing instinct in Margie's caring demeanour.

"Oh, that's a very good place. A lot of the greats stayed there. Room 126 belonged to Marcel Dennis when he came to camp back in the 70s, and Nick Logan was in 410."

"Really?" David laughed. "Well, I'm in 212, so let's make that the David Stone room and someday you can tell everyone about me."

"Well, I'd love to dear, but that was Johnny O'Grady's room. But if you get bigger than Johnny O, I'll tell them it was yours."

"It's a deal." David felt himself relaxing as they both broke out in laughter.

He felt an outpouring of gratitude for Margie. She had done her job. She made a lonely nervous rookie at his first camp feel a little bit better, even happy, if only for a few moments. For an instant he was not brooding over the tremendous task in front of him. Instead, he felt a small sense of belonging, found comfort in knowing that all those stars before him had shared this same experience and likely many of the same trepidations that he felt right now.

The odd pairing entered the auditorium and walked up to four draped registration tables. David saw, for the first time, some of the other 56 rookies and walk-ons that he would be competing against for a shot at the main training camp. It was like his first day of school all over again. Back then it had been his mother by his side holding his hand. Today it was Margie. Only she was holding his hand metaphorically.

"You know, Johnny O was a walk-on too," Margie stated in a matter-of-fact manner. "Came to camp and no one even knew who he was. Drank like a sailor, that one, but boy, could he score. 50 goals one year, 52 the next. I'm telling you, David, that 212's a lucky room, you just remember that." She reached down and warmly shook David's hand before returning to the main foyer.

David walked up to table four, where the S's were categorized. He had a brief meet and greet with the registrar, filled out a few boiler-plate liability release waivers and a player registration form, then received a beautifully bound, Red Wing binder full of information and a bright, emerald-green training camp jersey with his name on the back and the number 14. Officially, David now had proof in hand that he was a pro hockey player and no one would ever be able to take that away from him.

He left the registration table and found a seat at the front of the auditorium. Looking around, he saw a diverse group of rookies, draft picks, walk-ons and even a grandson of team owner, Mike Layton. There would be four teams of 14 players. It looked as though six invitees had decided to not even show up, so the total roster of competitors was already down to 50. *The odds are getting better by the minute*, mused David with a touch of optimism.

A man came out on stage and everyone went silent, listening intently.

"Good morning," the speaker greeted them in a booming voice. "My name is Bryce Anderson and I'm the rookie training camp director. There are seven main camp invites up for grabs, but chances are five of those will go to our highest draft picks from this year—if they don't fuck things up too badly and fail to live up to expectations. But, let me be clear: no spot is guaranteed. If we don't like what we see, we have no problem sending any of you back to juniors or college, so don't think that just because you got drafted you're a lock for main camp. It doesn't work that way. Every day, everyone here has to earn it. There's no freebies given and no one gets the benefit of the doubt. You guys need to prove you belong every minute, every day, both on and off the ice. You need to prove you have what it takes to be a Red Wing." He paused, letting his words sink in before continuing.

    David's eyes landed on Sawyer, just now entering the auditorium and joining them late. The future star casually dropped into a corner chair in the front row. He was barely recognizable with his Yankee's cap pulled low and dark sunglasses hiding his eyes. He certainly appeared far more interested in whatever was on his cell phone than anything Bryce had to say. The way he slouched in his seat seemed to indicate his general boredom with these initial proceedings.

    Bryce gave Riley and his late entrance an ominous look, then ignored him. "We have five days of classroom sessions, on-ice drills and physical tests. It's going to be gruelling and intense. That's not a lot of time for you to show us what you've got. So, do not take anything for granted. Do not think that you'll get a second chance to make up for mistakes. There aren't any. On day five, we have an inter-squad game with all the coaches, scouts, GM and owner in attendance, plus about 5,500 fans. After that, we wrap things up. Some of you will be invited to our main camp. Some of you may earn assignments to the farm teams in Adirondack or Johnstown. The rest of you will be given your out-right releases to go and pursue try-outs with other teams. We wish everyone a safe and exciting training camp. Make us notice you—in a good way. That's your job over the next five days."

    Bryce's instructions were loud and clear. David felt a serious attack of butterflies coming on again. He searched the anxious faces of his peers. They all seemed so big and serious. Some were youngsters just out of high school while others appeared to be larger, mature men. All of them seemed to be bigger, tougher and more confident than he felt right now.

It was then Dave Hellan's turn to address everyone from the podium. As General Manager, he would be the individual with the most input into which players would move on to the main camp. He outlined the team's general expectations for all its players. It was a lot of values this and hard work that kind of commentary, regular boiler plate stuff you'd expect at this type of presentation. He also outlined team behaviour policies for players regarding booze, drugs, gambling and women. Specifically, leave them alone and don't touch them at all this week. Don't go looking for trouble he noted more than once as there was plenty of it around, especially in the many night clubs and casinos that had overtaken Detroit and to a lesser extent Auburn Hills since the great recession.

Hellan's point was pretty straight forward: rookies had much bigger issues to deal with just to survive this camp. Screwing up would mean an automatic dismissal from the team, regardless of who you were.

Buzz Lanyard, Detroit's senior trainer, was the final speaker. He discussed player safety, equipment protocols, injury policies, insurance requirements, medical emergency procedures, and the booking criteria for taping, massage and other athletic services that might help rookies get through the next five days. Then he handed out dressing room allocations. Each player was assigned a personalized locker emblazoned with a Red Wings crested nameplate, featuring letters done in a stylish, san serif font. For many, this and the jerseys would be their only souvenirs of the week and perhaps of their pro hockey careers. These lockers would become each players two and a half by six foot home away from home for the duration of camp, complete with loud obnoxious neighbours and prying busy-bodies watching you all day.

Every day there would be two on-ice workouts of two hours each, one video session, and fitness training. When you were required to spend eight to 10 hours per day at the rink, it was great to know you had a little place of your own, even if it was just a cubbyhole refuge with a piece of padded bench a few shelves and some coat-hooks.

With the speeches ended, players obediently grabbed their gear and began embarking to their assigned dressing rooms. David was in dressing room three, home to the Green team. He was elated to see he had received an extra wide corner stall at the end of a row with a side wall. This meant greater privacy and only one neighbour to deal with. He felt another surge of optimism. *Things are definitely going my way*, he thought. It might seem silly and superstitious to base his feelings on such random events as others not showing up or getting a good locker, but he took them as fateful signs and that helped him build more confidence.

Professional athletes have obsessive personalities, a success trait personified in David Stone. They're hyper competitive and physically superior. Outside, it was common for them to project personalities with an indomitable spirit, unflinching determination and alpha-type character traits. Yet, they were still human. Self-doubt and insecurity could easily seep in and run rampant, especially at times like your first professional training camp, where outcomes are unknown and well beyond individual control, for the most part. That uncertainty leads to a yearning for predictability and certainty making many athletes extremely superstitious.

Waking up on time and having a great tooth-brushing, before enjoying a quick and easy cab ride to the rink could set the stage for a brilliant on-ice performance inspired by all the positive karma. On the other hand, waking up 10 minutes late, forgetting to brush your teeth and then not being able to get a cab to the rink and arriving late could be interpreted as the universe being against you, insecurity setting in and a terrible on-ice performance. Perception is everything and positive routine equates to control. When success and failure are measured in milliseconds and precision execution is essential on every shift and with every action, superstition and luck might just give you the confidence edge you need.

Most of the time, being positive mentally is far more important than one's physicality. Everyone who makes it to the pros has extraordinary physical attributes and specialized skills, but the truly great ones have a superior mental game as well. They intuitively sense outcomes before they occur, deal with split second situations a trifle faster and can will themselves to do precisely the right thing at the perfect time. More importantly, they remain steady, overcoming doubts and insecurities so as to ensure personal and team success. Still, even for them, superstition has its place. Players overcome superstition by creating habits and routines that produce predictability and predictability nurtures confidence. And confidence fosters improved performance. Successfully executing one's positive routines could provide the confidence and edge that may determine who wins or who loses on any given day.

It looked and felt to David that today might be a winner for him. Thus his confidence rose and he began to overcome some of his initial fears.

David opened his locker and laid out his pristine, yet experienced, equipment, piece by piece, doing so in the exact same order he had relied on for years. It was important that his surroundings look and feel familiar and this was a starting point. While hanging his skates on the side hooks of his locker, David glanced across the room and recognized Robbie Freeze. He nodded to him.

Robbie had played junior hockey in Prince Albert a few years ago and David, a rookie then, had faced off against the older player. Robbie had been a much-vaunted, high-scoring winger with a penchant for one timers from the face-off circle that had terrified goaltenders throughout the league. After a respectable junior career, he'd been overlooked in the draft due to his smallish stature. It was an unfair, yet all-too-common assessment that scouts readily made on these types of quality players. Since then, Robbie had tried out for a few NHL teams as a free agent without success. After a pretty good stint in the ECHL the previous season, where he had developed a reputation as a reliable penalty killer that could chip in a few goals here and there, Robbie earned himself a shot at Detroit's rookie camp. But, like David, Robbie was more likely fodder for the real prospects rather than someone with a bona fide chance at making it.

He looked nervous, thought David. I can certainly empathize with that.

The Green's head coach turned out to be none other than Mike McCroy, a fellow, good ole' Saskatchewan boy.

Another good sign, thought David.

"Okay everyone," Mike announced as he looked around the room. "We're on at 1 PM. If you're late, don't bother coming out. Just pack your bags and Uber yourself out of here. We demand professionalism, punctuality and effort here. The first hour will be skating and shooting drills, followed by line-rushes and, finally, a series of half hour scrimmages. I see a few familiar faces among us, so, from everyone in management, welcome, or welcome back. By day three, you'll be playing live full-contact scrimmages against the other teams. This is about your only shot, gents, so leave it all on the ice. There's nothing to save it for except a long drive or plane ride back to where you came from. Thanks for coming to our camp and thank you for wanting to be part of this great organization."

David raced to get the rest of his equipment on. He had been listening so intently to McCroy, that he had not noticed it was already 12:47. Only 13 minutes to launch.

* * *

"GO!" shouted the head coach.

On command, David's muscles flexed and he took off. They were 15 minutes into a good old-fashioned bag skate and the current drill was rink races. Two guys lined up on opposite sides of centre ice and raced to see who would cross their finish line first. Legs pumping, David felt good and the ice seemed to caress his razor sharp Super Tack blades. Enthusiastic hollers let David know that he must be doing well, but then, skating had always been his greatest strength. He blew past the finish line and stood up. Looking back across the rink, he still had time to see Andy Givens just crossing his finish line.

"Fuck, Bolt. Nice scamper!" exclaimed a seriously impressed Darcy Hilton, the resident tough guy from Detroit's farm system. He was a perennial close-but-no-cigar, rookie camp participant. "Keep thrashing like that, man. They love speed here."

If you were going to make a friend on your first day of camp, Darcy was the guy you would want to know. Few others in the organization could throw punches like Hilts and he had a reputation as a solid guy, if he liked you. He was an ominous presence that would always have your back and stood up for his teammates regardless of the cost to him personally. That commitment was what kept getting him invited back to rookie camp. Sadly, it hadn't been enough to get him through to main camp in any of his three previous attempts.

"Thanks man," David exhaled, chest heaving. The next set of participants lined up and the whistle went. David noticed McCroy looking in his direction.

The coach nodded and smiled as the next race was ending in a dead heat.

Uncertain that he was the coach's intended target, David looked over his shoulder to make sure he had not been acknowledging someone else. But, sure enough, nobody was there.

Riley Sawyer took his spot on the line for the next race. At the whistle, he took off quickly, sped around the rink and raced over the finish line to win his heat by about 15 feet. Not a huge margin, but convincing enough to satisfy the coaching staff's expectations.

Following Sawyer's race, David could not help but notice the dozens of reporters and fans watching and critiquing Riley's every movement on the ice.

"Way to go, Riley!" screamed a young boy with SAWYER boldly emblazoned across the back of his brand new Red Wings jersey.

The races eventually ended. This session's final drill would be the dreaded line rushes—a skating staple for any first day of training camp. It was a time-honoured cardio torture test that highlighted within minutes which players had pushed their physical training to the max prior to camp and, consequently, who had the stamina to make it through a real pro camp should they be lucky enough to get an invite.

This is it. I busted my ass all summer for this, so let's get to it, David thought as he glided toward the end boards where his peers were gathering.

10 skaters lined up along the goal line. On the whistle, they would race at top speed to the opposite line on the ice, then sprint back to the goal line they'd started from, then go to the opposite blue line and back to the original goal line. They would do each of the four lines on the rink at top speed before enjoying a short respite while a second group of players did the same drill. The first group would then do it again and then again in rotation. Each squad would do the drill about six times, which was an almost inhuman strain on your thighs, heart, lungs and often your ego.

David won three of his line rushes before catching an edge in a deep rut on the ice. Given his fatigue, he crashed heavily, shoulder first, into the end boards. He lay motionless for a moment, wincing in pain and trying to catch his breath, before instinct told him to get up and keep going. No one liked a quitter. This was not the time, and these were certainly not the people, to give a first impression to that you were injury prone or soft. They'd write you off immediately. His shoulder, the same shoulder injured playing football years ago, ached and his eyes watered a bit as he got up, but it did not feel like anything had been structurally damaged.

Christ! He screamed silently. *Nothing like fucking everything up in the first hour of camp. Be more careful. Get some control. That could have ended everything before it even started.* He shook his head and smashed his stick against the boards in frustration while the throbbing in his shoulder intensified.

As the players slowly glided around the rink during a recovery period, David was pleased to see Riley bent over, stick on his knees, gasping for air as if there was none to be had.

* * *

God, I'm going to puke, Riley thought. *I should have trained more. I really should have trained more. This is brutal. I can't catch my breath.*

"Okay, guys, back on the line. Time for more rushes," hollered the coach.

"What?" gasped an exasperated Sawyer. "There's more? Shit."

"Go after us, you pussy," sneered journeyman minor leaguer, Brent Hagen. "Wouldn't want you to get all queasy and out of sorts, would we?"

A few older players laughed and pushed their way past Sawyer to get on the goal line. At the whistle, they exploded forward. Riley squinted upwards at an oversized bank of metal lights, desperately trying to catch his breath. Then he tried to refocus as best as he could and prepare for his next set of sprints. The speed and skill of camp participants and the heightened expectations of management had taken him by surprise. And this was just rookie camp. Main camp would be even tougher.

Fuck. I'm better than these guys, he thought to himself. At least, that's what central scouting had reported with much fanfare last June. So what the hell was going on? This was no cakewalk. The competition was fierce.

He steadied his blades on the goal line and waited for a whistle blast.

The coach spoke without looking over. "Sawyer! Let's show

a little life for the media guys and all your fans. Ready!"

The coach's sarcasm was exacerbated by hoots of derision and catcalls from a few of the other players. Then the whistle came and he took off. All he could hear was the sound of blades thundering across the ice and his heart pounding with effort.

As he laboured through the lines, with nothing on his mind other than finishing this wretched drill without passing out, Riley could see fans screaming along the end boards. From the corner of his eye he could feel hulking, sweaty beasts pursuing him, each one determined to best Detroit's new boy wonder. At the end, it was not really close, with Riley finishing sixth amongst the skaters in his group.

It was not really the debut his teammates or management had expected or hoped for, but it was just the first day and this was just skating drills. There was a lot more to hockey than sprinting down the ice and Riley had many more weapons in his arsenal. Still, you never wanted to under impress on the first day, or any other day for that matter. It was bad form and would leave a negative impression with both management and teammates that would be tough to shake, especially for someone with a first overall draft pedigree.

* * *

The last session of the day for team Green was a video class focused on Detroit's highly-vaunted breakout and fore-check systems. Over and over the players watched what seemed to be the exact same play, yet each time the execution morphed ever so slightly. Almost imperceptible changes that were so subtle they would be indistinguishable to the average fan. But, to a pro hockey player, they were the essence of managing pressure while creating or eliminating time and space. These standard repetitive actions, as outlined by the special teams coach, gave you time when, in reality, you had none. They took the place of thinking when you really needed to act or react on pure instinct, something that happened a lot when ten skaters and four officials were flying around a 40 foot by 200 foot patch of ice on razor sharp blades at about 35 miles per hour, and some of them were trying to knock you senseless in the process.

The bright fluorescent lights came on and David squinted.

Wrap-up comments for the video session were completed and the first day of camp wound down.

Coach McCroy addressed his Green squad. "Good job out there today everyone. Some of you had pretty impressive performances. I strongly advise you to have supper this evening with some of the guys in this room. Become teammates. That's very important here. Get to know each other. Learn to trust each other. And, follow the personal diet guide in your orientation binder. Come back tomorrow well rested and refreshed. We start at 8 AM sharp in the fitness centre for physical endurance testing. Then we're on the ice for a light skate and more drills in the afternoon and evening. It's going to be a very long and physically demanding day. It will make your work today seem like a casual skate at the mall, so be ready."

"Well, that's fucking delightful," groaned Darcy Hilton in David's direction.

"Yeah, no shit," David replied, attempting to match the gruff tone and manliness that the older Hilton exuded. It didn't really come off too well.

"Listen, Bolt, I know a great Italian joint not too far from here. Why don't you come and join me and a few of the boys for some cannelloni that'll make your taste buds orgasm? It'll be a chance to get to know some of the guys who have been through this before. We'll give you some tips. Though with that hot-foot skating display you put on, you may not need any."

David beamed. "Wow, that'd be awesome. Thanks, Mr. Hilton."

"Seriously, kid? Call me Darcy. Mr. Hilton is some billionaire with two smoking hot daughters blowing his money and making sex tapes. That ain't me."

"Uh, by the way, what's with Bolt?" David asked, referring to the nickname that Hilton seemed to have given him.

"Bolt! Usain Bolt, kid. Fastest guy in the world. Come on, man. You gotta' pick up on the lingo a bit. Like seriously, do you want me to call you DAAAAVVEY?" he asked in a high pitch squeal.

The two laughed, strolled out of the meeting room and into the evening dusk. His first day was in the books and David had nothing more than a throbbing shoulder to show for it. *Not bad*, he thought. *I hope that Bolt handle sticks.*

Chapter 6

"Work it!" hollered an intense fitness evaluator dressed in a white smock and analysing what appeared to be a hand-held diagnostic monitor that reported an athlete's fitness data in real time. "You have to push yourself this last 15 minutes. Make your body do more. Feel the burn. Do you feel it?"

Beads of sweat poured down David's brow and stung his eyes, but he maintained focus through the encouraging comments of his evaluator and a few team mates waiting to do the test next. His lips were firmly fastened to a sterile breathing tube connected to a digital dashboard which methodically and precisely measured, recorded and presented David's bio-metric performance on over 20 variables.

David's concentration needed to be complete because every rookie knew that the cardio-cycle evaluation was the most gruelling and telling fitness assessment they would endure. Generally, the player scoring highest on this test was deemed the fittest player at camp and David felt the title was his for the taking. It was also one of the most important set of results team management and coaches used in determining which guys were professionally prepared for camp and committed to an NHL career.

As Bryce Anderson had said at orientation, "You need to stand out, gentlemen. Make us notice you." This evaluation was the highest profile way to achieve that notoriety in a hurry. So, as the minutes ticked by, David fought to maintain a steady pace, regulated his breathing as best he could and stared like a zombie at the blinking heart monitor pulsating on the digital screen in front of him.

His evaluator's comments and the rhythmic hum of rotating pedals barely registered in David's consciousness as his thoughts drifted back to last summer's morning runs, Anne's warm smile as he arrived home each evening, and of course the long conversations with Mel about life as a professional athlete. Even with all the pain of the moment these memories brought a slight smile to David's lips.

An excellent strategy for excelling during times of extreme physical stress was to release your mind and let it drift wherever it wanted to go. This is the body's natural defence against the harsh effects of fatigue, pain and self-doubt that accompanied such activity. You just let the physical happen.

David knew that he was fit, but this challenge was proving to be over the top by even the high standards of professional athletics, so he just had to have faith his muscles and everything attached to them would not seize up. Then, without notice, the trainer raised the resistance level to its highest allowable setting for the final five minutes.

David felt his legs and thighs spasm from the increased tension. His heart almost exploded as it was forced to pump harder to supply greater amounts of oxygenated blood to every extremity of his struggling body. His calves burned and his quads ached from the strain. Chest heaves and the rhythm of his breathing interrupted the random thoughts and became more elevated and at times irregular. *Am I going into shock?* He thought through the fog. Yet his legs continued to pump furiously though it took every ounce of willpower and determination he had just to stay upright on the seat.

"Just two more minutes, Mr. Stone! Great job, kid! Keep pushin' it."

David barely heard the trainer, or anyone else now. He was growing disoriented. He felt he couldn't push the pedal down one more time. But he couldn't stop either. And then mercifully it was over. The tension of the cycle eased back until the pedals seemed to be turning themselves. Finally, his legs gave out and stopped moving. Two of his team mates standing on either side of the stationary bike helped him from the seat and steadied him on his feet as he moaned in relief. The primary monitor by the trainer's station blinked intermittently before registering his final performance score which included an 8.85 out of 9 endurance level with an oxygen efficiency rating of 98.3 percent. Unimaginable scores for a hockey player.

Buzz walked over and placed his hand on David's soaked t-shirt. "That's a pretty special thing you just did there. Great job, amazing really. Are you okay?"

David tried to speak through the tube still taped to his mouth. "Did I win, Buzz?"

"Don't know yet." Buzz laughed as he gently removed the tape, tube and electrodes from his face. "But with those stats you would have won last year so I'm pretty sure you'll be up there. You need to relax now for about five minutes. Just sit on the bench over there and take some sips of cool water to get your body temp down and your heart rate normalized. Then go change for the video session. Really well done, son." Buzz placed his large hand on the back of David's head and nodded before turning away.

* * *

Mike McCroy walked over to the coffee machine. He shook his head and poured himself another dark roast with vanilla creamer. "I'm telling you, Larry, this Stone kid is incredible. He's as fast as a jet. And today it looks like he won the endurance test. I think he should get a look at the main camp."

"Are you kidding?" spat Larry Davies, the Red squad coach. "He's a freakin' walk-on and that's just fitness testing. I've got lots of great kids too, fast and drafted. We're not picking a cycling team here, we're building a hockey team. You Saskatchewan guys, you're always trying to find the next Gordie Howe. We've still got a long way to go."

Buzz chimed in. "Larry, you had to see him on that stationary bike today. It was primitive, man, beyond human. His eyes and focus were amazing. Stone-cold fearless and determined. I thought he was going to collapse a few times but then he would just seem to reset and keep going. That kid, he's special in a profound way whether it's a cycling team, hockey team or swim team you're putting together. There's no quit in him."

Dave Hellan, sitting off to the side of the room in a comfy Lazy Boy lounger with a stack of test results, snickered at the impassioned bickering among his key staff. He liked that. He wanted his guys to fight for their kids and push them to be great. It was the only way that his team could improve and certainly the only way each player could realize their God-given potential. "Settle down, guys, it's only the second day. We've got lots of things to evaluate yet, so it's probably a little early to be handing out invites. There's still scrimmages, then some games. We'll see what he's got then. Who is he, again?"

"David Stone. Saskatchewan kid. Farm boy. Played in Saskatoon on a pretty shitty team. Did okay, but nothing to write home about," McCroy explained.

"Well there's always one that flies under the radar," Hellan acknowledged. "Watch him and see if he's really a diamond in the rough or just fool's gold. Scrimmages and games always tell the true story. This fitness stuff is just window dressing. That said, winning the endurance test, well that takes some balls for sure." He stood up. "Let's get 'em back on the ice and see how good they are with a puck. By the way, how's Sawyer doing? Heard he's been struggling a bit."

"No, not really!" protested Davies, Sawyer's coach. "He's just getting warmed up. That kids got great instincts and tools, though he probably could have come to camp in a little better shape."

"How'd he do in testing?" Hellan questioned Davies point blank.

"Uhhh, looks like 18th or so," the Red squad's coach replied a bit sheepishly, flipping through his clipboard.

"And Stone?"

"Looks like he'll win it," Davies admitted.

"Good for him. Watch him, guys, that's a big accomplishment. He came ready to play. And remember, fans love an underdog. Let's see how he performs in scrimmages this afternoon. Mike, put him in a few jams. Let's see what happens when he's under game conditions."

* * *

Criss-crossing line-rushes proceeded down the ice at lightning speed. Wave after wave they came, with each rush hopefully ending in a shot on net and a goal. The idea was to see if defensemen could break up offensive attacks by planting the attacking forwards on their butts or driving them into the boards. If they could also get control of the puck and safely clear it from the zone, well that was a bonus.

Riley peered over at his linemates and fired a crisp pass to the right, then followed the puck over to the area.

Teammate Russ Williams caught the pass and threw the puck back across ice to left-winger Anson Dee, then moved quickly toward centre.

Dee carried the puck across the blue line as time and space

between forwards and defensemen disappeared, first to a few yards and within seconds to a few feet. He noted Sawyer speeding back across the frozen surface toward him and dropped him the puck.

Sawyer neatly picked up the black orb and accelerated instinctively toward a small crack between the two hulking defensemen. The rear guards realized immediately what was happening and pinched together in an effort to close off Riley's route to the net. But, Sawyer's size and speed were deceiving and just before the tiny fissure closed he skirted through and blasted a major league wrist shot into the top right corner of the goal.

His linemates roared a callous Bronx cheer for the young stud as a dejected goalie fished the puck from the back of the net.

Riley celebrated and headed back to centre ice to prepare for the next line rush. As he grabbed a water bottle off the board dasher to get some fluids, he could hear the coaches talking at the other end of the bench.

"Fuck!" exclaimed Coach Davies in genuine shock. "You just can't teach that move—a guy's either got it or he doesn't."

Buzz nodded. "No shit. That was a big-league goal to be sure. Great move. Wicked wrister."

Anson Dee cruised over to the boards next to Riley. "Oooeee, that was sweet!" he enthused. "Great play, man!"

Riley smiled. This was more like it. Enough of those fitness tests. This is where he shone, with a stick, a puck and ice under his blades. David Stone might have shown him up on the stationary bike, but this is where things really counted. And Riley was going to show everyone why he had been the number one pick.

***

Danielle watched as Sawyer perfectly split the defencemen and scored his highlight reel goal. The pretty reporter and her accompanying photographer stood adjacent to the net. The photographer had snapped a photo series of Riley's moves from a perfect angle, capturing every instant up to his shot. She watched as the other players cheered the goal and made a few notes on her phone. She had come to see Sawyer and knew that her readers, eager for any news, would be enthralled by that play and the hope it garnered for many more such highlights.

But there was more to this camp than just Riley Sawyer. Danielle moved quietly around the rink, watching each scrimmage, trying to determine which rookies might make the cut and become difference-makers during the coming season. While Riley Sawyer was the odds on favourite to make the team and many fans wanted to see Darcy Hilton moved up to add some toughness to the line-up, it was the blazing speed, work ethic, rugged good looks and self-deprecating style of some Saskatchewan farm boy, a walk-on named David Stone that had been making the biggest impression on the leggy reporter. In fact, she was heading over to check out his scrimmage now. The unknown, the underdog, fired up her journalistic instinct. And he was kind of cute too.

* * *

In Arena C, David was flying into the corner to retrieve a loose puck. Over his shoulder he caught a glimpse of a quickly closing defenseman who was preparing to deliver a crushing body check on him. The young forward braced for the contact he knew was coming while maintaining his focus on the path of the puck. At just the right instant, he threw himself into the boards and let the laws of physics go to work for him. The collision felt nuclear. David's body catapulted back off the boards at twice the velocity and blasted into the defenceman's chest causing him to fall backward from the blow and collapse on the ice with a thud. In obvious distress he rolled into the fetal position and lay motionless.

David, having survived the contact, deftly scooped up the puck as it careened to his side of the boards and in a seamless transition he angled toward the net. Deftly he slipped the disk through the skates of a back-checking winger and, in one fluid motion, slid a seeing-eye saucer pass under his outstretched stick to Robbie Freeze, who slammed it into the back of the net.

The two leaped into each other's arms like they had just scored a seventh game overtime winner.

Darcy Hilton screamed like a wild child and leaped into the gaggle of players congregating by the goal. Everyone was laughing and celebrating—if only just to relieve some of the pressure they were feeling. David extricated himself from the group as others arrived and flashed a broad grin toward the bench.

Mike McCroy looked over at Buzz and the two nodded knowingly. These were rare moments for them. It appeared there might be something special going on here.

NHL rookie camps were emotionally difficult for coaches and trainers because the odds of one of these young men defying expectations and having a career in pro hockey were infinitesimal. So many dreams were dashed here, crushed actually. And many other fresh-starts and do-overs died here too. It was little moments like these, unexpected eye openers, that let everyone just enjoy the moment. That play was perfect and had profiled David's genuine professional talent and extraordinary mental focus. It was a great moment for a great guy that both the coach and trainer were rooting for.

Buzz rushed out onto the ice to tend to the groggy defenseman that David had body slammed so perfectly. First some smelling salts and then the three-finger counting test. He would be fine Buzz concluded, his problem being more hurt pride than anything physical.

David glided over to the trainer as he helped the defensemen to his bench.

"Nice hit, tough guy." Buzz laughed. "Better keep your head up now."

David couldn't keep the grin off his face. "Will do. How's buddy doing?"

"Gonna be fine. You just winded him. Good hit. Good shift."

* * *

Danielle smiled at the mass of grown men celebrating on the ice like little leaguers over a meaningless goal in a nothing scrimmage. *Boys will be boys*, she thought. They sure didn't need much stimulation to act like idiots. However, the play by Stone was spectacular. Her eyes followed him across the ice. *I think it's time I introduce myself to this farm boy.*

* * *

The media scrum after practice was large by training camp standards. Video cameras and hand held recorders competed for face time in front of various players. Old guard reporters could not get enough of Riley Sawyer's glib, cliché comments. Yet today, a growing number of scribes were hanging around the locker of a virtual unknown, the Saskatchewan kid named Stone. Dave Hellan and Buzz Lanyard watched from the doorway as the media horde circulating around David continued to grow.

"So, David, the word around camp is you're the fastest guy here. Care to comment?" asked a radio reporter shoving his recorder in David's face.

"No," stated a deadpan Stone, much to the joy of everyone.

If there's one thing the media loves it's an unlikely hero and these reporters were looking at David like there was a big-league fairy tale brewing.

"David, how would you rate your camp so far?" The second question came from a shapely blonde who seemed familiar to him. In answering the question he had to work hard not to gaze at her inappropriately or for too long.

"Well, I think it's been okay. The guys have been really great and the coaches love to work us - hard. With so many great players around, I'm learning a lot and just pushing myself to do my best.

She cocked a challenging eyebrow at him. "What do you think of your chances for a real camp invite?"

David swallowed hard, then shrugged. "Lots of this camp left. Not sure there's been anything to write home about just yet."

She gave him a sexy, enticing smile. "But, didn't you win the fitness challenge? That must have felt pretty satisfying."

He looked down with a sheepish grin. "Actually ma'am, that may have been the worst 60 minutes of my life, I'm really happy to have just survived."

The group exploded in laughter as the media's full-fledged love affair with David Stone – walk on – elevated itself into a frenzy.

Dave Hellan and Buzz Lanyard watched in awe as the reporters around David's locker enthused over his honest responses and innocent nuances. They marvelled at the kid's humble attitude and infectious personality.

"Look at him Buzz. They love him. A nowhere, no name, honest to God nice guy and they love him. How many season tickets do you think that sells?"

Buzz nodded in agreement. "Forget tickets Dave, the kids got game. Not only can he skate but he thinks the game like a veteran. Plus, he's got moxie. He did a blow-back check off the boards and just about killed that Henderson kid from Denver, the giant defenseman. It was fucking hilarious. I haven't seen that move done so well in years."

"I got it Buzz, you like him. We'll watch him real close the next few days. If he stays on keel we'll give him an invite. Hell, if he can get that motley media crowd to cheer for him, he's already earned it."

* * *

From his vantage point down the corridor, Riley's head snapped around when a roar of laughter erupted from outside another dressing room. "What's going on up there?" he asked no one in particular.

"Not sure," replied Dex Watson, sports anchor with KLMO TV Detroit. "So, Riley, back to my question. Has this camp been tougher than you thought or pretty much what you expected?"

"Well it's been interesting, Dex, I can tell you that. Guys are a bit bigger and the speed of everything moves a whole lot faster than back in junior. But, I did some pretty good things today and so I'm hoping to keep improving every day, show them all what I can do."

Another blast of raucous laughter emerged from the media scrum down the hall, one that had grown much larger than his. Riley stared at the cluster of reporters and unexpectedly caught a glimpse of the beautiful female writer who had submarined him at his first Detroit presser. She was emerging from the boisterous crowd. His pulse quickened. What was her name again? Danielle! He quickly asked Dex and the others to excuse him for a moment and strode purposefully down the hall toward the action.

"Hey, Riley, I'm not done here!" called Dex after him.

Riley ignored the reporter. He stepped abruptly in front of Danielle, who was leaning against a pillar, listening to her recorder. "Your question was rude," he blurted out.

"Excuse me?" Danielle responded, somewhat taken aback by Riley's aggressive tone.

"I wasn't trying to be conceited you know, but you made me look like a jerk. I'm still taking flak for it."

Daniel shrugged. "Yeah, sorry about that. But consider it your first lesson in professional sports media relations. The questions for you are only going to get tougher from here on and you're going to need to be better prepared. And, maybe a little less arrogant." She smirked. "Be more like Stone."

Riley frowned. "What the hell is that supposed to mean?" he spat.

"Stone's kicking your ass on the ice, winning fitness tests and working the media like a pro, even if he doesn't know it. And everyone loves him. Frankly, he's a much better story than you right now. So you better get your game face on superstar or you could be in for a rough ride. And just wait until main camp starts, you're going to have some bridges to mend there with the veterans for sure."

Riley rolled his eyes. "Stone? Seriously? Who the fuck is he? Some flash-in-the-pan nobody. We're just getting started here. Still lots of time for that halo he's got hanging over his head to vaporize. I'm not worried about him. But between us, I'll definitely be ready the next time you try to set me up."

Danielle laughed. "Okay, I guess I've been warned. Thanks for the heads up. Sorry, what's your name again? Sawyer, right?"

Riley smiled. "Great, I'm glad we got that out of the way. Now, maybe you and me can get out of here and grab a drink or dinner? I'd be happy to give you another interview."

Danielle pulled her head back in a mock state of shock. She stared at him, brows raised. "Really? Did you actually just ask me out? Sorry, heart throb, but I've got a story to finish. Besides, I don't date hockey players. I just write about them. But thanks for the invite. Maybe I'll take you up on that interview if you make the main camp." With that Danielle swung around on her stylish heels and briskly walked off down the corridor.

Riley watched her go, determined not to give her the upper hand. "Okay then, another time. I can wait. But remember, I'll be ready for you."

* * *

As Danielle walked out the large double doors and into the late summer sun, she couldn't help but burst out laughing at the surreal confrontation that had just occurred. That Sawyer was unbelievable. And cocky. *He's ready for me. He'd better be more worried about the 25 guys he pissed off with his press conference comments.*

"Riley, Riley, Riley," she whispered shaking her head.

Chapter 7

One more day, thought David as he slid his feet from under the crisp white sheets and into Room 212's cool morning air. Rookie camp had gone pretty well until now, but the range in his sore shoulder had continued to deteriorate and this morning he was in significant pain. The focus of camp today would be the much-anticipated final scrimmage, a show down between his surprising Green team and the heavily favoured Red squad powered by Riley Sawyer and Anson Dee. The last day and last chance to earn that invite. He just had to make it through one final day.

As he gingerly stepped into the thick streams of steaming water that cascaded from a rain styled shower head, the throbbing pain and stiffness in his shoulder seemed to flow from his body and down the drain. "Ohhh," he sighed. "God, that feels good." He rested his head on the white tiled wall and slowly let it roll from side to side in homage to the healing properties of the heat and moisture.

Fortunately, David had had the foresight to book a physio treatment with Buzz at 10 AM, just after the team's film review. He wanted to get some professional diagnosis of his injury and figure out how he could protect it during the scrimmage. Hopefully, Buzz's magic and a few shots of cortisone would get him through the rest of the day and then he could heal during his week off before main camp, assuming that was even in his future.

Later, when David walked into the Coffee Bean for his morning caffeine fix, he could not help but sense that many customers, including those standing in the ordering queue, were staring at him. First, he recalled that his cabbie had been glancing in the rear view mirror a lot more than normal during the drive. Now, a young girl behind him in the line kept popping her head to the side and watching him before slowly moving back into place. Did she seriously think he couldn't see her. And now, as he placed his order, the barista's stare seemed to linger a bit longer than usual, before she turned to her co-worker and whispered something. Simultaneously, they both turned and looked him up and down.

"Here you go," said the pretty young server. She hesitated. "Do you think I could get your autograph?"

"Huh?" David grunted, not sure that he had heard right. "You want my autograph?" he asked in true surprise.

"Well, yeah, you're one of the Red Wings, aren't you? David Stone, right?"

"Uh yes. Sort of, I guess. I mean yes, I'm David Stone. But I'm not a Red Wing – yet. We're still in camp."

"Great! So, can I have your autograph?" The young girl grinned and looked at him longingly, endeared by his discomfort with celebrity.

"Uh, what do you want me to sign?" David fumbled, embarrassed to be asked and now stressed by how much time he was wasting for those standing behind him.

"How about your picture?" With that she reached under the counter and pulled out a newspaper. She handed David the day's edition of the Detroit Free Press, the city's most senior and respected publication.

David's eyes popped wide open and he almost dropped his coffee. There, on the front page of the sports section was a huge picture of him, leaping into the air during yesterday's practice. The story's headline, written by one Danielle Wright, proclaimed his performance at camp, "Solid As A Stone?"

He scribbled his name across the page. To Cindy. My first autograph as a Red Wing. David Stone.

Then, there was another page from a guy behind him, a napkin from a female bus driver who wanted it made out to Mark, her son, and within seconds he had signed about five autographs. Realizing the growing angst of customers behind him – regardless if they were Red Wing fans or not - he hastily bowed out of the coffee shop and sprinted to his cab.

"Hey, do you think you could find me a newspaper box?" he asked the driver. "I need to get a paper before we get to the rink."

"You can read mine, Mr. Stone." The cabbie smiled and held out his own copy of the Free Press to his now famous fare.

The very flattering story chronicled David's stellar play at rookie camp since his inauspicious arrival. It then proceeded to break down and rationalize how and why he was now a leading candidate for an invitation to Detroit's main camp. It also had a bit of background story. The surprising walk-on was defying the odds and likely moving on while other, more notable names were struggling or had downright blown their opportunities. There were interviews with his hometown trainer, Mel Simms, as well as his mom and Luke. And there were some very complimentary reviews from Detroit GM Dave Hellan and Coach McCroy. He could hardly contain the smile that grew wider and wider across his face as they drove.

This is awesome, thought David as he scribbled his name across the front page picture like a seasoned autograph veteran. To Vince, My Favourite Driver. Best Wishes, David Stone #—. The crash back to reality was abrupt as David realized in that moment that he did not have a number. In fact, he wasn't even an actual Red Wing. He hadn't made the team yet. Hell, he hadn't even been invited to the real training camp. And he had a very important day in front of him. He might be a contender, but he could still blow it all. He had to stay focused.

He passed the signed newspaper back to the front seat and stared out the window at all the beautiful red and orange foliage lining the streets as they approached the practice facility. The rinks appeared and with it came a renewed sense of foreboding. Could he do this? Today he would find out?

* * *

The door to dressing room three had barely opened when the classic R&B tune, Solid As A Rock, started blaring, compliments of Darcy Hilton. In unison, all the players held up copies of the Free Press, parodied the main chorus of the song and bowed in mock deference to David as he walked by them to his locker. He was barely able to contain the giant grin that had formed across his face as he revelled in his fifteen minutes of fame.

"Okay, you idiots, shut that off," bellowed Mike McCroy over the noise, which quickly dropped to dead silence. "Alright, we've got one more day and this is the big one. Dave Hellan will be here. Bryce Anderson will be here. Hell, I've even heard Mr. Layton might drop by. This is make it or break it day, guys. Everything you've done up to now doesn't really matter if you blow it here. It's all about today. You need to capitalize on every moment if you hope to make it to the show. This is the pros. So stop acting like assholes and get focused. Film and playbook until 10 AM, then a light on-ice session. Pre-game prep starts at 4 PM. The game goes at 6 and apparently it's completely sold out. So let's give them a major league show. Good luck gentlemen."

The room remained silent as each player processed the gravity of Mike's comments and their own precarious situations.

Their rookie camp was almost over. When the arena lights dimmed tonight following the game, so would the fleeting friendships, great memories and funny stories that defined this moment of their lives.

David quietly gathered his thoughts, grabbed his playbook from the top shelf and strolled off down the hall to the video room with Darcy and Brent Hagen. It was time to get his game face on.

* * *

"Hey, Buzz," said David as he walked into the trainer's room. "My shoulder's killing me. Anything you can do about that?"

"Guess you're not quite as solid as they seem to think," joked Buzz.

The irony of his comment made them both chuckle.

David shook his head as he took a seat. "Yeah, that was pretty weird alright. You should have seen how people treated me this morning. Strangers at the coffee shop asking for autographs, shaking my hand, taking selfies. Then the cabbie. It was pretty cool."

"Kid, it's only cool on the way up, remember that. The day you stop moving up it can get real ugly in a hurry. You're getting a break because the story went your way this week. Don't blow it by having a shitty game tonight. You've still got to prove that you belong, that you can handle the pressure and still perform." His fingers pressed into David's flesh as he began to treat his patient. "So, I've gotta' get this shoulder better. I'm gonna' need some more ice so just lay here and relax on the slab for a bit. I'll be right back."

Buzz left the room and David laid his head on the training table's raised pillow staring at the ceiling. He felt nervous and excited at the same time. Happy, yet scared. He laughed to himself at the thought of Darcy bowing down to him in the locker room and that stupid song. What a day it had been already.

The door crashed open, almost causing David to fall off his perch. He looked up suddenly to see Riley Sawyer standing over him.

"Oh. Sorry, dude. Didn't know you were in here. Is the old man around?"

"Uh, no. He went to get some ice."

"What's the matter? Bum shoulder?"

"Yeah. Took a spill the first day and it hasn't been quite right since. Hoping Buzz can take some of the sting out."

Riley studied him for a long moment. "So, you're Stone," he stated with a slight sneer. "The farm boy that made good, huh? Congrats man, you turned a lot of heads this week."

"Thanks, Riley. I wasn't sure how this would go, but it's been good. I saw some of your game yesterday against the Blue team. You got great stuff, man. I guess that's what made you number one."

"Yeah, right. Don't blow sunshine up my ass. This has been a brutal week, with guys like you making me look like a pylon." He hesitated. "But, thanks for the effort."

David stood and offered his hand. "Good luck out there."

Riley looked down at the hand for a moment as if contemplating not taking it. Then he reached out his own.

The two shook hands.

Riley broke the handshake first. "OK. You have a good one too. Watch that shoulder, if you know what I mean. When the old man gets back, tell him I need some early taping and I'll see him at around 4:45 PM or so."

Riley left and David again laid down and stared up at the ceiling. *Is that guy okay or is he gonna' kill me tonight now that he knows my weak spot?* Buzz returned with the ice and began his treatment and while the ice and cortisone numbed the pain, it did little to counter the uncertainty of the night's big scrimmage and David's future.

Chapter 8

David had prepared for hundreds of hockey games, many far more prestigious than the rookie scrimmage he would play in tonight. But, none ever meant as much to him. He had done everything possible to get noticed and earn one of the golden invites to main camp. But, it could all be undone by a so-so performance tonight. Everyone loves an underdog except when they play like an underdog.

With a few hours to himself before he needed to get ready for the game, David stared at his few scattered press clippings spread out on his dated and cheaply crafted bureau. If nothing else, he had a few mementos to share with the folks back home. Proof for a future date that would authenticate his stories of NHL grandeur and disappointment. He clicked the remote and his television burst to life pre-set on ESPN – the single greatest time waster for a pro athlete. It was rolling through the day's headlines.

Baseball highlights were first and longest because that sport was heading into its playoffs, with the World Series only weeks away. Then came football. The NFL was just starting and it was by far the most popular television property in America, so there was plenty of coverage there. They talked about golf and the upcoming FedEx Cup tournaments, a bit of soccer and, finally, hockey.

Normally, ESPN wouldn't spend a lot of time on something like NHL rookie camps. But, this year, thanks to number one draft pick Riley Sawyer, the camp was getting an above average amount of media attention. In fact, Detroit's rookie camp had been attended by an astounding 89 accredited reporters from almost every credible national and international hockey broadcaster and publication.

Following a final mind-numbing flash-back to baseball highlights that all seemed the same, the coming soon hockey feature was highlighted as an interview with a Detroit affiliate on the final scrimmage game to be played later that evening. *Cool*, thought David. Enough time for a bathroom break, grab another water and be back in time for the interview. As he plunged back onto the bed the stunning features of Danielle Wright appeared on screen, much to his satisfaction. *God, she's gorgeous.*

"So, Danielle, what's the competition really like right now in

Detroit?" asked the ESPN studio anchor in Atlanta.

Danielle flashed a brilliant smile that no doubt captured hearts nation-wide. It certainly captured David's. "Well, it's been pretty interesting here, Don. Of course, all eyes have been on Riley Sawyer since the day he was drafted. But, after the first day or two, a lot of eyes have shifted to a couple of unknowns also: David Stone, a rugged physical centre from Saskatchewan and Anson Dee, a set-up winger from Toronto. They have really worked their way into the story. Tonight they'll all be going head-to-head in the final scrimmage to see which players will go on to the main training camp with the veterans."

"Eyes have shifted. So, are you saying Sawyer's looked bad?"

"No, not at all. He's shown some flashes of brilliance at times, the kind of things you'd expect from a first overall draft pick. But what's surprised everyone is that other guys have just performed better. Guys like David Stone, a walk-on and virtual unknown that has looked really good. Not a lot of undrafted players make it through this tough process, but he just might. There's a lot riding on this game tonight for a lot of guys – especially Stone and Dee."

David had never been a ladies man—in fact he had never even had a real girlfriend—but for the first time in his life he knew he was in love. Had she just said on national television that he had a good chance of getting through to main camp? He felt an incredible welling of happiness and confidence that had been in short supply over the last week – maybe months. David shook his head and again focused on the interview.

"So everyone here is very anxious to see these three guys under live fire tonight in a real game situation with a lot on the line," Danielle continued. "Then we'll have a much better idea of who's got the right stuff to move on."

"Well thank you Danielle for that bit of insight from Detroit. Next hour we'll be talking NASCAR and are these guys cheating with new engine fuels? Story coming up in two minutes."

David threw his head back into the pillow and winced as the movement caused discomfort in his sore shoulder. *I should phone mom.* He picked up his cell phone to make the call, then paused. He put the phone back down. *Stay focused. I'll call mom after the game. After I get an invite.* His thoughts drifted again. *Boy that Danielle is amazing. She's gorgeous, smart and strong. And, I think she likes me. God, what a loser I am.* David chuckled. Maybe, after tonight's game, if everything went well he would try to bump into her and see where things went. It was time to head back to the rink.

David's cab pulled up 13 minutes later.

"So? You got something to do with the Wings?" his driver asked.

"Yeah. I'm at the rookie camp."

"No shit? You don't look that big dude. How's it you don't get killed?"

"Actually, I'm sort of average size for a player. That equipment puts on a lot of bulk. Kind of an optical illusion, I guess."

"Hmmm, well, I'm mostly a Tigers and Pistons fan. But this year I might start following the Wings too 'cause they got that new kid, Stone. Some big super star.

"Uh, I think you're talking about Riley Sawyer, he's the number one pick."

"Really? I thought it was Stone. Solid as a Stone, they say."

"No, it's definitely Sawyer." David protested. "He's the big stud, trust me."

"Hmm. But there's a Stone too, right? You know him?"

"Yeah, we've met and he is a really good guy. Great player too. I think he could make it."

The yellow cab pulled into the parking lot of the Coffee Bean and after a few minutes waiting while David got his java fix, it headed to the arena and to David Stone's appointment with destiny. What a great day this was turning into for the nobody, soon to be somebody, from Saskatchewan.

Chapter 9

"One minute remaining in the second period," blared a voice from the arena's deafening public address system. *Someone, really should have done a sound check on that*, thought David. But, in true minor-league fashion no one really seemed to care.

David sat on the bench, waiting for his line to be called. He had a great sweat going and felt totally in synch with the moment. He was having a strong performance with one goal and a sweet primary assist on Brent Hagen's go ahead marker. His green team was leading Riley's red team 3 to 2 and just 20 minutes to go.

Anyone watching the game, except maybe the most star struck female teeny-bopper, would have to admit Stone was the best rookie on the ice followed by Brent Hagen. Both were tough and fast, seemingly in love with the dirty area in front of the goal crease where the hits were the hardest and most of the goals were scored.

Riley Sawyer? He seemed to play around the edges too often and appeared to have no interest in crashing the net. In a hard-hitting fast game like hockey, that makes it very hard to show your skills and be effective.

"What the hell are you guys doing out there," yelled Larry Davies the Red team coach, after his players had settled in their dressing room following the period. "This is fucking embarrassing. You guys look completely disinterested. Stone, Hilton and Hagen are destroying you out there. Where's your pride! Sawyer, you may be getting a free ride to main camp, but believe me the way you're playing you'll be back in the Soo before they hand out practice jerseys. Now, all of you, sit here and think about what you're going to do to have a better third period and maybe save your pro careers. Nobody in this room deserves to be a Red Wing based on what I saw out there in the first forty minutes." Davies turned and slammed the door behind him as he left the room.

Dave Hellan was in the hallway reviewing some stat sheets as his seething assistant coach stormed towards him. "Wow, this is not going so well," understated the coach. I can't seem to light a fire under that kid. He's playing like a pussy and its spreading through the whole line-up. I'd bench the little prick if I could."

"Don't be crazy, Larry" smirked the GM. "He's just an immature kid. We've seen this a million times. These star types show up all full of themselves after the draft and realize pretty fast this place is primal. It's survival of the fittest and remember Stone – he was the fittest." Larry laughed at the all too true metaphor based on David's earlier fitness testing achievements.

"Yeah, you may have been right Dave. Anyway I'm going to double shift Sawyer in the third and see if I can wake him up. I know he's got the skill. He's just disconnected."

Darcy Hilton elbowed David as they sat in the dressing room between periods. "Man, you're on fire tonight." His face contorted in an ear-to-ear grin.

"Give me a break, Darce. You know how it goes, great game tonight, bad game tomorrow. I just have to keep going. Do more. And by the way, you're playing fucking awesome as well. We can win this thing," David stated emphatically to his new found friend slapping the thick thigh pads on his nylon pants.

The two had bonded quickly over the past week and David loved playing with Hilt's on the same line. He hoped Darcy would make the cut, but knew that might be an even longer shot than his own chances.

"Listen Bolt. It couldn't happen to a better guy. I'm proud of you. Now let's go kick their sorry asses in the third and I want you to get one more. Let's shove this down Sawyer's throat – with authority." Hilton laughed and pulled on his helmet.

The buzzer sounded and the players marched toward the ice for the final 20 minutes of play and possibly their careers. David could barely contain his excitement as he strode down the covered tunnel like some mythical warrior heading into battle. With each step the noisy crowd got louder and closer elevating his testosterone levels and energy. It was such a rush. Unlike anything he'd ever experienced before. A crescendo was reached as he stepped on the ice and a huge roar went up that seemed to rock the stadium's metal roof.

Darcy skated up and tapped David's shin pads. "That one's for you kid, enjoy the moment, they don't come along very often. David smiled and the two skated in circles prior to heading to the bench.

"OK, we start with Stone's line, let's go boys, big effort

now." Coach McCroy waved David, Hilton and Hagen onto the ice and then laughed as Hilton moved past him. "Hey Hilts, if Stone can score again with you on his line, then he really is ready for the pros."

"Up yours, coach." Darcy laughed at his superior and then turned to David. "Don't worry, I won't let anything happen to pretty boy here on my watch." McCroy winked and the three glided out to centre ice.

The puck dropped and the capacity crowd of 5,996 roared in unison as play began.

David fired the puck into the red team's end. A defenseman tried to blast it around the boards and back out.

Riley Sawyer saw the puck approach his blue line and deftly poked it by a slow-footed rear-guard, creating a perfect two-on-one. He raced for the net.

David saw the play developing. He put his head down and skated as fast as he could toward his defensive zone. The burn in his thighs reminded him of those long summer runs. This would be where it all paid off. With a burst of energy he found a new gear, one he hadn't even known he had. He caught Sawyer from behind and lifted his stick, easily letting him steal the puck.

Riley spun around and stared in shock unable to believe Stone had caught up to him.

David wheeled around abruptly with the puck, sending a spray of ice into the air. The crowd leapt to their feet shrieking approval. Instinctively, David reoriented himself on the ice. To his right, he saw Hilton heading toward the red team's goal. David fired a perfect tape-to-tape pass to Darcy and then took off at full speed toward the slot in front of the net.

Hilton cut deftly around a rather clumsy red team defenseman and threw the puck back to David.

David faked a shot, pulling the goaltender completely out of his yawning cage. Then to everyone's surprise considering the easy shot on goal he would have, David slid the puck back to Darcy, who was steaming in from the wing. The somewhat surprised Hilton happily slammed the puck into the open net and then leaped into the end boards in ecstasy.

David and Hagen joined the celebration as Guns and Roses, Welcome To The Jungle blared from the public address speakers and the red goal light flooded the arena with pulsating lumens.

Boisterous fans hammered on the glass with their fists and the building erupted. It was a moment in time David would never forget.

Success comes in so many ways, David thought, *some big and some so small they barely get noticed. But, this small moment was the best.* Darcy Hilton, his friend, protector, mentor, and teammate for the most important week of his life, was aptly the centre of attention at a very critical time and, for David, that gave him a far better feeling than anything that could have happened for him.

"What a pass, man!" Hagen shrieked in the huddle of players. "All world, baby! All world!"

Darcy grinned in sheer euphoria. "Awesome, Bolt! Beauty pass man. Fuck I wasn't even going to go to the net. Figured you'd shoot. Loved that play man. That was great. Seriously, I owe you—big."

"Never, buddy, you deserve it. You're playing great."

They skated back to the bench as the crowd roared its approval.

"Green team goal scored by number 15, Darcy Hilton," boomed the metallic PA system voice.

The crowd's noise level increased again.

"Assist number 14, David Stone."

Wild cheering reverberated off the walls of Auburn Hills Sports Plex as David took his place on the bench. He bowed his head and quietly thanked God for everything that had just happened in that instant. Then he pinched the inside of his leg just to make sure this was all real and smiled at the pain that shot up his thigh.

* * *

Watching the game from seat 18 in row seven was Dave Hellan. "He's in," commanded the general manager emphatically. So is Hagen and that mutt, Hilton. Those guys have something special going on. Hope they can keep it up. Sawyer and Dee get them too. The rest are up to you guys. Training camp director, Bryce Anderson nodded his approval and took the bulging clip board from the GM with the five names scribbled across the top page.

"Unreal Dave. I don't remember a camp like this ever. A kid comes in and steals the show, an old fart finally has his day and the fans are eating it up. I really do love our jobs sometimes."

"Don't get too touchy feely Bryce, it's only rookie camp. The next round gets a lot tougher." The general manager calmly collected his things and after flashing a thumbs up to the Green team coach, he left the arena.

The scrimmage ended 5 to 3 for David's Green team, thanks to an empty net goal by someone that no one will ever remember. In the dressing room after the game, music blasted from a boom box. Everyone was talking and hugging and enjoying the final moments of their pro experience. For most, it would be the end of the dream. Precious few would move on to a major league career. Most would simply return to the minors or junior hockey, while some would give Europe a try or give up altogether and enter a new phase of life.

Buzz grinned at the happiness all around him. For a moment, the pressure was off and they were just a team, celebrating a win. He was proud.

David, Brent and Darcy couldn't stop reliving highlights from the game.

Brent pretended to announce Hilton's goal. "Hilton streaks over the blue line, slides a pass to Stone who, ooohhhhh what a pass back and Hilton scoooooorres!"

Everyone, including Coach McCroy, laughed at the impromptu play by play while Buzz carefully collected the player's game jerseys.

"Hey Buzz, any chance I could hang onto this?" asked over-aged junior, Mark Jansen, quietly. He was holding the folded jersey like a priceless crystal. "I'd be happy to pay you for it. It would mean a lot."

Though the invites weren't handed out yet, Jansen may have felt that weird premonition athletes get when they know they haven't quite measured up. Tonight would likely be the end of Jansen's professional career. His play had been utilitarian, not stellar enough to earn him a camp invite, and likely not even a minor league deal. He might end up in Switzerland or, God forbid, England, but right now his world and the hockey opportunities it presented seemed pretty limited.

"Of course, son. We've got lots of these and no, you don't have to pay for it. You earned it, my friend." Buzz felt awful as he stared at the youthful face in front of him.

"Thanks, Buzz. It's been a dream week for me but I guess reality's here. Not sure what I'll do after this, but this jersey will always be special. I was sort of a Red Wing for a week. That's something I'll never forget."

"And no one can ever take that away from you, Mark." Buzz stated, before taking his hand and shaking it. "You were indeed a Red Wing, part of our proud family, if only for a while. Be very proud of that no matter what you end up doing."

The player flashed a thankful smile at the trainer and nodded. He carefully refolded his jersey like the Shroud of Turin and placed it gently among his personal effects as he cleared out his locker.

Buzz could not help but get a lump in his throat for this most excellent young man. For all the David Stones who made the cut, there were hundreds more Mark Jansen's who didn't. They were talented, salt of the earth guys the system simply spit out.

He always felt bad for them and as he got older, he seemed to feel worse and worse. Being so young and at such a critical crossroad in their lives, they often felt alone and disillusioned. Buzz hoped that Mark would get over the disappointment. That he'd bounce back and move on to something else, enjoy a great life, even though there would always be a little bitterness in the back of his mind, a little heartache. He just hoped that Mark wouldn't be one of those who succumbed to the disappointment, seeking solace in drugs or booze to help dull the pain of rejection and the insurmountable insecurity that flourished within them once they realized their dream would never be.

In the background more laughter and catcalls erupted as Anson Dee led his losing Red squad into the winning team's dressing room for wrap-up announcements and presentation of the invites. He launched into an even more over the top play by play performance of Hilton's goal accompanied by some crazy street style dance moves with a perfectly choreographed slap on the back for David Stone at just the right time, much to the delight of everyone in the room.

Buzz looked on grinning and shaking his head. *Good for Stone*, he thought. For with David's story, every youngster like Mark Jansen could keep dreaming. Sometimes the good guys did win. They beat the scouting systems, the media prognosticators and they beat the odds. And, in their wake they left a belief in others that they to could achieve something special, no matter how many people told them they could not. Buzz loved them all, but he loved the David Stones the best.

The revelry began to wind down and players sat by others, patiently awaiting the invite selections. David and Darcy sat quietly in their lockers slowly placing pieces of equipment in their duffle bags. "It's been a real blast, Bolt."

"What do you mean, man? We're going to main camp—you and me."

"Yeah, right. Listen, I've been here before. I know the drill. But this year I got a few goals and that last one was a beauty. That's all I need. Next week I'll be back in Adirondack, hoping to get another minor league deal. But, who knows, maybe someone will get injured and I'll get a game or two in the show this season. I had a pretty good camp. That would be awesome. But you! Man, you got the world by the short hairs. Pull hard, Stone. Pull very hard."

Bryce Anderson walked into the centre of the room with an iPad tucked under his arm. The players immediately went silent. "Okay, listen up guys. Thank you to everyone for your amazing effort this week. For the last seven days, you've all been Red Wings. No matter where you go this year or in life, you have been a part of this incredible hockey club. That said, we only have seven invites to main camp and I've got them here. When I call your name, please come and get your invite and accept the sincere congratulations of your teammates and the entire Red Wing organization for your accomplishment."

The silence deepened as everyone seemed to take a breath almost simultaneously.

"Anson Dee, you're going to main camp."

The big winger jumped for joy and his triumphant cry shook the room, causing everyone to laugh. He raced over and wrapped Bryce in a bear hug that raised him off the floor, shaking him like a rag doll. Then he thrust the Red Wings-emblazoned envelope into the air and closed his eyes, raising both hands in one-finger salutes to the man upstairs before returning to his seat.

Bryce read out an invite for Riley Sawyer, no surprise there. It was an obvious selection that garnered respectful applause. The next two selections seemed to surprise no one either. Then came one for Brent Hagen, the power forward, drafted in the second round. He had both size and a cannon for a slap shot, the kind of player who was always in demand. He would surely get a good look in main camp. Only two invites remained.

Bryce smiled. "David Stone. Congratulations, you're going to the main camp."

The room erupted in cheers. David sat there for a moment, obviously stunned. Finally, Darcy pushed him out of his seat and towards the camp director. Players reached out to shake his hand, give him a heartfelt hug or slap him on the back. It was a special moment and David felt his eyes filling with tears as he shook hands with Bryce and received the beautifully emblazoned envelope with his official training camp invite inside. He returned to his seat trying not to trip over any of the equipment, duffle bags or sleek carbon sticks lying in chaos on the floor. Darcy smiled warmly to his friend as he continued to methodically place his gear into his bag.

The room went silent again. This was it, the final invite. It was odd, but it seemed as if Bryce was getting a bit choked up as he stared at the last name on his tablet.

"Just get it over with," Hilton murmured to David. "Some of us have to get going. I've got a long fucking drive ahead of me."

Bryce cleared his throat. "And finally, I'm so proud to say this name. Darcy Hilton, you're going to our main camp. Congratulations my friend, you really broke through this year." Bryce beamed at the rugged winger across the room.

The aging rookie sat completely stunned in his seat as the room exploded in heartfelt happiness for him. When he seemed incapable of moving, David punched him in the arm causing a smile to form on his face that lit up the depressingly small smelly area where they sat. A few tears began leaking from the corners of Darcy's eyes and as he stared at all the smiling faces around him they evolved into a flood of happiness. Such good news! His quest had been so long and gruelling and he had felt such shame each year as his parents, siblings and friends had tried to stay positive despite another career failure. But, not this time. He could finally call home with good news. News they had all been waiting a lifetime to hear. With his knees shaking, Darcy began his walk across the room through a cavalcade of well-wishers that had formed a clapping receiving line that stretched from his locker to Bryce. Upon arrival, he wiped his eyes and then respectfully shook the camp director's hand and clasped his envelope. Then without explanation he hugged a shocked Bryce Anderson in a meaningful embrace that moistened the eyes of everyone in the room.

Finally after three tries and so much heart-ache, Darcy Hilton was heading to the main camp and his first shot at the big leagues. With that he acknowledged the support of his friends in the room with a wave, wiped his eyes again and gave a thumbs up to David, who was standing and clapping by their lockers.

* * *

Media swarmed each of the players as they emerged from the congested dressing room. Riley Sawyer, one of the three Red team members to earn an invite was already in the hallway when David emerged. He was surrounded by a dozen local and national reporters, all hanging on his every word. The number one draft pick's manner seemed a bit more understated than in his first televised interview, a touch more humble. Perhaps, Adonis had realized that his bankable good looks, first pick pedigree and natural athletic ability might not be enough to get him a spot on the Red Wing's regular season roster. He wasn't as far above everyone else as he thought, and now he would be facing the best of the best. It turned out that the junior leagues were a far cry from the NHL.

Darcy Hilton was clearly the media's sentimental favourite, thought David as he watched a growing number of reporters congregating around his friend. *Good for him.* David continued to quietly finish packing his equipment bag. His efforts were quickly undone by a cadre of excited reporters wanting comments on just about everything. However, none was the one he had been hoping to see. Today was such a great day, such a huge achievement. If only she had been here to share it with him. He peered over the tops of heads and around microphones at the dozens of adoring fans, media, training camp personnel and departing players, but Danielle was nowhere to be found.

After an hour or so, things were beginning to wind down. Reporters wrapped up their questions and players collected their kits and headed for the exits. A rejuvenated Darcy Hilton spotted David doing his final one-on-one interview and called over.

"Hey, Bolt! The boys are heading to The Sports Den for

drinks. You gotta come. It's the last unofficial act of camp. Everyone's in. Even that pussy Sawyer."

"No problem!" David shouted back. "I'll meet you there. Just let me finish up."

David's final interview was with a pale, pimply-faced reporter from a local university cable TV sports show, who clearly had no clue about hockey. This must have been for a class project or something because he lacked any instincts or understanding about the significance of this moment or the unlikely outcome of this camp for David. "So, David, were you surprised how easy this camp was?"

David shook his head. "Well, it certainly wasn't easy. I worked very hard preparing over the summer and I was ready. That's why I think things went pretty well, but it certainly was not easy. The competition at this camp was formidable and these guys are all great athletes. No free passes were given out. I'm psyched about going to the main camp." David rubbed his eyes, exhausted after the long day. His attention wandered from the reporter in front of him and down a rapidly emptying concourse.

"I think what he meant was that you made it look so easy. Did that surprise you?" came a follow-up question from behind.

David's heart jumped and began pounding in his chest. He whipped around to face his new inquisitor and was elated to be staring into the beautiful angular face and sparkling green eyes of Danielle Wright, his favourite reporter and secret crush.

The university reporter glared at the leggy blonde who seemed to be subverting his rather lame interview.

"Well, I think sometimes it's best to not know what's coming," David answered her. "That way you just push yourself to be your best. That was all I did and, by the grace of God, it worked out."

Her smile wasn't just in the lips, it genuinely reached all the way to her eyes. "Boy, did it ever, Mr. Stone. You made the cut. Now what can you do for an encore?" she teased.

The handsome couple stared at each other expressionless for a moment but the romantic tension between them was palpable and made the third wheel university reporter very uncomfortable.

David continued. "My encore will apparently be going to the main training camp where I will continue to bust my ass and eventually work my way onto the opening day roster of the Detroit

Red Wings – real simple. But, before I do that I must phone home and tell my mom what a great day I had today."

"Aw, your mom? That's so cute." Danielle laughed.

The university reporter sensed he was involved in something deeper than a sports interview and clicked off his recorder in disgust. "Not very fucking professional," he muttered, just loud enough for Danielle and David to overhear as he turned and stormed down the hallway.

Metal doors closed in the distance and someone began turning out the lights.

"Any other questions I can answer for you?" David asked, unable to take his eyes off Danielle. "I've got all night," he blurted, then winced at how obvious and direct that sounded. "Uh, I mean—"

"Really? All night?" She pretended to think it over. "I would have thought that a star of the Red Wings' rookie camp would want to go out celebrating with the boys. The Sports Den, I believe?"

David thought fast. "Uh, actually, we were told, first day at camp in our orientation, that, as Red Wings, we always have to take care of the media first. So, whatever you need. I'm all yours." He was working hard to drag out this moment as long as he could.

"So, you'd ditch the boys, for little ole' me?" she asked with mock innocence.

"Yeah. Absolutely. Coffee? Drinks? Late dinner?" I've got an in with the owner of the Coffee Bean at Auburn Plaza. He said if I made the team I can have all the free latte's I want." David felt himself starting to babble.

She pretended to give his suggestion serious thought, but reluctantly shook her head. "That sounds delightful, Mr. Stone—"

"David, please."

"David. But I think tonight, you'd better join your buddies. You're going to main camp, so I'll have lots of chances to interview you. And I'll definitely need to interview you—thoroughly. So, can I take a rain check on that coffee? We can have it when you make the real team. Then the coffees are free."

David felt a mixture of disappointment and triumph. She hadn't said yes, but she hadn't said no either.

"Sounds good, Miss Wright."

"Danielle, please."

More lights shut down and the hallway went completely dark

except for a few emergency lights and some illuminated exit signs.

"Hey, you two!" a voice called from down the hall. "We're closing up—ya gotta go."

"No problem!" shouted David. "We're just leaving."

The two moved slowly towards the exit, neither eager to separate. They reached the heavy aluminum and glass doors and departed the arena. David's cab was waiting in the parking lot.

"So, I guess I'll see you around the rink?" David asked, eyes once more locked on hers.

"Oh, you'll see me around a lot during main camp. I'll be watching you." Danielle responded. "I think I may have found one of the great stories in Detroit Red Wing history. And, when I find a great story, I am very persistent."

"Great, I can't wait to read the story – see how things turn out." David grinned as he looked down and pawed the concrete with his foot.

"And, you have a great night and a great main camp, so I can write that story." Danielle winked at him, then turned with a wave and headed for the parking lot.

David sighed and walked toward the cab. As he climbed into the back seat he turned to look for Danielle. She was standing by her car, looking at him. He waved and she waved back. The cab pulled away from the curb and headed out into a beautiful Detroit evening. David pulled out his phone.

"Hi, Mom, it's me. Guess what? We had a really, really good day today."

Chapter 10

For Riley Sawyer, the best part of being a pro athlete was—without question—the sex. As he laid back on his luxurious, king-size bed, barely covered by an exquisite, beige, 300-thread-count sheet, with his head pushed deep into massive goose down pillows, a sense of exhilaration flowed through his body.

At the foot of his bed, a shapely brunette named Jesse let her pastel, flowered sun dress slip off her shoulders and drop to the floor, revealing satin skin kissed by the summer sun. Riley couldn't take his eyes off her perfectly sculpted form: curved, lean and luscious. It was a body honed to its taught condition through endless hours of dance training, Bikram yoga and spin classes. Plentiful rounded breasts strained against her crimson Victoria Secret bra and a matching lace thong accented the joys of her hips and the pleasures that would soon present themselves to Detroit's newest high-profile celebrity. Jesse was perfection by any standard. And yet, she was just another in a string of chance encounters that would become one of the young phenom's conquests.

As she prowled seductively across the bed and inched her way up his body, Riley felt a rush of anticipation and closed his eyes to heighten the sensation of her skin against his. Her flawless flesh would soon be beaded in the musky aroma of sex sweat. It would mingle with his game-strained muscles to create a perfect therapy that was both physically and mentally blissful. Riley opened his eyes as Jesse slid beneath the sheets and pressed against him, caressing his fully engorged penis. Riley forced himself to breathe.

Jesse closed her ample, moistened lips around his erect member, prompting an intense moan of satisfaction that filled the room. Lithe fingers tenderly enveloped his testes. The movements of her lips and tongue edged him further and further towards climax.

Sawyer's breathing deepened. He writhed, driving his head deeper into the down pillows. Trembling hands instinctively reached down and pulled Jesse's beautiful face further into him, pushing himself deeper into her throat. He looked down and watched the genesis of his pleasure, connecting with the sensual eyes staring back up at him. She stared longingly as if seeking approval, as if her sole purpose in life was his sexual gratification.

Riley shuddered at how sexy that thought was. "I want you. Now," he moaned.

Without a hint of reservation, Jesse pulled herself up and above his stiff shaft. In one quick motion she placed him inside her.

The warmth and moisture of her body sent a spasm through Riley. He convulsed momentarily before gaining control. She gave him a moment to recover, then settled into a perfect rhythm of lust. He glanced up at her and could not help but be transfixed by her natural perfection. The sensual motion of her hips and the moist heat enveloping him intensified. Each thrust eased his stress, replacing it with an indomitable sense of invincibility and power, two of the most precious assets any pro athlete could hope for.

Riley came alive with passion, unable to restrain himself any longer. He reached up and grabbed her wonderfully toned arms and thrust himself into her, harder and harder, causing Jesse to lean back and her breasts to rise before him. His excitement quickened. He clutched her lean waist and slowly moved her into a position from which he could exercise complete control.

Jesse grinned up at him and pulled hard on his buttocks while tightly wrapping her legs around him and digging her heels into his back.

The love making continued for an hour or more before they collapsed from a combination of orgasms and pleasant exhaustion. Heavy breathing punctuated the darkness and sex's sweet odour lingered in the air.

Jesse possessively threw her leg over Riley and laid her head softly on his rising and falling chest.

He stroked cascading streams of auburn hair, pushing it tenderly behind her ears. Neither spoke. The moment had been everything each had hoped for. And perhaps a bit more. "God, you're beautiful," Riley whispered into the darkness.

Jesse pulled him tighter to her and exhaled a contented sigh. "I know."

The pair giggled like the kids they were. Riley gently kissed the top of her head. He guessed it was probably 3 or 4 AM, but really, did anyone care? In the post-coital lull, his mind drifted back to hockey. In seven days, he would start his first real pro training camp and he hoped that change would make everything normal again. He knew his rookie camp performance had been a disappointment for both him and the team, a point rather stridently brought home to him by his agent and his stern, no-nonsense father. But all that would change now. He was, after all, Riley Sawyer—the next great one, according to central scouting, the fans and throngs of mainstream media.

He looked down at the young model draped across his chest and a slight smile creased his lips. He thought about all the things that life had blessed him with. The world really was his for the taking. He was a star and everything was within his grasp. He would step up his game at main camp and put any nay-sayers in their place, including Danielle Wright, that bitch reporter who ignored him after the rookie game so she could interview Stone and caused him so much grief in his first press conference.

David Stone? Really? Riley fumed. The guy was a bum from nowhere and she was interviewing him instead of me. What a rube. Just wait. At main camp, Riley would show his true brilliance and kick that country loser off his high horse. There would be no doubt then who was number one.

Why am I wasting my time thinking about Stone, Riley thought in frustration. I have Jesse. I have perfection in my arms. Adrenaline coursed through his body again as he extricated himself from the lightly sleeping Jesse and rolled her onto her back, exposing that exquisite body to some limited street light peeking through the blinds. He ran his fingers across her neck and studied the bewitching face of his sleeping goddess. He lowered himself and began to nibble and softly bite her breasts. His hand slipped between her legs and he massaged her moistening vagina. Jesse slowly responded and began to moan with each of his quickening thrusts.

As the erotica began anew, Jesse's desire intensified. Eager to be done with the foreplay, he positioned himself above her, opened her legs and thrust himself inside her, back to the warmth.

Jesse whimpered and rolled her head back and forth in pleasure. She willingly let him control her body, submitting herself completely to his every whim, letting him use her as he pleased.

It was exactly what Riley wanted: to dominate her, just like he dominated everything else in life. Just like he would dominate the media, the team, and that bastard, Stone.

The sex was vigorous. Riley pushed and moved Jesse into

different positions, exploring all of it, pouring out all of his pent up frustration and stress, taking as much pleasure as he could from her and, from the sounds she made, giving as much too.

They built up to another exhausting climax, then, collapsed, panting, on the sheets. And finally a deep sleep overtook them.

Riley loved hockey and he loved being a superstar. But, at this moment, Riley Sawyer just loved being Riley Sawyer more than anything else. Outside the first crest of morning sunlight peaked over the horizon.

Chapter 11

The pace of play seemed to increase ten-fold from rookie camp to the main camp and the atmosphere here was strictly business. These were not young men trying to establish a career in hockey; these were seasoned professionals and some of the best athletes in the world. This was their day job and they did not like it one bit that each year a platoon of cocky young punks would again try to make them irrelevant. Only the best of the best remained at the top and veterans fought just as hard to keep their spots as they had to earn them in the first place.

In the dressing room there was no real love displayed for the seven rookies. It was nothing personal, just business. David had never experienced anything like it. This was generally a sport known for camaraderie and sportsmanship. But once you added in million-dollar contracts and giant egos, everything became impersonal and cold and the rookies were outsiders who still needed to prove they belonged at this level. Luckily for Stone, Hilton and Sawyer, the three newbies were thrown together as linemates for scrimmages and line rushes, an ironic twist of fate given the feelings Riley had for David.

The three rookies had been unceremoniously nicknamed the "Wee Winners" line, in reference to their age and a not-so-subtle shot at Riley's initial press conference comments. Sadly, all the rookies got painted by the same Sawyeresque brush. David really didn't care, but it deeply irritated the older and more established professional, Darcy Hilton. Every time Hilts heard the nickname, he made a mental note of who said it and then committed to punch his lights out at the first possible opportunity. After only two days of practices that list was getting uncomfortably long.

Mike McCroy was the main man at this training camp. That gave David a bit of comfort because he felt their relationship had grown stronger thanks to his rookie camp performance.

"Okay guys gather in here," hollered McCroy, as the hulking athletes glided toward centre ice. "This year we need to improve our team play. We've become a collection of talented individuals and it killed us late last year. Only great teams succeed, not great players.

So, I need you to think about that in everything we do. Check your egos at the door every day and commit to helping each other. That'll help us build a great team again. Now, that's gonna be harder for some of you, but just know it's essential if you want to be on this team. If you think I'm kidding, you're a fool. If—anyone—here isn't ready to be a team player, not only won't you be on our starting roster you likely won't be on the team. So, don't test me. Now, let's have a bit of scrimmage to end things off. And remember what I said about teamwork. Stone, your line and Abramov's line will be reds, everyone else in blue. I'll coach red. Trent, you take the blues."

With a shrill blast of his whistle the teams divided up and scrimmage began.

Scrimmage had always been David's favourite part of practice. It reminded him of playing on the backyard rink at home. You got to rediscover the game in its most free-style form without all the interruptions of rules, refs, and systems that were foundational for more formal games. Of course, you still had to do the basics well, but every now and then you could freelance a bit and maybe even show off a move or two. Just enough to make an impression.

Much to his chagrin however, his line struggled to make much of an impression at this outing. Within the first few minutes, they'd been scored on twice and McCroy was visibly frustrated by their poor defensive effort and overall positioning at both ends of the ice. David knew they had better improve in a hurry. Following a severe dressing down from McCroy, he leaned over to Darcy on the bench. "I don't see anyone hitting out there. What do you say we throw a few body checks and at least show Coach we've got some balls?"

Darcy laughed through his heavy breathing. "Not a good idea, kid. First days of camp, these guys don't like to get hit. They got a lot riding on those fancy blades in terms of dollars and cents and they don't wanna get hurt, you get me?"

"C'mon, Darce. You gotta be with me on this. If we're gonna make an impression we have to make something happen." He paused, then nodded toward Sawyer, who sat on the other side of Darcy. "Tell him to."

"It's a bad move, kid." Hilton groaned. "They're gonna remember this and kill us for it. But what the hell it's only our careers."

"We're minus two, bonehead. They're already killing us." David countered.

Darcy leaned over to Riley and jabbed him with an elbow. "We're going to start hitting next shift. Try to change the momentum a bit. Take your guy in the offensive zone. Stone will go after the puck. I'll clean up the garbage – got it."

"Are you fucking crazy! I'm not hitting these guys this early, they already hate me."

"So what have you got to lose?" Hilts stared menacingly at the young brow-beaten teenager. "Do it or I'll hit you myself."

Riley stared back dejectedly. "Aww shit, fine." He shook his head unconvinced and glared at David, who gave him a quick nod back and flashed a broad grin.

At that moment, McCroy called for a change. "Stone, get your line out there! And try not to get scored on again. Sawyer, do something, anything, to prove we didn't waste that precious first round pick on you. Please."

They lined up for a face off at center ice. David noticed they were against the blue team's second line, made up of Detroit's regular fourth-line guys from last year. Generally, these were the team's grittiest players, the most likely to get physical because they were not always the most talented. He leaned over the face-off dot and wondered if he should call off his plan. All of a sudden, hitting guys in an early scrimmage didn't seem all that clever. Before he could think about it too much, the puck dropped and he took a forearm shiver in the cheek from Nate Andrews, last year's runner up penalty leader in the NHL. The puck went through his skates and he fell backwards from the force of Andrews' blow.

A red defenseman promptly carried the puck to centre and fired it into the blue team's end.

David picked himself up off the ice in time to see the puck slide into the far corner. He skated furiously towards the offensive zone.

Hilton was already chugging toward the puck as blue defenseman Byron Rogers swiftly turned to pick it up. Rogers grabbed the disk and deftly turned for safety behind his own net. He stop abruptly, instinctively preparing to set up a standard break-out play. What he did not expect was a crushing body check.

Seemingly out of nowhere, Riley Sawyer obliterated the

rugged defenseman with a clean, hard hit and grabbed the loose puck. His eyes widened as he looked around for someone coming to punish him, but nothing came.

David saw a gap open as the defenseman in front of the net moved to cover for his fallen teammate. That left the whole slot wide open.

Riley saw Stone streaking for the space and waited for the perfect moment to dump a saucer pass to his line mate. David didn't waste the chance, hammering a hard one-timer past Bob Hendricks, the Red Wing's regular goaltender.

The whistle blew, but it did little to stop the action.

"You little shit!" screamed Rogers. He jumped up from where Riley had knocked him down, grabbed Sawyer's jersey and began to throw punches wildly. "Who the fuck do you think you are?"

Other players on the ice quickly paired off and everyone on the benches rose to their feet and began either yelling support or screaming, "Kill him!"

The first punch hit Riley in the jaw and hurt, but the second glanced off his helmet. Riley, looking a bit disoriented, pulled away from the larger defenseman and moved into a bit of a crouch to shield his face. Then he exploded back into his opponent's chest.

The quick movement caught Rogers by surprise and he winced when Riley's helmet crashed up into his chin, knocking him backwards.

Sawyer threw two more blows, neither which did much other than look pretty good, before teammates pulled the scrappers apart.

"Okay, superstar, easy there. We don't want you breaking one of your million-dollar mitts on that cement head of his," joked acting referee, Larry Davies, normally the Wings' special teams coach. He pulled Riley away.

David, who was holding Anson Dee by the scruff of the neck, quickly let go and raced over to Sawyer, giving him a congratulatory slap on the pads just before Darcy arrived.

David laughed. "Fuck, what a hit, what a great play! But, next time leave the fighting to you know who." He nodded toward Hilton who was barreling toward them with Riley's stick and gloves.

Riley grinned and winced from the pain in his jaw and a growing red welt. The three skated slowly back to their bench amid a combination of cheers and jeers from the other players.

McCroy shook his head as the trio clamoured through the gate. "Good hands, Stone. My grandmother could have shot that in. Hilton, where the fuck were you when the shit started flyin'. That's why you're here. Sawyer, good job out there! Not very smart, but a great play. You finally showed some game out there. Keep your head up though, kid. They're gonna try to kill you now, but I'm sure you know that."

"Kind of had that feeling, sir."

Stone and Sawyer looked up at their coach and then at each other. David couldn't help but laugh and when he did, Riley grinned and started laughing too.

Main camp's second day ended with a bag skate for the losing team, which happened to be the blues thanks to David's goal. The red team was rewarded with some fun penalty shot drills, while at the other end players were paraded through rounds of wind sprints across the width of the rink.

*** * ***

When players finally headed down the tunnel to their dressing rooms, Byron Rogers caught up to Riley and slammed him up against the white concrete wall. "Not cool, motherfucker. Remember me? I'm the fucking guy that's gonna knock your pussy-pampered ass all the way back to junior."

Riley didn't speak. He glared into Rogers' eyes, not backing down. It was a primal thing. When the alpha male tries to dominate, don't look away. Stare straight back, be fearless, no matter how hard your heart might be pounding. Don't let anyone see or smell your fear.

Dave Hellan interrupted the confrontation. "Making friends, I see? Rogers, knock it off and hit the showers."

At the sight of the team's General Manager, Rogers released his grip and headed to his dressing room, still enraged by the audacity of the rookie upstart and his band of idiot linemates.

"Don't worry about him or anyone else," Hellan began. "That was a great play. The kind of play I expect to see from our first round pick. Don't forget it. That's how we play in the NHL, so it's how we should practice too. He'll get over it and maybe try a little harder from here on." The smirking GM slapped Riley's shoulder pads and moved on to where a group of coaches were gathering to assess the day's performances.

Riley proceeded to the dressing room with a self-satisfied grin on his face. When he passed through the door, he was celebrated with a series of mock cheers and platitudes for his highlight reel hit. As he acknowledged their jokes and support, he couldn't help but feel a bit relieved. Riley knew he'd done the right thing. That hit had felt good and if guys came after him now, so be it. For the first time since joining the Red Wings, Riley Sawyer actually felt like a first round draft pick and part of the team. And, oddly enough, he had David Stone to thank for it.

* * *

The press moved through the dressing rooms like hounds in search of prey. They gathered around the dank stalls of the most popular and relevant players. Starting goalie, Bob Hendricks laughed with a few. Captain Phil Davis provided quotes for three or four others. A couple of reporters enthusiastically prompted Riley for his version of "the hit" and the fight that had followed the play.

None approached David, but he accepted and liked that he was not being showered with attention at this training camp. He was happy to fly a bit under the radar.

During the week between camps, David had been the subject of much media attention. It wasn't every day that a non-drafted player moved up to a big-league training camp. However, with the start of main camp, news coverage quickly moved on to heightened team expectations given their high profile first-round draft pick, updates on the veteran stars and interviews with the new free agents Detroit had signed over the summer. All interest in a kid from some backwater hole in Saskatchewan had fallen significantly down the media's priority list and his making the main camp was almost forgotten, for now. David Stone was yesterday's news and he was just fine with that.

Contented, he pulled off his practice jersey and began placing his pads and gear in his locker, carefully observing every superstitious nuance developed over a decade and a half of playing the game.

"So, still scoring. Even at the big league level," came a verbal dart in that biting tone he had learned to expect and love from Danielle.

He turned to see her moving towards him as he struggled to rip his head from a skin tight Under Armour t-shirt and writhed to extricate his arms from its strait-jacket grip. She was the one exception to his lack of media attention that he was okay with. He grinned, happy to see her and instinctively stopped removing his equipment.

She had her smart phone in hand, ready to record, a look in her eyes just for him and a smile that mirrored his own. "I told you we'd have lots of time for that coffee interview," she stated in a matter-of-fact tone. "Sweet goal, stud."

"Thanks." David responded and then questioned her honestly.

"I find it odd they let you in the dressing room right now, like with everyone changing and showering and stuff. It seems wrong. Is that proper protocol?"

"Really farm boy. Where are you from again? 1945? It's the job. Nothing here I haven't seen lots of times before." She clicked on her recorder. "Now, what was it like playing with Sawyer?"

"Pretty good, actually." David gushed in genuine excitement. "He's got great instincts. Made some sweet passes, and that big hit, that was awesome. Me and Hilts had a lot of fun playing with him today."

"Looks like they tried to give you a hard time after that hit and goal."

"Yeah, but we managed to hold our own. Rooks gotta' stick together, you know."

"Did anyone else impress you?" Danielle continued.

"Pretty much everyone, except maybe Hilton." David laughed. "I mean, seriously, I'm on the ice with Pavel Abramov, Eric Richards and Phil Davis. This is all so cool considering I never expected to even be here. So I'm just taking it one day at a time, trying to do my best and chip in wherever I can. I still haven't made the team, so I'm still trying to prove myself."

Danielle clicked the recorder off. Her eyes roamed David's bare chest for a couple of long moments. Then her eyes rose to meet his. "Oh, I think quite a bit has changed Mr. Stone. You know, maybe we should have that coffee now."

Chapter 12

Their laughter was real and the myriad of stories they told each other ribald and robust. David's genuine decency and thankfulness for his current lot in life was infectious for Danielle. She loved listening to his accounts of life on the farm, summer training with his old football coach, looking up to his older brother and the deep respect he showed when discussing his mom and dad. David was not only a special hockey player, he was a special person. A good human being. It didn't take very long into their meandering conversation before Danielle realized how much she liked being with him. How comfortable it felt.

"Can I get you something else?" David asked, nodding at Danielle's oversized coffee cup. It was empty and bone dry, with remnants of long ago foam fossilized along its edges.

"No, it's fine. I've had so much coffee I won't sleep for a week. What time is it anyway?"

David looked around and immediately knew what the answer was: closing time. They were the only two left in the barren cafe and a barista appeared to be finishing up the final floor mop of the day. A kitchen staffer grudgingly lifted chairs and stools onto the counter tops and tables, only steps ahead of the whirling mop head his partner was steering around the table legs.

Deep down David groaned. He loved this. Just talking and spending time with Danielle. She was fun, high energy, a bit edgy and sarcastic, a bit intimidating at times and so beautiful. He wanted this time to just keep going, but he knew it was drawing to a close.

"Uh, I think it's close to 11 PM." He shifted in the hard wooden chair and winced. "Wow, I think my butt's cramping up, we've been here so long."

"Now that would be a pretty tough injury to explain to McCroy." Danielle mimicked a man's voice. "Hey coach, I can't play today because I've got butt cramps from sitting on my ass too long." The two broke into laughter.

"I guess we'd better go," David remarked quietly, as a row of lights at the back of the café went dark and only a prism of street light illuminated Danielle's angular features.

She nodded in agreement and they headed outside.

The cool fall air was refreshing after hours in the musky interior of a crowded coffee house filled with the pungent odour of exotic coffee beans.

David waved to a cab parked along the street and the driver flashed his lights and started the engine.

"Don't be silly," Danielle protested. "You're not taking a cab. Let me drive you home. You do have a home, right?"

David turned to her and thought about his answer. "Actually no, I don't really have a home. I'm at the Motel 6 on Auburn Palace Drive, but I'm not sure you can really call that home. I guess in a way I'm sort of homeless right now. Between places." He grinned as he stared into Danielle's stunning green eyes, suddenly glistening in the moonlight.

Without hesitation Danielle leaned in and kissed David much to his surprise. She pressed into him and moved her hand up to caress his cheek. The kiss was so unexpected that David was lifted back onto his heels and almost stepped off the curb before he recalibrated his stance. He then simply gave into the moment and wrapped his muscular arms around her slight shoulders as she retreated into the warmth of his embrace. The kiss lingered for several minutes and then they were staring again into each other's eyes.

"You are, without a doubt, the handsomest homeless guy I've ever seen," Danielle whispered into his ear and softly kissed his neck. David closed his eyes and gently swayed back while he savoured the moment he had imagined a hundred times since first seeing Danielle on TV. He exhaled and a wave of peace swept through him. "Why don't you come home with me tonight, hobo. I think you need some time in a nice homey atmosphere after all those weeks of hotel living. C'mon." Without another word, the two strolled off to her car arm in arm and drove off into the darkness.

* * *

A quorum of coaches sat at a long boardroom table poring over stacks of day two player performance summaries. Mike McCroy was the first to speak. "So, what did you guys think of Sawyer today?"

"I liked him," responded Trent Caplan, who had been one of Riley's biggest boosters during rookie camp. "He seemed to have a lot more energy today. Maybe he just needed to be up against better competition."

Larry Davies chimed in. "That hit was fucking hilarious. I almost upchucked my coffee, and then when Rogers jumped him, that was classic. The kid did okay though. Gave him a shot or two. I liked him too – a lot."

GM Dave Hellan then entered the conversation. "What about Stone?"

The room went silent for a moment as if they were all waiting for someone else to speak. Finally Davies broke the silence. "That kid's pretty damn good, Dave. The competitions way better here and he doesn't look at all out of place. Plus, he's tough and he's got some chops. Mike told me he heard him chatting up Hilton and Sawyer about hitting guys. They both said no but he got them on side. He's got some leadership skills. And, of course, he's fucking fast."

"Anson Dee? Anyone notice him." Hellan continued.

"Can't really say I did," nodded McCroy in a disappointed tone. "He seemed slow and scared. Like he'd seen a ghost."

"Or three ghosts named Abramov, Richards and Davis," Trent Caplan joked in his spookiest voice. The rest of the table laughed.

It was early in the camp but management did not have a lot of time to evaluate the rookies. Their first exhibition game was Saturday in New York and they needed to decide who'd make the trip. Training camps were no longer month long affairs. Today, teams had only a few weeks to learn about players, see them in game situations, get systems in place and play up to five exhibition matches. With Detroit in transition mode, the need to make player decisions quickly had been magnified and this always favoured the veterans.

"Alright, let's see how things go on the ice tomorrow. Then, Wednesday is the Fitness Challenge. Watch and see how Stone does against this crowd and let's hope Sawyer can keep improving after that dismal rookie camp effort." Hellan closed his comments by raising a beer in toast to the coaches and everyone joined in. "Salut!"

* * *

Danielle's classic brick townhouse was nestled along a perfect suburban boulevard. Tall mature trees, neat black metal fencing and wilting floral blooms, that had seen better days during the summer, welcomed the couple home. The air felt crisp and clean. David stepped quietly up the four concrete steps to a thick, heavy oak door. In the distance, a barking dog gave the neighbourhood an almost idyllic ambiance.

Danielle stuck her key in the gold-plated lock then stood back and let it swing open into total darkness. "Homeless first." She grinned as she waved David in.

He moved past her and clicked on the foyer light. He looked around. "Very nice" was all he got out before the two were again embraced in a kiss.

"You like it?" Danielle purred.

"Ohhh, very much," exhaled David.

"Wait 'till you see the bedroom. It's truly spectacular."

With that, Danielle turned out the light and they moved quickly toward the second level. Hours later, exhausted from love making, they collapsed into each other's arms. Despite the incredible caffeine intake over the previous four hours, both drifted off to sleep peacefully, happy to be together.

* * *

A bolt of brilliant sunlight broke through the morning sky and splashed across David's face. He slowly opened one eye and reached out with his leg to the other side of the bed. He wanted to make sure he wasn't dreaming. Danielle's silky skin and long, slender legs assured him that everything had been only too real. He grinned and then, in panic, shot his arm out from under the sheets to check his watch. He sighed in relief. It was only 7:45 AM. He didn't need to be at the rink until 10 AM.

He rolled over to look at Danielle and was genuinely stunned to realize she was even more beautiful in the soft glow of morning sun then she had been the night before. He touched her golden hair and felt deeply contented, a smile broadening across his face.

"You're amazing," he whispered, leaning over to gently kiss

her forehead. "Anne would love you."

With that small touch, Danielle smiled and opened her eyes. She thrust her arms skyward in a huge early morning stretch. "Well, Hellan will be happy to see you've been doing your part to build good relations with the media, Mr. Stone." She laughed.

"I told him I'd do anything to make the team, even if it meant being nice to you guys," David responded. He ran his fingers over her soft, ample lips and leaned in for a kiss.

She kissed him back. "Mmm, score one for the home side."

With that David jumped out of bed and headed to the bathroom, grabbing the clothes he had strewn across the floor the night before. "Will you be at the rink today?" he hollered over his shoulder.

"No. I've got to do an update on the Pistons, so I may have to sleep with one of them tonight."

David froze for a split second while pulling on his denim shirt, then relaxed and chuckled at Danielle's caustic wit. "Okay, that sounds great. Maybe I'll see you later then? After you're done with him?"

"Hmm. Probably not. I have to cover their game and then file my story, so I'll be pretty late. Give me a call tomorrow or Thursday. When do you guys leave for New York?"

"I don't know." David said. "I just hope I'm going." He came out of the bathroom, now fully dressed.

Danielle was sitting up in her bed with knees tucked up under her chin and wrapped in a big fluffy pillow. She watched as the boy from Saskatchewan confidently headed out of her room.

"Of course you're going," she yelled after him, no trace of doubt in her voice. Then she counted quietly in her head. One. Two. Three.

David got halfway down the stairs and had a cab company on the phone before realizing he had a problem. He turned around and returned to the bedroom.

"So, where the hell am I, anyway?"

Danielle laughed. Life was perfect in Detroit.

Chapter 13

The overpowering scent of the harbour, screeching gulls, and the chatter of New York's Russian citizenry made Brighton Beach an exotic, cosmopolitan, yet strangely uncomfortable place for many. Brighton Beach had always been a haven for immigrants from its first English esquires in 1645, who astutely purchased all the land from Sheepshead Bay to Sea Gate from the Native American tribes for the unjustifiable sum of a gun, a blanket and a kettle.

Next, a flood of Jewish refugees and concentration camp survivors would migrate to the area from 1945 to the early 1950s following the liberation of Europe after World War II.

Later, following the collapse of the Soviet Union, tens of thousands of Eastern Europeans would emigrate to the region, resulting in its most recent cultural nickname - Little Odessa. With those migrants came many of the worst manifestations of the new mother Russia, an empire built on the cold merciless foundation of political corruption, greedy oligarchs, and ruthless mobsters intent on establishing brutal fiefdoms. First, focused on their homeland, but later metastasizing like a cancer to surrounding countries and ultimately, to the fertile economic soil of the United States. Brighton became the beach head for their social, cultural and criminal ways. Russian restaurants, stores, clubs, gaming houses and essentially a transplanted society flourished in the area just down the road from popular Coney Island on the southern tip of New York City.

It was well known this borough belonged to, and its residents had succumbed to, the control of Odessa, known in local circles and law enforcement as the most brutal and powerful Russian crime family in the western hemisphere. Like some ancient secret society of power brokers, they governed with impunity, regulating everything from commerce, construction and local government to their more lucrative dealings in drugs, guns, prostitution, extortion, racketeering and gambling.

As the gang had evolved over decades, it carved out an enviable and highly profitable position in New York's burgeoning organized crime industry. A niche paid for with the blood of thousands of loyal soldiers who had battled Italians, Mexicans,

Aryan Nations, Latinos, and of course the NYPD, FBI and DEA for this prized turf. And, they guarded their domain and its chattels with a fanatical zeal that would have impressed Stalin.

Odessa's most powerful figure currently was Alexi Tsarnov. He had been born some 46 years ago, though his exact age was unknown, into a mining family and abject poverty in the coal region of Donetsk, Ukraine, under the old Soviet regime. At the age of five, his father had died in a mine explosion and his mother, an alcoholic who preferred cheap vodka to her children, simply walked out on Alexi, his brother and two sisters, leaving them on the street to fend for themselves, defenceless and alone.

Alexi, the youngest, was picked up by police one night in a homeless sweep and placed in the nightmarish Soviet orphanage system. For years he endured regular beatings from staff, other children and a myriad of brutal foster parents who generally took the children in to work as slaves in their fields or homes. By the time he was twelve, Alexi had brutally tortured and killed two foster parents, he believed with good reason, and was considered a pariah to everyone he came in contact with. But this was when he learned to survive by whatever means possible. Eventually he was sold to a top lieutenant in a Moscow crime family to serve as a drug dealer on the mean and deadly streets of the Soviet capital. Somehow, he survived.

Later, as opportunities blossomed for organized crime following the fall of the Soviet regime in the early 1990's, Alexi was smuggled into America among other refugees to work in Odessa's expanding North American operations. He was housed in an Odessa lock-up and each day assigned tasks ranging from simple shoplifting and car thefts to running drugs, pimping young Russian girls or working in Brighton Beach's raucous gambling houses.

As Alexi grew into a young man, his ruthlessness and sheer cruelty helped him rapidly move up the organizational ladder. He readily took on the more vicious assignments like protecting turf and carrying out targeted executions of Odessa's enemies, a specialized skill he seemed to enjoy far too much.

Odessa's American leader at the time had been an ex-KGB intelligence officer named Yuri Zherdev. He marvelled at Alexi's efficiency and psychopathy. Alexi never balked at a request and performed each assignment, no matter how despicable it was, with such calculated coldness and lack of emotion that Yuri made him a key associate in his inner circle. Here, Alexi learned the management philosophy and operational systems of Odessa's far reaching criminal empire. He absorbed everything with the comprehension and executive savvy of a Harvard MBA. By combining formal knowledge, fearlessness and strict loyalty, Alexi continued his meteoric rise through the ranks and further established his credentials as one of the country's most prolific hit men and brutal mob thugs.

Eventually, after 15 years of service, even Yuri began to worry about Alexi's career aspirations. His lust for power and sheer brutality seemed to have no limits and, instead of moderating over time with his rise in rank and responsibility, it appeared to be growing in intensity. Even more worrisome was the ability of Odessa's top bosses to control a growing faction of Alexi's bloodthirsty disciples, gangsters that were becoming more demanding and unpredictable. It was decided the young assassin had served his purpose for Odessa and should be taken out for the long-term protection of the business and everyone in the organization - namely Yuri.

Bad idea! When Alexi caught wind of the "order," he turned his considerable skills and loyalists to the task of taking out Zherdev and all his followers in one of the bloodiest and most violent mob takeovers ever orchestrated in American history. It lasted over two years and left thousands of Russian mobsters, their families and regular citizens dead or injured through direct assassinations or as collateral damage during bloody rampages and attacks. It also severely weakened the Russian mob in New York. Smelling fresh blood and opportunity, other crime families attempted to move in on their trade. This caused many more armed conflicts between crime families and further hardened the experienced soldiers of Odessa, transforming them into a formidable and professional militia.

But, that was then and this was now. After two decades at the top, Alexi had grown Odessa back into a many-headed criminal hydra that had firmly re-established its dominance once again over the Italians, Chinese, Serbs, Africans, Mexicans and others, taking control of the criminal marketplace along the northeast seaboard.

"Have another vodka, my friend," Alexi said to his key lieutenant, Andriy Korpikosky. Alexi loved to relax at the Moscow

Café patio on the Brighton Beach boardwalk. He was fascinated as he watched so many of his countrymen clamour before him, each grasping at the American dream without much success. He had come a long way since his Donetsk childhood, marching mercilessly down a road drenched in blood and chaos. But these days, his life was quieter. More predictable. Like any alpha predator, many of his threats had been eliminated in the short term and he now enjoyed the windfall profits of a successful though brutal business.

"Look at these pathetic bastards," Alexi muttered aloud as he held his thumb and forefinger to his eye and pulled an imaginary trigger in the direction of two somewhat chunky Slavic mothers pushing baby strollers and discussing their problems at home far too loudly for his liking. "Do we have any problems that need fixing, Andriy?"

"Well, actually boss, word is the Gambino's have pushed themselves a bit more into our area down in the east. They claim they aren't, but our intel says otherwise. We need to have a sit-down with 'em and stop it, before it gets ugly."

"It's always ugly, my dear Andriy." Alexi grinned. "That's why I have you around and it's why we are so good at what we do. Ugly does not scare us. It motivates us, excites us. Sit-down? I say we give them a beat down. I think I know what's happening. Since the old man Gambino's death, they've been waiting for someone to take over, someone new to lead. And, some fool in their ranks thinks his rise to power comes by making inroads at our expense. That's a big fucking miscalculation if you ask me. Fucking stupid wops."

"So what you saying, Alexi? You want us to fuck them up?"

"Let's just say wake them up. The Gambino's have gotten fat and stupid, with whoring wives making reality shows and spoiled kids taking business school at Yale and Cornell. They forgot how the business that made it all possible operates, and they no more respect the energy and work ethic it takes. They don't want to, or know how to, fight anymore and need to be reminded of that. Do some fieldwork this weekend. Find out which of their guys are targeting our turf. Then, we'll send him home in a body bag. They'll need a team of forensic scientists to figure out who he is when we're done. By the way, when does hockey start again? I heard training camps are going."

"Nothing but exhibitions for a while, boss. A waste of time."

"Oh, you're so wrong, Andriy. There's never a waste of time when it comes to hockey. It's in our blood. Any of our boys in town?"

"Detroit's coming in Saturday. I'll try to get some tickets. They've got two Russians, Abramov, who's not ours and they traded for Valeri Voyov. He's not a real money maker. Earns a mill or so a year, pretty small time to waste many resources on."

After the fall of the Iron Curtain, organized crime quickly filled the power vortex left by a crumbling political system. As the government's sports authority disintegrated, dozens, if not hundreds, of professional athletes escaped the country to ply their trade for multi-millions across Europe, Scandinavia and North America. Hockey, tennis, soccer, basketball and many other sports offered them wealth and fame. As their pay cheques grew fatter so did their exposure to protection and extortion schemes which were being orchestrated by crime families back home. There were threats of abductions, harm and even death to their loved ones if they didn't hand over a significant part of their wealth to the gangsters. It was just another of the dark new realities of Russia's first flirtations with capitalism.

At the current time, Odessa was providing protection for 39 Russian athletes abroad, all of whom felt it more expeditious to just pay a "reasonable" security tax to the group than to risk the wrath of its management and teams of enforcers. And, business was expanding rapidly as fear of the organization spread through various countries, sports and professional leagues. Even the International Olympic Committee was feeling repercussions from the growth of this new criminal cottage industry.

"You watch those guys on Detroit and find out their situations." Alexi ordered. "You never know who might have a good year and then a good contract."

"Da." Andriy nodded his head obediently and stared across the pier towards the Atlantic. He casually shot back his second iced vodka. "Can't believe there's great white sharks out there right now who could tear you to bits," he mused nonchalantly as he sucked back on his cigarette and stared straight ahead.

Alexi's eyes narrowed at the dismissive nature of Andriy's comments. It was disrespectful. He sneered and shook his head. Kids today, they were so arrogant and smug, they hadn't suffered like he did. They didn't care. They were weak, lazy and stupid. Down deep Alexi wondered if he could trust Andriy. In reality, he didn't trust anyone.

* * *

David strolled into the arena feeling on top of the world. "Thank you for this, thank you for this, thank you for this," he sang under his breath as he skipped up some steps and through the dressing room doors toward the trainer's room. 12 to 15 guys were already milling around in various states of dress and swagger. He noticed Anson Dee leaning against the doorway, staring at the ceiling.

"Hey man, what's up?" David asked. "How late were you out last night?"

"Left pretty early," Anson responded without looking to see who'd asked the question.

"Hey, earth to Anson! What the fuck?"

Dee's eyes focused on David and he shot back, "What the fuck? I'm playing like shit, that's what the fuck. They got me in a black jersey today. Fuck, it's only the third day. I didn't even think they brought those out this early." He shook his head, kicked at the base of the wall and stared at his feet. "Dammit!"

David felt guilty all of a sudden and toned down the everything-is-great vibe he'd been effusing. Being tagged with a black jersey was the symbolic mark of death at a training camp. It signified what players were most likely to be among the first cuts. Practically, it meant you didn't have a line to practice with during skill drills and line rushes. It was the equivalent of hockey excommunication.

"Sorry, man. I didn't know."

"Yeah, whatever. Just forget it. This is on me, not you." Anson sighed and looked down at the floor.

David clasped his fellow rookie on the shoulder and moved past him into the dressing room, settling in at locker 12. He had 45 minutes until practice but still needed to get his shoulder strapped and tape a new stick. The shoulder he'd hurt during rookie camp was still tender and providing some limitations for the centerman. Taking draws and battling for the puck against opposing players put immense pressure and strain on his damaged ligaments and clavicle. This had him wincing in agony at every face-off, regardless of the pain-killer cocktail being administered by Buzz.

While face-offs hurt the most, what was really weighing on David's mind was that he was only winning 38 percent of them. Certainly not a good enough ratio to challenge for a full-time position on the team. Body checking also sent searing pain the length of his arm that seemed to shoot straight into his brain. Fighting for position in the slot was a special kind of hell, especially when massive defensemen would lay cross-checks into his back as a means of moving him out of shooting lanes.

He needed to dodge more he chided himself, leaning back in his locker and closing his eyes. David's analysis was rudely interrupted by a kick to the legs from Darcy.

"Hey, did you hit that reporter last night?" Hilton asked with a grin. "She is some kind of wonderful. What would she want with you?"

"Really Darce. Have a little class. My lips are sealed. And, if you don't mind, I'm visioning for today's practice, so back off."

Darcy decided to bug his friend a bit more. "Great. Are you visualizing Sawyer fighting again while you float around the slot avoiding all the hits?"

"Ouch, that was nasty. Look, I gave you guy's great advice yesterday and it was probably Sawyers biggest moment at camp," David shot back.

"Yeah, whatever. Well, don't get too cocky. I'm pretty sure we're targets today, so you better play tough. If we get through scrimmage without getting killed, things could be interesting the rest of the way."

Hilt's ended his mentoring just as Riley entered the room and nodded at his linemates. Buzz followed him in and looked over in David's direction, signalling for him to follow and pointing at his shoulder.

"Time to get fixed, my friend," David moaned to Darcy as he got up and headed for the trainer's table.

*** * * ***

Following David's exit, Mike McCroy strolled across the

dressing room and stopped at locker 13.

"Hey, Darcy. We really like what you're doing out there. Listen, we need to get a read on Levins to see if he's still up for the physical stuff. I want you to go at him in practice and drop the gloves. We won't step in."

Brent Levins had been Detroit's tough guy for the last four years and had done an admirable job on a club that was too small and not mean enough. Night after night, he had fought the good fight. That, and time, had perhaps taken its toll on the 34-year-old utility winger. Darcy had a lot of respect for Brent. There was no tougher job in sports than being the enforcer on an NHL hockey team, even though some of the game's focus on fighting had begun to wane in recent years.

"Sure, coach, whatever," Darcy responded with a knowing nod of his head. But, deep down, he felt bad for Levins and sick to his stomach.

This was one of the primitive aspects of pro sports—only the fittest and the toughest survived.

"Okay, thanks. Have a good one," Mike said with a pained look, well aware of what he had asked the rookie to do. He turned and walked off, leaving Darcy to ponder how he would initiate things on the ice.

It was also obvious that this was an important audition for him to make the team. It was likely the Wings would keep either him or Levins at the end of camp so he had to make his moment count. Playing with the kids had earned him a look but he knew only too well that sticking around would depend on his ability to protect Detroit's stars.

* * *

The shrill double whistle meant drills were done and scrimmages would now begin. The black–clad players sat quietly on the bench, hoping someone would screw up worse than they had, and thereby earn them another look on a regular line.

"Stone, you guys start," McCroy directed as he motioned them to centre ice.

On the other bench, Trent Caplan called over Anson Dee and told him he would be a substitute on his fourth line, which included

Brent Levins, and that they would be out first against David's line. Dee was ecstatic and quickly pulled on a blue practice jersey. As a black ace, the last thing you expected was to start a scrimmage. Something must be up.

Levins lined up beside Darcy and both stared straight ahead at the face-off dot.

"You ready to go?" Darcy murmured barely moving his lips.

"Might as well get this over with. I was wondering who they'd pick." Levins answered back casually. "We'll get into the shift a bit and then go."

"Sounds good." Darcy replied. "Good luck, man, nothing personal."

The puck dropped and scrimmage began with Anson Dee losing the face-off to David. The puck moved quickly to Riley, who caromed it off the boards and into the offensive zone. Game on.

David raced down the ice, instantly recognizing how to attack the defenseman who was circling to pick up the puck and set up a breakout from behind his net.

Darcy lumbered down the ice with Levins close to his side trying to hook him and impede his progress. Phil Davis, the Wing's most accomplished defenseman, got to the puck ahead of David, but, as he headed behind the net, he didn't notice an accelerating Riley Sawyer coming from behind, who with a deft stick check stole the puck from him.

"Where'd he come from?" David murmured in amazement.

Sawyer powered past the shocked rear-guard who reached out and tried to grab the rookie star, but stumbled and fell. Sawyer cut around the net and, in an instant, fired a perfect pass onto the stick of Hilton, who really could do nothing other than shoot it into the gaping net. It was a brilliant play that brought both benches to their feet, cheering while the "wee winner" line huddled in celebration.

Anson Dee hung his head. He leaned over, stick on his thigh pads and glided back to the blue team's player's box. *Could things really get any worse*, he thought? After a cold stare from coach Caplan, he assumed his position at the end of the bench. The slot is a center's cover zone. He had clearly missed his check, on top of losing the draw and not picking up his man in the neutral zone. Another handful of nails in his career coffin.

Levins skated past the celebration and grimaced at the smiling Hilton. He nodded knowing the next shift would be their time to dance—no more delays.

"Sweet pass, Saw," David exclaimed on the bench slapping his former nemesis on the shin pads. "You beat Davis like a mule. That was awesome. Fuck, I love it. You're like the stealthiest dude in the league."

The two laughed.

Riley could barely contain his excitement. "It felt good man, real good. I think it's starting to come. Thanks for the advice yesterday; it helped. Anyway let's get another one next go. It's your turn."

"Happily, Saw. Happily." David could not wait to get back on the ice.

Within minutes the blue team tied the score and the rookie trio headed over the boards following an icing call. The face-off was left of the blue team net, so David glided past Sawyer and motioned where he should position himself. He then nodded at Darcy to move further away from Levins, who had coincidentally come off the bench also. Hilton moved only a foot or so, seemingly ignoring his centre.

Fine, thought David, *be difficult.* He leaned over to get low on the face-off. The puck hit the ice and David pulled a perfect draw back to Sawyer. The next instant all hell broke loose. David saw gloves flying and sticks sliding across the ice as Levins and Hilton squared off in a battle of heavyweights. Everyone stopped immediately and stood by, stunned. This was not like a game where referees would move in quickly to break up the fight to avoid injuries. No, this was a primitive ritual amongst the titans to see who would dominate and survive to fight another day. And, sadly, there would be only one survivor.

Darcy seemed to get the upper hand early with two big blasts to the jaw and side of Levins' head. But Levins yanked the smaller Hilton forward and delivered a crushing uppercut square into Hilton's nose. Blood exploded into the air and seemed to heighten the hostility of everyone on the ice.

"C'mon, Darce, you can do this," David whispered as everyone crowded around and paired off instinctively with someone in a different colour jersey. The blow staggered Hilton momentarily, but the sight of his own blood seemed to elevate his determination to its apex. With a quick, forceful thrust to the side, he pulled Levins off balance for just an instant and that opened the flood gates. Punch after punch piled into the veteran's face and opened a deep cut over and around his left eye. After the fourth or fifth punch landed squarely, Darcy could feel a sense of give in the power of his opponent's punches and the intensity of his grasp. It was over. Hilton knew it, and with a final thrust he landed one more solid blast into Levins' mouth. Not where he had been aiming, but that was the problem with hockey fights, they were random though the damage inflicted was all too real. It was brutal and ugly from beginning to end.

    Darcy flinched at the sharp pain that shot through his knuckles and fingers as Levins' jagged teeth and jaw bone opened huge gashes across hands. Then Levins slipped and fell to the ice in a heap. Hilton stood over the larger man in agony, breathing erratically, and then shifted his wild-eyed stare at the assembled players around him. For an instant he became detached from reality. Right now it was him against the world. He was on his own. Everyone was the enemy.

    "Lots more where that came from, you assholes," he shrieked at the collection of players. With that he straightened his mangled jersey and started the long skate to a penalty box where he sat down and gingerly wrapped his bleeding hands in a wet towel. David quietly picked up Darcy's stick and gloves as two other players and a trainer helped Levins to his feet. The beaten forward was not really hurt that bad physically, though he had taken a number of very big blows, but the mental anguish of knowing you had just lost your supremacy in the one thing the Red Wings valued you for, left him distraught. He glided aimlessly to the opposite penalty box with the aid of his teammates and tried to push two of his teeth back into place. He would need a good dentist and a miracle to save them, let alone keep his job as a Red Wing.

    "Get them ice and towels," yelled Trent Caplan at a young assistant trainer. "Buzz, make sure those two are okay. They were throwing some bombs out there."

    Buzz raced across the ice to the penalty boxes to meet with the players and check their condition.

    "OOhh, fuck, Buzz, I'm pretty sure I broke two fingers,"

moaned Darcy as he held up the mangled bloody pulp of his punching hand that had struck Levins' mouth multiple times.

"We'd better get some antiseptic on that mess." Buzz stared at the savage gashes and winced. "Jesus, those cuts are deep and they'll get infected fast. You're done, Darce. Go to the dressing room right now."

At the next stoppage in play, Darcy left the penalty box and skated over to the Green team bench, his throbbing hand wrapped in a bloody white towel.

"You okay man?" David stood up as he got near.

"Yeah, I've had worse I think, just bad timing. Third fucking day at camp. Fuck this hurts."

David swung open the heavy gate and helped his friend, the injured warrior, through a maze of water bottles, sticks and tape as the other players looked on.

* * *

From row 16, seat eight, Dave Hellan watched the drama unfold below. He leaned over to Larry Davies and said, "Unless that kid, Stone, breaks his leg or gets arrested for something heinous, I want him on my team. He just never disappoints. And, I sure do like Hilton so far. Those two might just have something. Hope he didn't break his hand or worse. Let me know what's up after you talk to Buzz."

* * *

David entered the sterile reception room of Auburn Hills Hospital Emergency Center. "Ahh, excuse me. Is Darcy Hilton in here somewhere?" he asked.

A large and extremely disinterested black woman looked up from her computer screen and asked, with a hint of derision, "You family?"

"Not really. Well sort of. I'm a teammate."

"Uh-huh. Then as far as you concerned he ain't here," she snapped, just to establish between the two who directed the chain of command.

"Well, as teammates go, he's like family and he got hurt in

practice today playing on my line. And then he had to come up here, so I just thought I would—"

"Oh please, boy. Spare me any more details. I don't care. He's in room 654 getting his mangled paws cleaned up and stitched. He's got some big old gashes, that's for sure. What the hell are you guys playing, for mercy's sake? The gang bangers don't mess each other up that bad. You boys playin' way to rough for me. Now, I'm busy, so good day."

"Thanks," said David. He walked down the hall to a small treatment room. "Hey! What's up big guy? Why couldn't they stitch you up at the rink?"

Hilton looked up and smiled at his friend. "Can you believe it? They made me get a tetanus shot. A fucking tetanus shot 'cause I hit the bastard in the mouth. Said it's like getting bit by a dog. God, my hands are killing me. Then they had to take X-rays because I might have broken a few knuckles. I landed more punches on the side of his hat than on his melon."

"Listen, I'll wait here until they finish up and then we'll go get supper."

"Thanks, Bolt. Anybody talkin' about my goal in the media scrums?"

"Hmm, not so much. But, they were all talking about the beating you laid on Levins. How did you come up with that?"

"Wasn't me, Davey boy, it was McCroy. That's the only way I'm making this fucking team. He knows it and I know it. That's why if my hand's broke I'm fucked. A scrapper with a bad flipper is, well, pumping gas as they say."

The two buddies burst into laughter at Hilton's insightful metaphor just as Dr. Ernst Raddison pivoted on his crisp white medical shoes at the door and strode into the room. He asked David to leave and began carefully cutting away the damaged skin and suturing the four major gashes on the trembling gnarled hands and knuckles of Darcy Hilton.

"Oh God, that's brutal," David whispered to himself as he left the confined area and paced the hallway outside.

Chapter 14

The squeak of Nike's on the gym's hardwood floor echoed through the building, accompanied by grunts, moans and shouts. Fitness testing day was a unique occasion at a pro hockey camp. It was a chance for the best athletes to shine and for no-names to make an impression that might be the difference between playing an NHL season or languishing in the minors. On some level, every athlete, regardless of the sport, admires and respects the superhuman endurance of the fitness freaks among them. Those few who excel through physical excellence and rise above the already exalted expectations of a pro athlete's strength and power.

David Stone had prepared a lifetime for this and he planned to go the distance today. He had retired after an early supper with Darcy the evening before, enjoyed the perfect dose of caffeine in his morning latte and felt lean and mean after the first days of practice. Hopefully, this would be his professional coming out party. Endurance testing had helped turn a few heads at rookie camp, but that felt like a lifetime ago and the competition then was far inferior to what he was facing today.

David's interval at the bench press station was coming to an end. He had requested another ten pounds on the bar following his previous set, making the total load 255 pounds. The rule of thumb was if you could bench press your weight - that was respectable. Anything above that was impressive. And way above that was "make an impression time". David was 55 pounds over his weight and still adding. The test required three clean presses at each weight, followed by a five minute rest and then more weight. Each station hosted a team of four and Stone's group included Riley Sawyer, Pavel Abramov and Phil Davis.

Just being in the same physical space as Abramov, Detroit's veteran superstar, intimidated David, but he had work to do and his focus needed to remain constant. With his three lifts easily completed, he jumped up off the bench and moved to the back of the station where his vitals would be recorded by a training supervisor. Riley Sawyer, some 15 pounds heavier than David, whipped off the first two presses and then noticeably struggled on the third.

"What's happening over there?" asked GM Hellan as he peered at the bench press station.

"That'd be Sawyer, Stone, Abs and Davis doing strength testing," noted Buzz casually.

"How's Stone doing?"

"He looks good, I gotta say. Makin' the others push it just to keep up. They're onto the VO test next. That's the big one."

"Okay, I look forward to seeing Stone's results. We'll see if that rookie camp performance was just a fluke."

Hellan left and walked by another station where four guys were grabbing a steel bar with all their might to get a reading of grip strength.

Back at the bench press, David finally tapped out at 285 pounds, easily winning his group by 20 pounds and setting a rookie record.

Abramov nodded to David. "Very impressive, Stone. You seem extremely well prepared and you showed up in great shape. Good luck at camp."

David stood transfixed as the smallish Russian forward spoke and nodded modestly. "Thank you, Mr. Abramov. Thanks so much, I only hope—"

"Call me Pavel."

"Pavel." David grinned.

"Okay you guys," Buzz motioned them away from the bench press, "over to the VO station and grab a treadmill. Ross will fit you up for evaluation."

60 minutes later, David could feel his leg muscles aching and stress building in his pounding heart. Yet oddly he did not feel all that tired. He turned his head, careful not to disturb the various hoses and electrodes Ross had attached to him. Down the row of 12 athletes, he noted three were gone and the others were in various stages of fatigue. David turned and stared forward at the wall. It was go time. The rubberized road beneath him increased to its final level for speed and grade and the sudden change impacted those still running like an upper cut to the jaw. In less than a minute, three more guys quit from the extra strain and stepped off the treadmills leaving only half the original group still going. Sweat streamed down David's face but still he ran, undaunted. After another minute his body seemed to accept the new resistance levels.

Riley's knees almost buckled with the change in speed, but he would not let himself stop. He had to keep fighting. There was no way he could lose again to Stone. He was the guy destined to bring the Cup back to Detroit, not that hick from Saskatchewan or wherever. *I've got to keep going*, his mind screamed, but his lungs and legs were fading fast. Three more agonizing minutes passed and finally just David, Abramov and one other remained.

Abramov was a physical phenom, often competing in triathlons throughout the summer in preparation for training camp. It was no surprise he had won the fitness challenge each of the last three years. He glanced sideways, surprised at David's persistence. *This fucking kid is unreal*, he thought to himself noting how smooth David's stride remained and how little stress seemed to show on his face.

Don't let them see you sweat, David thought over and over, noting the rest of his team watching. The words of his home town trainer, Mel Simms, made a lot more sense to him now and he found strength in them. It was time to let his body just run while his mind drifted back to those gruelling summer training sessions with Mel pushing him to keep going around the dusty high school track, making his way over weeds and tufts of grass, while he chased the dream of a lifetime. He remembered Anne driving him to the airport, her tears forming as they hugged for the last time at the security check point. He visualized the old beat up tractor his father would drive around and around from sun up until sun down, never complaining, never wishing life had dealt him a different hand. Then of course there was Luke, saying he would kill David if he didn't give this opportunity his best shot. David felt a smile purse his lips at the thought of his brother. His eyes opened as a slight spasm in his right calf surged up his leg. To David's surprise, staring him in the face was not some white-coated fitness analyst, but the steely eyes of Dave Hellan.

Hellan smiled at the shocked expression on David's face.

David looked left, there were no other runners. To his right, no one. In fact, the whole team had formed a semi-circle around him, staring in awe as he continued to pound out the miles. David's pace slowed as he realized he did not have to keep going and the twinge in his leg finally made him stop.

In unison, the GM, coaches, players, trainers and everyone

gathered around his treadmill and began clapping. Then came the congratulatory expressions of grown men who had just witnessed something truly impressive. David felt stinging sweat drip into his eyes and as he stepped off the treadmill he stumbled. His cramping calves and the pain in his thighs were finally taking their toll.

"Easy does it boy," cautioned Buzz as he and Phil Davis reached up to stabilize the young man, moving him over to a bench. "You are one amazing dude, I'll tell you that. Pavel quit over two minutes ago and no one saw that coming."

David smiled through the pain and applause though he began to feel some dizziness.

Buzz patted him on the back. "Put your head between your knees until things settle a bit. If you think you're gonna puke, you probably are. Hit this garbage can. You beat Abs man, and no one's done that for a very long time."

Buzz stood over the slumped shoulders, hand on David's back. "I'll get you some ice chips and water - that might help." He grinned at Hellan as he strode past him.

"Well, what do you think of that?" The trainer asked the GM.

"Not much to say my friend. That was just - inspired. I sure do like what I'm seeing."

Buzz laughed and continued walking. "You and me both boss, you and me both."

He returned a minute later to find David still disoriented. "Here son, sip some water. We'll take a few minutes and then head back to the conference room for Dave's final session. But we got time so don't rush it."

David slowly lifted his head and felt a wave of relief sweep through him at the sight of ice and water. He grasped the plastic cup and raised it to his lips before pouring the life-giving liquid down his throat.

"Does that help a bit?" Buzz placed his hand on David's shoulder searching his face for any signs of problems.

"The little shit's fine," boomed Darcy. Hand in a stiff gauze wrap, he reached down and began to lift his line mate to his feet.

"C'mon, Kip Keno, let's get to the conference room," said Hilts, referencing the famous Olympic marathoner.

David struggled to stand, his legs devoid of any feeling or strength. "What the fuck is up?" he muttered.

"You might of hit the wall, Bolt. But don't worry, your timing was impeccable. If you're going to leave it all out there, this was the time to do it. Big, big, impression you made today."

The three were the last to arrive at the conference room where everyone was assembled following the off-ice testing. Before them, reviewing some procedural items concerning the weekend's first road trip stood GM Hellan. When he saw the three arrive, he nodded and pulled his bifocals down just a touch.

"Nice of you and your friends to join us." Hellan wisecracked into the microphone, causing almost everyone to turn their heads. Buzz, David and Darcy took seats in the back row.

"Okay," began the GM. "Day four is over and generally we like what we're seeing. A lot of incredible effort out here from many of you. Thank you for that. The real test starts Saturday in New York. We're playing our first pre-season game against the Rangers and the travel team will be posted tomorrow morning. If you're not on that team, it's not the end of the world, so don't think or do anything rash. We can't take everyone. I will tell you now, the team will have a lot of younger guys and rookies so we can see if any of them can actually play at this level. You old farts, we already know what you can and can't do."

Sporadic chuckles arose across the room.

"We'll make our first cuts Sunday after the game and we'll have the team picked about eight days from now, so things are going to move fast. Go home, get some sleep everyone—especially you Stone. I don't expect to see you until the afternoon sessions tomorrow."

David froze upon hearing his name and noted that everyone had again turned to look at him.

Hellan continued. "That was some job you did in there. Abs is the fittest human being I'd ever seen until today. Well done kid. The rest of you, we're back on the ice this afternoon at 3 PM. Don't be late."

With that endorsement, Hellan finished his comments and everyone disbursed. The room emptied quickly as players retreated to their lockers and then took off for a few hours of relaxation. What David encountered, however, was a phalanx of reporters, anxious to find out more about him. If he thought the VO test had been gruelling, he would soon learn it was nothing compared to the endurance required to face a throng of frenzied deadline driven sports writers.

Everyone loves a feel good story, and David's was building at a fever pitch. The buzz from his VO test victory had spread like a flu and every scribe was suddenly clamouring to interview him and own a piece of his rising star.

After an hour of questions in various stages of dress, David was leaning against the shower wall, steaming rivulets of water coursing down his back and legs. He was oblivious to the other players' rowdy conversations going on around him as he luxuriated in the water's deep healing power. His joints and legs felt soothed and he imagined he could easily fall asleep right there. When he emerged from the concrete shower room only two people were still working: a young trainer picking up towels and Buzz, who was sitting by his stall.

"You okay, kid?" Buzz asked.

"Yeah, I feel a lot better now. I really needed that shower. Felt a little woozy before that."

"Not surprising. According to that VO test you're either an antelope or your heart should have stopped about three quarters of the way through. I've never seen such a high threshold for stamina and pain under duress. That was unreal. Where did you get that from?"

"I guess my trainer back home, Mel Simms. He put me through some pretty crazy shit this last year, but I didn't think it was all that special."

"Well, you owe him big. Maybe your whole career, if indeed you get one. What happened today was special, son. Now, get dressed and I'll give you a lift to the hotel."

"Thanks, Buzz." David began to pull on his clothes and realized for the first time that Danielle had not been in the room with the other reporters. That seemed odd. Oh well, he'd call her when he got to his room.

The 2012 Ford Edge pulled into the hotel parking lot and stopped in front of the main doors. "Get some rest, David. You need to take it easy tonight after what you put your body through. One more practice tomorrow and then off to New York."

"Am I going, Buzz? Do you know?"

"Can't really say, David, not my call. But if I were a betting man, I'd say yes. But, honestly, I don't know."

Perhaps Buzz did not want to wreck the joy he suspected David would feel when he saw the list in the morning for the first time. David thanked his trainer for the ride and slowly climbed from the vehicle, turning to wave as the tail lights pulled away.

"Ohhh God, my legs hurt," he mused quietly as he leaned over and took a deep breath.

Room 212 felt like it was miles away as he groped his way through the lobby. At mid-week it was bustling with budget-minded salesmen and older couples taking holidays in the city. Regardless, it felt great to be back, even if it wasn't really home.

In his room, he called his mother. "Hey, mom. How's it going?"

"Oh, David! Wait a minute while I get your father."

The sound of the handset hitting the counter top made David chuckle as he visualized their old beige land-line telephone in the kitchen with the touch-tone buttons. After a great deal of consternation, his mom and dad had switched from their rotary phone only five years before, and to this day refused to get a cell phone or an answering machine.

"No real need for one," his father had stated emphatically. "I don't need those big telephone buggers getting rich off every word I speak. Cockroaches!" The thought of that conversation actually had David chuckling to himself as he waited.

Within a minute, both parents came on the line.

"So, did you make it?" they asked in unison, the positive tone belying their fear of what they might hear.

"Not yet, but camp's going okay. Just got to keep powering through as Luke would say. I've met some great people though and the Wings are a first class outfit. How's everything at home?"

His father began with a frustrated blast. "Well, this harvest has been a bitch. I swear it's been raining since the day you left and Luke, well, he's fit to be tied."

Then Anne added, "We need some sun, David, and some heat. But we're all fine. Your dad's just a complainer. Stop complaining, you. He didn't call to hear all this."

David grinned and realized how perfect his parents were. Through thick and thin they pushed and prodded, yet no couple ever had such a deep love for each other or their children.

"Mom, it's okay really. I want to hear about the harvest."

"So what are you up to, David? What do they have you doing?" His mom continued.

"Well, tomorrow they're picking the travel team for our first exhibition game, so I've got my fingers crossed. The trainer thinks I have a shot."

"Well of course you do, David. You're such a fast skater. Why wouldn't they pick you?" She seemed indignant at the thought of her son not being on the exhibition game roster.

"Oh, Anne, they don't care about just that, this is the pros, not little league," David's father cut in.

"Thanks, you two. I appreciate all your support and Dad, thank Luke. I kind of left you guys high and dry this year."

"Don't be silly, David, we're all cheering for you, especially Luke. So make us proud. And, if you get in that game, kick some New York ass. Let them taste a little bit of prairie pride."

The conversation drifted to a bit of local gossip and David mentioned he was starting to enjoy life as a minor celebrity, even if it was only at the coffee shop so far. The call ended after about 20 minutes with loving thoughts and his parents' prayers for their son's success the next day. David clicked off his cell and stared at the ceiling in silence.

"Wow!" he exclaimed. "What a trip. God, please let me be on that team tomorrow. Even if I only get one game in the NHL, let it be in New York City at Madison Square Garden. Amen."

He closed his eyes and winced at the pain and stiffness settling into his legs and hips, so he rolled onto his side. What a great day.

* * *

The call went to voicemail for a third time. Danielle was sitting in her bed with an animated frown on her face.

Where's my hockey player? She thought.

The buzz around the sports desk had been about David winning the fitness challenge and beating Abramov in the VO test. Of course, she had been assigned to cover the Lions latest fiasco: three of its red-shirted players had pleaded guilty that day to drug possession and illegal possession of firearms. Maybe that was why she liked the hockey players. They just seemed so regular and well balanced. A bit nerdy, almost, in the realm of professional sports. They had a sense of decency about them she just did not see very often anymore in players from the other major leagues.

And David Stone. He seemed pretty much perfect. A good guy. A great story. Tomorrow she had to make a point of getting back to the rink to cover his ascent to stardom or whatever level of success he would achieve. He was probably just too tired to call. But really, would a call be so tough? She shook her head at her silliness. She felt like a teeny bopper fretting over a new crush. They barely knew each other. But he was special and she wanted to hear his voice.

She dialled again but this time it was to the desk chief at work. More voicemail.

"Derek, hi. It's Danielle. Listen, I interviewed those psycho football players today and left my notes and final story on the server for you to review tonight or in the morning. It's probably not as big a story as it first sounded like, so, tomorrow, I would like to get back to the Wings camp for the first travel team announcement. Want to see how the super star is making out and that new guy—Stone. That's going to be a great rivalry for the rest of camp and I'd like to explore it more. Maybe have Dennis follow up on the Lions thing. He seems really into it and loves talking to those guys. Okay, thanks, and have a good night."

She set down her phone and hugged her pillow. It felt warm and comforting but was a poor substitute for what she had been hoping for.

* * *

"...Abramov, Sawyer, Davis, Hilton, Benson, and last but not least, yes you, Stone."

David's heart leaped. *Really? They had to wait until the very end to say my name?* He felt a mix of complete exhilaration and abject fear all at once. He had not realized how much stress was weighing on him until now.

"That's the travel roster for Saturday in New York. Anyone not on the team, we'll be practicing the next two days and scrimmaging on our regular schedule. We'll post Tuesday's game roster on Sunday, so get ready if you weren't on this one."

Darcy Hilton leaned back in his locker and slapped David on the thigh.

"We made it, Bolt. We're goin' to New York. The Big Apple. Manhattan. Willie Joe and all that. Hope these knuckles are ready to go by then. Be a real waste if they weren't".

David laughed and sighed in relief. "Yeah, it would be."

The doors opened and reporters poured into the musky dressing room full of sweaty players. Each received a roster for the Saturday game and immediately scoured the room for participating players.

From across the room, David could make out the shapeliness of Danielle huddled over at Riley Sawyer's locker, jockeying for position with a few other writers. He continued to remove his equipment and methodically massaged his calves and thighs, which were still aching a bit from the previous day's fitness testing and today's practice. He was happy tomorrow would be a travel day. He needed some down time off the ice.

As he turned to hang up his shoulder pads, the misery of Anson Dee came into full view. The lonely forward sat slumped in his locker. No reporters, no coaches, hell, he didn't even have another player to talk to. David finished removing his gear and towelled up for a short walk to the showers. He took a detour by Anson.

"Wow, pretty tough out there today." David said at Dee's locker. "I thought I might drop. How about you?"

Anson looked up and his face cracked into a forced smile. "It was definitely shitty Stone, because I'm on the bubble and not in the first game. Hell, if a rookie doesn't make the first roster team he may as well forget it. They've already given up on you. But thanks, Stone, you're alright. You're a good guy and I appreciate you stopping by. Congrats on playing Saturday and I'll be cheering for you. You deserve to make this fucking team."

David stared at his friend. "It's a little early to be checking out, my man. You still got lots of time and you got the skills. Refocus. Power through and get in the Tuesday game. Hilts and I are going to PF Chang's tonight. Want to come?"

"How could I say no to that?" Anson laughed.

"Perfect. We're meeting at 6 PM. Don't be late." David

reached out his hand.

Dee grabbed it tightly and held on just a little longer than usual. David noticed. "Will do, Stone. Thanks again man."

* * *

As David returned from showering, he saw Danielle at his locker, talking into her recorder. Mmmm, that face. He stopped and just savoured her natural beauty. He wanted to grab her and give her a huge kiss, but of course that was not going to happen. Not here. Then he felt a quiver under his towel and quickly walked back into the shower area hoping his amorous thoughts would soon subside. *How embarrassing is this*, he thought.

Danielle smiled as he eventually walked gingerly back to his stall. "Well, if it isn't the fittest guy on the planet."

She had barely finished the statement when three other reporters and two cameras pushed into his space and questions began flying. After 15 minutes the interviews ended and it was just him and Danielle again.

"Thought you'd lost interest when you weren't here yesterday."

"You're such a wimp." She responded in mock disdain. "And yes, I think I am losing interest in you. So now, on with my interview. What's it like for you right now? You gotta feel pretty darn good."

"Actually, it's a dream and totally scary at the same time. I feel so close and yet today I almost threw up with each name they read ahead of mine. They put me on the very bottom. Last fucking name. It's like they're trying to kill me. It's all good, for sure, and yet every moment I realize it could end with one bad move, an injury, anything, and it's all out of my hands. So, in fact, I'm just scaring the shit out of myself right now so let's just go with, it's scary, no, nerve wracking. Change scary to nerve wracking."

"Wow, you're an idiot," Danielle snapped, shaking her head. "You beat Abramov in the fitness test, you're scoring or setting guys up in every scrimmage. Guys like Hilton, who's a cross between a bulldog and a fire hydrant. And the rumours are Hellan loves you to death. Your nemesis, Sawyer over there, he can barely sleep thinking about how you're upstaging him. And you're scared! Oh, I mean nerve wracked. C'mon, give me something to work with here."

David was genuinely stunned at the outburst. "Well, what should I say? That's how I feel. I'm proud and things are okay but, Danielle, I'm not there yet. Not even close. I'm a walk on. I don't care who loves me or what I've won so far, I still need to make this team. And then, I have to stick for the year. So, hopefully that's not too boring. It's just the truth."

"Okay, that's better. A little passion. That's what I need. Now, what's up with not calling me last night?"

"Is that an interview question or a personal one?" David responded.

"It's mildly unprofessional and mostly personal." Danielle grinned.

"To be honest, I called home and then fell asleep. Slept a full 13 hours. Thought I was dead until I woke up."

The pretty reporter raised her brows in a questioning manner. "Okay, I'll give you that one. Any chance we can continue this interview later, say over dinner?"

"I've got a bit of morale building to do with Dee and Hilts, but happy to join you for a night cap—actually no. Join us. Come to dinner with us."

"Are you crazy? I don't want me and you becoming the story right now. No, you go with them and then maybe head home early because you're feeling so exhausted. Then maybe we can have a little work out of our own."

"Sounds like a plan, Miss Wright. See you about 9:30 or 10 PM. I'll bring some cocktails to celebrate making the roster today."

"Can't wait."

Chapter 15

A steady rain was falling outside the Baklava Café just north of Brighton Beach Avenue and 2nd Street as Andriy pulled up for his 9:30 AM meeting. He had received a late night call from Alexi, who had sounded far more agitated than usual. He jumped from his car and hurried to get inside before his very expensive, but untreated, black leather jacket was ruined by the downpour. Once inside he spotted Alexi and one of his stone faced henchman sitting in a secluded corner of the cafe. He waved and hurried to the table without stopping to place an order. He would do that later. As he approached his boss, Alexi thrust a black and white photo of three men laughing at a posh cigar bar on the Upper West Side into his hands.

Andriy took the photo and stared in disbelief. He scratched his head and then looked back at his boss. "What are we going to do about him?" the gangster asked.

"What do we do with anyone like him?" Alexi sneered over the burnt smell of his double espresso.

Andriy knew the answer, it was what he did. "I guess we should make him disappear?"

"No. Not this time my friend. This guy, his betrayal has earned him a special kind of hell." Alexi's eyes never wavered from his coffee cup which he clutched with both hands in silent rage. "I want you to get this piece of trash and take him to the warehouse. I'll meet you there. He needs to experience how horribly things end when you help others move into Alexi Tsarnov's town. A little bird told me he'll be at Plush on Saturday, feeding cash to strippers and sucking their titties. Take him there, quietly. Use one of our girls to make sure everything is controlled. Mind you, he's so stupid you could probably send a pig to his table and he would pay it to dance and then try to fuck it."

The triumvirate of black-clad killers burst into laughter at the thought of Alexi's once trusted lawyer, Mike Denman, drinking and cavorting at the strip club completely unaware of the bloody demise that would soon befall him.

Denman had been an important mob lawyer for Alexi over

the last 11 years, helping him through many legal issues and perilous times. But, as the new cash-rich Mexican cartels began moving into the northeastern US, Mr. Denman had decided their millions were worth a lot more to him than the hundreds of thousands Odessa was willing to pay. At first he had just distanced himself from the Russians, frequently complaining about his meagre fees and how he could not work for peanuts when he was such a vital cog in their cash machine. Over the last year, however, he had started turning down work altogether, a non-to subtle disrespect to Alexi that had left him seething.

"It's just business," Denman had told him on a few of those occasions. He had done a great job for Odessa and now he felt he was entitled to move on to larger more lucrative deals, wherever they might be found.

But nothing was that easy with Odessa. Once you were in, you were in for life - or death.

* * *

The jet's screeching wheels upon landing always made David jump a little. As the plane's reverse thrusters powered up, he pushed his head into the thick leather headrest and squeezed his eyes shut. In the darkness he recalled the spectacular views of Manhattan's concrete towers and Lady Liberty, which he had seen so often on TV shows, usually of the cops and robbers genre. His thoughts then drifted further back to memories of a small boy on a freezing rink, struggling to keep up. Of an older brother who mentored, taught and protected him. And, of two caring parents who poured their love and resources unselfishly into their children's lives so they could chase their dreams whatever they might be. So many people. So many paths crossed. And now, so much opportunity.

The team's commercial flight was in its final taxi to the gate and of course, the captives were getting antsy, pulling up stowed luggage from under seats and already planning their escape in spite of the Captain's announcement to remain seated until the aircraft had come to a complete stop.

Normally, the Red Wings travelled on a private plane—Red Wing II, a retro-fitted McDonnell Douglas 81 jet they shared with the Detroit Tigers. Following 911, all NHL teams were required to lease or purchase private planes, so the Layton family had purchased one to share between their professional sports teams. On rare occasions, this meant scheduling problems during times of the year when seasons overlapped. This was one of those times and David would have to wait to enjoy the private pleasures of Red Wing II. He really didn't care however. He would have flown on the back of a goose if it meant playing an NHL game in the "Gahden".

"Okay, Bolt, here we are—the big apple and the big leagues," mused a philosophic Darcy Hilton. "No matter what happens tomorrow, I honestly don't care, it will be my night. This is what I've always wanted, and sore knuckles or not, I'm ready. How you feeling?"

"Pretty good, I guess. Actually, real good. Hey, Darce, this reporter asked me how I felt the other day and when I told her I felt scared about the way camp was going she nearly bit my head off. Said that was boring. She wanted something more dramatic. It seemed odd. Since when is saying what's true not good enough?"

"Since you became the poster boy for everything good about pro sports. Don't you get it? Every nobody in the world wants to be a guy like Riley Sawyer: young, rich, good looking, successful. Just show up and it's done. But you, you're the real fantasy, something everybody thinks they can be. The walk-on that beats the odds. A Mr. Nobody who is now likely gonna make this team and become Mr. Somebody. And, even better—you could be the star who all the experts missed or overlooked in spite of their integrated scouting systems and computerized stats analysis. You're what every average motherfucker dreams about. We all need you, kid. Your little adventure here helps us get up in the morning and live another day knowing that we got a chance to do something big. Fuck, sometimes you even inspire me, man. You're a great story right now. No one wants to hear that you're scared; they want to hear that you've got this by the throat and you're living proof we all have better days ahead."

"Wow, that's a lot deeper than I expected," David responded with raised eyebrows. "I thought you might give me a few clichés that would work better. You know, like give it 110% or whatever."

"You idiot. Just soak it up for all us shills who are going to bust our ass and end up in Adirondack anyway. You are going to be a Detroit Red Wing when the smoke clears, and not a lot of us can say that. But, you gotta believe it or this league will eat you alive. The players, the management, the fans and for sure the media."

The plane steadied and a beam of light shot through the cabin as a metal door opened onto a humid New York day. David and Darcy grabbed their carry-ons and stood in silence as others awkwardly pulled down oversized suitcases and satchels from the overhead bins and deplaned. Some were Red Wings or coaches, but most were just everyday people going to or from work, visiting family or starting a new life. Regardless of the challenges ahead, David knew he needed to make his future happen. He wanted to enjoy it too, not be scared he might screw up all the time. Tomorrow might be Darcy's biggest moment, but from here on David promised himself that every day would be a new chapter in the best career he could put together. His life would be about preparation, performance and passion in everything he did whether that was in pro hockey or whatever else fate handed him.

Maybe that would be his legacy from this experience, a fresh perspective on how great life could be, not clinging to, and struggling with, the insecurities of his past. All his time and all the roads taken had landed David right here. At JFK International with the Detroit Red Wings and he was only 33 hours from his first NHL game.

As the cadre of well dressed, perfectly toned players moved through the terminal, it was obvious they were a sports team. They had that look and swagger. David nodded to each person who stared at him, none having a clue who he was, but knowing he was something special.

They moved as a pack through the corridor and into the main baggage collection area where they stood like a military platoon while waiting for luggage. David felt so proud to be part of this team. From the corner of his eye he noticed everyone staring at them and he loved that people were snapping photos from almost every direction. A buzz went through the crowd, starting with the few hockey fans who recognized Abramov, Davis and some of the other veterans who made the trip.

David felt a tap on his leg and looked down to see a small boy with a Yankees cap.

"Hey, mister, are you a baseball player?"

"Uh no. I play hockey."

"Oh," replied the boy. "Well, who do you play for?"

"Uh, the Detroit Red Wings," David replied under the glare of the kid's sparkling blue eyes.

"Are you good?"

Hilton smirked at the child's innocent interrogation.

"Well, I think I'm pretty—"

"Hey, son," Darcy cut in. "Do you know who this is?"

"No, sir," chirped the small voice.

"This is the best player in the NHL. Superstar David Stone. He's the most famous hockey player in the world right now and if you get his autograph today it'll be worth a ton of dough by the time you're old enough to drive."

"My dad doesn't really like hockey. We're baseball fans," answered the youngster solemnly.

"Really?" David said, stunned at the brutal honesty.

"But, if you're really that famous, could I get your autograph, please?"

"You bet," David replied with relief.

It wasn't really the way he had imagined his first airport autograph request but, what the hell, it was better than going unnoticed altogether. The boy held out a wrinkled piece of paper his dad had found in his back pocket. David pulled out the black sharpie Buzz had provided each player with just for these occasions. Then David froze and stared in horror at Hilton.

"Now what? Jesus, just sign the goddamn paper," moaned Hilton.

David whispered in the direction of his confidant. "What number should I put? I always put a number before I sign my name and I don't have one yet. It's kind of weird for the most famous hockey player in the world not to have a number, isn't it?"

Hilton laughed out loud. "Number one, stupid. Put number one. You think this kid's going to remember you? That paper won't even make it out of the car when they get home. Fuck, you really are a rube."

David nodded at Hilt's logic and quickly scribbled his name and a number one on the paper. By design, David wrote the number so that it would be hard to determine whether it was a one, seven or nine, convincing himself that was better than a lie. And his signature, well that wouldn't be any more legible, so the whole exercise was really quite benign in the end. A few more minutes and one more autograph later, David had his bags and was heading onto the team charter that would drop them at the Trump Plaza Hotel, adjacent to Central Park.

From his room on the thirty-third floor, he looked over the massive green swatch of park that carved its way through this world-famous concrete metropolis. He pulled open the balcony door and stepped out onto a tiny perch to revel in the city's sounds. A symphony of movement and life. The dank smelling air, pungent with exhaust and exotic cultural spices, seemed a perfect sensory metaphor for America's most cosmopolitan destination. Horns honked. Various voices raised and went. The din of hustle and activity filled his ears. David just leaned on the railing and tried to take it all in. This was big.

* * *

"Very good, Mr. Sawyer. Is there anything else I can do for you?" The bellman carefully loaded Riley's bags onto a cart.

"Nah, I'm good. Actually, I'm getting pretty hungry is there a steak place around here. I might want some supper later. Though I'm not sure what we're doing yet."

"Yes indeed, sir, that's easy. I recommend Morton's over on Fifth Avenue and 45th Street. Best steak in America, people say. Would you like me to make a reservation for you? It's very important you make a reservation and I may have to grease the wheels a bit even now as it's a very popular establishment."

"Uh no, I'm not sure how the food thing works for the team, so I'll call down once I find out. But thanks for the intel." Riley pulled out a ten dollar bill and handed it to the bellman for the tip and bag service. One thing about New York, you tipped for everything: bags, advice, nightclub referrals, and of course, girls. But that wasn't really the main thing on Riley's mind right now. His agent had been power calling and texting him since they landed. So, after settling in, he would have to give him a call back.

"Hey, roomie." Team Captain Phil Davis called to Riley in his distinctly mid-western twang. "Looks like they want me to teach you a few things while we're here. A guy can get into a heap of trouble if he doesn't pay attention to what's going on around him in the Apple."

"Thanks, sounds good. So, what do we do for supper? Is it like a team thing or are we on our own? I'm kind of getting hungry."

"We have a team meeting at 2 PM and then a light skate at 3 PM to get our legs and see what the lines are. Then we're pretty much on our own after that. But curfew is 11 PM sharp on a pre-game night. And, we will be here at 11 PM, okay? Don't make me look bad on my first babysitting assignment."

"You're safe, Mr. Davis. I kind of need to focus on my game right now. I haven't really been lighting it up. Certainly not the way I imagined."

"You got the shock, kid. Happens all the time, especially to you first-round, can't-miss types. You think since you've always been the team stud that you're gonna march into the NHL and everything will just be the same. Trust me, it's not. Guys here, they're pros. We do this for a living. A very good living. And, we're not giving that up to anybody without one hell of a fight. Then there's the other guys, like Stone. They're scared tough kids with something to prove and nothing to lose. They don't have your luxury of selection so they fight to the death. Us veterans, we really don't give a shit who you are, unless you help us win. And even then, you better know your place in the pecking order for a while. You're a gifted player, Saw, no doubt, but you gotta learn to bring it every night and respect the older guys. You don't right now. You'll be okay, I'll make sure of that. But don't think for a minute you're entitled to this job or this life. Right now you're just an unproven punk and no one here is going to give you an inch."

"Wow, that's some brutal honesty, but actually, thanks. You're right, I probably wasn't ready for this competition. I thought I'd be doing better."

"You will, kid. Listen, I'm going to take a nap for an hour. Can you get me up at one and we'll head to the rink? And call me Phil."

"Thanks, Phil. I'll get you up at one."

* * *

"Oh Davey-boy, are you in for a treat tomorrow," Darcy announced. "After the game, we're all hittin' Plush."

"And what, pray tell, is Plush?" David asked.

"Well, my dim-witted country friend, it's only the hottest club in all New York. Home of the famous, the high rollers and the most beautiful women in the world. It's pure heaven, man. Every girl's a Victoria Secret model or better. It'll blow your freakin' hillbilly brain. Not to mention kick the shit out of your wallet. So bring cash. Lots of cash. You're gonna need it, man. This place ain't cheap."

"Listen, Darce, I don't want to do anything stupid. And why are we talking about a club? We have to play the game first. I'm focusing on that."

"Of course you are, Bolt. But then you gotta have something to play for and you're playing that game to the max, so you can really play at Plush afterwards. It's the kind of reward that shows you why we work so fucking hard to be pros and put up with all this bullshit. There's nothing like marching into Plush through the VIP door and having first pick of all that sexy merchandise. Trust me, it'll be a night you'll never forget. And you only get to experience it for the first time once—so do it up right. Remember, lots of cash!"

David shook his head.

* * *

The bus ride to Madison Square Garden was everything David had hoped it would be. Massive concrete towers cut off the sun. So many people. He had ever increasing butterflies in his stomach as the massive complex came into sight. Their chartered coach pulled into the visiting team's entrance. A small band of Red Wing-emblazoned fans rushed out of nowhere toward its doors, hoping to catch a glimpse of their favourite players, get an autograph or maybe snap a selfie. These hard-core followers were mostly interested in the veteran stars, but a surprising number picked out Riley Sawyer for special attention.

"Hey, Riley, over here," called a rotund man in his 30's, thrusting a Red Wing, game day press sheet towards him.

Riley abruptly stopped to scribble his name, causing David to pull up quickly. When Riley turned to see who had bumped him, David nodded and moved ahead as best he could. "See you on the inside, Saw," was all David could say before a throng of fans encircled Sawyer.

Well, that was disappointing, thought David as he strode toward the arena doors. *Nobody wants my autograph. Oh, stop being such an idiot and just play. There'll be lots of time for autographs later.*

That voice in his head had always sounded an awful lot like Luke. David continued through the massive entry doors with a few other unknown Red Wings, realizing in that instant how easy it was to get caught up in the trappings of this business while forgetting what it was that got you there. He needed to just focus now. There was still work to do.

* * *

The speed of the shot caroming around the boards was like a bullet and it hit David at the same instant that a giant Ranger defenseman crushed him into the glass. The sound was deafening, but was nothing compared to the roar of approval from 18,000-plus deranged Garden fans. Surprisingly, David felt the full force of the dual blows but not a lot of pain as he fell to the ice.

Awesome, get up and get back into the play. He looked around. *Fuck, I'm out of position.* He got back up on his blades just in time to see Todd Granger, the Ranger's leading sniper, deposit a perfect wrist shot over the glove of Bob Hendricks, Detroit's starting goalie. A deafening horn blared and two sirens cascaded colourful light around the arena, much to the delight of the Ranger faithful.

A dejected Stone, accompanied by linemates Sawyer and Hilton, slowly skated back to the bench, heads down after allowing a second Ranger goal to be scored against them. With the Rangers leading 4–1, the young guns had to get their heads and hearts into the game. Everyone was playing lousy and seemed out of synch. It was far different than the scrimmages at Auburn Hills.

"What the fuck is up with you guys?" blasted coach McCroy. "C'mon! You aren't shooting, your zone coverage is the shits and, Hilton, what the fuck—hit somebody. Let's get into it. You're not pussy-footing around at training camp now. This is a game, so make something happen or sure as shit you won't play in the third period."

David couldn't believe the pace. He was getting checked the instant he touched the puck and neither, Riley or Hilts could get open or feed him a pass.

"Bolt, I'm gonna go next shift. My hands are killing me and it's not going to be pretty, but I think I gotta go."

"Don't be crazy. You just got the bandages off yesterday. You can't fight now. You can barely hold a stick."

"If I'm here in this game, I know why. That's my job. So stay clear."

"Don't do it. We'll get a goal, that'll keep them fucking happy and once we get close, the fight's not important. Riley, can you get open anywhere?"

"It's super tight out there. There's just no space. They're jamming the front so much, I can't even see the net."

"Okay, how about Saw blasts the puck low at the net and then me and Hilts just crash the slot for any garbage. No more fancy passes. Darcy, you can still crash the net, right? Don't need hands for that."

"A lot easier and less painful than punching somebody, that's for sure."

"Good, we should get out there with two minutes left—we gotta get a goal or Hilts is screwed." David let his plan percolate with his linemates while he looked at the score clock and repeated to himself, "gotta get one now, gotta get one now."

With 2:18 left in the period, David lined up opposite Reg Dexter, a Ranger rookie, for the face off. He motioned for Riley to move a little further behind him so he would have a clean shot on goal if he won the draw.

Sure enough, before Riley could even get his stick into shooting position, the puck flew back from the face off dot and hit the tape on his blade. In one instinctual motion, and with only a mental image of the net, Riley fired a wicked snap shot before taking a crushing cross check to the face, causing tears to stream down his cheeks.

The unmistakable clank of frozen rubber hitting metal brought a giant groan from the crowd followed by a few scattered cheers for the hit.

1:59 left.

The puck bounced into Darcy's corner off the post and David watched Riley, in obvious pain, get up after the check and slide into the slot, just above the defensive positions, yet behind the forwards who had moved out toward the Wing's defensemen. For a split second he was open.

Darcy spun to get the puck and in an awkward motion slashed the unruly orb in Sawyer's direction. As it arrived, Riley braced his feet and hammered a hard slap shot that hit New York's goalie square in the mask, knocking him and the puck down in the crease.

David watched the puck drop and quickly pushed through his coverage. The Ranger goalie fell to the ice, slightly dazed, and began frantically searching for the disk. With deft hands, David pulled the puck from the goalie's grasp and lifted a back hand into the yawning cage just as two Rangers arrived. The blinding red goal light signalled David's first NHL goal, even if it was only pre-season. He leaped into the glass surrounding the rink as happy linemates joined the celebration.

Rangers 4; Red Wings 2. 1:09 left in the second.

The Red Wing dressing room hummed with energy during the intermission. Darcy had his swollen hands on ice trying to get them ready for a seemingly inevitable third period tilt.

"Let me see those big paws," Buzz ordered as he pulled one out of the compress. "God, those look awful. You can't fight with these, not this game. I'll let them know."

"No, Buzz. Stay out of this. I've got an assist and if I hold my own with Phillips, I'll take a big step toward making the team. I can do it, Buzz, I'm okay."

"Hilts, if you break a knuckle, assuming one or two aren't broken already, it will be lights-out for maybe your whole fucking career, so don't tell me you've got to do it. You don't."

"Buzz, I'm begging you, leave it alone. I'm okay. Don't say anything. I've been in worse shape than this and survived. I need this."

"Ahhhhh. You guys are just plain stupid sometimes. But if that's the way you want it, I'll shut up. You're on your own. I think it's crazy and don't say I never warned you."

The energy level dropped noticeably as an unhappy McCroy began to address his team. "Okay, this game has been awful so far and so have most of you. 12 hits. 12 fucking hits. 13 shots on goal. 16 turnovers. Are you guys kidding me? You want to play in the NHL? Really? Not with these numbers. And great goal Stone. Now you're only minus one. We're lucky to even have an outside chance to win this game. So get out there and compete like you don't have a tomorrow. This will be the last chance for a few of you and don't forget it. You need to perform—now. Sawyer, nice shots on goal but you've got to be tougher in the slot and create some space for yourself. Bobby, we're going with Wade in goal this period. Tough night out there. Everybody, shoot the puck and stop making bone-headed passes. That shot in the melon should have shaken up their goalie, so use that. Okay, get ready—let's go."

Riley acknowledged the coach's assessment of his play though his head was still aching from the vicious hit he'd taken to the face. *Dammit*, he thought, *I can barely focus my eyes*.

The siren's wail announced the third period's start and Abramov's line took the first shift.

David settled on the bench with Hilton on one side and Riley on the other. "OK guys, we've got to do this. We got one, now let's get the next. We're the guys."

Darcy glanced at the young centre. "Love your spirit, Bolt. I'm in."

"Me too." agreed Sawyer, wiping his eyes trying to clear his vision.

A crash from the boards let everyone know another smallish Red Wing had been crushed by a Ranger forward and another offensive foray had been easily repelled.

"Stone, get your line out there and cycle the puck more in their end. They're outworking you guys. Don't stand still. Move to the openings."

"Got it!" David nodded as the "wee winners" line jumped over the boards.

With the period half over, the Rangers were content to play defence and just check the daylights out of their opposition.

"Hey, newbie. Ready to go?" Ranger tough guy John Phillips murmured to Darcy.

"I'd love to, but I've gotta score this shift. It's my turn. Let me score and then we'll go."

"You're not scoring, you chicken shit. Drop your gloves."

"No can do, cement. Just let me get my goal."

"Fucking candy ass pussy." Phillips sneered slashing at Hilton's stick.

As the puck hit the ice, David scooped it back to a defenseman, who promptly fired it into the Ranger end. At the same moment, Phillips pushed his stick between Hilton's legs in an inexplicable display of poor judgement that promptly earned him a penalty.

As the players reset to the left of the Ranger net, David gathered his line. "OK, guys, they're letting us stay out, not sure why, but let's make this work for us. Riley, go behind me and I'll try to draw it back. Hilts, head for the net and set up. We'll fire at your feet, just try to get a stick on it."

Hilton responded with an uninspired nod. "Okay, boss, but that hasn't worked all night."

"They're jammin' the front way too much. That'll never work," Sawyer also complained.

"Yeah, that's been a problem for you, not Hilts. So shut up and let's do this. If guys are in the way run over them."

The puck skidded back to Sawyer as David won his third face off in a row. Sawyer blasted a wicked wrist shot off a defenseman's ankle that hobbled him.

Hilton muscled his way towards the front of the net pushing a Ranger defenceman aside.

Riley grabbed the loose puck off the injured player and threw a beautiful pass to David, who circled around the boards to pull the penalty killers out of their box formation. They didn't go for it.

Seeing they stuck in position he burst through a small opening on the right side, forcing two guys to try and stop him.

As they closed in, Lonnie Raymond pinched from the point and took a pass from David. He hammered a slap shot towards the net that Hilts saw at the last minute. It hit his stick's shaft and dropped under the screened Ranger goalie. Suddenly, it was 4–3 and the Red Wings were flying high.

Hilton beamed from ear to ear as he pushed his way into the back of the net to retrieve the puck. It was his first NHL goal after three long years trying to get into a game, and he was not sure he'd get another chance.

The power play goal gave the Red Wings new life and they stormed the Ranger end for the rest of the game. But, they couldn't get another goal despite firing 19 shots at the net. Final score: New York Rangers, 4, Detroit Red Wings, 3.

The wee winners' line ended the game minus one, giving up two goals and scoring one. Though, they also had a power play tally. They had had an excellent third period. David finished with a goal and an assist, Darcy, a goal, assist and, eventually, a pretty good tilt with Phillips to complete the Gordie Howe hat trick. And Riley had two assists.

The dressing room was quiet following the game as each player knew they had lost the contest early because they had not been mentally prepared.

McCroy dressed down everyone but saved his most biting comments for the veterans, who had played invisible the whole night. Following McCroy's analysis, the players finished their physical therapies, showered and prepared to hit the clubs.

"Ya know, Hilts, I'm not sure I want to go out," David said quietly. "I'm really beat. Those hits are starting to take a toll on me."

"Shut up you pussy. We're going to Plush, so get your country ass into that lame suit and get your cash. How much did you bring?"

"Well, I took out $200."

"$200? You're kidding, right? Have you ever been to a city before? This is New York. $200 won't get you a drink and a hand job."

"What is this place, Darce? It doesn't really sound like my kind of bar."

"Ask, super stud there. Hey Sawyer, you in for Plush tonight?"

"Absolutely. Wouldn't miss it. Is the cowboy coming?"

"I guess so," David finally relinquished, "but I'm not sure I can take out much more."

Phil Davis who had been listening in, spoke up. "Don't worry sport, I'll spot you some cash. It's a good time. Have fun; you played great."

Phil's comment shocked the rookies, but they nodded and smiled in unison."

"Thanks, Phil but it's okay. I'll take it easy, and if I need any cash, I'll let you know and certainly pay you back every cent, with interest." David replied respectfully.

"Kid, the way you played tonight, I won't have to worry about getting paid back; you'll be good for it. I got an extra grand

and it's yours. Don't spend it all at once, which is a lot easier than you might think."

The group laughed and rushed to get dressed. From the sounds of it, almost everyone was going. A few interviews and a quick discussion with Buzz later, David, Riley and Hilts were in front of the Garden trying to hail a cab.

The crush of New York's busy streets on a warmish fall Saturday night was exhilarating for David. He couldn't believe the energy around him. After six unsuccessful attempts at a cab, Darcy decided to take things to another level. As one cab drove past the arena and stopped at a red light on the corner of Pennsylvania Plaza, Darcy ran over and opened the door, much to the cabbie's horror.

"Get out, you crazy! I have to pick up a fare, not you. Get out!"

"Listen buddy, my friends and I gotta get to Plush, the night club. It's not far." He shoved five Andrew Jackson's into the cabbie's face.

"You're fucking crazy, man. But get in, the meter's running."

Though it was only a few miles away, the ride took over 35 minutes and cost $265 once they added in a second tip.

"Welcome to New York, Bolt." laughed Hilton.

"Geez, I can barely afford the cab ride," David replied as he pulled two $20's from his rapidly depleting wad of bills to pay his share of the fare.

The three rookies ran like school kids down the darkish alley to Plush's bright pink VIP door, which was perfectly set back into the side of an old, two-storey, brick-a-brack building. It had the aura of an old-time flapper house from the roaring 20s, but the entertainment behind the brightly coloured door was pure 21st century.

Darcy hammered on the steel reinforced entry. A small light appeared as the door cracked open, revealing a massive security guard with 13 inch biceps and a distinct Jersey accent.

"Yeah?" The doorman sneered.

Darcy answered. "Just played at the Garden. We're with Detroit and wanted to blow off a little steam. Hoped you could help us out."

"Yo, no problem. Some of your boys already here. They're at the back of the club. Welcome to Plush."

"Thanks, man."

Darcy peeled off a stack of bills and squeezed $100 into the doorman's palm. The rookie entourage strutted confidently into the noise, lights and lust of New York's most excessive club, famous for its strong drinks, bewitching women and the complete fulfillment of every male fantasy.

David squinted as they entered the vastness of this modern day home of hedonism. A massive mirrored stage to his right flashed wildly with colourful strobe lights amidst dry ice plumes that created a sci-fi-like context for the perfectly silhouetted female forms that writhed in and out of the clouds. His observations were interrupted when be bumped into the broad back of Darcy, who had stopped to chat up his first femme fatale of the evening.

"Watch out will ya?" Hilts barked.

David stepped around him and his face broke into a broad grin as he stared into an entire section filled with New York's most beautiful women, each in various states of dress, mingling and cavorting with his Red Wing brethren.

"Oh wow, I probably should have brought more money," David muttered quietly.

"Prepare to enter paradise, my friend. It's time to get down, big league style". Riley blew past David and was instantly greeted by a tall brunette with long dreamy legs and Sophia Miacova features. As he pulled her into him, Sawyer glanced over his shoulder, flashed a thumbs-up and then moved toward the Red Wing party space.

David reached into his pocket to rearrange his money. He felt a brush from behind and turned to see an exquisite Nordic blonde running her fingers through his hair.

"You are mine," she whispered in his ear in her sexiest Finnish accent possible.

"Oh man, I think you're gonna be a lot of trouble for me," David stammered.

She placed her stiletto shaped fingernail on his lips and escorted him to a thick chaise lounge located near his teammates and curled up in his lap. Softly she stroked the back of his neck, then his cheeks and lips.

Across the way, David could see Darcy cozying up to a raven-haired beauty with the brightest red lips he had ever seen.

Hilts was playing the high roller, barking orders at scrambling servers for bottles of champagne that retailed for about 700 dollars each. David smiled at his chaotic surroundings.

"What is your name?" His date asked as she stroked his head.

"I'm David. David Stone."

"Mmm, such a strong name. A real man's name. What do you do, David Stone?"

"Well, I play hockey, like all these guys. And you are?"

"I am Erika. And the minute I saw you, I wanted us to be together."

"Well. I must say I'm happy you did, because I really want us to be together too. You're just flat out stunning." David blurted out his comment without really thinking as he stared into her exotic, angular face.

"Thank you, David. You are too kind. And handsome." Erika placed her hand at the top of David's shirt and after loosening his tie and opening some buttons, she began to caress his chest.

"Are you Finnish?" David asked loudly as he leaned toward her ear so she could hear him above the pounding electronic club music.

Erika's eyes lit up in genuine surprise.

"Yes, how did you know this? Americans never know this."

"Well, actually, I'm Canadian and I've played a few times against Finns and I even went over to Finland once with my midget team. Love the country and its women."

"You played midgets in Finland?" Erika responded with a questioning look.

David laughed at the absurdity of trying to have a conversation while surrounded by the pulsating beats of the club's sound system. It was obvious refined conversation was not the reason one went to Plush, no matter how inspiring the company might be. "No, when I was younger I played some games in Finland, as a kid," he yelled back.

"Finland is a great country. And we have many great hockey players, but none are greater than Canadians. This is right, yes?"

"We like to think so. Do you know anything about hockey?" David was having trouble keeping his eyes from drifting down to the perfect breasts heaving under his chin and the bronzed thighs resting on his lap. "Sorry, I just can't stop staring. You're very beautiful.

Not many girls like you where I come from. Geez, now I feel like a schmuck."

"You are not a schuck, David. That is so sweet. I like you. How about we have a bottle and get to know each other better, okay?" Her head lifted quickly off his shoulder and she snapped her fingers like a Russian General.

On cue, a server appeared instantly out of nowhere.

"What do you want?" David asked Erika.

"Bring us a red Cab," she told the server bluntly then returned her gaze to David and softened her tone. "You like red wine, yes?"

The transformation of Erika from doting super model to cold hard revenue generator was simply amazing to David, almost worth the hundreds of dollars it would cost him.

"Sure, I'll drink whatever. I'm good."

"Oh, you are so sweet. Are all Canadians sweet like you? You seem not shitty like Americans."

"Well, not sure about that, there are some pretty shitty Canadians too. So, I have to ask, how do you keep your body so incredibly fit? You must work out like crazy."

"Thank you, David. Yes, three hours a day I go to gym or dance. And, I do Bikram yoga—hot yoga. We sweat so much David. Many girls here use trainers to stay in shape and do the hot yoga. Better body, better money, you know."

"Well, whoever your trainer is, I want his job. This is the most impressive collection of bodies I've ever seen, but you—you're incredible."

Erika's face beamed with a spellbinding smile that actually heightened her aquiline features even more. She leaned in and kissed David very softly at first and then with more intensity. At that moment, his every care melted away and an overwhelming sense of calm flooded through him. He moved his hands slowly up her thighs, across her curvaceous hips and onto the small of her back. He rested his head on her wonderfully sculptured breasts and let out a sigh as, again, her touch stroked his neck. Amidst all the noise and chaos of this glammed-up, heathen paradise, David was at peace. The irony was delicious. This was the reward Hilts had been talking about.

The server interrupted his perfect moment. "Who wants to taste?"

"Just set it here," snapped Erika with an irritated glare. Then she looked back. "David, would you like to taste?"

"Yeah, great. Let's give it a try." David pulled himself up in the seat, moaning as he extricated himself from its deep cushioning. He sampled Erika's vintage and nodded his approval to the server.

"That's $650. Cash or credit?" The stone faced server pushed a service check into his face.

David bristled and stiffened as he heard the price. He shot an angry glance at the server. "What? How much?" He instinctively questioned raising his voice above the music.

"David, it is $650 for the wine. Plus, you will need to tip." Erika purred as she pursed her lips and moved them closer to his ear. "Just give him $800."

David looked again at his jovial teammates but none were paying any attention to him. They also had their hands full of bottles and women, and wads of cash were flowing like the Hudson River.

"What, you don't like this wine?" Erika asked.

David looked into her deep blue eyes and decided to just go with it like everyone else. After all this was the big leagues. "No, no it's fine. I just couldn't hear him." He peeled off six $100 bills and a wad of $20s, which significantly diminished his cash flow. He placed the pitifully small wad back in his pocket.

The blaring music, constant barrage of women, lust and never ending spending continued unabated for hours. Riley Sawyer seemed especially overindulged in the entertainment and moved every half hour from one gorgeous vixen to another with a dogged determination that had seldom been seen during his training camp debut. He began to aggressively pound back double shots of whiskey and exotic shooters, while constantly flashing cash or his ebony American Express card, so he could order anything he or his new friends desired.

David and Hilts laughed at the suddenly, almost likeable, super star. All the players contributed to simultaneous cheers and jeers at various actions by their peers. At one point, Sawyer and a lithe, sexy, blonde, Russian dancer staggered onto a small corner stage and began Cossack dancing, though it was painfully obvious he had no idea how to do it or how terribly foolish he looked. The good news for him was no one could pull out a cell phone to video anything without being immediately grabbed by security and their device crushed beneath black military assault boots. Privacy reigned supreme at Plush, for the protection of the girls, its patrons and of course the club owners, who, according to other players, were rumoured to be a shadowy group of eastern Europeans.

Vodka, wine, whiskey. The drinks added up and eventually Riley succumbed to their influences. With his Russian beauty in tow, Riley stumbled over to a couch adjacent to where David and Erika were now embraced in a most promiscuous state.

"Hey, cowboy," greeted Riley, "this is Katrina or something."

"He is American?" Erika whispered in David's ear.

"No, he's one of those shitty Canadians I told you about."

Erika nodded in agreement.

"Hi, nice to meet you, Katrina. I'm David and this is Erika."

"My name is Katarina. Yes, we know each other. All girls here know each other," Riley's date responded coldly in thickly accented english.

"Well, what you ladies don't know is this is Riley Sawyer, the NHL's number one draft pick and future superstar," David heralded in animated overtures. "He's one of the best hockey players in the world, though he might not look like it right now."

The group laughed as David and Riley raised their glasses in a celebratory toast.

"Salut! You know, I hated you cowboy, with all your down-home charm and aw-shucks interviews. You really pissed me off. But man, you're a player. The real deal. And I hope we get to play together a lot."

The touching moment was slightly marred by Sawyer's drunken delivery but did elicit a moan from the two girls who then quickly pulled their respective partners apart for a brief session of high school-style petting. After a few seconds, David's head popped up over Erika's shoulder.

"Thanks, Riley. It's good playing with you too and let's keep it going," he slurred slightly. The wine and fatigue were beginning to take their toll.

"Wow! Does your chick have great tits!" Riley shot back, ruining the special aura that was encompassing the group. "Can we switch girls, bud?"

"Uh, Riley, being a linemate only goes so far and that's way over the line."

"Aw, what the fuck? C'mon, Andrea. You don't care, do you?"

Erika glared at Sawyer. The awkward moment ended when the two interlopers moved away thanks to Katarina sensing it was time for her to take her mark to a more private and potentially profitable area.

David and Erika laughed as Riley stumbled away, then cuddled and chatted, drank and laughed for a bit. They then moved to a private corner table for some extra special fun that cleaned out the rest of David's meagre bank roll.

* * *

Darcy Hilton had assumed the role of protector for some of the younger, less experienced players. His tough, minor league tenure, living on the fringe of pro sports, had given him invaluable insights into what was fun, and what was bordering on destructive and dangerous behaviour. As he watched Riley's antics with the girls and booze, he felt a growing sense of trepidation.

These were not the star-struck high school groupies, Riley was accustomed to and had led around on a leash during his junior days. These were spectacular, vetted and selected works of female art, professionals in the dark science of separating drunk, wannabe men from their money. They always had the upper hand and wielded their control with a ruthless precision, seeking more cash and financial opportunities. The minute your finances were drained so was the superficial affection they peddled. If anyone thought this crowd was being exploited by their floundering clientele, they only needed a few minutes with one of these she-beasts to understand how cutthroat and pragmatic they could be.

By Darcy's rather generous standards, Riley was way too drunk for his own good and was bordering on out of control. He got up and went over to the youngster, who had opened his shirt and was now flopped half-conscious in a lounge chair with his grinning Russian captor.

"Sawyer, you okay man? You gotta take it easy. It's like a mine field in here. Give me your credit card and cool it with the booze."

"OOOHHH, go away, you big buzz kill!" Katarina snarled as she toyed with Riley like a devilish feline might toy with a mouse before killing it. "Go! Leave us alone."

Through half closed eyes, Sawyer looked up at Hilts. "Yeah, I'm not feeling so great, Darce. I think I need some air." He tried to remove himself from Katarina's grip but she fought to hold on and keep him for her own in the chair.

"Let him go for a minute," Hilts shouted at the girl as he grabbed Sawyer and abruptly pulled him to his feet.

"Fuck you, jerk," Katarina screamed and took a swing at Darcy.

This was unexpected and, within seconds, two security men were rushing toward Hilton, one grabbing the arm that had helped Riley.

"Easy, mister, don't make trouble. We don't want no trouble here," yelled the first security man to reach Hilton.

"Hey, I'm cool." yelled Hilts, raising his hands and not reacting to the confrontation. "My buddy here just needs some air. Your girl's gotta let him go. He needs some air. I'm gonna take him—"

A slight sense of panic set in as Darcy looked past the security duo and realized there was no Sawyer. Where had he gone? Katarina was now standing beside the security guys and screaming insults at Hilton, in both English and Russian, but no one paid much attention after a few minutes as the drama began to die down.

* * *

From a few booths away, David noticed the security detail and Hilts. He jumped up from Erika.

"Listen, gimme a minute. I'll be right back." He pushed his way through the crowd toward Darcy. "You okay? What's going on?"

"Aww, that fucking Sawyer. He's drunk as a skunk and now I can't find the little shit. Anyway, I'm gonna go see if I can find him. It's fine. Go back to your girl. Man, she is hot. Don't see that very much down on the farm, do you, cowboy?"

* * *

Riley bounced off a wall in the dank dimly lit bathroom hallway at the back of Plush. The sounds and lights were all distorted by the alcohol-infused state of his brain. He saw a shape under a brightly lit, red exit sign.

"Need air. Where can I get some fresh—" he gasped to no one in particular as a surge of nausea began to form in his stomach and a hot flash shot through his contorting body.

A dark figure standing at the back door to the club rudely grabbed the drunken youth, thinking he was some trust-fund college kid in town for a few thrills, and unceremoniously threw him out the door into a dark empty alley. "Lots of air out there, asshole. Hope ya had fun." The heavy door slammed shut and a bouncer walked back inside the noisy club.

Riley hit the pavement with a thud and laid in the stench of a New York alley for what seemed like an eternity. His tongue touched his lips just to make sure he was still conscious. He dragged himself to his feet. "Oh fuck, I gotta get back to the hotel, gotta get back to the hotel," whispered the increasingly distressed hockey player.

He saw a bright light at the end of the alley and began stumbling towards it, using walls and industrial garbage cans as crutches to keep himself upright. He continued staggering toward the light, thinking quite incorrectly it was a main road. In his clouded reasoning he believed he could hail a cab there and get back to the hotel. All would be good then. He staggered along the alley towards the light, twice tripping over loading pallets at the back of businesses and once stopping to throw up, hitting his leg in the process.

As he reached the end of the alley, the lights came into perspective. But it was nothing more than a few loading dock lights. He had three directions to choose from now and he went right. Unaware of what was around him, he stared at his feet to make sure one kept going in front of the other, then felt a serious rush of head spins. He stumbled to his left, hit a railing and fell down beside a smelly old loading dock attached to a metal and wood warehouse. He laid on the pavement for a few minutes trying to collect his faculties—then rolled himself toward a large window with wire grills that looked into the basement of a building.

Oh fuck, he thought, in his muddled consciousness, *this is so not good. I need to rest a minute and sober up and then I'll go back to the club and find the team. Oh fuck, I'm so hammered. This is not good.*

* * *

"Denman. Name's Mike Denman," the slightly pudgy lawyer beamed at Giselle. "I'm a lawyer."

"Oooo, a lawyer. So impressive. What law do you do?" the tall brunette from Columbia asked.

"Pretty much everything for some very important people. Big people mean big money, you know. That's my business."

"Say, Mike, Mr. Big Money, why don't we go to one of the private rooms?" Gisele whispered in his ear and then kissed his neck, which she had to lean down a fair bit to reach.

Denman felt an immediate stirring in his tan cotton pants and had visions of savagely ripping off the tiny thong Gisele was wearing, pushing her down on a bed, and having hot, primitive, animal sex with her. He growled at the thought. "Show me the way, honey. Show me the way to heaven. Woo!" He punched his fist into the air elated at his good fortune. This was going to be a night unlike any other.

The couple, tangled in an awkward embrace, staggered through the door of a private room and Gisele seductively motioned Mike toward a king-sized bed at the centre.

"I need to get some protection," she said, pulling away and heading toward what appeared to be a bathroom door.

Mike laid on the bed and stared gleefully at the ceiling, burping up a little red wine and then reaching down to undo his belt. All he could think about was the incredible sexual experience he was about to embark on. He hoped he was sober enough to enjoy it properly. Within a few minutes he heard the door open and waited for the long-legged, Amazon beauty to return and begin his pleasuring. He waited. And waited. Finally, he turned his head only to see two brutish-looking thugs clad in long black leather coats standing beside him with looks of pure cruelty and hatred as they glared at their helpless prey.

Before he could open his mouth, a massive fist fitted with bone-crushing bronze knuckledusters crashed into his face. A burst of blood shot down his throat.

"A friend of ours wants to talk to you, asshole."

"Oh God," Denman whimpered as he felt some teeth come loose against his tongue.

After a few more head shots, the dazed and terrified lawyer was tied up, bundled into a blanket, and with his mouth taped shut was pushed into the back of a van waiting in the alley. The van drove a very short distance, turned a corner and stopped abruptly beside a warehouse loading dock. The two henchmen jumped from the vehicle, took a quick glance around, swung open the side door and grabbed the tightly bound, sobbing lawyer.

Denman's head crashed into the frame of the van as his handlers clumsily extricated him from the cargo hold and lugged him up the dock stairs.

"Hey, careful, you idiot."

Yeah, like it really matters."

The two laughed.

Chapter 16

Screeching brakes and the flash of red tail lights by the loading dock startled Riley's rum-soaked brain. His eyes opened slowly and he saw the back of a dark van sitting about twenty yards in front of him. Then there were noises, like a chair scraping a concrete floor, coming through the window he was lying beside. Bright illumination from the bulb inside the room blinded him until his eyes adjusted and the activities taking place in the room began to come into focus.

Okay, I've got to get out of here, Riley thought. *Fuck, how long have I been out?* Just then, a second set of car lights turned into the alley and shone directly in Riley's direction. He instinctively turned away from the light and rolled under a concrete outcropping on the side of the warehouse dock that protected lower level windows from vandalism.

A black Cadillac SUV pulled up in front of the van and three more hardened-looking men got out.

Riley was sobering up fast as adrenaline pumped through his body and his heart raced. This did not look good but being paralyzed with fear he dared not move from his covered position.

His face was now staring directly into the window, hidden only by some long wide and extremely uncomfortable crab grass that had broken through a crack in the pavement where it intersected with the warehouse foundation. He was too afraid to move—or even breathe.

In the room, a bloodied but well-dressed man with a gag stuffed in his mouth was slumped in a chair. Two oversized captors calmly lit cigarettes by the door. Riley's drunken haze, combined with the thickness and age of the glass, made it hard to hear anything more than muffled sounds from the room. The view, while dramatic, was still at a difficult angle and he was unable to get a clear perspective of what was happening. He saw the door to the room swing open and the three men who had left the Cadillac strode in. The last one through quietly closed the door.

One of the men, a mean-looking, sinister character in a long, camel trench coat, seemed to be in charge and moved close to the chair. He then punched the prisoner full fisted in the face. The chair fell backwards from the force of the blow.

Two of the goons moved in quickly to pick up the tortured body of the victim and placed him back upright.

Riley felt himself convulse at the savagery and, for an instant, he began to cry, then stopped himself. What was he seeing? This was horrible. "Am I dreaming?" he murmured, hoping to wake himself from this nightmarish moment with the soft utterances of his voice. Sadly, the long grass poking his eyes and face and the sharp stinging it delivered provided sensory evidence his sorry situation was all too real.

"So, Mr. Denman, you like Giselle, huh?" asked Alexi in his tortured English. "She is very fine. One of my favourites. And so beautiful; those legs and tight ass you were dreaming about. They will not be yours, Mike. Not tonight. Not ever. Tonight unfortunately will be your last night on earth, Mr. Denman, because you have tried to fuck Alexi Tsarnov and Odessa."

The terrified lawyer shrieked in muffled tones through the gag and his hysterical eyes belied vividly the terror that was welling through him.

"Why would you ever think you could do such a thing? We paid you so well. Obviously too well. Then you became Mr. Big Money or something. And this is how you repay us—with betrayal. You know, those Arabs have a good way of dealing with traitors. They cut off their heads. What do you think of that, Mike? Not very civilized, is it?"

A prolonged moan escaped from the lawyer's bloody mouth. Tsarnov raised his hand and snapped his fingers.

One of his associates standing by the door calmly walked over. From beneath his black full length trench coat he pulled a three-and-a-half foot samurai sword. The lawyer wept openly now at the inevitability of his fate.

Tsarnov grabbed the sword and continued to stride around the chair, wielding the beautiful instrument of death in artistic movements. A subtle dance of death, timed to some haunting whistling.

From Riley's awkward vantage point it appeared as though the crazy bastard in the camel trench coat had a sword or machete and was kind of prancing around the guy in the chair like an executioner. While his fear threshold likely couldn't go much higher without causing him to stroke out, the side benefit of all that adrenaline was how heightened his senses were all of a sudden. "Oh come on man, don't do this. Please don't do this," Riley whimpered to himself.

"Mike, you must be a man now. You are likely going to die tonight, but I am going to give you one chance to tell me why you would betray me for some Mexicans. And, who are they?"

One of the thugs savagely ripped the gag out of the terrified lawyer's bloodied mouth.

"Alexi, what are you doing? We're friends. I never betrayed you. They only work their turf—I directed them away from you and your business. They are no threat. Honest, I was always thinking of you and protecting your business. You and me—we go way back. We've done so much. Please don't do this."

"I said: who are they?"

"They call themselves Poncho Villas—you know, after the guy that saved Mexico from the Americans. They're pretty lame. They're not you, they're not Odessa. They are small-time. Little fish."

"And what little fish runs the show, my friend?"

"Some punk named Alejandro Rodrigues. He's a new guy. I think he's from Jaurez or—"

"Times up!" The crazed Russian swung the sword in a single violent stroke and it cut clean through the lawyer's neck like butter.

Denman's head fell to the floor, bloodied lips still moving, red liquid spurting from the headless torso.

Riley stopped breathing and went into shock. He felt urine fill his pants from the terror. No matter what happened, he had to get out of there—now. He pushed against the window frame to escape from under the ledge and began to run. Sadly, he was not as sober as he had thought, stumbling and falling twice. Each time, he picked himself up as fast as he could and ran again toward another light at the end of the alley.

* * *

"What the fuck was that?" Alexi shrieked. "Is someone out there? Find out who or more heads will roll!"

The black-clad Odessa soldiers pushed their way out the door and headed up the steps two-at-a-time towards the loading dock. As they hustled, they drew machine pistols from chest holsters, each filled with 60-shot magazines. The large metal door of the loading dock burst open and four gangsters rushed out into the night. Their view of the alley was restricted by the large cargo van and black Caddy. The street was pitch black and not illuminated by the loading dock lights anymore. A minor, life-saving bonus for Riley.

Andriy Korpikosky leaped onto the hood of the black Caddy. Like a panther, he glided across it and back onto the empty road, his gun cocked and ready to fire. At first he saw nothing. But then, in the distant street, he thought he heard faint footsteps in a disorderly pattern. But his accomplices were talking too loud among themselves for him to hear clearly. "Shut up, you idiots!" Andriy snapped. "Or I'll shoot you myself."

Instantly, silence on the loading dock. Yes, there were definitely footsteps—far down the alley toward the brightly lit main street. Then he glimpsed a movement. Someone was running in the shadows, trying to stay out of sight. But they looked hurt. They were not in control. As a trained killer and mob soldier, Andriy knew every aspect of an execution. Prey had to be hunted. You had to know them. Know their state of mind. What they would do. This one was hurt, so he would head for the brightest lights. The busy street. That would mean safety, or so he would think.

"Fool," spat Andriy. He wasn't scared of a busy street. All the better to kill someone and escape in the chaos. "Come on, follow me. He's going to the street."

There was another glimpse of a person under a porch light far down the alley. It was a guy and he was wearing a suit, his jacket flapping open. He was more than a block and a half ahead of them— a mere silhouette against many drab walls. Andriy charged towards him with the other soldiers in pursuit. It was kill time.

* * *

"Okay, where the fuck is Sawyer?" Hilts yelled. "Dammit, I haven't seen him for two hours. This is really fucked up, man. He was a mess."

David felt scared but tried to stay positive. "He's okay, Darcy, forget it. He probably went back to the hotel. Wait— how many hours? What time is it, anyway?"

"It's 3:30 AM. We've got to get out of here—but not without Sawyer. Call his cell phone again."

* * *

Riley bounced off of a metal garbage bin and struggled to stay erect. *Just another block and I'm safe*, he thought. Then, for some reason, he looked back. Maybe it was the instinct of an athlete in the heat of competition, but he sensed a new presence. In the alley's shadows he could see men charging after him and they were gaining quickly. They all had long coats and he was only too aware of who they must be.

At that very moment, a piece of brick shattered above his head, blasted apart by a bullet. They were shooting at him.

He summoned all his faculties and miraculously ran with the dexterity of an Olympian, weaving slightly to take away any steady shot his pursuers might have. Half a block to go.

Another shot broke a window.

"Oh God, get me out of this alley."

Then: blinding light. Riley couldn't stop; he had to keep going.

A massive truck was turning the corner and would soon come down the alley towards him. With many industrial garbage bins along the walls, the truck would fill the entire width of the alley and virtually seal off any escape he had. He knew he had to beat the truck to the end of the bins to escape. Riley Sawyer was in for the race of his life. For some reason, he recalled the training camp treadmill test. Thank God he was in good shape.

The lights from the garbage truck lit him up, along with the entire alley. For a fleeting instant, Andriy got a steady look at his prey even though it was through a blinding light. He looked young. Sort of big. Athletic. He even thought he knew the face. But where from. It didn't really matter. He had to die. Andriy could see the truck was going to cut them off once it got to the rows of waste bins. The runner in front of them had disappeared into the lights.

"Go that way! Go back and down the alley by the club and get him if he goes left on the main street!" I'll go straight and under the truck. The hunter always had a plan.

Riley ran straight into the lights and everything went completely white as he squeezed past the last garbage can and through the tiniest of openings between the five-ton garbage truck and the first of the huge metal dumpsters. The truck's horn blared as Riley bounced off a slightly protruding metal lever at the back of the vehicle which struck his upper arm. He winced in pain.

"You idiot! What are you trying to do? Kill yourself?" shrieked the horrified driver. He also received distinctive middle finger salutes from two guys riding along on the the steps at the rear of the truck.

Made it! Riley's heart pounded as he sprinted the final 20 yards to the main street. It was well lit but not that crowded. A few bar-hopping drunks were on their way home after pulling late nights. Not the crowds he had hoped to find and lose himself among.

I need a taxi, he thought. *Oh shit, where's a taxi?* Instinct told him to keep moving, find cover and change his look. He knew those guys would not be stopped for long and he was only a minute or so in front of them and not feeling all that great, his arm throbbing in pain.

He quickly pulled off his coat and stuffed it in a trash can, much to the surprise of a semi-conscious street bum. Riley turned right and headed off in search of a public place with lots of other people. Though he was not sure that would change his odds at all with these guys.

Coffee shop. No. Little lounge. No. Then, right in front of him, a lady appeared, staring him in the face. She was just coming out of a brownstone walk-up and was taking her garbage to the curb. The door to the building was closing. That was his escape. Quick and lockable. He charged past the stunned woman and into the building.

"Hey! What's the hurry?" she yelled, adjusting the cigarette between her lips. "Do you live here?"

Riley slammed the door behind him and headed straight down a long, narrow hall. There had to be a rear entrance. Hopefully he had lost them. But he had to keep going.

* * *

In one fluid motion, Andriy slid under the chassis of the garbage truck, to the even greater shock and horror of the sanitation engineers operating the massive arms of the vehicle. They could have sworn the well-dressed guy in the trench coat had a pretty cool looking gun, but they weren't about to be heroes. In New York, it was best to stay out of things. As Andriy turned the corner of the main street, all he saw was a few meandering fools, his idiot sidekicks racing around the corner to the far left, a drunk leaning up against the wall and a lady, clearly frustrated by something, taking her garbage out.

"Hey, you!" he yelled up the street at the lady. "Did you see a young guy run by here? Don't worry, I'm a cop."

"Run by me! He practically knocked me over," she stated angrily.

Andriy ran towards the lady. Then, from the corner of his eye, he saw some fine fabric sticking out of a public trash can. Really? Had he been dumb enough to throw his coat in the garbage? What an amateur. He grabbed the coat and pulled it out.

"Hey, mister! I got dibs on that," came the slurred rebuke of the wall-flower drunk.

Andriy raised his deadly assault weapon at the old man and pointed it between his deeply blood-shot eyes. "You got dibs on dying too?"

"Okay, okay, it's yours. All yours. Geez," moaned the hard-luck street person, bested by someone who really did not have any need for that suit jacket. Life was truly unfair.

The women watched with growing anxiety as four burly men approached her—with big guns in plain view. After 58 years in the neighbourhood she knew cops and no cops dressed like this, had guns like those and none she had ever met had heavy Russian accents. They certainly did not point guns in the faces of street people.

"Which way?" Andriy grilled the terrified lady.

For her own preservation, she pointed at the door and then immediately regretted it.

The men charged up the steps and kicked the door open, leaving glass and shattered wood everywhere. Within seconds, faces appeared from open doorways and then quickly retreated when they saw the hit team and their drawn weapons.

Andriy closely monitored their faces. No one helping the target would have come out to see the commotion. He must have gone out the back door. It was the only logical move. "Dante, stay here and look for him. See if he sneaks out from somewhere. The rest of you, follow me. We need to find this guy—or else."

* * *

Riley was alone and running down another alley to nowhere. He had no idea where he was or what was coming next. He just knew he had to get away. Had they seen him? He had to assume they had and were likely right behind him. He kept turning down random streets, both to take him out of sight and to cause them some delay as they tried to guess his moves, maybe even to split their ranks.

Down one of the alleys, he jumped a fence and went through a backyard to a front street with beautiful big trees, some four-storey apartment blocks and rows of classic walk-up brick townhomes. There were no commercial buildings, which, at this time of night and in his current situation, was not a good thing. He ran across the street and hopped into another backyard, then over another fence and into the backyard of an older townhome. He paused, tired. A hiding place. He needed a hiding place.

At the end of the alley, he could see a densely treed park. Perhaps he could hide in the trees. He could bury himself in them and just fall asleep. And when he awoke he would realize this was all a bad dream and his blessed lifestyle would reappear.

Suddenly, in the quiet of the night and the still of the moonlight, he heard distant low-level Russian accents.

"He'll go to the park. Check the park."

Riley froze and frantically scanned the yard for cover. A shed. Too obvious. A pile of wood. Too noisy. A wooden deck? Again, obvious.

He could hear the scuffling of one of the goons heading down the paved alley. Time was running out. As he frantically scanned his surroundings he noticed a giant black space at the back of the home's east side. Of course, a giant elm tree. It was perfect. As a boy, growing up in Toronto's posh Rosedale district, Riley and his friends, Laurie Walsa and Alan Higgins, had played war and his favourite hiding place had been the trees. His first girlfriend, the lovely eight year old Laurie, had dubbed him the human chimpanzee for his climbing prowess and many a time had he sought the dense cover of thick branches and massive leaves while waiting for his prey. That had been a childhood adventure. Tonight it was life and death. A sudden surge of childlike reflex and honest excitement hit him as Riley transformed from hunted prey to Ralph, motivated survivor and lead character in Lord of the Flies, the iconic novel by William Golding.

He leaped up to the first thick branch and quickly pulled himself higher with smooth instinctual motions, despite the pain that was shooting through his upper arm. The rustling of massive green leaves in the night wind perfectly muted any sounds related to his out-of-practice climbing. Riley felt eight years old again and moved deftly through the branches, higher and higher into the thick canopy, which was still largely unaffected by fall's colour transformation. Then he moved to the back side of the massive trunk and peered over the back yard with only the moonlight as illumination.

He had a perfect vantage point, with dense coverage and, for the first time in the last six hours, felt in control, even if it was by the slimmest of margins. Through the whistling wind and rustling leaves he thought he heard the sound of a gate opening. In the moonlight, he noticed a shadowy figure stealthily moving along the west wall of the yard. He stopped breathing and tightened his grip on the branches. *Don't move. Oh God, don't move*, he thought as his eyes closed tightly.

The figure moved in a crouch toward the shed, weapon raised, then thrust his head around a corner ready to fire. He stood up. There was nothing. He then quickly moved toward the deck and casually looked underneath it. Much to Riley's horror a bright security porch light burst on due to the stalkers motion, filling the lower yard with illumination and breaking the cover of darkness that hid his Russian adversary. The killer jumped back and, realizing his exposure, began to run toward the back of the yard.

Lights immediately went on in the house and within seconds an old man in bright green pyjama's burst out of the back door. "Get the hell out of here, you asshole," he screamed into the darkness. "We've called the cops and they're on their way and I've got a shotgun, you son of a bitch. Show your face here, you bastard, and I'll blow your fucking head off. C'mon, show it. Chicken-shit! Don't come back!"

Riley could barely contain his laughter and pressed his head against the tree. The Russian mobster had been sent running by an old man and a security light.

"Thank you, God," he whispered.

Riley heard the sound of men scrambling in the alley and numerous footsteps heading in the opposite direction of the house. For an instant he felt safe. He pulled up his sleeve and looked at his watch.

It was 4:45 AM. In a few hours the sun would start coming up. He would wait here, not move, and after the heat died down, leave his lair and get the hell out of here. He watched as the elderly gentlemen, quite satisfied with himself, turned on his heel and headed back inside the house.

"Roger! What's going on down there?"

"Oh it's probably some fucking kids trying to steal stuff. Little bastards. I'd like to put about 20 of these pellets in their asses and send them on their way. Did you call the cops?"

"Yes, dear. They said they would try to come by, but they're awfully busy tonight."

"Fucking police. What the hell do we pay taxes for? I gotta get me a real gun."

From his perch, Riley watched the scene below and thanked his lucky stars for this brave and loud New Yorker who had likely saved his life. If he only knew just who the man sneaking around his yard was, an armed killer, he might not have rushed onto the porch so aggressively.

The back door closed and complete darkness, except for the soft moonlight, enveloped the yard again. Riley's breathing was controlled and he placed his tired head in his hands. His last thoughts that night were of three faces: Laurie Walsa, Alan Higgins, and some crazy killer with a large sword that had cut off some dude's head. Then sleep, fatigue and drunkenness overtook him.

Chapter 17

One of New York's famous yellow cabs pulled up to the front doors of the hotel. Three players jumped from the back seat and made for the entrance.

"When I get my hands on that fucking Sawyer, I'm gonna kill him," growled Hilton as the trio ran up the hotel's stairs three at a time. "He's with that hooker for sure. He's probably up in his room banging her head into the headboard while we're running all over New York looking for him. Jerk off."

"Easy, Darce, I don't think so. That girl he was with, she was still there when we left. He just vanished, I swear," groaned Brent Hagen. "One minute he's there and then gone. Something happened. It had to. He's not that stupid."

"If I get cut because of that little shit, I'll kill him."

"Yeah, we got it, Darce." David replied. "Let's just get to his room. What is his room number, do you guys know?"

"No, but we can ask at the desk. I think he's with Davis. But I'm not sure."

They walked briskly to the front desk and stood while a completely disinterested Night Captain finished entering some data into the computer.

"Hey, pal!" shouted Hilton. "We need some help. Now."

The Night Captain glared at Hilton as he looked up. "How may I help you, sir?" he asked in an acidic tone.

"We need the room number for Riley Sawyer."

"Oh, I'm sorry sir, I can't give that information out to you. It's against our security policy." The clearly amused staffer smiled.

Hilton's face turned crimson and just as he seemed ready to grab the guy, Mike McCroy came around the corner. The look of his face scared even the Night Captain.

"What the fuck are you three doing here at this hour? Curfew for tonight was 1:00 AM. And where the fuck is Sawyer? He's not in his room according to Davis. Dave is fucking pissed and sent me out to find you guys. Jesus, are you really this stupid? Hilton, you've been around. You know better than this."

"Listen, coach, we think Riley might be in trouble. He just

disappeared from the club. We've been looking for him all night. Maybe he got kidnapped." Hilton was desperate to make the scenario better for himself.

"For your fucking sake, you'd better hope so. They fucking send rookies to the minors for this shit, especially you, Darcy. Fuck, you're lucky to still be here. Now get the fuck up to your rooms. We have to meet Hellan in his room at 8:30 AM. And it's not going to be pretty. Jesus. What club were you tools at, anyway? Maybe I'll head back there to look around."

"Plush, Coach. It was Plush." The dejected Hilton shrugged.

"Yeah, of course it was," stated the angry coach under his breath as he headed for the hotel doors and out into the night.

* * *

The twinkling of morning sunlight and a cool breeze awoke an almost sober but very hung over Riley Sawyer, still perched in his tree. It was 7:35 AM. He'd been asleep for over two hours. Not bad, Riley thought. Time to get out of here. But just in case his pursuers were still prowling around, and he assumed they could be, he needed to be careful. In broad daylight and from his perch, he had a pretty good view of the surrounding yards and roads. He was in a pretty neighbourhood with classic Bronx character. Across the street was the small park he had seen the night before, but he noticed now that the homes surrounded it.

A few cars moved slowly along the roads but, other than some guy delivering milk, there was no one else on the street. He methodically climbed down the tree, being careful not to expose himself or make any overt noise. He did not want an ass full of pellets and he knew that was a distinct possibility if the owner of this fine home entered the fray again. As he crouched at the base of the tree, he listened to see if there were any sounds that should not be there. Like low guttural voices or the sound of fine leather soles on pavement. There was nothing.

He moved quietly to the back gate and eased his way through it and into the alley. It was pretty open out there, but so was the front. At least here he could weave and duck through the rear fences, garbage can holders and garages until he got to a public place. He could not phone a cab in case they were watching the street. For some reason he felt they were likely still around. It made sense they too would wait until daybreak and then continue searching for him. As he stood behind the cover of a garage, down the alley came the sound of a car turning the corner and moving slowly along the paved surface. He ducked into deeper cover once again. He pulled back and pushed his head against the wall. Through the wood slats of the fence he saw shard views of the oncoming vehicle and a thankful smile spilled across his face. It was New York's finest.

True to their word they had had been busy last night, but finally, almost three hours after the call, a blue and white patrol car crawled down the alley looking for anything or anyone suspicious. Riley stood up and walked out of his hiding place and waved at the car. Instantly, red and blue lights came on and the car stopped. Two officers got out and shouted at the relieved hockey player. "Put your hands up and walk slowly towards us!"

"Actually, I'd rather run," stated a relieved Sawyer.

"Just walk, buddy, and keep those hands high."

As he reached the car, one of the officers quickly turned him toward the hood and told him to spread his legs.

"Listen, I spent the night out here because some guys were chasing me. I was at a bar and—"

"Just be quiet, we had a complaint last night from a resident about some creep trying to break into their house. Was that you?"

"No!" pleaded Riley. "I was trying to not get killed and so I was hiding in this backyard. These guys were chasing me."

The smell of liquor was very strong on Riley's breath as he spoke and his clothes reeked of cigarettes and pot smoke.

"Been drinking, buddy?"

"Yeah, I drank a lot last night at a club and then when I went out for air I got chased by these guys, but not before I saw a guy in a trench coat cut off this other guy's head. It was fucking crazy."

"Yeah, sure you did. Get in the back seat and shut up. And don't make any trouble or I'll crack you over the head with my flashlight. Got that?"

* * *

The Russians had seen a police car pass them a few blocks from the house they had scrambled away from the previous night.

"New York's finest. Right." Dante sneered.

"We've got nothing here. The guy's long gone, probably never even went this way."

"You idiot, do you want to tell Alexi that? It'll be our fucking heads rolling around on the floor. Dumb shit. I've got his coat and my guess is he was at Plush. It's a very expensive jacket—the kind of stuff real money buys. It smells of smoke and broads. I'm sure he had one of ours draped all over him. Now we just find out who he is—and go kill him.

Chapter 18

Ozzie was sitting back in his chair, throwing a tennis ball against the wall and catching it as he tried to make sense of his current case. This tourist comes to New York, goes to a fetish club and ends up with two rounds in the back of his head in the middle of Times Square and no one sees or knows a thing. *God*, he thought, *New Yorkers can be real pricks at times.*

"Hey, Ozzie. Rangers lookin' good again this year? Hope you aren't betting on those bums doing anything." The jibe was an obvious shot at the years of Ranger playoff futility, made by the only Islanders fan in the Bronx's 40th Precinct.

"Yeah? Up yours, Shiller," Ozzie yelled back. "You guys even still gotta team? It's hard to keep up with them and that crazy owner."

"Oz! You gotta see who's sittin' in holding. You'll shit yourself."

"Don't care, Bing, don't care." the distracted detective said without looking up. "Got a case to solve here. You should really try it sometime."

"No, ya do care. It's fuckin' Riley Sawyer from the Red Wings. Couple of uniforms just picked him up on a B&E."

"Yeah? That's good. The NHL's first round draft pick doin' a B&E. Am I just surrounded by stupid here?"

"I'm not shittin' you, man. He's in lockup, I just saw him. It's fuckin' him. I think he's drunk or stoned or something and talking shit about some murder."

Ozzie leaned back in his chair and stared at the ceiling in disgust. *It's like a daycare here*, he thought shaking his head from side to side. "Okay, I'll bite—but if you're shittin' me, Bing, I'll shoot you with your own gun. I'm really busy here."

Ozzie Stark was a detective, first grade. A lonely figure who lived for his work, the Rangers, and, well, that was about it. His home was really the office or the streets of New York, and when he did take down-time it was in a small, depressing Brooklyn apartment. Ozzie pulled himself from his chair, slammed his tennis ball on the desk and headed down the bland institutional hallway towards holding, which at this hour would be populated by a collection of last night's hookers, brawlers, drunks and thieves. It would be an extremely odd place to find a pro hockey player—even if he was a Red Wing.

As he strode around the corner and glanced towards the pen, a surprised grin crossed his face. Sure as Ozzie was Irish Catholic, sitting behind bars was the most hyped guy in pro sports, scared and curled up in the corner surrounded by the worst of Saturday night's riff raff who, by all appearances, were not hockey fans. He certainly looked wasted and was absent his belt, shoes, watch, tie and jacket. His clothes were ripped and dirty and his bright, lime-green dress socks made for quite a fashion contrast. *What a dick-head*, thought Stark.

"Hey, Scooby, get me rookie-of-the-year there from holding for questioning. That would be the puke in the green socks. And bring him to interrogation three. Be careful, he's very valuable. Worth more today than we'll see in our whole lifetime and then some."

At the sound of the rookie comment, Riley lifted his head and sheepishly looked toward the detective staring down at him.

"Okay, so what the fuck is the NHL's top draft pick doin' sittin' in lock up in New York for doin' a B&E? This has got to be good," the detective demanded of Riley.

"Can I get a coffee or something?" the traumatized hockey player mumbled. "Can I make a phone call? I've got to call the team."

"Yeah, I bet you do. What time does the plane leave?"

"I don't know, but I did not do a B&E. Some guys were chasing me last night and trying to kill me, and I ended up hiding out in this yard. The guy who owns the place, he had a gun and confronted one of the thugs chasing me, and that's when he called the cops. I was in a tree the whole time."

Oh fuck, Ozzie thought. *This is gonna be fun.* "Let me get you that coffee, kid, and maybe when I get back you'll have come up with a real story that makes sense." Ozzie walked out of the room and right into the confused stare of his Captain.

"You really got Riley Sawyer in there? What'd he do, punch his girlfriend or something?"

"No, boss. My guess is he got drunk, probably pissed off

some broad's boyfriend at the bar and they wanted to give him some New York justice when he tried to go home. Give me ten minutes and I'll find out. In the meantime, you should try to get a hold of the Wings' management and tell them wonder boy is here. Their probably freaking out right about now. I saw their GM was at the game last night. His name's Dave Hellan and they're probably stayin' at the Westin down on Third Street. Don't let anyone know he's here or we'll have a media gong show on our hands. He's a pretty hot property actually, though you wouldn't know it to look at him right now."

"Fuckin' jocks. They get all the money and chicks. Life is so unfair," groaned the captain. He spun around and headed back to his office.

* * *

An irate Dave Hellan was frantically waiting in his hotel room for some kind of report on Riley Sawyer. His assistants had been out all night looking for him and now that he'd heard the story of his late night running buddies, a deep fear was replacing his sheer rage. At the end of the day, all these guys were still basically kids, and with all they had, they were easy targets for the dark, unseemly dregs of any major American city, especially New York. Hellan had heard of mobsters kidnapping rich kids, executives, and yes, even some athletes to achieve some pretty handsome paydays and to make statements in various places around the world. There were even very real terrorist considerations today. But it would still be something unparalleled for the NHL.

The Red Wings had beefed up security over the last couple of years due to some unsubstantiated threats from international crime families trying to extort their countrymen out of most of what they made. It was certainly not the game he had grown up with in Burlington, Ontario, but it was his reality today. And, right now, it was all too real.

A quiet rap on the door caused Hellan to jump from his chair. His nerves were really fried right now. He stormed over to the door and pulled it open. Before him stood Darcy Hilton, David Stone and Brent Hagen. All looked appropriately sombre and stared at the floor. "Okay, get in here," spat the angry GM. "Where were you idiots and what happened last night? I got McCroy's version of your story but what more do you know?"

"There's not a lot more, sir," stammered Hagen. "We were out for drinks, a bunch of us, and Riley was just havin' a few and dancing, and then he was gone. We looked everywhere around the club, but there was no sign of him. Then we thought he might have got a girl and headed back to the hotel, but he wasn't there either. That was around 1:30 AM or so."

"David called the cops when we got back but they couldn't tell us anything, so here we are, still waiting," added a dejected Hilton.

"Well, that's great. We'll deal with your situations later, but right now go back to your rooms, stay there, and do not talk to anyone. No one! No teammates, no friends or family. Nobody. Who knows what stories are floating out there today? The press will have a goddamn field day on my grave."

The three turned to exit the luxury suite just as a cream desk phone rang and the anxious GM rushed to it. "Hellan here."

"Hello. This is the NYPD. My name is James Murray and I'm the Captain at Precinct 40 in the Bronx. I think we've got something you may have lost last night. He's fine, just drunk and probably a little scared. He's being questioned right now by one of my detectives about a B&E, which we don't think he had anything to do with, but you might want to get a lawyer down here before he admits to killing someone or worse."

The stressed out GM's shoulders slumped in relief. "Oh God, thank you. Thank you so much. That is such good news. Please hang onto him and I'll be over there as fast as I can, Captain..."

"Captain James Murray. Just ask for me when you get here."

"I'll get you season tickets for this, I promise," the GM enthused.

"Yeah? That's great, but I'm a Knicks fan. Don't follow hockey too much."

Hellan waved at the three players standing anxiously at his door. "They've got Sawyer at the police station. I'm going down to get him and hopefully clear this up. Get back to your fucking rooms and do not say a word about this to anyone. Are we clear?"

"Crystal," stated Hilton, as the other two nodded and they headed off to their rooms at double time. They were exhausted and nervous at what their fates might be, but this was the best outcome they could have hoped for.

"This is good, right Darcy." David asked the older rookie.

"Not if you're Riley Sawyer," spat his angry friend, lamenting the terrible failure his first chaperoning assignment had been.

* * *

"OK, so let's try this again, kid." Ozzie said. "You leave Plush nightclub and for some unknown reason some guys start chasin' you down the street and shooting at you. Is that your story?"

Riley's hands trembled as he clutched his lukewarm styrofoam cup. "No. I remember leaving the club because I had way too much to drink. I was in an alley and then I was laying by a window. I think I saw someone cut somebody's head off and that's when I started running and the guys started chasing me. It's sort of a blur right now, but I ran through some buildings and alleys and just wanted to hide. That's when I went into a backyard because it was really dark and I climbed up a big, leafy tree. I knew they'd never look up there and if they did the leaves would keep me hidden."

"Pure genius, kid," mumbled the detective as he doodled characters on a piece of yellow scratch-pad paper.

"I saw one of the guys enter the yard and that's when the man came out with a shotgun and started yelling. But he was yelling at the killer—not me. He's lucky to be alive. These guys meant business."

The detective leaned in his chair and looked into the hockey player's panicked eyes. "So, you're telling me you saw a murder? And, not just any murder, but a beheading. And then the guys who did it came after you. Wow, that's very Robert Ludlum, but, okay, I'll give you points for originality. And I think you're too dumb to be that creative. Can you tell me what building?"

"Like I said, I don't really know where I was. I was really drunk and it was so dark. There was a big truck in the alley that I ran past and some kind of buildings, and a lady putting out garbage or something. It's all just fragments."

"Well, that's great. We'll just go find a building with a truck on the street and a lady taking out garbage and we'll find a headless corpse. You realize how fucking terrible this information is, right?"

"One more thing: the guys had accents, sounded Russian. I've played with lots of Russians and I know how they sound and it was like those guys. I don't know what they were saying."

Stark stopped scribbling on his note pad at the sound of Russians. Plush was a notorious club for Russian mob activity and there had been a lot of chatter lately about some new crime groups moving in on their operation. Experience had told him it would not be long before the bodies started piling up. He straightened up in his chair. "Do you think you could show us the building if we took you back there?"

"Uh, I'm not going back there. What if they're waiting? No, I just want to get the hell out of this city—as soon as possible."

"Yeah? Well that won't be happening until you write out this fairy tale and we check out the scene of your alleged murder. You said it was in the back alley of Plush?"

"Actually, it was around the club not in the alley. I think I turned, I just don't remember what direction or where. I was under some kind of ledge and staring through a window. I think it had a thick metal screen on it. There was a loading dock and a big car pulled up—black. I ran the opposite way."

"Okay, write it all down, every detail, and sit tight. We'll go over there. If there really was a homicide, you could be the only witness, so, kid, you're in this. You'd better hope we find something to support this crazy story. Because if this is some bullshit excuse you cooked up to save your hockey-playing ass, you'll have even more trouble from me, and some serious legal problems." The detective tossed his yellow pad across the table and threw Riley a pen. "Start writing."

Ozzie got up and left the interrogation room. He walked quietly down the hall towards the Captain's office, mulling over the bits and pieces of information he had just been given. Russians. Plush. Beheadings. Shooting at a witness. Warehouses. Oddly enough, the fragments did have a line of logic that fit together. But right now, he had no evidence and no reason to think this was anything more than the story of a drunk, scared kid trying to avoid trouble with his boss.

"Cap, the kid had quite the story about Russians, a murder and him hiding in a tree. It honestly sounds completely bonkers, but somehow parts of it make sense. I'm taking Fergus and heading over to the club to look around and ask some questions. Could you have the patrol guys stop by the house of the guy who called in the complaint and see if he has a huge, leafy tree in his backyard? If he does, we'll cut the kid loose. His only crime is being young, rich and stupid. We should all be so lucky."

"Got it," replied his captain.

As Stark grabbed his coat and headed toward the front doors, a black limousine pulled up to the curb and two well-dressed, but very harried, gentlemen jumped out and ran past him. It was Detroit's GM and a bookish looking intellectual type—New York's top criminal defense lawyer—Tom Baines.

Chapter 19

The tension in the 58th story penthouse office was palpable as Alexi stared over the massive city below and the Hudson River. "So, you bumbling fools couldn't catch a fucking drunk kid running in the night alone. Are you kidding me?"

The henchmen sat quietly, heads down.

"The body. Where is it?" Alexi continued.

"The Hudson. Deep, deep in the Hudson. No one will ever find it. Properly weighted, it will decompose or be eaten before anyone ever finds any part of it. We're good there," replied Andriy.

"Are we? What about the basement?"

"Clean as a whistle. Not a spec of blood anywhere. Nothing. Everything's perfect. We burned the plastic sheets in the blast furnace and bleached all the walls. No evidence there—ever."

"Well, at least it sounds like you did that right. Perhaps your job should be more janitorial in the future and less homicidal. We don't know what that kid knows or who he is. We need to know that and get rid of him—permanently. We cannot have any loose ends."

"Boss, we think we might be able to figure out who he is. We found a really expensive suit jacket stuffed into a garbage during the chase. We think it's his. It's BOSS, so the kids got some cash. Think he must have been at Plush earlier. Maybe went out for some air or something. I got a pretty good look at him and, weirdly enough, he looked sort of familiar, but I can't place the face."

"Well, isn't this great? My hired soldiers are now New York City detectives. That's just fucking great. If you had done your job last night this would all be so unnecessary. Find this miserable brat however you have to and eliminate him. You know the price of failure, right?"

The team nodded and headed out of the palatial office.

Andriy directed the others as they headed down the austere hallways and waited at the elevators. "Call Plush and get all the girls who were working last night there at 4 PM sharp. Every single one of them. I'm sure they'll have met our mystery man or know who he is. Actually, get all the security guys too,"

* * *

The Red Wings' private plane had been delayed almost four hours and it did not have Riley Sawyer or Dave Hellan on it. This seemed odd to Danielle. She was waiting in the press area of private terminal three to get comments on the Ranger game and first performances of the rookies, but surprisingly there was no GM nor the biggest rookie of them all. Where was Riley Sawyer? Her reporter's instincts spiked.

David grabbed his bag from the cart and turned into her sightline. *My God, David*, she thought, *you look awful*.

As the extremely grim-faced rookie walked towards her, his pained expression and depressed demeanour took on even greater veracity. But, it wasn't just him. Everyone seemed down. This certainly did not look like a young team that had just played a pretty good road game against the Rangers the night before and would now be preparing for their first home tilt. Something certainly seemed out of whack here.

Captain Phil Davis was the first Wing to arrive at the press area and attracted the greatest attention. He did not look at all happy and gave only short, curt answers about the game.

Danielle focused her interview on the rookies, starting with her own David Stone. She held up her microphone to his face and grinned as he approached. "So, where's Riley?"

The question seemed to hit the young centerman like a full on punch to the face. "Huh? What? What kind of question is that? I don't know."

"You don't know where one of your teammates is?"

David snapped his head around to see who was watching and then quickly covered the microphone with his hand. "Turn this thing off. Now," he shot back, clearly upset at her line of questioning.

"What are you doing?" responded Danielle in anger. "What's going on with you?" The red record light faded to black.

"Riley missed the plane and will come back on a later one with Hellan. It's no big deal, but we've all caught hell for the game in New York. As far as Riley we've been told to shut up about it. So, don't ask me that. Or maybe ask a coach. I've got enough issues to deal with right now."

"Ok, this is crazy. Did something happen in New York? You

guys played okay but everyone here looks like they're coming back from a funeral. Did Riley get hurt?"

"No comment!" David stated stoically. Then he turned and walked away from the stunned reporter toward a taxi stand.

Danielle wasn't sure what hurt more, David's unexpected negative tone or the fact he did not trust her enough to share his thoughts. Either way, she was ready now to let her reporter's instincts take full control. She quickly walked over to Mike McCroy who was doing his best to get out of the airport.

"Coach, that had to be a satisfying game last night, care to comment?"

Still walking, Mike replied, "Sure we're always happy when the young guys play well, even if it was just exhibition, and I thought our kids played really well, so it was an okay night. Would have been nice to win though."

"Was it okay, coach? I noticed one of your kids didn't make the flight home. Where is Riley Sawyer? Did he get hurt? Is he still in New York? Where's Dave Hellan? He usually travels with the team to the first exhibition game and he's not here either. What's going on, coach?"

McCroy stopped and his tired eyes looked into Danielle's. "Riley is fine. He just missed a flight and Dave is coming back with him later. No story here, though we will issue a formal statement later today, so you all get the same commentary. That's your big scoop, Miss Wright. Is that all?"

"Well, not really. Why did Riley miss the plane? It seems like the team is really down. Did something off the ice happen in New York?"

"No, nothing. We're all fine."

"Did Riley miss curfew? Did he get in trouble in New York?"

"For the last time, no, he's fine. We are all fine. There is nothing to report except he's coming on a later flight."

"Will it be a private flight or a commercial flight, coach?"

The drained coach stopped one final time and glimpsed toward the floor. "I have no idea. Check with our travel guy or trainer, maybe they know something." At that, the coach disappeared out the door and into a waiting SUV where he kissed his wife on the cheek and the vehicle sped off.

When Danielle looked back into the terminal she noticed everyone was almost gone. There had not been a lot of reporters, but this may have been the biggest drive-by press conference ever given. And the most pained. Her instincts told her there was a lot more to the story than anyone was admitting and she was determined to find out what. She could not blame David, he had his career to worry about. But she had her career to think about too, and at the moment those two careers appeared to be colliding.

* * *

David rubbed his temples as he sat alone in the cab. What a disaster New York had turned into. He wondered what had become of Riley. After checking out late, the team had made a decision to leave without Sawyer and issue a press release later. The players were sworn to say nothing about anything that had happened, or that they thought had happened, in New York. They were instructed to only address the media with "no comment" or "I don't know" if asked anything. Riley was coming on a later flight with Mr. Hellan. It didn't seem to be that big of a deal to him, but then David was not a reporter versed in the art of investigation and sensing every nuance of misdirection, lies or spin.

He couldn't wait to get back to his little hotel hideaway and have everything return to normal with the team meeting on Monday morning. He needed some sleep and, in the short term, some space from Danielle until the press release was issued. He knew she would not let it rest. That was just not her nature. It's what made her so good at her job and such a pain in the ass—all at the same time. He felt bad about his airport outburst and storming off, but oddly enough he was not even sure what the implications of the night before might be on his career. There were just too many unknowns right now.

* * *

Nothing. There was really nothing Ozzie could find out of place in the alleys around Plush. He and Fergus, his partner, combed up and down the alley directly behind the club, but other than a few broken bottles and some dried vomit—nothing. They reached the alley's end and he turned his head right. People tend to follow habitual behaviour when in distress he recalled from some old police crisis training seminar he had attended. Sawyer was a right-winger, so he was likely a right-hand shot. If he was loaded and out of control, chances are he would follow instinct and go right. The detective turned and began walking down an adjacent alley. About 150 yards along the narrow asphalt strip, he saw a loading dock just as Riley had described. He leaned over to examine a concrete overhang on the left of the dock and found an area under it where tufts of weeds and grass growing through the cracked pavement were crushed and flat, as if someone fairly heavy had been laying on them for an extended time.

He had Fergus snap a series of crime scene reference photos of the site and then lowered his body and rolled into the space. He turned his head and in the late morning sunlight found himself staring into a bland, empty room of no real interest—except that it might be his crime scene. They would need a warrant to investigate the room. First, he needed to find out who owned the building and why it was so completely empty.

Okay, if this was the murder scene, Sawyer must have ran to his left in fear, the two officers decided. After casing the loading dock area carefully they found nothing. No shell casings. No fresh tire tracks. Certainly, no drops of blood and really nothing out of the ordinary. They walked west down the alley, away from the loading dock—Sawyer's escape route according to his tall tale. In front of them, Stark saw a broken lamp on the side of a building with shattered glass on the asphalt. The broken glass appeared to be recent. If it was old it would have been cleaned up by now or disturbed by traffic moving through the alley. He stared further west down the alley at a bustling main street and sure enough there were rows of empty industrial garbage bins lining both sides. They had obviously been emptied a short time ago—like the night before.

"Ok, kid, so far so good," mused Ozzie as he directed Fergus to photograph the garbage bins and broken glass. He would have to find out what time garbage pick-up had been scheduled for these businesses and by what company. He noted FLG Waste Company's name and contact information in his note pad. It was the most common brand on all the bins and therefore the most likely to be doing a late night pick-up in the area.

Then, at just above head height, he saw two marks freshly etched into the old scarred brick facade of a building. Those could be bullet marks, if he was not mistaken. Shots taken that missed and ricocheted off into the distance, clearly not hitting their target. He collected some brick fragments from the ground and placed them in a small evidence bag and again more photos.

Around the corner to the north were numerous garbage cans and piled trash that had probably been put out the night before based on their orderly arrangement. It was still too early for the street people who roamed through the area to have moved, dissected or ripped apart the bags.

Up the street about a block away, Ozzie saw a building superintendent cursing at the top of his lungs while trying to reset the front door on a small walk-up apartment.

"Hey, buddy, what happened to your door?"

"You a cop or something? Well, thanks for showing up now. You guys are useless. Four assholes bust my door down, scare the shit out of my tenants and you don't show up until now. Yeah, thanks for nothin'."

"Listen, can anyone identify the guys who did this or did anyone see them? If they did, I really need to talk to them. This is very important."

"Old lady Rosen said they ran right past her, chasing some kid who went flying through the building first. They said they were cops but she knew they weren't. All sounded like fucking Russians. She won't be home for a while, if at all. She's gone to her kid's place in Vermont. She was pretty shaken up by what happened. Said they all had guns. This city is turning into a pile of shit what with all these crazy bars and clubs opening everywhere. It's a bloody disaster."

Ozzie got the address for Estell Rosen and looked at Fergus. "That goddamn kid was telling the truth. Every miserable word of his stupid story is true. Wow, he had one hell of a night, that's for sure."

The building with the broken door was about four blocks from a backyard where an old man had reported intruders the previous night. Sawyer's story and circumstantial evidence fit perfectly. Just no sign of a murder, no body and no report of any murder from the night before. But, there was certainly enough here to pique the detective's interest.

The two detectives were walking back to their unmarked car in the alley behind Plush, when they noticed a long line of beautiful women streaming through the club's back door. Staff meeting? Not likely. Sunday at 3:25 PM? That would be highly unlikely. Plush was normally closed Sunday and its staff were certainly nocturnal by nature. They'd been working until the wee hours of the morning and would not be showing up on their day off unless summoned by someone high up—very high up. Ozzie and Fergus quietly settled in their non-descript car and continued to watch the activity.

At 4:09 PM a black cargo van pulled around the corner and into the alley stopping outside the club. It was the kind of van usually commandeered for clean-up jobs after a hit, sort of a discount hearse for unfortunate souls. Three men, clad in black leather and military-grade boots, climbed out and, after glancing up and down the alley like good soldiers, hurried into the club.

Fergus furiously snapped photos of the men in rapid succession with a telescopic lens from the moment they left the van until the last one disappeared through the doors. Could these be the killers? Why were they at the club now?

"Looks like we stumbled ass backwards into another murder, Fergus. Now all we got to do is find the body, the motive and the killers. We need a warrant for that warehouse, like now, and that van. Make sure you get a shot of those plates and send it for identification." Ozzie rang the precinct to make a report. "Hi, Cap. Yeah looks like you can let the superstar go, his story has legs. He may be very lucky he's still alive if the thugs we just saw were the guys chasing him and they may be looking to finish the job. We need a forensics team out here immediately to document and examine some trace in the alley. We're at the back of Plush nightclub and my spidey senses tell me something went down here last night. And the kid is in the middle of it."

* * *

The hunched-over figure in a Yankees cap and dark glasses soberly retrieved his belongings from a portal window surrounded by a thick wire screen. An officer escorted him from the precinct's holding area to a waiting town car where two, older, distinguished-looking gentlemen were seated. The car silently pulled into the chaos of New York's Sunday evening traffic and headed out to LaGuardia Airport for a 10 PM Delta Airlines flight to Flint, Michigan, and then a one hour, eleven minute drive down the John C Lodge Freeway to Detroit. This would be the quietest off-the-grid homecoming ever orchestrated by Red Wings' management.

Chapter 20

The player's entrance at Joe Louis Arena was bustling with reporters at 8:30 AM Monday as players arrived for their game debriefing and practice. David paid his cab fare and kept his head down as he headed for the door, trying to avoid questions. The issuing of an evening press release about Riley's absence from the team's flight had set off a scandal among the locals, given his reputation, the team's pre-season loss and growing speculation on social media and some New York scandal websites about Detroit's out of control team partying on the weekend. There was a picture of Riley looking very drunk with a half-naked girl on his lap, trending on Facebook and Instagram and it was helping shape and sensationalize the ever-evolving negative story of Detroit's first-round draft pick.

Reporters were buzzing the arena like hornets around a disturbed nest and David was determined not to get stung by any of them. He heard nothing, knew nothing and would say nothing, as instructed.

David looked up sheepishly as he passed Danielle, nodding, made a call-me sign and then disappeared into the vast chasm of the rink.

Red Wing PR maven, Pat Thompson, was standing in the midst of the turmoil, professionally answering questions while denying everything and saying absolutely nothing. The players avoided almost all contact and quickly vanished behind the entrance doors and down the hall to meeting room 110.

As players discussed the New York trip over their morning coffees and sport drinks, each peered around the room for the cause celeb, Mr. Sawyer. He was nowhere to be seen with the clock quickly approaching the 9:00 AM meeting time.

Darcy pulled in beside David. "So where is the little prick?" he spat in his ear.

"Don't know Darcy. Haven't heard a thing. Maybe still in New York."

"If he's smart, he should just stay there. Guys are pretty pissed about this. Not the way to start our season that's for sure."

Without notice the door slammed and the sight of a fatigued

Dave Hellan moving to the podium silenced everyone. He pulled the microphone up to his lips and turned it on. This caused a loud humming and then sharp squeal that only heightened the tension and made everything even more awkward—if that was even possible. After clearing his throat, he took a sip of water, placed both hands on the lectern and spoke.

"As you all know, we had an incident in New York. Riley Sawyer and some others got a bit out of control while they were partying at a night club and he ended up drunk and lost in the city. He was picked up early Sunday morning and detained by NYPD for his own safety. The police contacted me Sunday morning and he was released to us yesterday. I flew home with him very late last night. That's it. Nothing more. Riley and the others will be disciplined, just as any of you would be for doing something equally stupid. Sadly, despite all the orientation time we spend on this issue, this is not the first time it's happened, and likely won't be the last. The team has issued a media release stating that Riley missed curfew and will be disciplined internally for his breach of conduct. That will be the end of this incident as far as you players are concerned. None of you are to speak to the media about any of the silly conjecture that might blow up from this story. What I have told you is the team's official position on what happened and you are required to stick to that narrative. And, that narrative only. Is that clear?"

The room remained silent.

Hellan lifted his hand and hammered it on the lectern setting off a sonic boom that reverberated off the walls. "I said, is that clear!" He yelled.

"Yes, sir!" was the quick uniform response from across the room.

"Thank you, gentlemen. Now, have a good meeting and a good practice. We have Chicago coming here in two days and they would love nothing more than to add to our humiliation by kicking our asses. Finally, let's have no more negative incidents at camp— on or off the ice." Hellan turned from the microphone quietly and walked out of the room with only the scuffling of his hard-soled shoes making a sound.

Mike McCroy approached the lectern. "Larry, hit the lights. I want to run some video. Pay attention guys."

The meeting began.

***

Danielle watched the afternoon's on-ice session. It seemed exceptionally hard for a practice just 48 hours prior to their second preseason game. It was basically a bag skate with no pucks or scrimmage and it left no one happy.

Gasping for air, Darcy pulled up next to David and Anson Dee. "When I get my fucking hands on Sawyer, I'm going to rip out his eyeballs and piss in his—"

"HILTON, what the hell are you doing? Get back on the line and shut up. This isn't a gab fest," shouted assistant coach Davies.

His shrill whistle blast started another round of lines that had become far too numerous to count.

Danielle winced at the exhaustion showing on the faces of some less fit players. "Wow, this is brutal," she whispered to her colleague, Dan Norris, a friend and hockey reporter for television rival, KMOV-TV.

"Yeah, somebody's pretty pissed about something," he chuckled, before scribbling in his notebook.

"What do you want to bet it has something to do with Riley Sawyer?" Danielle grinned.

"Duh, gee, ya think?" He laughed. "Great insight Sherlock. Sometimes you really are as dumb as you are good looking."

Danielle punched his arm and stuck out her tongue at him. "What do you think happened?" she continued.

"Well, I heard from a buddy of mine who works at the Ledger in Jersey that a police scanner picked up a report of some NHL player getting collared for being drunk and doing a B&E. You know, break and enter."

"Yeah, I know what it means. Duh, back at ya." Danielle sneered good-naturedly.

"But that sounds just plain nuts. No one really thinks it's true. Rumour has it he did get hauled off to jail for something after leaving a strip joint called Plush or Pure or something. I guess the whole team was there," Dan concluded casually.

"Really?" grimaced Danielle, suddenly facing a new reality that for some reason had not bothered her before. "Were all the rookies there?"

"Who knows? I guess so. The first road game is always kind of a big initiation for the kids. They usually go to a nightclub, some high priced den of iniquity. Then everyone blows off a little steam and the rooks get to feel like celebrities for the first time—big city style. Why? You think there's a scoop about a bunch of overpaid jocks getting drunk? Forget it, honey, it's the worst story in sports, unless of course they kill somebody—then maybe you've got something."

Danielle stared coldly at David hustling down the ice as she felt a sense of anger rising with each word Dan spoke. *That would explain his cold reception at the airport and the brush-off last night,* she thought. *What an asshole. First trip out of town and he's whoring around New York like a rock star. Screw him.*

Mercifully, practice ended while Danielle was in midthought. The players began to muster at centre ice for final instructions.

"Tomorrow we'll post the Chicago roster. If you didn't play in New York, this is your shot. After the game, everyone, and I mean everyone, is on lock down. No going out until camp's over. Break the rule and, well, you'll wish you hadn't," instructed Davies.

David, bent at the knees and breathing heavily, was happy to hear the new team edict. It gave him a built-in excuse to forget about New York and just focus on making the team. What had started out as such a great experience in the Big Apple had shown him how quickly traps could be sprung on the young and stupid. He just prayed there would be limited fallout for him and the others.

Everyone moaned about the lock down and dejectedly glided off the ice. As David entered the tunnel, he caught a glimpse of Danielle's shapely backside heading for the dressing rooms and was happy for the chance to see her now that the team had issued a formal statement. It would give him a chance to make up with her after last night's disgraceful homecoming and his rudeness. He should have been more respectful of her job. But he was just a bit out of his element right now and had a lot on the line. She would understand.

The dressing room was a sombre place, completely opposite of what was normal for an NHL training camp. Various players whispered in hushed tones about the Sawyer stories that were now swirling on social and traditional media.

"So, I wonder where he is." Hilts moaned to David.

"Don't know, Darce. And in reality, we don't know the whole story. He got drunk, that's for sure, but we don't really know anything else. Don't judge until—"

"Really? You're going to defend that little turd? His fucking around could cost us our careers. And, I was trying to help him. Ingrate."

"We're all to blame man," shot back David. "We were all stupid. Fuck, I spent $1,400 in one night and had like four drinks. My mom would kill me if she knew. We didn't do anything less stupid than him; we just didn't end up in jail. So cut him some slack. He's our teammate.

"Listen kid, up here you take care of yourself. No one's crying for you when they ship your ass down to the minors because you have an attitude problem, so don't give me the we're all in this together crap. You don't have a clue about life in the minors or how things work up here. This is likely my last shot and I'm not some special rookie with soft hands or a thoroughbred pedigree. I'm a labelled minor league lifer who maybe, just maybe, had a shot this year. So don't—"

"I got it, Hilts, I got it. Everything's just messed up right now and it bugs me so much because we were on a roll."

"Yeah, I know and we got to stay on that roll. Say, where's your girl? Thought I saw her in the tunnel. You're usually her lead story. Bloom off the rose?"

"No, no. She just had to spread around the coverage. She'll probably be along later."

The two friends were among the last players to leave the dressing room. David was surprised he had not seen Danielle. She was probably trying to pry more information out of poor McCroy. He walked into the corridor as the last reporters left the arena. None of them was Danielle.

Chapter 21

"Boss, I think we might have a bad situation here."

"Andriy, how many times I tell you, we never have bad situations, we just have things that need to be fixed," Alexi stated matter-of-factly as he coldly stared up at his lieutenant. "What's your situation?"

"We talked to the girls and one of them thought she recognized the suit coat. She claims she was all over the guy in it, at the club for a couple of hours or so. We could even smell her perfume on it. You're never gonna guess whose it was."

"Stop playing fucking games with me. Just tell me, you imbecile." Any hint of smugness was gone from the crime boss's retort.

"It was that high-prized rookie, Riley Sawyer from the Red Wings. I think he may have been the kid we were chasing. He's the right size and I thought the guy looked familiar when I caught a glimpse of him in the alley. I just never thought it would be a guy like that. Then today, there's some media rags saying the cops arrested a hockey player on Sunday morning. It all fits. We chased him into that alley and he must have hung out there until the cops found him."

Alexi's face went ashen as the words spewed out like little daggers into his black soul. This was very, very bad news. Killing a mobster was akin to community service, so you never really had to worry about the cops. Killing a regular citizen, well that was bad, but it could still usually be kept under the radar and made to disappear. Hell, decapitating a sleazy mob lawyer was probably even acceptable as long as the current in the Hudson stayed strong. But, a fucking celebrity athlete with major-league security, agents, access to lawyers and DA's, and all the professional protection they had from the teams. That was an almost unprecedented situation.

What did the kid know? What had he seen? Worse yet, what had he already told the cops? Yes, this was very bad indeed but Alexi would deal with it the way any alpha predator would.

"Yes, it certainly is a situation, Andriy, and it needs to be fixed, fast. Better find out where the Wings are playing. We're going to need a guy over there? One with a family?"

Chapter 22

The smile on Anson Dee's face was enough to light up the cavernous hallway leading to the dressing room.

"What the hell are you grinning about?" David asked with a smile.

"I'm playing tomorrow against the Hawks. I'm second line. I got a chance to make things right again."

"Oh, yeah. I forgot they were posting the team this morning. That's great news, man, I'm happy for you. Am I playing?"

"Hmmm, can't say I saw your name, but then I didn't really look that close," Dee responded.

David's heart skipped a beat. Everybody had surely scanned that roster and committed it to memory. These games were the difference between a year in the minors or in the big leagues. You paid attention. David felt a bit queasy as his pace quickened down the hall. A group of guys were standing outside the door, mulling over the roster, including Darcy.

"Don't rush, Bolt, we're not on it," he lamented with a beaten down look. "And now the pain begins."

"What does that mean?" David asked, somewhat afraid of what the answer might be.

"Means we're getting iced for that New York fuck up. How stupid are you? After the game we had, our line should be playing. None of us are on the roster and the black aces and older veterans are. Not a good sign."

"Darcy, they have to look at everyone, we aren't going to play every game."

"Yeah, actually you do if you're a rookie and they think you've got a shot. That's what this camp is about. Have you heard anything about Riley? Where is he? No one's seen him since New York."

"Nah, haven't heard a thing," replied a suddenly very disheartened David.

* * *

It had been three terrible days for Riley and now he was sitting in Dave Hellan's office waiting to find out his fate. He had already received a mandatory suspension for missing the flight while the media were having a heyday making up stories about his New York adventures. He only hoped the damage was not irreparable. Plus, he couldn't sleep. He kept having flashbacks of that night. The slashing of a long blade, the falling head, the running. Every time it entered his psyche, his stomach constricted with nausea and he almost wretched. *If only this would all go away*, he thought, placing his head into his trembling hands.

What about those guys chasing him? Who were they? Did they know who he was? What a mess things had become. He shook his head slowly and clenched his eyes tighter. Adding to the stress, his father and mother were flying in today, with his agent in tow. How awkward was that going to be?

"Mr. Hellan will see you now," came the stern direction from the GM's Executive Assistant.

Hellan's voice was curt. "So, that was quite a night you had!"

"Yes, sir. Things certainly got out of hand. I feel awful and-"

At that moment a back door in the office burst open and Detroit's iconic owner, Mike Layton, stormed into the room. Riley froze in mid-sentence.

"Maybe you'd like to start again for Mr. Layton," Hellan quietly and coldly stated, staring directly into Sawyer's eyes.

"As, I was saying—" Riley began, but he was cut off a second time.

"Son, do you know how much money we'll invest in you? What with all the scouting, promoting, pampering, coaching, training? Well, the amount is in the hundreds of thousands—and that's just to get you ready for the team. Then, we're expected to pay you a king's ransom to do what it is you do. And so, when you embarrass our entire organization, making us look like assholes in the biggest media market in the world," his voice began to tremble, "Well, I get really pissed off. Now, Dave here, he's a good man and he's got a lot more patience with punks like you then I do. I worked damn hard for every nickel I've got and I try to treat my players well, but when you do this, you break the bond. It's just not what

Red Wings do. We never sully the brand. The team and that jersey are sacrosanct, above everyone and you need to get that very simple premise into that thick skull of yours. I don't want to hear another thing about this weekend's stupidity from you or anyone else. I don't care what happened." The red-faced owner stopped to take a breath. "And, you are not to speak about it to anyone, ever. Is that clear. The facts are, you got drunk, cops found you, took you to the precinct for your own protection. We picked you up. Stupid kid makes an immature mistake. That's the story we're all sticking with and this embarrassment is over."

"Well, actually sir, I was just going out for air and ended up in this alley."

Mike's hand shot up immediately an inch or two from Riley's lips. "No! No! No! You're not hearing me, son. You were drunk. The cops found you. That's it. You do not utter another word about this to anyone. Our PR people will take over from here. I want this behind us. You have a week to prove to everyone in this organization that we did not waste our number one draft pick and money on you. Right now, we're not sure of that. You're suspended until Friday and will miss the next two games. So, in fact, you have four days to impress us. Am I clear?"

"Yes, sir," Riley mumbled, head bowed.

"Now get to your hotel and meet your family. Don't discuss this incident any further than what I told you. As far as we're concerned it's done. No stupid stories of people chasing you, hiding in trees or any other bullshit."

Riley knew better than to try and retell his tale now. Besides, who was going to believe him? The cop had thought he'd made the whole thing up to get out of trouble. They had no evidence. He better do as he was told. Shut up, stick to the party line and just put this behind him.

"You look like shit." Hellan's comment broke the silence. "Go to your hotel. I've asked Dr. Bracken to come by and look you over. Try to get some sleep, son. When the suspension ends you're going to have a lot of work and catching up to do and not a lot of time to do it in."

"Yes. Thank you, sir, I will. I haven't been sleeping very well lately."

"Yeah, I bet." Hellan glared.

Riley left the room and closed the door quietly behind him, leaving the two executives sitting on opposite sides of the desk.

"Did we make a mistake on this kid, Dave?" Layton queried.

"He's had moments, but he's all over the place. He's certainly been a bit disappointing."

"What about that Stone? I heard he was part of this fiasco too."

Hellan peered ahead. "Him, I'm just pissed at. He's fine, just let him sweat a little. Hilton, I don't know about him. He led the idiot parade to that bar. Not sure that's the influence these kids need at this point in their careers."

"Who?" asked Detroit's owner.

"Oh, nobody," replied the GM. "Nobody at all."

* * *

Danielle was sitting at her desk perusing an alleged police report on the arrest of Riley Sawyer in New York. Nothing in it made sense. This kid gets arrested somewhere in Brooklyn, early on Sunday morning, walking down an alley, for an alleged break and enter that some guy complained about late the night before.

Bullshit, Danielle thought, *that's just too far out there. Clearly, this has to be wrong. And, if it's not then there really is no story here. Oh well, maybe I'll call the officers later, do a follow up and then let it go.*

Knowing young professional athletes as she did, it made sense they went to a strip bar, got really drunk and just got stupid. After all, they were hockey players, many of them in the big city for the first time. That's what they do.

Chapter 23

The detective sat staring at a collection of non-descript photos from the alley. To his left was a newly-issued search warrant for a warehouse owned by an untraceable, numbered company in the Cayman Islands. Nothing overt jumped out at Ozzie about a murder taking place except every detail in the kid's story seemed to fit perfectly. His timeline was credible and there was even a photo of the backyard of a townhome on West 121 Street with a giant elm tree that now seemed like pretty compelling evidence of Sawyer's alibi. The puzzle pieces had begun to fall into place.

Ozzie chuckled as he thought of the pampered prima donna pissing his pants in fear and scurrying up a tree in the dead of night. That takes some balls when you think killers are chasing you. But, given his situation, it was actually pretty quick thinking that likely saved his life. For sure the kid had been involved in something and it looked like it might involve some pretty bad dudes.

He stared again at the photos and, with renewed vigour, summoned Fergus as he grabbed the warrants. "Let's go, buddy. Back to the warehouse and we'll see what the fuck went on there. Maybe we'll hit the clubs tonight too. Time to rattle some nerves in the hood."

As he grabbed his coat and headed down the hallway his desk phone caller ID lit up—D. Wright, and it had Detroit's 313 area code.

"—at the beep please leave a message."

"Uh, hello. I was given your name as one of the investigating officers in the Riley Sawyer arrest. My name is Danielle Wright and I'm a reporter with Detroit's Free Press. Could you give me a call back at 313-456-7768. I have a few questions about the facts of the case and wanted to get some clarifications on a few police report details provided to us by the Red Wings. Thank you."

Chapter 24

The only good news for David and his linemates was the Chicago game was a total disaster. A 7 to 1 thrashing has a way of moderating a lot of the coach's messaging to players. This would be the case for David and Hilts. The Chicago catastrophe was followed up with a close 4 to 2 loss in Toronto, including an empty-net goal. A better effort to be sure, but still, something was missing and everyone knew it.

Danielle had penned an especially critical article of the club's handling of the Riley Sawyer incident and ripped into team management and the coaching staff for not playing their stellar new centre David Stone, underdog favourite Darcy Hilton and, of course, "the star of their future", Riley Sawyer. What was going on? She demanded to know.

The article initiated a flood of calls from angry fans to local sports radio shows in support of her questions. Those feelings festered through the week and eventually created a full-blown scandal. Surely, the Wings were not going to burn two, bright, young prospects for simply breaking curfew and getting drunk during a training camp road trip? That just seemed like a complete overreaction to most of the Red Wing faithful. Hell, compared to the far more serious allegations directed at Lions and Pistons players, this was a nothing. Clearly the "wee winners" brought something to the team that was not there now. With only two pre-season games remaining though, these players were running out of time.

Five cuts that morning before practice brought home, with surgical precision, how precarious a player's future was. David watched his friend Anson Dee get tapped on the shoulder and, after a brief chat, head to the coach's office. He had cast a last look at David as he pulled off his shin pads. It was a sad and dejected expression, the kind a person makes as they head into a doctor's office. Fearful, questioning, but ultimately just sad.

"Take care man," were the last words he mouthed in David's direction and then disappeared from the room.

David stared at Anson's now empty and lifeless locker. There'd be no more boisterous celebrations or dreams fulfilled in that two foot by six foot piece of real estate—a players sole sanctuary during this difficult grind.

"Okay God, please let me have a good practice today. Please," David quietly whispered to himself.

* * *

Practice was fast and hard. David focused on winning everything possible. Skating races. Shooting drills. Line rushes. Face-offs.

"Hey, sport, lighten up. You're making the rest of us look bad," joked Pavel Abramov.

"No can do, Pav. Today is about redemption. I'm playing to impress, so stay outta my way."

The final whistle blew and players formed a circle around Mike McCroy.

"Good practice boys. It's nice to see some familiar faces back today. What happened in New York is over and now it's business as usual again. We've had enough distractions and controversy to last us for a whole season, so everyone take a deep breath and get ready for the stretch run. For some of you it will be your last shot to make the team."

David could not help but feel Mike's glare move in his direction and then to Darcy.

"Line-ups will be posted tomorrow morning for the St. Louis and Edmonton games. Lots of rooks going to St. Lou and likely the regular season line-up will be back here for the last game. Good luck, guys, let's get this thing back on track."

The players began hammering sticks on the ice like some tribal ritual and chanted, "Kill St. Lou, Kill St. Lou."

David picked up the chant and felt a grin break across his face for the first time in days. The team's gloom seemed to be lifting ever so slowly, replaced by an aura of excitement again for the final leg of training camp.

A few die-hard fans watching practice picked up on the chant and players raised their sticks to them in salute to a fresh start.

Amidst all the revelry, no one noticed that a shadowy figure in a black Calvin Klein leather jacket and beige pants remained seated, nodding his head as he spoke calmly into a cell phone.

* * *

The reenergized Red Wings crushed St. Louis, 6 to 2, with David recording two assists and Riley chipping in a power play goal. Not a bad night for the kids, Danielle Wright would report in her game coverage the next day, as the rest of the city waited anxiously for the final pre-season game roster against Edmonton.

No one was waiting more anxiously than David. His game had been okay, but on one St. Louis goal, it had been his man that broke free and got a sweet one-timer. *Dammit*, thought David as he stared into the creamy abyss that was his morning latte. *I should have stayed on that guy. I thought I could break out and—*

"Looking pretty intense, rook. What's up? No confidence?" came a familiar jab from Danielle.

David lurched and looked up into the most beautiful face he had ever known and someone he had been missing very much over the last week.

"I thought you might be here." She shrugged. "And I needed a coffee."

"Hi," he quietly murmured. The next words poured from his lips, almost by accident. "I'm really happy to see you. I know things have been kind of bad the last little—"

"Well, a girl can't hear enough of that, so I guess it's an invitation to join you," she cut him off in her regular fashion.

David smiled and stared into her sparkling eyes, so perfectly shaped and dancing with inquisitiveness.

"I'm so sorry," he began again. "I've been a total ass this last week and I want to apologize." He shook his head in submission. "You're actually all I've thought about but, yes, I'm a bit scared of what happens today and I just thought—"

"Okay, okay, you can stop falling on your sword. Yes, you are an ass. A great big ass. Actually, you're an arse," Danielle playfully responded in a matter-of-fact tone. "But, my dear, you are forgiven this one time. And unlike you, I have a very good feeling about today."

David's head shot up and his eyes widened in anticipation. "Did you hear something? Am I in? Did I make it?"

"No. I mean no as in I don't know. But apparently, unlike

yourself, I'm an excellent judge of talent, and in spite of your rather pitiful defensive zone coverage in St. Louis the other night, no one has had as good a camp or shown more determination and professionalism than you. New York party fuck-up excluded. I think you're exactly what the Red Wings need and I believe you should be on that team. Cheers."

The stunning blonde raised her lipstick-stained coffee mug towards David and he felt his heart skip a beat and melt at the exact same time. In a mere five minutes, Danielle had rescued him. Taken him from the depths of insecurity to the mountain top of positive anticipation. "You really are the best." He smiled. "And, I promise I will never be an arse again, regardless of what happens today. Maybe tonight we can have dinner and relax—together."

Danielle moved her head in to David's and pursed her lips. "That sounds so perfect, but I've got to cover the Tiger's game for Troy. Wanna come?"

"Now that's perfect." David beamed.

* * *

Media personalities of all types were milling around the foyer, waiting for players to arrive, but most importantly waiting for the Edmonton game roster. This would likely be the team starting the season and it was always every reporter and fan's favourite day because, after it, all the second guessing and criticizing could begin in earnest.

"Hey, Stone, do you know if you're in?" screamed a television reporter from KMOV.

David grinned and waved a thumbs up to his inquisitor, heading quickly for the safety of his dressing room. As he walked in, he saw Darcy sitting by his locker, hands folded and head down, staring at the floor. "What's up, Hilts? No confidence?" David tried to be funny.

Darcy raised his head and growled. "My, aren't we chipper this morning? Are you too dumb to know what the next fifteen minutes mean?"

"Nah, I just kind of got nothing more to give. I can't be any more nervous, so I guess I'm just beyond nervous and back at calm. Que sera sera."

"What the fuck are you jabbering about? Sit down and shut up."

"What do you think is the best way to hear it?" David asked as he sat beside his friend. "Should you go down the minute the list is up and look for your name, or wait for someone else to come and tell you?"

"I've always stood and looked at the list and never made it, so this year I'm just going to let someone else deliver the bad news. I couldn't stand going through that torture again."

The two waited in the quiet of the room, David staring at the second hand on the clock and Hilts at the floor.

At 9 AM, they both took a deep breath. The list would be posted right about now and soon the cheers or wails would begin. It started with the distant sounds of chatter and a few boisterous echoes from afar. Then the clear pounding of designer shoes on concrete floors outside the dressing room. Then a bursting door. David's head jerked left only to be obstructed by Darcy's.

First through the door was none other than Riley Sawyer, grin beaming from ear to ear.

"Looks like I'm in the Edmonton game," he screamed at David and Darcy.

Pause. Nothing. Riley extended his fist for a bump.

"C'mon, aren't you guys happy for me?"

Darcy hung his head; he knew the protocol. "Yeah, sure, man. Congrats."

David's heart dived. They had not made it. Riley would have told them.

"Oh, by the way, SO ARE YOU TWO BOZO's!" Sawyer screamed.

David impulsively leaped into the air and punched Riley's extended fist so hard, both men recoiled in momentary pain. The room was filling with jovial teammates who had waited outside while Riley set and triggered the emotional trap for the other two rooks.

Darcy did not even raise his head. He just pulled his hands to the back of his scalp and grabbed his thinning hair. He felt tears welling up in his eyes uncontrollably. So long. It had been so long. And finally good news. Teammates paraded past the rookies offering congratulations and ribald comments about what lay ahead for them in the show.

It was a big day for everyone, but for the rookies it was the top of the mountain. Everest. The end of the quest.

In unison the room began chanting, "Hiltsy, Hiltsy, Hiltsy".

It was always better for the older guys. The underdogs. Darcy couldn't stop the tears from streaming down his face though he tried hard and the lump in his throat almost choked him. Amid the noise and celebrations, he looked at David, who could not stop jitterbugging around his little locker space. The energy and stress release was more than he ever imagined it could be.

"We made it!" David shrieked, almost in disbelief. "Can you believe it? We made it! We're Red Wings!"

The celebrations carried on for ten minutes or so and subsided as the media descended like locusts into the dressing room. Leading the pack was Danielle, big smile on her face. She nodded at David and headed for team captain, Phil Davis. One reporter from a local Chinese newspaper and another from a free city publication came over to David and Hilts while a crush of media surrounded Riley.

David stared at the ceiling. For an instant, everything in his life was complete.

* * *

It was an unseasonably cold day in Saskatchewan for late September and, worst of all, there was still lots of work to do. With David gone, the farm was down a man and the fall harvest was taking longer than usual due to heavy rains.

"Never really thought David did that much," Luke spat as he rotated his steaming cup of Maxwell House coffee in his hands.

"Oh, Luke, you're always picking on your brother," said Anne as she brought out servings of maple oatmeal and berries.

"Well, we need to get back in those fields and this weather is killing us," moaned the eldest son.

An ear-splitting ring from the telephone interrupted their conversation and the CBC news telecast that had been droning on in the background.

"Hello," said Anne.

"Hi, mom, how are you and dad?"

"Oh, David!" she waved frantically at Luke and his father to come over. "We're all fine, David. How are things going, son? Are you okay?"

"You bet, mom, I'm great. I made it. I'm a full blown Detroit Red Wing."

Anne gasped. She stood speechless and quickly handed the receiver to Luke. She began to cry as Paul wrapped his thick arms and worn hands around her shoulders and gently kissed the top of her head. These were not tears of sadness, just the tears of unconditional love and support that a mother sheds when expressing the joy she feels for her child's achievements. It didn't matter whether they were little league or big league in scale.

Paul stared at Anne in anticipation as she nodded her head up and down with Luke wildly talking and laughing into the handset. It had just officially become a very good day in the Stone household, weather be damned.

Chapter 25

"Good evening, sir, enjoy the game," chirped a smiling gate attendant as she scanned the final pre-season ticket of a burly, Slavic-looking man.

"Yeah, I will," grunted the man in his thick Russian accent.

From behind his dark prescription lenses, Andriy quickly looked around the crowded corridors of Joe Louis Arena for signage that would point him to his seat. A couple of half-drunk teens with bright red, painted faces and Steve Yzerman jerseys slammed into his back and then meekly apologized for their actions. The mobster glared at them and angrily tried to rub the red paint off his designer jacket. He moved toward his section and, upon arriving at the aisle to his seat, asked an usher, "So, where do the Wings come onto the ice?" He tried to sound like an excited fan.

The pimply young man graciously pointed at the other end of the rink. "That's where the Wing's dressing rooms are and their goal is at that end twice and this end once."

"Can you go down and see the players?" he asked.

"Hmm, not really. Though if you go to the club lounge, you can line up and watch them as they come and go onto the ice. A lot of cops and security there though, so you don't always get a very good look."

"Thank you." The Russian nodded. "Maybe I will try to get a look after the game."

"Not likely. After the second period intermission, they close that area completely and only the media can get in. But, a lot of fans wait outside in the parking lot after the games and catch the players for autographs when they go to their cars."

"Really?" mused the hit man. "You've been so helpful. Spasibo."

"Anytime, sir," replied the slightly confused usher, unaware of the Russian term for thank you. "I've been working here five years. Nobody knows the Wings better than I do."

"Yes, you certainly know your stuff."

The usher turned his attention to another enquiring patron and Andriy proceeded to his seat, oblivious to the excitement around him regarding Detroit's tilt with the Oilers. He grinned as he watched the players burst onto the ice from the two dressing room tunnels for their pre-game warm-ups. Sure enough, within seconds the familiar face he had seen and shot at in a dark New York alley flashed by him, completely ignorant he was within ear shot of his executioner.

Riley Sawyer was a dead man skating, Andriy Korpikosky thought to himself. The question was not if, just when and how.

* * *

"Starting lines for tonight are Sloan, Abramov and Miller. Next, Stone, Sawyer and Hilts. Third is..."

David could barely believe his ears as Assistant Coach Trent Caplan yelled out the lines. Everyone was focused. Jacked. A constant growing din of white noise from the rink permeated the thick concrete tomb that was Detroit's dressing room. David's heart pulsed in anticipation. *Just open the door and let me go*, he thought.

"Hey, Stone, easy. You got a whole game to go yet. Don't burn up all that energy sitting here."

"Right Hilts, good advice. Got some pretty big butterflies, bro."

"Me too. But, if we're lucky, we've got at least 80 more of these to go, so let's just try and stay cool."

"Ok, let's go," screamed team captain, Phil Davis.

David jumped out of his stall, grabbed his gloves and marched to the door, running right smack into the back of Riley Sawyer.

"Easy, big guy. Save it for the other team."

Both players grinned at the spectacle of this moment and proceeded to the home team's tunnel.

In seconds, excited children's faces, beautiful young women, doting parents and scores of middle aged men in game jerseys greeted the players as they strode toward the ice. Each held up his gloves for the adoring fans to touch.

David, couldn't help but grin. It actually hurt his face. As he approached the ice surface a thunderous roar of over 21,000 crazed Red Wing fans consumed and overwhelmed his senses. With an explosive blast of adrenaline he leaped onto the ice, skating as fast as he could to nowhere in particular. David Stone had realized his dream. He was playing his first NHL game as a bona fide member of the Detroit Red Wings—even if it was still exhibition. *Nothing could top this,* he thought as the faces and people whirred past him in a blur.

* * *

The game was turning into an ugly boring affair due to the close checking, defensive game of the Oilers. Road teams never worried about pleasing the fans, they simply wanted to get a win and get out of town. The "wee winners" line was struggling to do anything. A few harmless shots, no real scoring chances and a few bad giveaways in the neutral zone were pretty much the tale of their tape.

"C'mon, guys, we're sucking out there," said David to his linemates. "We've gotta get going. Technically, we still haven't made the team."

"Like we're not trying," moaned Sawyer. "I feel like I'm in a straitjacket. I touch the puck and boom, it's gone. We got no flow."

"Shut up you two, it's a long game," said Hilts. "Let the game come to you. Take what it gives. We're all just gettin in the groove."

"Seriously? You're going all philosophic on us? You of all people?"

Hilts glared at Sawyer for the comment and they turned their eyes back toward the ice.

"Stone, get your line out there and do something. You guys look slower than molasses. And remember, I can still cut your asses from this team." McCroy slapped Hilts and Sawyer on the back as the rookies jumped over the boards to join the action.

The puck raced around the boards and up the ice on a perfect pass from Byron Rogers, Detroit's all-star defenseman. It hit the tape on Riley's stick. Sawyer lifted his head just in time to see David cut through centre and he threw the black saucer into an area where Stone seemed to be heading.

David had a full head of steam and saw the play developing in front of him. Using the blinding speed that had defined him through training camp, he grabbed the puck and headed directly through a narrow gap between two Oiler defensemen who had gotten caught a bit by the pace of the attack.

With precision timing, David bumped the puck through the two flailing players and literally jumped over their sticks and hips before heading home free for the net. About twelve feet out, he threw a wicked head fake that froze Edmonton's goalie and then cut hard left.

As the goaltender tried to move to the side, David slid the puck through a widening space between his pads and watched in sheer disbelief as the red goal light burst on and the crowd rose as one, cheering wildly. He leaped into the air and fell into the open arms of Hilts and, soon after, Riley.

"Detroit's first goal scored by number 14, David Stooooone," bellowed the announcer over the roar of the crowd.

"Assist to number 86, Riley Sawyer and number three, Byron Rogers. Time of the goal 16:45."

After what seemed like an endless celebration with all the requisite hugs, fist bumps and head shakes, the players lined up and prepared for the puck drop at centre ice.

* * *

"Well, that's a big one for David Stone of the Detroit Red Wings." said an announcer on TSN Hockey's game of the week which was being televised in rural Saskatchewan.

Luke was dancing around the room with a chicken wing in one hand and an Alexander Keith's beer in the other. Anne had her head in her hands, while their neighbours and family friends hugged her and patted her on the back. Paul sat grinning in his recliner, thankful for the moment. It wasn't often the Stone's left their fields early, but tonight was special. Very special. They got to watch their boy on TV and the crops could damn well wait their turn. There'd be lots of time tomorrow to finish combining.

"What a move," continued the commentator. "That kid has speed to burn and sweet hands. He's a great player and to think, he wasn't even drafted. Stone was a walk-on. Did you know that?"

A second announcer chipped in. "Yessiree, Detroit, there is a God and it appears he's given you David Stone." The two laughed at the comment and the game continued.

***

"Great play, kid. You and Sawyer are on the microphones tonight," said McCroy as the final buzzer sounded.

The teams had exchanged goals for a ho-hum, 2–1 Detroit win, but goal difference didn't matter. Detroit had won. David was second star behind the acrobatic magic of goalie Bob Hendricks, who was speaking to reporters as Riley and the other players filed off the ice.

"What do you mean, coach?" David asked.

"He means we're going to talk at the post-game press conference, you hick," blurted Riley.

Following a few softball questions at the presser like "How are you preparing for your first real NHL game?" and "What are your thoughts on the team's chances to win a Stanley Cup?" a pretty, local reporter fired a missile at Riley. He recognized her at once.

"So, Mr. Sawyer," she began boldly, "during the pre-season you were involved in an incident in New York that never really got explained to the press. Is it true you were involved in a major crime in that city, and the team covered it up?"

The levity in the press room dropped to zero and Riley froze at the microphone. It went so quiet you could hear a pin drop, a very unusual state for a post-game press gathering after a win.

After what seemed like hours, Riley nervously leaned toward the mike and, in a level tone, stated, "No, that's not true. We were just out after a game and—"

A Red Wing media supervisor grabbed the microphone in front of Riley and immediately ended the presser, "That's all the questions we'll be taking this evening. Thank you everyone. The Red Wings have issued a formal release on that incident and it has been put to rest. Certainly it is not an issue to be discussed at a post-game press conference. I'm not sure why you would think that's appropriate to bring up, Miss."

"But," Danielle continued, "a New York detective has told this reporter that a Red Wing player was involved in or witnessed criminal activity in New York and he was investigating it. Can Mr. Sawyer or the team comment on that?"

The room buzzed as security officials came on the stage and

ushered the two players behind a curtain and back to the dressing room.

Riley felt pale and shook as he sat in his locker area. He stared at the floor. "How did she find out?" he mumbled to himself. If she knew, who else knew? The thought scared him to death as a fleeting image of a sword slashing through the air and a human head falling to the floor overwhelmed his mind.

"Hey, easy dude. You okay?" asked Darcy Wade, the back-up goalie.

"Yeah, yeah, I'm fine." But in reality Riley Sawyer was anything but fine.

* * *

A small crowd of excited Red Wing-attired fans were congregating in a poorly lit parking area adjacent the arena's back doors. Two security guards, one slightly rotund and the other a whiff of a man, were gabbing with those at the front of the rag-tag cluster and every few minutes they'd exert their authority by waving a few kids to the back for trying to cut-in.

"Is this where the Red Wing players come out?" Andriy asked a father and son watching eagerly for the door to open.

"You bet it is," squealed a slightly undersized nine year old fighting to see past the crowd toward the darkened doors.

"Oh, that's great. Do they ever give autographs or can you get close enough to get a picture?" The man continued his enquiry.

"Not unless they come over here. Security can be pretty tight, but a few usually come by and sign some things and maybe take a selfie. Mostly the rookies," the father answered.

The Russian looked at the security guards in their ill-fitting uniforms and responded, "Yes, I can see security would certainly be an issue if you were trying to get close. Have you guys ever seen Riley Sawyer? Does he ever come by here?"

"No, can't say we've seen him. But, you know, he's the new big star in town, so he probably doesn't think he has to," snapped the father with a hint of disgust toward the young protégé. "We're gonna try and get David Stone's autograph. Now that guy's a real Red Wing. Like a young Gordie Howe. That'll be worth something someday."

"Really? Can't say I've heard of him. Thanks for the heads up though."

Andriy stood back as players began leaving the arena as singles or in small tightly-knit groups of two or three. He carefully analysed what each did after leaving the building. He noticed Riley's distinctive shape appear under the exit lights and snapped a few quick pics while he was illuminated. He also made a mental note that Sawyer headed straight for a brightly coloured Corvette without acknowledging the fans. He was alone with his head down, as if he didn't want anyone knowing who he was.

"Hey, mister! I think that's Sawyer there. He's heading towards that 'Vette," the enthusiastic father commented while nudging Andriy's arm.

"Yes. I guess I will have to wait for another time. He does not seem that friendly. You were right." The Russian laughed as he slowly drifted back into the darkness of the parking lot.

* * *

David walked toward the small boy with an ill-fitting Red Wings cap. With a gracious smile, he grabbed the cap when it was thrust in front of him and scribbled his autograph on its visor.

A collection of fans immediately surged toward him, clamouring to get close and began pushing every type of logo paraphernalia at him, while others hastily snapped photos or tried to awkwardly pose for selfies. David laughed at all the commotion.

From the corner of his eye, one thing did seem odd. A tall, blond-haired guy, built like a linebacker, was standing by himself way back in the parking lot, taking in everything. He stood like one of those security guys that travels with the president or something, all sullen and serious. He didn't seem to want an autograph and he didn't seem to be with anyone in the crowd. And, he certainly didn't care to interact with any of the players who made their way over to the fan group. His clothes also seemed wrong. Too dark and ominous. He just looked oddly out of place and David committed his face and body type to memory for no real reason.

Maybe he was just a bored father waiting for his son or nephew. But, if that was your dad, poor you. He was one scary looking guy, like the villain in an action movie.

A frenzied fan handed David a water bottle. *Never signed one of those before,* he thought as his attention turned again to the kids and parents in front of him and away from the out of place character he had been observing.

Chapter 26

Ozzie and Fergus entered the bland, empty warehouse with the assistance of a rental management company supervisor.

"So, what you guys looking for?" the supervisor queried in his most helpful tone.

"Just a routine search on account of a complaint," Ozzie responded.

"Complaint? That's weird, nobody been in this building for over a year. Nothing goes on here. We haven't had so much as a nibble on it. And hell, the rent is, like, dirt cheap. It's too fucking boring for any of those hi-tech geeks to put their office here. They all want brick and concrete and shit like—"

"Thanks for the synopsis," interrupted Ozzie, "but could you just let us do our investigation? Who owns this shithole?"

"The ownership is some offshore group, or so I've been told by my boss," the curious agent responded.

"Have you ever let anyone in here or given anyone a set of keys?" Fergus asked.

"Uhhh, about six months ago, I let some Russians in here to look around. They were gonna set up some kind of investment business—you know big time money guys—but nothing ever came of it. They looked like they worked for some super rich Ruskie oligarch or something. Probably connected with Putin, you know the type."

"Yeah, sure. Do you have names for those guys?"

"I just show the place, I don't get a lot of details. But my boss might have something. I'll call him."

"Okay, good. You go call him and let us take a look around."

The two detectives headed straight for a basement room with one barren hanging light. They opened the door and the whiff of bleach immediately caused irritation in their eyes.

"Okay, that's not too old, is it?" spat Fergus. "I can taste that shit."

"Wow, that's strong," replied Stark.

They closed the door behind them and stared straight into the back window overlooking the room from the alley. Given the light, the height of the window and the grass in front of it, and the grime on the outside of the glass, you could never have seen out from the room into the street at a glance. But, as he had noticed in the alley, you could very clearly see into the room had it been night and the room well-lit, compliments of the one hundred watt, incandescent bulb hanging from a thread.

"Turn out the light, Fergus."

Stark went outside to another storage room and brought back an old cardboard box that he tore apart and placed in the window, making the room almost completely dark. Then he took out an infrared light and shone it on the walls in search of blood spatter. Nothing appeared.

"These guys cleaned up real good," he muttered to himself. "Must have been pros."

Fergus nodded. "Try the floor, man, especially the corners. No matter what, they can never quite get the corners completely clean."

The room seemed pretty large, Stark thought to himself, *for blood to hit the corners, but it did make sense that splatter from a decapitation would fly pretty far.* He shone the infrared in a low methodical search pattern over the floor keenly looking for any hint of dense purple light.

"Bingo," he yelled, as a small smear appeared in the angular moulding closest to the back corner and just down from the window. If some guy got his head hacked off in the centre of the room, it was possible random spurts from a severed artery could have shot in this direction and it was the only area that had not been meticulously wiped clean. "Fergus, we now might have a crime scene here. Let's get forensics moving on this. And don't let a soul in here until they get onsite."

Fergus nodded and began furiously tapping on his cell phone. Ozzie placed a small yellow tab in the general location of the smear. As small as it was, it might be the only evidence they had of a crime being committed in the room.

The supervisor returned. "Okay, so the boss man tells me we aren't supposed to be in here and we have to get out."

"Tell your boss man we're coming over to talk to him and he'd better stay put. What's his name?"

"Jeff. Jeffrey Deschamps."

"Okay, let's go see your boss and no one comes in here or leaves this building. It's now the site of a police investigation. Got it?"

"Fuck, I just show the place man. Talk to Deschamps."

* * *

"Okay, so what's Riley hiding?" Danielle quietly asked David as she climbed into bed beside him.

"Seriously, Danielle," moaned David. "Can you please let it go? There's no story there. We all went to a club and stupid Riley got pissed backwards, stumbled out of the club, I guess, and got arrested for something stupid. The guy's just an idiot, but he was pretty funny at the club, Cossack dancing and stuff."

The soft, silk negligee caressed David's skin as Danielle pushed up beside him. It felt more like therapy for his growing number of bruises and abrasions than a strategic garment designed to create arousal. Her satin legs moved up his and he felt an overwhelming lust creep through his aching muscles. It was a kind of beautiful pain that was impossible to control.

"Well, if you want to have any more fun than this tonight, you'd better start talking, mister," cooed Danielle.

"Okay, you're way out of line here, missy. That's blackmail and I won't stand for it," David said in mock rage as he rolled on top of the curvaceous beauty and his hips fell between her thighs. "It was all so stupid," he lamented as he stared into her face, slowly shaking his head from side to side. "One minute he was there and then he was gone. I thought he left to go back to the hotel, but when he wasn't, we went looking for him. I thought Hellan was going to stroke out when we got back to the hotel without him. But the cops called and said they had him and we were just told to shut up and get back to our room. Which I did."

"Is that why neither of them was on the plane home?"

"What do you think?" David kissed her neck and ears. "You tell me. You're the reporter."

"Ohhh, you've been a very bad boy," moaned Danielle at the tickling by her ear and slowly the silk began to rise as the two collapsed into a long passionate night of love-making.

"By the way, you played great," Danielle whispered.

* * *

Riley turned his car into the carriageway of his luxury rental condo and wheeled up to the curb. He had spoken to his agent, Alex Moore, after the game and, during his call, a weird telephone number had appeared on his screen. It had looked like a random telemarketing number so he'd ignored it. But, he noticed there was a message, so he viewed the text version first. He hated listening to voice mail. It was such a pain and most of the time you couldn't understand what they were saying. Why didn't people just text? So much quieter and unobtrusive.

TEXT: Call dizzie spark, NYPD, 212.765.4565 imedatli. Any hour. Call me.

The only thing that stood out to Riley were the letters NYPD. This did not look at all like a call he wanted to take, but he had caused enough problems, so he thought it wiser to play things straight and not screw around with any follow-up issues. The real season was now underway and the last thing he or the Red Wings needed was more scandal.

Perhaps he should call Mike to see what the club wanted him to do. Coach McCroy could give him some direction. Or should he call his agent? Or his dad? God, this thing was a mess. He just closed his eyes, shook his head and pushed his skull deeply into the leather headrest with such force he thought it would snap. His telephone rang again and this number he did recognize: it was his father.

* * *

30 yards behind Riley's Corvette, a mid-sized rental pulled slowly around the corner and parked silently in the dark shrouds of some overhanging branches, shielded from the street lights.

Andriy stared at Sawyer's vehicle and slowly reached inside his coat, removing a Glock G17 semi-automatic pistol—the preferred weapon of assassins around the world. His eyes never left Riley's car.

A youngish couple left the condo and strolled hand-in-hand into the carriageway, stopping every few steps to kiss passionately. Weaving up the street were two very drunk college guys, stumbling along a sidewalk towards Riley's car.

If things went well, perhaps instead of just getting to know his victim tonight, he would just kill him now and get it over with. The sooner the better. Less chance the kid would have had time to talk. Andriy opened his car door and tucked the long-barrelled pistol into his belt. He put on a dark cap.

* * *

A loud thud on the passenger side of the car caused Riley to almost soil himself. "Christ!" he yelled loudly as he tried to control his breathing.

"What's going on, Riley," screamed his dad from the phone.

"Dad, I'll call you back. Something hit my car." He jumped out and became enraged at the sight of an inebriated idiot slumped beside his front wheel.

"Hey sorry, dude, I'm a little wasted," gurgled the teen sitting on the pavement, while his friend laughed hysterically.

"Really, man? C'mon, I gotta go. Can you get away from my car? And hurry." Riley moved to the front of the car to help move the obnoxious youth when he noticed a man in a bomber-style jacket moving quick-time towards the three of them. He felt his heart sink and fear gripped him. "You gotta get away from my car," Riley gasped, his heart pounding.

"Chill, man. What's the problem? Lighten up," the second teen slurred in a drug-addled dialogue that was barely comprehensible.

Riley looked around, panicking, but could not see the man on the street. Where had he gone? Who was he?

A set of flashing blue and red lights appeared on the street and blinded him momentarily.

"What's going on here?" came the stern command from a car-mounted speaker. Everyone froze where they were.

Riley squinted into the lights of the private security patrol vehicle that watched over the development's high-valued tenants.

"It's okay, officer. This guy just fell into my car and he's leaving now so we're all good," a relieved Sawyer replied to the patrolman as lights began to come on in many of the suites overlooking the front entry and a few residents emerged onto their balconies to see what all the noise and commotion was about.

Two officers stepped from their vehicle with flashlights.

"I live here, guys. Suite 319. Just taking a cell call and then going to the parkade."

"Who are these two?" questioned an officer.

"Uh, one of them was just walking up the drive and fell into my car. Kind of spooked me."

The two college kids were now standing at attention beside each other, saying absolutely nothing.

Riley scanned the street and grounds, desperately searching for the man he'd seen coming at them from down the street. There was nothing.

"Okay, everyone, get out of here. It's late and you can't park at the front doors. This is a pick-up and drop-off area only. So move it. All of you."

Riley dropped the car into gear and pulled away quickly toward the parking garage. His car disappeared into the night with nothing but the sound of a closing metal parkade door to punctuate the darkness.

* * *

The security officers were too busy examining identification from the two youths to notice a shadowy figure move from behind the carriageway's tall cedars and make his way back across the street.

Andriy grinned as he looked at the building's slick contemporary architecture. "You won't be living here long," he mused quietly, sliding back into his rental. He watched the action wind down and then started up his vehicle.

I should have just gone and popped the little creep, Andriy thought in disgust. *I could have finished this and been on my way back to New York.*

Generally, it was an Odessa best practice to hunt your prey first, then set up a flawless, non-traceable kill. And finally, execute the target. Base the plan on the habits, weird fantasies or foolish judgment of your victim.

Tonight, Andriy had gotten ahead of himself, perhaps been a bit sloppy. He tried to take a short cut and it had not worked out.

Professionals never took short cuts. Amateurs took short cuts. He would need more self-control next time. He knew Sawyer would be an easy kill, just not tonight. He was an egotistical twat and they always did stupid things he could exploit.

A blue glow beamed up from his buzzing phone.

"Yes, I've got him under surveillance. Probably could have offed him tonight but things didn't work out. His demise though is imminent, sir."

"Very good, Andriy. Plan carefully. This one will have lots of security and I want nothing coming back on us. You got that? Lots of distance between him and us."

"Da, Alexi."

The phone went dark.

* * *

"What? You can't get nothin from all that blood? Can somebody else? The FBI? There's got to be some DNA there. That's a great sample."

"I'm sorry, Stark, but the sample is actually pretty small and it was terribly degraded by a bunch of chemicals—one of them bleach. Sample size isn't the only thing we deal with here. Garbage in, garbage out—got it, Detective?"

Ozzie slammed the telephone handle back into its antiquated cradle and put his hands on his hips. "Fuck!" He yelled.

"Hey, what's up, Oz?" asked Fergus as he looked up from his desk.

"Can't get a thing off that blood trace from the warehouse, so we're back to zero. That sample looked fine to me. Now what are we going to do?"

"We could go back to the club and pull security video and see if anybody that was there maybe hasn't been seen around for a while. Like gone missing in the last three weeks or so. Plus, I'll check with missing persons and see what pops." Fergus got up from his desk and headed for the door.

"Sure, like that's going to work. Everybody there's paying cash and they ain't using real names, but yeah check it out. At least we get to look at some babes for a few hours."

His ancient telephone burst to life again.

"Yeah, Stark here."

"Hi, you left a message on my phone," trembled the voice on the other end of the line.

"Hey, is this the hockey player? Sawyer?"

"Yes, it is. How can I help you?"

"Well, kid, we're having a bitch of a time trying to find clues in this case. Lots of pieces fit but nothing tangible. We found a place that could be the crime scene, and maybe if you came back and took a look, it might jar some memories or something that could help us."

"Listen, I'd love to help, but that night is a blur. I can't really remember anything more than I told you."

"Kid, sometimes you need to push yourself to make your brain work and I don't think you're trying hard enough. Fuck, you had the sense to get away so you weren't that pissed. Now think. Is there anything? What did the guy in the chair look like? That room would have been lit up like a candle if you were outside looking in."

"Honestly, I've tried to remember, but I can't. And, I certainly can't just come back to New York. We're starting our regular season. I've got to focus on my game and that crazy night has to go away."

"Kid, let me be very clear here. The guys you told me about who killed our vic with a sword, ninja style, and then came after you, if they are who I think they are, they will quickly piece together who you are. And, if you think they're going to let you walk around until you have an ah-hah moment and rat them out, then you are as dumb as you are a dead man walking. They're planning your execution right now and you gotta get in front of this. What you described sounds like a Russian mob killing. These are mean, barbaric motherfuckers who actually enjoy butchering people. You're nothing to them, no matter how important you or your team might think you are. Now I need you to give me something."

A half-sobbing Sawyer slammed his cell phone down on the glass table top, cracking its thick pane in the process. He hit it once, twice, and finally demolished it with a third violent thrust.

"Why? Why me? What's going on? I'm a hockey player. This is too fucked up," he moaned in the darkness. "What am I going to do?"

All of a sudden, Riley became very aware of his vulnerability to these professional murderers. Before this, they hadn't seemed real to him, in spite of all he had seen and been through. They felt like comic book characters or TV villains and this had been a bad dream.

Then there was that guy tonight, coming down the street. Was he one of them? Surely no one would hurt Riley Sawyer, first round draft pick—he was special. But now, after Detective Stark's comments, what engulfed his mind was how profoundly dangerous his situation was. He could die—at any moment—and at the hand of anyone around him. His broad shoulders slumped and his head dropped into a decorative pillow on the sofa.

He curled up on the thick leather cusions and stuck his hands between his legs as his eyes closed and his stomach churned with revulsion.

"God, dear God, please help me."

Chapter 27

The Wings finished their home stand and first road games with a three and three record. David had impressed everyone with his blazing speed, a knack for winning key face-offs and some lethal wrist shots that seemed to always find the back of the net. He finished the six games with three goals and two assists, one of them on a classic garbage goal by Darcy Hilton, who continued to solidify his fan favourite stature with a crash-and-bash style of game and a lunch-bucket readiness to drop his gloves should anyone get heavy with his teammates.

Sadly, Riley was not living up to his pre-season hype and was struggling with only one assist in the season opener. Since then, nothing. Compounding the problem was his lacklustre defensive play and a penchant for taking lazy penalties at awful times. So pronounced were his shortcomings that by the time the team headed back to Detroit for their seventh game, he had played his way off David's line. Riley's internal team stats showed he had six costly defensive zone turnovers, three of which caused Red Wing losses, four selfish penalties and a minus five rating in his six games. He was languishing on the fourth line and prior to his seventh big league game, was being considered for a healthy scratch.

As practice ended and the game roster was posted, Riley sat dejected in his locker, staring down into a concrete abyss. Most of the team had long since cleared out and Riley was alone, sitting in full gear, minus the black practice jersey he had been assigned—another ignominy for a player of his status. How had everything gone so wrong?

The media was ruthless, harassing the young star with verbal darts about his poor play and failing skills that had destroyed any semblance of confidence he had. And now, he was a black ace. The "next one" was now the "great bust." Riley saw it, heard it and felt it everywhere he went.

"Hey, Saw, what's up? You gonna sleep here?" David asked as he finished pulling on his coat and was preparing to leave.

Riley's head turned slowly as he pondered the question. "Might be a good idea," he answered and returned his gaze to the floor.

"Listen, why don't we get some food? We can shoot the bull and relax a bit. Might help clear your head, make you feel better."

"You're a good guy, Stone, but I'm fucked, so why don't you just go hang with that reporter chick. She's so hot. Man, you got the world by the balls. You're what I was supposed to be—the next big thing. Shit."

"Uh, not exactly where I was going with the food suggestion, but seriously, you need to get your head out of your sad sack ass and grow up a bit. You think I'm doing you a favour here? Forget it. I need to get you focused so you can get back on our line. I think Hilts actually misses you. As much as Andrews is a good guy and all, well, he's not Riley Sawyer. Not even playing as shitty as you are right now." Stone chuckled and tossed a towel at his tortured ex-linemate. "So, get out of that smelly gear and let's go. I'll be back in 10 to get you. Get going!"

Sawyer shot a pained grin back at Stone. "You got some kind of bed-side manner, cowboy. Thanks. I'll be ready."

* * *

Ozzie stared at the list of missing and unaccounted for people in New York over the last month. It was a tragic reality of life in the city. Runaways. College girls. Stolen babies. Kidnapped children. Sex slaves. Drug addicts. Single moms. Every month, dozens of people simply vanished off the streets of New York. Some would eventually show up in the East River or the Hudson. Others in shallow graves. Some might even be found living on the street or under a bridge. But for most of them, this list would be their epitaph. Their 15 minutes of fame, noticed fleetingly by a few cops and then filed somewhere as a cold case. A few would get passed along to another officer when new information surfaced, but eventually no one would remember them.

It was for these people that Ozzie had become a cop. He'd grown up in a broken home with an alcoholic father and doting Catholic mother. He had lived a rough and tumble life in Hell's Kitchen and, at an early age, had decided to channel his aggression and ruthless determination into doing good things instead of bad. He could have gone either way, given his neighbourhood, friends and acquaintances, but he had ended up at the police academy and then walking a beat with lots of people similar to those on his list.

He saw them every day, struggling to get by or just survive. They lived in alleys, appliance boxes, pushed shopping carts and wore foul, filthy clothes, and yet many would smile and say hi to him as he patrolled their streets, thanking him for keeping them safe. Ironically, they were often covered in abrasions and bruises from a hellish existence few could imagine, yet they thanked him. He remembered a small Puerto Rican kid living in an alley that had given him some key clues that helped solve a high profile murder case. That had been the catalyst that eventually elevated him to a gold shield. Now he wondered where that kid might be. Was he a name on a list somewhere? Passed along, unknown and undervalued?

Denman, Mike. Lawyer. Failed to report to work. Missing 26 days. The report was filed by a receptionist at Denman & Associates, a Ms. Bonnie Skyler.

The name jumped off the page as it certainly didn't fit the regular profile of NYPD's missing persons. However, with all the greed and largesse on Wall Street, this Denman wouldn't be the first lawyer to "go missing" from work over insider trading, embezzlement or some other innocuous white-collar crime. He was probably laying on a beach in the Seychelles with a beautiful girl on each arm, fruity drinks and a big fat Swiss bank account.

"Hmm, Denman," he mumbled, looking at his desk calendar.

26 days was around the right time frame for his headless victim. It had been almost a month since the crazy night with the hockey player. He'd check into Mr. Denman's disappearance. Ozzie quickly located the address of Denman & Associates on his computer and grabbed his coat.

"Fergus, take a ride with me, I might have something on that headless dude the hockey player told us about."

* * *

"I'll have a pulled-pork bunwich and a Keith's, please."

"A what?" asked the server, obviously unaware of Canada's finest lager. "We don't have Keith's, never heard of it."

"Okay, how about a Coors Light? Have you heard of that?"

teased David, staring at the pretty 20-something server with an unabashed style that made her perfect to work in a sports bar.

"Yeah, I can probably find you one of those," she responded scanning the handsome faces that were decompressing in her section.

"I'll have the soup," said the second guy without lifting his eyes from the table.

"You'll have to excuse my buddy here," David grinned. "His horse just died."

The server laughed and then her face lit up in recognition. "Hey, you're that guy from the Wings. I saw you on TV the other night being interviewed. This is so cool. Can I get a pic with you? Do you mind?"

David could not help but grin. "Sure, fire away."

The girl leaned in and then surprisingly plunged herself on David's lap, raising her cell phone to arm's length. She thrust her head back onto his shoulder and mouthed "Cheeeese!" as the camera whirred off a dozen pics from every conceivable angle. David felt like he was getting mauled as she flung her long hair back and forth, exaggerated facial expressions and thrust her legs in and out simultaneously.

"That was awesome. I've got to post these. Thanks. Oh, do you play hockey too?" The girl looked at Riley.

"Uh, not very well," he deadpanned.

The server flashed a grin back at David and scribbled her name and telephone number on a small chit of paper. She placed her fingers by her ears in the call me sign and passed the note to him while she mouthed the words.

David nodded and stuffed the paper in his shirt pocket.

Riley slowly shook his head and stared at the huge wall-mounted TV which, at that very moment, just happened to be showing a David Stone interview. He noticed their server giggling with the other staff as she pointed at their table and then looked up at the TV. They gasped in unison before looking back at the table again.

Such was the life of an NHL player in Detroit. A good life—no, great life—to be sure. But, only if you lived up to your part of the deal and helped the team win. If not, you were nobody, regardless of hype or pedigree. In hockey town, if you weren't a producer, you were a disappointment. And Riley had been more of a disappointment so far.

"So what gives, Saw?" David stated bluntly. You seem completely out of it lately, both on and off the ice. New York is old news my friend, not even Danielle is bugging me about it anymore."

"Man, things are so bad right now, you can't even imagine." Riley raised his head and stared at David, sheer sadness filling his eyes.

David was surprised at the intensity of Riley's response. "Well, as your teammate, I hope you know how bad that sounds. What's so awful? You've got this. You're a great player. You skate better than most guys on the team. Killer shot. Defence might be a bit dodgy at times, but not that bad. You're better than this, and then all of a sudden it's just gone."

Riley shook his head and returned his stare downward to the table. His face trembled with stress and he quickly raised his hand to wipe a tear off his cheek before David could see it.

David pushed. "C'mon, man. Talk to me. You've got to get past whatever it is. Is someone in your family sick? Is it a girl? What could be this big a deal? Oh no, did you get some chick pregnant?"

"No, no. Just stop, David. You don't need to know this shit. It's my problem. I just need to figure it out."

"Riley, you don't have time to figure this out. You need help. Your career depends on it. You can't keep fucking up with all these eyes on you. Not in this line of work. We're a team. So I want to help if I can."

Sawyer wiped his nose as the server brought out their food. She set down the plates and smiled again at David, interrupting their conversation. After she left, David returned his gaze to Riley.

"I saw some shit in New York that was bad, Stone. Real bad. I can't even understand what I saw, but now I think some guys are after me. And this cop in New York, he thinks so too. They could come after me at any time. Any place. Right here. Right now. Yeah, I'm a bit out of it, alright. At any fuckin' minute some crazy motherfucker could waste me and the longer we go on, the more likely that is. So, it's not really my career I'm worried about. It's my life. That's my first priority. Stayin' alive."

As David listened to the incredible story, he felt his heart sink. "Okay, wait a minute. Are you shittin' me? You've got killers chasing you and you haven't told anyone? Go tell McCroy or maybe

Buzz. You gotta let them know. They think you're just a fuck-up that doesn't care."

"I care, David. I care about surviving—in hockey and life. McCroy knows. He heard the whole story in New York with Hellan. They were so pissed the next morning, I thought they were going to kick my ass down the road right there. They don't want to hear any more about it. Nada. They think I made the whole thing up. Even Layton told me to never mention it again, or else. But now, I'm giving them another reason to hate me - for how I play. I can't pile this crap back on them again — not now."

"What about your agent?" David asked.

"Moore? Are you kidding? He doesn't give a shit about me. Him and my old man have pretty much mapped out what they're going to do with all my money and this does not register in their plans. He told me I'm crazy. Imagining things. Even after he talked to Stark—that's the cop in New York. David, you can't say a word about this to anyone. I have to figure it out—and for sure don't you dare tell your girlfriend. She's already snooping around this story, as you well know."

"Yeah, wow, she'd love this, alright." David shook his head. "Why don't you let me help? We can go to McCroy quietly, at least get security beefed up. I talk to Mike all the time—we're tight. Let me...help you!"

The two started laughing at one of Hollywood's most famous movie lines, from Jerry Maguire.

"Can't do it, David. If whoever this is caught wind you knew anything, chances are they'd kill us both."

"Hey, dummy. Strength in numbers. They can't kill the whole team."

"But, David, the whole team doesn't know. And you can't tell them. I'll say you're insane. No, it's best if I just try to work it out until I know more."

"Riley, I'm telling McCroy on the down low. At least give me that. Let's get a bit more security. The good news is we're leaving town tomorrow morning. That buys us a bit of time. You don't need to stress about being alone at home. Stick by me or Hilts at all times for a while. We got your back."

"You're not telling Hilts. Absolutely not. You might as well tell your girlfriend."

"No, but I will tell him you're secretly gay, not that there's anything wrong with that, and you're having an episode where you need some extra companionship. You'll never be out of our sight."

The two chuckled and began eating. After an hour they paid the bill and posed for a few more selfies with patrons and servers, then left to get ready for a new adventure in their young careers.

* * *

"Nikolai, I need favour."

"Anything, Alexi. It is so good to hear your voice again. How are things in the Big Apple these days?"

"Well, this is why I'm calling. We have a problem that needs a solution and we think it would be best done outside New York. Possibly Miami, and that's your town. I have Andriy doing research and we think it could be done if you helped us a bit. You know in this business—always best to work with the locals."

"Yes, of course. Is Andriy there? I've not seen him for ages. How is the big brute?"

"I am here, Nik. I'm coming to Miami in three weeks and we can work out details. Maybe just need a few guys to help and coordinate things. Can I count on you?"

"Of course. You are the boss; we're just the minions doing what we're told. Whatever you need, you can always count on us."

"That's great, Nik, but this job may have some complications, so only top talent. Pros all around. No low-level types."

"Ooh, that sounds ominous, but not a problem. Anything for you, Alexi."

"That is why I love you, Nik, you always say the right thing. Say hello to Rita. And, how are your girls?"

"Doin' great, boss, though they miss New York. And the wife, she's constantly harping about how the humidity is ruining her hair."

Laughter broke out at the comment followed by the setting of dates for Andriy's arrival: November 23.

Chapter 28

"Yeah, Stark here."

"Good afternoon, Mr. Stark, this is Danielle Wright of the Detroit Free Press calling again. How are you today?"

"I'm fine, Danielle, and to what do I owe the great pleasure of your call?"

"Well, I'm just wondering if you have any further details on the investigation into Riley Sawyer."

"Whoa, lady. No one is investigating Riley Sawyer, so don't say shit like that. Don't put words in my mouth or I'll hang up right now."

"Okay, sorry. I just meant you were investigating something to do with Mr. Sawyer, right?" Danielle continued.

"First of all, everything said during this call is off the record—got it?" Ozzie then insisted Danielle turn off any recording devices she may be using on the call.

"Fine." Danielle agreed.

"Secondly then, no. We really don't have anything out of the ordinary with Mr. Sawyer. He was drunk and stupid and that's my official comment. Is that clear enough for you?"

"He's playing awful, you know?" Danielle probed. "Any idea why?"

"God, lady, you got some moxie I'll give you that. No, I don't know why he's playing bad and couldn't care less."

"Have you contacted him since he left New York?"

"That's none of your business." Ozzie answered impatiently, massaging his forehead as the questions continued fast and furious.

"So, that's a yes, then?"

"Danielle, if you ever get tired of working in the media, call me. We could use an interrogator like you at the precinct. However, the answer is still that it's none of your business. Actually, let me just say no comment to that."

"You certainly would not be following up with a kid in Detroit for being drunk and disorderly. You're a New York City detective, first grade. That's a homicide-level designation."

"Impressive, you did your homework. Very good Miss

Wright. No comment. I'll call you if anything relevant breaks. Hear that? I'll call you; don't call me. Good day, ma'am." Ozzie calmly placed the telephone back in its cradle as Danielle's feverish questioning in the receiver faded away.

Girl is determined, Ozzie thought to himself. *Wonder how I could use that to my advantage? Kid's playing the shits—gee, that's a surprise. He's probably tied up in knots with fear. I'm surprised he can bend over to tie his skates. Wonder when the Wings are back in town again.*

Ozzie searched online for the Red Wings' schedule and reviewed its contents. Detroit was on an extended road trip as far down as Florida in late November and then would be working their way up the eastern sea board and back home for mid-December. It was their longest road trip of the season. They would be back in the New York area from December 15th to 18th. Ozzie leaned back in his chair and threw his ball against the dull green wall. *Wonder if the kid will still be alive by then?*

"Hey, Fergus," Ozzie bellowed. "Let's go see what's up with that lawyer—Denman".

* * *

The Red Wings finished their most recent home games and their first test back on the road in good shape, with an overtime loss and two wins. David added two more goals and an assist while Riley had the unfathomable embarrassment of being a healthy scratch for the second home game — a Red Wings victory. That was never good.

"Hey, Coach. Got a minute?"

Mike McCroy loved waking up earlier than anyone else when the team was on the road and heading to a quiet coffee shop where he could be alone with his post-game stat sheet, a bulky daily newspaper and his iPad, reviewing player metrics and gauging media commentary. What he did not expect to see, was a player up at 5:30 AM the morning after a rugged physical game and standing beside his table.

"Sure, David. Sit down. What the hell are you doing up at this hour? How did you even find me? Nobody knows about this place. I made sure of that."

"Actually, Coach, I followed you from the hotel. And, I got news for you — we all know about this place. Sorry."

The two smiled as David pulled out a chair and sat down with his early morning latte.

"It's about Riley, sir. He's in a tough place and I think you need to know what's going on."

"Stone, you're a good kid—but you're a rookie. Don't say something here that's going to wreck what you've got going. Your teammates like you and respect your hard work. No one likes a rat. If Sawyer's got problems, then he needs to man up and face them. Come and see me himself."

"He can't, sir—so I am."

"What do you mean he can't? Of course he can. He was walking and talking last night in the press box. Though, not talking much, I must say."

"What do you know about the night he got picked up in New York, sir?"

"Oh fuck. Not that again. I thought that was over. Stupid little shit scared the hell out of all of us. Could have cost us our jobs, our careers. Anyway, I know he got drunk and acted like an asshole and got arrested for a break and enter or something. It was all just a big mistake. He's lucky we didn't can him then. Arrogant fool."

"Sir, you know that's not the real story. He witnessed a murder. A really gruesome murder. Might have been some kind of mob thing, and now he thinks they're coming after him. He's terrified. Scared to death. And, some cop from New York keeps calling him and telling him it could be any day they take him out. Sure, he's been a bit of a jerk, but he's just a kid like me and if we can get his head straight again he will be a huge asset for our team. He's so scared and he's got nowhere to go and no one to help him. The media's crucifying him. His own dad says he's imagining things and all you management guys just want to ignore it and hope it goes away. We had that security orientation in preseason and they talked about these types of criminals infiltrating sport and being major threats to players and their families. What if they reach out to someone on the ice? A foreign player getting blackmailed with instructions to kill Riley. This is more than a problem for Riley, sir. This could be a problem for the whole team's safety, the Red Wings and even the NHL. I really thought you needed to know what he's dealing with."

McCroy stared at the youngster in disbelief. "He told you all this?"

"Sort of. He told me the worst parts, but I know Danielle Wright from the Free Press thinks something is up too. And, she's smart, sir. She'll figure this out and then you guys might have an even bigger problem when the press hangs a cover-up tag on it. Riley and me, we're just young guys lucky enough to play pro hockey. But he's into something way over his head and he's getting no help from you or the team. He needs that now. I'm telling you this so we can act like a team and protect one of our own. Isn't that what being a team is all about - coach? At least that's what you've been preaching all year. Look, I know we all screwed up that night and broke every rule you guys told us about during training camp, but Riley needs us and we all need to step up. Everybody."

McCroy's mouth morphed into a crooked smile. "You're something, Stone. I had no clue things were this bad. I don't really like guys like Sawyer much, so I just thought the worst about him. Another silver spoon, trust-fund jerk who can't hack it when the chips are down. You're a good teammate and a good person. And, more importantly you're right, we need to act like a team. Okay, leave this with me."

"Sir, could you not spread this to anyone, but those who already know. Riley thinks if it got out things could be worse for a lot more people."

"I'll use my discretion, Stone, rest assured. Thanks. See you back at the hotel."

* * *

"Hello, I'm Detective Stark and this is Detective Fergus. Is Mike Denman in, please?"

The two officers flashed their blue and gold shields at middle-aged receptionist, Bonnie Skyler.

"Officers, we haven't seen Mr. Denman for a few weeks. I think he left town on business. He's been going away a lot lately."

"Is there anyone we could talk to about him or his work?"

"Well, there's his assistant, Patel Raven. He's a first year associate who's worked on some of his files. Maybe he could help."

The receptionist led the detectives through a narrow hallway and knocked on a thin wooden door with a number three on it. A smallish Pakistani man peered out from behind the door.

"Patel, these men would like to speak with you. They're detectives."

"Okay, thank you, Bonnie. How may I be of help, sirs?" Patel asked in a low voice while staring wide-eyed at the two solemn looking officers.

"So, Patel, when did you last see your boss?"

""It was the Friday, September 28. He gave me a bunch of files to work on and then said he was going out to start a big weekend. He was a very happy man that day."

"Why the big weekend? Something good happen at work? A girl? What?" Ozzie questioned the young associate as Fergus documented the details.

"He just seemed very happy. I think he had gotten much money because he was going car shopping in the afternoon and showed me some brochures of new Mercedes Benzes and Porsches. They were very, very nice—but I know they cost a lot."

The thought of anyone who worked in this office buying an expensive Benz seemed a bit out of whack given its pedestrian interior, lack of style and cubbish feel.

"Was he doing anything else on the weekend other than car shopping?"

"He liked to go to clubs sometimes. Very expensive clubs on weekends. He liked the pretty girls, you know?" Patel raised his eyebrows to make the point.

Ozzie rolled his eyes. "Yeah, we know the type, for sure. Any club in particular?"

"I don't know. I do not go with him and don't really discuss these things. He said he was meeting a new client over the weekend and it was going to be very, very big for us. That is very good."

"Let me guess, you don't know the client?" Fergus asked in frustration.

"No."

"What kind of law does Mr. Denman specialize in?"

"Some criminal cases—mostly drugs, some real estate and corporate stuff."

"Wow, if that's not a recipe for mob I don't know what is,"

Ozzie muttered to Fergus.

"Can we see his office? Has anything been removed or anyone been in it?" Ozzie asked as he turned back to Patel.

"Mostly just me and Bonnie putting in agreements and correspondence. One client came for a meeting and just sat in there for an hour and then left. That was about two weeks ago. After that, nothing."

Ozzie and Fergus walked into Denman's small corner office. It was stuffed with legal journals, books and files. Hundreds and hundreds of files and walls of filing cabinets. All filled with more files.

"Either this guy was the busiest lawyer in New York or a paper hoarder," laughed Fergus as the two moved awkwardly around the room.

"No computer," noted Ozzie immediately. We need to secure the server, like right now. Call HQ and get us a warrant. Tell them we're not leaving until we've got it. Get some back up also and sit in here. Don't let anyone touch anything."

The files appeared to be for an endless array of business incorporations and off-shore companies, the hallmark of the drug business's financial model. It was evident Mr. Denman had likely been setting up complex financial corporate structures for mobsters so they could launder drug money through other legitimate business revenues either out of the country or just out of sight. It was the easiest form of law but certainly a very dangerous type of practice, as sooner or later something always went wrong and these were not the type of clients who put up with errors and omissions, so to speak.

Ozzie motioned to Fergus. "Secure the office and get a forensic accounting team here to go through every room and catalogue all client and billing files. Let's find out who's paying for all this.

As Ozzie left Denman's office, word that two detectives were on site asking questions had spread and staff were congregating in the reception area.

A well-dressed lawyer, clearly quite full of himself, pushed to the front of a small group of about 15 people. "What's going on here? You have no right to burst into our office and disrupt business like this."

"Cool your jets, my friend. We're not sure, but we think your partner might have got on the wrong side of some very bad people and that's why he's not around. We're waiting on a warrant now and then we will have the right to disrupt your business."

His face immediately became distressed and the bellicose barrister backed down.

Ozzie pulled out his badge and flashed it to the group. "Does anyone here know anything about what your boss was working on in the last two months? Anything big and lucrative that he may have talked about or new clients he may have set up contact information for?"

The well-dressed lawyer, Bryce Richards, was partners of a sort with Denman. The two shared resources, office space and computer systems but had very little to do with each other's legal practices. Regardless of Mr. Richard's pompous attitude, according to staff it was Denman's billings that paid for most things and kept the office going. Richards' practice was mostly family disputes, minor estate consulting and some public service work, none of which was very lucrative. With Denman, he had found a modicum of financial stability. *But, why would Denman want to hook up with him,* thought Ozzie. *Man about town, big wheel type with this deadbeat. It seemed like an odd choice unless you were trying to fly under the radar of other law firms, regulators and the bar association.*

As employees offered up their tidbits of information, Ozzie noticed one girl drift back to her stall and begin shuffling through her handbag. She took out a cell phone and furiously tapped on the screen. With Fergus writing down details as fast as he could, while also trying to assure the panicked staff that everything was going to be okay, Ozzie subtly moved towards the girl's cubicle without drawing attention to himself.

"Who you texting?" Ozzie asked as he popped his head over the textured temporary wall.

The intrusion shocked the pleasant-looking brunette, who dropped her phone and looked into the detective's face.

Ozzie sensed she was frightened as he strode around the wall and leaned over to pick up her phone. The half-finished text was on the screen.

TEXT: I think Mike is in trouble have you -

"So, who are you talking to?" Ozzie began.

The girl breathed in deeply. "My brother. We grew up with Mike and he gave me this job because he knew he could trust all of his old friends from the neighbourhood. My brother Josh and him were close. I wanted to know if he had seen or heard from Mike."

"Are you close with Mike or just your brother?"

"Uhh, I used to be and then we went to Mexico earlier this year. Cabo San Lucas. Things got kind of weird while we were there so we sort of cooled it off when we got back."

"What happened in Mexico?"

"Mike was meeting with a lot of sleazy-looking guys. They were all driving black SUV's and arriving in three-car convoys at weird hours. I asked him what was going on and he said it was just business. That they might be new clients of ours. He said they were really rich businessmen from a Mexican beer company, Tecata I think, and they wanted to expand more in the US. He said they wanted him to set everything up and find them some real estate in New York for maybe a plant or something. We went for dinner with a few of them one night and they seemed pretty nice, but I just got a weird vibe. Like they were acting one way but they were very different. Ya know that feeling?"

Ozzie nodded.

"I saw one of them at the office about a week before Mike disappeared. Something bad has happened to him, I can just feel it."

The girl began to shake and then cry softly as Ozzie pulled out a tissue so she could dry the tears welling up in her eyes. "Who exactly were Mike's clients—other than the Mexicans?"

"Well, we had a few local businesses, restaurants and car shops mostly, a couple of clubs and a lot of private individuals, including some Russian bigwig that owned a lot of real estate. We also got referral work from Stitzgard & Wadkins, but a lot of that work seemed to have dried up lately."

Ozzie winced at the name Stitzgard & Wadkins. The firm was one of New York's toniest criminal defence firms, specializing in celebrity representation and catered to only the very richest of individuals. What kind of files would they be sending to this place? Ozzie wrote himself a note. "When did you last see Mike?"

"Um, likely Saturday, September 29th. I saw him at a coffee shop in Queens, the old neighbourhood. We used to hang there on Saturday mornings and reconnect with everyone. He was super happy that day and test-driving this crazy expensive car—a Porsche 911 GT or something. He brought it by to impress everyone. I asked him what he was doing with a car like that and he said he was going to buy it. He had a new client that was giving him a big retainer. I asked if it was the Mexicans, but he never said. He asked me and Josh if we wanted to go out and celebrate with him that night at Plush. It's a super expensive club in—"

"Oh, I know Plush," interrupted Ozzie. "So, you're telling me he was going to Plush that Saturday night, September 29th? For sure?"

"Yeah, I think so. He said he needed a night out. That he had been working really hard and wanted to blow off some steam. Josh and I weren't really into it so we just made up excuses and he left."

"Okay, thanks. That's great. Here's my card. Don't tell anyone we spoke, and I mean nobody. If I need anything else, I'll call you. If you see or hear anything, you can contact me directly at this number. But use somebody else's cell phone. Do not use yours—got it? And definitely don't discuss this on a company phone. What's your name?

"Dianne Esquirdo."

"Nice to meet you, Dianne. I'm Ozzie Stark, Detective Major Crimes. Remember, we did not have this conversation. Right?"

"Got it," she said, wiping her eyes. "The firm's not going to make it, are we? Mike is never coming back."

"Like I said, I'll be in touch."

Ozzie turned from the cubicle and walked quickly back toward the chaos breaking out by Fergus.

A team of uniformed NYPD officers had just arrived, throwing the staff into hysteria. Yellow police tape was being put over numerous office doors and boxes of files were being moved from Mike's office as everyone, including a completely dejected Bryce Richards, looked on helplessly.

This would likely be the last day of business for Denman and Associates, Ozzie suspected.

Chapter 29

Telling David his biggest secret had been a major breakthrough for Riley. For the first time in weeks, he felt less exposed and alone. Somehow, he felt safer on the road as the team was always together, almost like a wolf pack, and a security detail followed them everywhere. Plus, at night he had a roommate, and not just any roommate, but one of the Red Wings' biggest stars—Phil Davis.

Now, if only his new green shoots of confidence could transform his play on the ice.

At the first practice day in Nashville, Riley was confined to the black aces again, and while others were doing line-rushes at one end of the ice, he and the other aces were doing lung-busting skating drills at the other end.

"Sawyer, get over here!" screamed coach McCroy from center ice.

Riley nodded and skated over to the coach at full speed.

"You're skating well today, son."

"Thank you, Coach. I'm feelin' pretty good."

"You know, Stone thinks we need to get you back on his line, for the good of the team. What do you think?"

Riley could not hold back his smile, the first real one in weeks. "I think I love David Stone, sir. If you let me back in, I won't let you down. I promise."

"I got a feeling you won't. I know things are tough right now." Mike nodded at the young player knowingly. "But, we're a team, as I was reminded this morning, and we watch out for each other. We all got your back, Saw. You can count on us. That, I promise."

A surge of relief swept through Riley's body. He swallowed hard. "Thanks, Mike, I mean Mr. McCroy. Like I said, I won't let you down, sir. I swear."

"Go get a green jersey and do the second half of the practice with Stone's line. You gotta do something tomorrow, kid—that's your job. Like I said, we'll take care of everything else. You just play hockey, okay?"

Riley nodded enthusiastically and raced over to join the line-rushes.

McCroy laughed as Riley sped over to Hilts and gave him a big shoulder bump to announce his arrival. The three started celebrating as Hilts pulled Sawyer into a head lock and twisted him around. Yes, this was a team and, for the first time in a long while, it really felt that way.

Mike gestured toward Buzz.

"What's up, Coach?"

"Buzz, get me John Davis from security and have Hellan and Riley's agent join us when we arrive in Columbus, Thursday morning. We have something extremely important to discuss. Get all the security guys on Sawyer. They don't leave his side. And tell the hotel we want extra coverage on our floors. Also, let every rink know we want our dressing rooms buttoned down, plus extra tight identity checks on anyone from their staff working for us and on media credentials. And, I mean everyone."

"What the hell, Mike? What's going on?"

"Oh, nothing. I just think the team needs to circle the wagons right now and make sure these guys don't get too carried away while we're on the road. We don't need another episode like New York. That's why I want the guys on Sawyer, little shit troublemaker." McCroy grinned to himself.

"Aw, Coach, he's not that bad—" began Buzz.

"I'm kidding, Buzz, but get the security, please."

"Done, Coach."

* * *

"So, how's it going?" cooed Danielle into David's ear. "Any scoops for me from the road?"

David laughed into his phone. "Do you seriously think I'd tell you if there were?"

"Oh, come on. There must be a drunken foray from a night club in there somewhere or maybe some embarrassing team prank that went horribly awry."

"No, it's pretty quiet here. But we did get Riley back on our line for the next game. I guess McCroy thinks he's suffered enough, so Hilts and I are stoked about that."

"Really?" noted Danielle. "That's surprising, isn't it? How'd that happen? McCroy hates him and, let's face it, he hasn't done a thing to earn that spot back, has he?"

"He's not a bad guy, Danielle. And, if he ever gets his head straight, he does nothing but help us out. Honestly, I like playing with him. So, there's your scoop. Riley Sawyer is back and David Stone is happy about it."

"Sounds like a bromance that will have the Red Wing faithful retching in the aisles. No, I need something more, well, substantial. Like, I talked to that cop in New York and he thinks Riley may have something to do with a murder there. I don't know what, but he was—"

The light and fun tone of the call took on a much darker and disturbing tenor with Danielle's comments. David cut her off in mid-sentence. "Danielle, are you crazy? Like, seriously, you need to get off this weird thing you've got going with Riley and that stupid New York mess. Just let it go. You're not helping us. I'm not sure your reporting on this with all your imaginary details isn't what plunged him into the doldrums in the first place. We need Riley to start playing well and he's feeling a bit better now, so please don't screw that up for him—us—by dredging up New York again."

"Seems like that hit a nerve," Danielle responded, growing more indignant by the second. "Listen, David, we might like each other, but I know when I'm being played and everyone involved with this is lying. Sadly, even you. I won't report anything that's not true, you have my word on that, and certainly I would never write anything to hurt you or the team. But, I will do my job, you can be assured of that, and the chips can fall where they may. Got that?"

"You exhaust me," David quietly lamented. "Just give the guy a break. Do your job, for sure. That's what I love about you—how good you are, which is for me a double-edged sword. Just don't go creating bogeymen where none exist and hurt us in the process. I'll call you after the game tomorrow with some juicy road gossip, I promise. Even if I have to make it up. So, we're good?"

"Of course we're good. But, we'd be better if I knew everything you know about New York."

"Trust me, you likely know more than me and that's my final comment. Good night now and have a good sleep. Miss you."

David clicked off his phone and stared blankly at the muted television showing sports highlights. God, she's relentless, he thought to himself. It was only a matter of time until she figured things out and then it would go from news story to scandal or worse. David pushed his feet down into the end of the clean crisp sheets and closed his eyes. Visions of Danielle raced through his mind.

"God she's relentless and so beautiful," he whispered into the darkness.

Then sleep.

Chapter 30

Valeri Voyov was enjoying his new life in North America. The speedy forward had been born in Timonovo, Russia, a city of strategic importance located about an hour and a half northwest of Moscow. Timonovo's global significance stemmed from its principal institution, the Missile Attack Warning Centre. This critical piece of Russia's security infrastructure was a complex network of monitoring systems designed to identify any type of ballistic missile attack from across the globe. And, it was the only place that authorization to activate Russia's nuclear codes could come from. The network was linked 24/7 to the Kremlin's most senior officials who could from a secret location within the building or from a nuclear briefcase, should that option be required, initiate thermal nuclear war. This unique reality had always made the city an interesting mix of power brokering, politics, crime and intrigue.

Valeri's father had been a physical education instructor at a high school and his mother, Ava, was a nurse at St. Alexander's, a hospice for terminal AIDS patients. He had enjoyed a pretty average upbringing for a 21st century Russian. Add in his minor celebrity as one of the country's finest amateur hockey players and the family had perhaps even lived a privileged life.

Valeri had an especially close relationship with his mother and admired her hospice work as the ultimate validation of her sainthood. In Putin's Russia, with its anti-gay culture, AIDS was considered a disgraceful disease and a just indictment for society's most abhorrent citizenry—homosexuals and drug addicts. Ava did not care about Putin. Human suffering in every form was unacceptable to her. And she had passed that belief on to her beautiful Valeri. She brought her patients as much comfort as she could until they passed on to a better place. Valeri could not imagine a more perfect human being or example for him to follow.

Valeri had played recreational hockey in the local kid's leagues before graduating to the Timonovo Bears at just 15, the city's junior team. After starring in the world junior tournament at 17 and being chosen as a second team all-star, he had been drafted by HC Sparta of the Kontinental Hockey League. This was one of

Russia's premier franchises, located in Moscow.

After three years in Moscow, he had been offered a contract with the New York Islanders and in his first NHL season, at just 23 years of age, had come within a handful of votes of winning the Calder trophy as Rookie of the Year. Sadly, his sophomore season had been terrible and his third year had not gotten off to a great start when he had been abruptly traded to the Red Wings for a third-round draft pick. This was where he had hoped for a fresh start. But, the emergence of new teammates like David Stone, Darcy Hilton and, of course, Riley Sawyer, were putting a strain on his ice time. The pressure for Valeri to have a big redemption season was building daily. With only one goal and two assists after fourteen games, plus a few games missed due to a lower leg strain, his confidence was spiralling and problems had begun to arise in his relationships with some teammates and coaches.

Valeri's phone buzzed, interrupting his woeful introspection about his game. He placed his coffee on the table and pulled out his gold iPhone. "Da."

"I am a friend sitting right behind you and I have a message from Ava. Please come. Join me at my table. I think we have much to talk about."

A sudden chill shot down the young player's neck and spine. A friend? Ava? Much to talk about? He quickly glanced around the coffee shop, but other than a few university geeks and an older gentleman reading a magazine, he saw no one. A sense of apprehension began to grow in Valeri as he stared into his coffee cup. *What's going on*, he thought.

"Hi. Your friend asked me to give you this." A pretty barista smiled as she handed Valeri a folded piece of paper. "He said that you should come over and join him. That it would be great to catch up. So, I take it you're from Russia too?"

"Uh, yes," Valeri mumbled as he grabbed his coat from the back of his chair and turned to see what person he had missed in his search. Peering from behind a square, plaster pillar at the back of the coffee shop, he noticed a thick, Slavic-looking man staring at him coldly while he dipped a giant biscotti into his steaming cappuccino. Though Valeri was sure he didn't know the man, he knew he was no friend of Ava's, and his heart began to pound faster.

"Who are you?" Valeri demanded as he walked up to his new

acquaintance. "How do you know my mother? What do you want?" Valeri tried his best to look intimidating as he stood over his fellow Russian.

"Sit, Mr. Voyov. Sit. We have much to talk about. This is your lucky day."

Valeri was surprised by the man's disarming demeanour and pulled out the chair. With a queasy feeling growing ever stronger in the pit of his stomach, he sat down, never looking away from his antagonist.

"Do you read the news, Valeri?" the brutish thug queried as he thrust an open-faced Russian newspaper to the other side of the table.

Valeri stared down at the paper. The man had taped a photograph to it of his mom, apparently taken about 32 hours earlier, if the time stamp on the image was to be believed. On it was inscribed all her shift hours for the next week and notes about her daily routines and the current roster of patients she was attending to at the hospice. It also included some highlighted insights like when she would be travelling to work and home alone and times of the day that she was generally not around a lot of people during her shifts.

"What I need is very easy for you to give and it guarantees the safety of your wonderful mother, Ava—and your father for that matter. And, maybe even a few more members of your family, like cousin Danos, or your uncle, Mischa. You see, my friends in Russia, they are kind of in the insurance business and we have a very good life insurance policy for you and those you love."

Valeri felt revulsion well up through every pore in his body while huge beads of sweat formed across his forehead and brow. He was quite sure he knew what was coming next. How he wished some of those irritating Red Wing security guys he always laughed at would show up now and rescue him from this guy.

"And, Valeri, please, for your own sake and especially the well-being of all your family, do not go to any security or police. That would be so foolish. We will know instantly and our judgement will be swift, torturous and final, you know. We own the Timonovo police and they will make sure we know those things that are important to us. Plus, that would also unleash terrible problems for your new family here in Detroit too—including you."

"Wh—what do you want? How much?" The words, dripping

with fear and terror, fell weakly from Voyov's lips.

"No, no money," laughed his tormentor. "No, we have very much money now. We don't need money. We just need to know things. Simple, easy things. Things you will know and we would not. So, when I call you, you will tell me what I need to know and then we are all good. It is so easy really. Like I said, this is your lucky day. Nobody gets off this easy when dealing with Odessa."

Valeri's heart sank as he heard the word. Odessa was every Russian athlete's worst fear and now they had set their cruel sights on him. But why? What information could he give them? He didn't know anything.

"By the way, Valeri, Ava is doing great. It is a depressing place she works, but she seems so nice, truly kind as she helps those scum faggots that she loves so much. It is hard to understand what motivates her, but surely the world needs more people like her. Agreed?"

Valeri nodded his head in the affirmative and dejectedly stared down at the table.

"Agreed, Valeri?" the man's voice became aggressive and angry as he awaited a verbal cue that everything he had communicated to the hockey player was clearly and unquestionably understood on the deepest level.

"Yes," he responded meekly.

"Excellent then. Enjoy your coffee, my friend. We will be in touch soon. Make sure your cell is on at all times, because we would hate for any little thing to go wrong and cancel this incredible life-giving insurance policy we have so graciously granted you. And have a good game tomorrow and a good season. My name is Yuri. Remember it and make sure you tell me the truth. Always the truth, Mr. Voyov. The truth will set you and those you love free, as they say." With that, Yuri rose and walked out of the coffee shop waving happily at the barista as he strode through the door.

Valeri sat alone at the table, staring sadly into its dark, naturally-grained, wood texture. He'd been warned about this upon arriving in the United States, but nothing had happened for four years. Why now? What could he possibly do for them? Who could he talk to? He unfolded the picture of his mother comforting one of her patients at the hospice. *Oh my God*, he thought, *they could kill her in an instant, at any moment.* He decided right then, whatever they needed to know, they would know. No one mattered more to him than his mother, father and family. Certainly not a room full of hockey players, most of whom didn't really like him anyway. *Screw them*, he thought in frustration.

"So, was it fun to see your friend?" the bubbly young server who had handed Valeri the note gushed as she came over to his table. "That must be so awesome after all this time to catch up with someone from your home town when you're all the way over here." She grinned.

"Da, it was really great." He waved her off and with a forlorn look stared out the window onto a street bustling with people going about their daily lives much as he had been an hour ago. His life would never be the same after today, he just knew it.

Chapter 31

"Could this finally be the real Riley Sawyer? The dominant force we've all been waiting for?" gushed Detroit's play-by-play announcer as the three stars were paraded onto the ice. Two goals and an assist in a 5–1 Detroit win over Nashville was what the stats page would show, but that was far from the reality of the game. Riley, Hilts and David had dominated the Predators in every way. Hits. Shots. Face-offs. Goals. Assists. Passion.

"I hope that was Riley's first of many big games for us," Mike McCroy dead-panned at the post-game presser. "We all know he's got the talent, he just needs to focus on his game and forget all the outside stuff. So, great game and good for him. We're anxious to see a lot more of this. He was the best player on the ice tonight although that whole line was working well together."

David, with a goal and an assist in the game, had taken over Detroit's early season scoring lead. But, the growing media scrum was buzzing around Riley's locker. It was only mid-November and no one was worrying too much about a bad effort by Nashville or scoring leads, however everyone was still watching Riley Sawyer.

* * *

"We matched DNA from a headless corpse some flat-foots found along the Hudson to some taken from a hair brush at Mike Denman's townhouse. I think it's safe to conclude the headless body is Mr. Denman. At least that will be my conclusion following the autopsy," stated the Brooklyn District pathologist as she tossed a case file on Ozzie's desk. "Cause of death? Well, that was pretty easy—decapitation, but the body also showed signs of torture and a severe beating. A brutal, cruel beating. There was pre-mortem bruising on his arms, legs and chest, plus ligature marks on this arms and ankles. I would say he was tied to a chair and beaten for a while, and then decapitated as a final indignity. Not a pretty way to go. Very likely Russians. We've seen this type of execution before—a few of them linked to the Odessa crime group. A real nasty bunch, those guys. They save this savagery for those they really dislike."

"Un-fucking real," Ozzie mouthed quietly into the air. It had happened just the way Riley had said and he'd seen the killer. He knows who he is. "Fergus get me everything Organized Crime has on Odessa. I want to know who its head guys are, lieutenants, wise guys and look for any connection to Denman. Finally, we got a real lead."

Ozzie picked up his phone and buzzed the Captain. "Boss, I gotta go out of town and meet with that hockey player. We got a break in the headless horseman case."

M-I-K-E D-E-N-M-A-N, was methodically typed into a search engine and within seconds a number of pictures of the New York lawyer appeared on Ozzie's computer screen. *He looks shady*, thought Stark, *and likely deserved what he got.* The pieces were falling into place as Ozzie printed out a picture and took it over to the evidence board. He stuck it above a picture of a decomposed corpse which had surfaced two weeks ago on a riverbank about three miles down the Hudson River on the shores of the Upper Bay. He drew a black line to some menacing looking Mexican guys in black SUV's. Then, he drew a second box and put the name Odessa in it and drew another line to the dead man's picture.

The puzzle was pretty simple and could not be clearer. Denman had done work for Odessa likely creating corporate shells for some money laundering schemes and then got a bigger, better offer from the new guys in town—likely the Mexican cartel, who wanted to expand their drug business in America—New York specifically.

"Wow, what was that guy thinking?" Ozzie whispered as he shook his head in disbelief. Denman had signed his own death warrant the minute he'd gone to Mexico to meet those guys. And the hockey player was right in the middle of it all—the one guy who could finger the killer and perhaps bring down one of New York's biggest and most violent criminal organizations.

Ozzie shook his head. "Oh fuck, they've gotta kill that kid to protect the operation. For sure they've got to kill this kid—hockey player or not, security or not. Odessa, with all its resources, would easily find a way to kill Riley and possibly a few others when it happened."

* * *

The red-eye from Nashville to Columbus was the worst flight David had ever experienced. A violent thunderstorm, fairly frequent for the time of year in the southeast, was howling outside and the turbulence was not only terrifying but making him nauseous as well.

"I gotta get off this fucking plane," mumbled Hilts, staring straight ahead. "This shit makes me crazy."

"Ahhh, the big tough guy is scared of a little thunder and lightning," mocked David, trying in vain to get the upper hand in the bravery department any way he knew how.

CRASH.

Lights in the plane flickered into darkness and only blue-filtered emergency lights illuminated the interior for a few seconds while the private aircraft dove and then steadied again.

Hilts let out a shriek and grabbed David's thigh with such force the latter yelled in pain and shock. Many players, more familiar with the pitfalls of NHL travel just grimly stared at their glowing tablets or cell phones as the regular lights flickered back on and the crackling of the intercom came to life.

"Sorry folks, but we're in some terrible weather here and may have to fly a bit off our route to avoid this storm. The plane was just struck by lightning, but that's not unusual and we came through it with no issues. Everything is fine, so don't be nervous. All the plane's avoidance and grounding systems worked perfectly and we are flying fine, but I know that last thunder clap probably shook everyone up a bit. Please, just bear with us while we look for better air up a little higher."

"Better air—is this guy kidding?" complained Hilts. "I think I shit myself."

David did not respond, he just sat and clutched the armrests of his seat, making no movements.

The big winger saw his seatmate's discomfort and began laughing. "You chicken shit, Stone. Giving me the gears and look at you—can't unwrap those pussy hands from the armrests. You need me, man. You and Sawyer, you both need me. No courage in either of you." Hilts laughed smugly and turned back to his edition of the Hockey News.

"What I need is for this plane to land," David said quietly.

"Did you see if Riley's okay?"

"What do I look like, his fucking mother? He's fine; stop babying him. What the fuck is up with you?"

David slowly unbuckled his seat belt and, since the flight had settled somewhat, moved to an empty seat by Riley and Davis.

"What are you doing here?" Riley asked somewhat bewildered.

"Just thought I'd see how things were going. That last crash was a real shocker."

"Go back to your seat, Martha, I'm fine. When you've got the mob chasing you, a little lightning's no big deal and likely a much more civilized way to go." Riley whispered to David, his eyes wide.

David didn't know whether to laugh or console his friend.

Sawyer's face quickly changed. He grinned and slapped David on the shoulder. "I'm fine. Really. That was a joke."

David nodded and took comfort in the fact his friend was starting to come out of the stupor the New York experience had put him in. That was a big step forward.

Nashville gave way to Columbus and then Tampa Bay as the calendar drifted through November and the Wings' south-eastern road show limped out of town with a 4–3 loss. Next they would be moving on to the sunny shores of Miami's South Beach. The team usually played back-to-back games in Florida, but some strange concert scheduling problems had given them three days off in America's hippest coastal city (with all due respect to Los Angeles).

The team scheduled a meeting for the first night at the hotel, accompanied by a sizable cadre of dark-suited security guys who had joined the team in Columbus.

As Darcy stared at the platoon of suits moving around the hotel lobby, he leaned over to David. "Say there, Stone, I know you're doing pretty well in the points department, but did they go out and get you a private security detail to deal with all the broads that are after you?"

"Actually, Hilts, they did. Now that I'm the scoring leader they figure some other team might come and try to poach me or maybe knee-cap me, Tonya Harding style."

"Shit, give me a break." Hilton spat back.

"Okay, guys, listen up," came the stern voice of Mike

McCroy. "I know we're in Miami and it's a great place to party and hang out with celebs, but that last game in Tampa was pitiful and you guys need to keep your focus. So, we're on 11 PM curfew while…"

All the players moaned in unison at the news they knew had been coming.

"No way! Not in South Beach. It doesn't even get going 'til 1 AM. What are we supposed to do, go for tea at the Polo Club with the blue-hairs?" yelled Dan Lowe to much laughter from his teammates.

"I'm too old for curfew," chimed in Abramov from the back of the room.

McCroy raised his hands and, after a few seconds, the players were again silent. "I said we have an 11 PM curfew prior to the game. Now stop bitching; that's it. Secondly, after the New York fiasco during pre-season, you might notice we brought along a few security reinforcements for your protection. They'll be watching you guys closely, especially the rookies, so we don't expect any repeat performances. You got that Sawyer?"

"I got no problem with that, Coach," Sawyer responded immediately amidst numerous catcalls and groans from his teammates.

"Good. And finally, you old farts, watch out for the kids. While we're all professionals here, more importantly, we're a team. We watch out for each other. I want everyone watching for anyone or anything that might look suspicious out there. I mean at practice. At the hotel. In the seats. Keep your eyes on one another and make sure we pull together here."

"Ok, that's fucking crazy," Hilts whispered to David. "What are we, at a Pee Wee tournament, first time away from home?"

"Shhh". David threw a passing glare in his friend's direction.

McCroy continued. "We need a good game in Florida. I want a win. A big win. And that comes from everyone watching out for each other and helping each other, every minute of every day. Got it?"

"Yes, Coach," yelled the team.

"Okay, misfits. Tomorrow we've scheduled practice for 11 AM. So, sleep well. The bus arrives at 9:00 AM and practice is going to be a doozy 'cause it's an off-day, so relax and get some sleep. Stone, Hilts, Abs and Sawyer. You four will be sharing a suite. The more the merrier, okay?"

"So, what the fuck are we doing in a suite?" Hilts asked no one in particular as the players strolled toward the elevator.

"Not sure," replied Abramov. "But, if any of you snore really loud, we're going to have a big problem."

David looked at Sawyer and gave him a knowing grin. *"We got you."* he mouthed.

Chapter 32

A dark, shadowy figure moved across the front of Miami's Excelsior Hotel and quickly strode up its steps into a beautiful marble foyer, spectacularly lit by streaks of white light from a breathtaking crystal chandelier. The concierge nodded and closed the door behind the visitor. Upon entering the centre of the room, he took out his smart phone and pretended to be texting while, in reality, he slowly scanned the oversized space and snapped a number of reference pictures, particularly of the stairwells, elevator access and notable security features.

He then walked into the Continental Lounge and took up residence at a private corner table near the back where a portly middle-aged man was already seated, staring into his phone.

The seated man looked up. "Andriy, is that you?"

"Nik, it is me. Good to see you again. It has been much too long."

Nikolai rose from his chair and the two men embraced briefly, slapped each other on the back and took opposite seats across the table. "You look different, my friend. Life must be treating you well."

"Life is okay, but right now we have a problem." Andriy began rhythmically tapping his fingers on the table.

"Yes, Alexi tells me you might need some help while you're in town. No sweat, I'm your guy. What's the job?"

"I'm here to watch some hockey games and might need to take someone out from one of the teams," Andriy stated bluntly as he stared into Nikolai's eyes.

Nik exhaled deeply at the comment. "Oh man, pro sports. That's a very tough one. Those guys are surrounded by private security now at all times. Very professional guys. Black-ops, ex-seals and shit. Who is it you're after?"

"A guy on the Red Wings. A kid—names, Sawyer. Big star. Showed up at the wrong place, wrong time. Of course, he loves partying and the ladies so that opens up some opportunities. Regardless, we need him gone."

"Hmm. What are you thinking?"

"I'm thinking a robbery or mugging gone wrong. A fight at a club. Things got out of control and he's collateral damage. Perhaps in a private corner of the club with a girl, leaving the club, walking to the hotel. Make it look like gangs, a drug fight, beef with a pimp, some shit like that. Where do the hockey players go when they come to town?"

"Visiting team? Only one place: Pearlman's! Hottest club on the strip with the most beautiful women on earth. Always crawling with jocks, Hollywood types and reality stars. It's crazy every night. Never a dull moment. Athletes, models, singers, actors, flavours of the month—they all get priority and boy do they use it. I have a guy on the inside. He can help us."

"Who runs the girls?"

"Jews. Do you believe that shit? Jews. And not the little rabbi types with flat hats and dreadlocks. I mean big, hun-hatin', scary JDL guys, with tons of money, entertainment connections up the wazoo and they don't like Russians or Germans." Nikolai stared at Andriy with legitimate concern.

"No, I'm sure they don't. Racists. So, we can't get any of the girls to help us or someone on the bar staff?"

"Bad idea." Nik continued. "Word could get out way too easy. You need to keep this tied down tight. Two, three people, max. I've heard some of their security are ex-Mossad. You may be good, my friend, but you got nothin' on those guys. So don't be arrogant in your planning. These aren't mall cops."

"Hmm, that's a few more complications than I expected. Can you get me in there tonight to look around? Then I can tell you what I need." Andriy seemed a bit unsure of his plan.

Nik looked down at the table, not sure he really wanted this assignment. "Let me check." He got up and slowly walked to the middle of the bar, cell phone in hand. In about three minutes, he turned, smiled at Andriy, gave a thumbs up and walked back to the table. "Be there at 2 AM and go to the back door. Knock twice, loud, then wait three seconds and knock twice again, not as loud. He'll let you in. His name's Marco. I would trust him with my life."

"That's good, because you are," said Andriy coldly. "He's a Russian?"

"No, a Jew. So, no anti-Semite shit. He's touchy about that. But, he loves money more than blood, so this help is going to cost

Alexi. A hundred grand for everything."

"Are you fucking crazy?" Andriy leaned hard into the face of Nikolai. "This is at best a fifty, that's it."

Now Nikolai's eyes narrowed and he did not flinch from the aggressive posturing of his co-conspirator. "Crazy, you son of a bitch, is killing a pro hockey player in public. That's going to cost you—big! You, my friend, are the fucking crazy one."

Andriy was stunned at the sudden darkness of Nik's stare-down. Then a smile creased his scarred lips. "That may be the smartest thing you've said all night. Money is fine then. I'll get fifty wired tomorrow and the rest sent from New York upon success. Standard rules."

And, with that, the two Russians raised their eight-ounce tumblers of ice cold vodka and moved on to other topics.

Andriy glanced at his watch. It was close to midnight. He would have to leave soon.

* * *

Riley felt helpless. He pleaded for his life, but it didn't matter. He looked into that face. The face of a cruel killer and felt himself weep. A hot muzzle flash and the loud crack of a .357 was deafening and the last thing he heard. Then, black.

His heart was racing as he shot up into the stillness of the night. Sweat poured down his cheeks and his t-shirt was a hot, sticky mess despite him sleeping just two feet from an air conditioner.

In the darkness he could hear David's rhythmic breathing as he slept soundly. Hilts and Abramov had won the rock-paper-scissors show-down and gotten the suite's private bedrooms as their just rewards. Sawyer tried to control his irregular heaving and shook his head. The debilitating fear subsided as it always did and his head slumped down toward his chest. A final deep breath and he flopped back onto the damp pillow.

God, this is gross, he thought. He remembered the horrible face so vividly. It was actually getting clearer and the definition and details of that fateful evening were slowly coming back to him in nightmarish ways at the oddest times. For the first time, he recalled the sad, desperate look of the victim before his head fell from his body. He remembered the shapes of the crew that chased him down.

There were three, no four guys. Slowly, images were coming back to him, much to his anguish.

"Hey, what're you doing?" David mumbled drowsily as he slowly opened his eyes. "You okay?"

"Yeah. Yeah, I'm fine. Just some indigestion, I think. Go back to sleep. I'm fine."

"Okay, you too. Big game comin'..." David's voice trailed off.

Sawyer stared at the ceiling for hours after that as sleep only brought back to him haunting images of fear, death and that face. That heartless merciless killer that was now likely focused on him.

* * *

"Stark. Ozzie Stark. I booked the room through some web site. It said I had a room and that it was paid in full."

"I'm sorry, Mr. Stork, but I don't have a reservation. Are you sure you're at the right Holiday Inn? There are 23 in the greater Miami area."

"Of course, I'm sure. It was Holiday Shores or something, I wrote it down here on this piece of paper." Ozzie awkwardly pulled out a pile of receipts for magazines, fast food, gas, his car rental and lots of other completely useless shards of paper as the night clerk stared at him. Everything seemed to be there except the paper with his hotel information on it.

"Do you have a confirmation number, Mr. Stork?"

Ozzie glared up from the pile of junk in front of him. "Lady, my name is Stark—not Stork. I'm an NYPD detective and no, I don't have a confirmation number, it was on the paper too. Now look, I know you guys have a national database, so I know you can look up my name. Maybe this is the wrong place. Anyway, I got a room at one of your stupid hotels. So, can you please help me? I'm tired and need some sleep."

"I can try, but we really don't like to do that." The rotund older lady lumbered out of the desk area to a private room and emerged about ten minutes later. "Okay, Mr. Stark, I did find your online reservation and it's at the Holiday Inn Miami West. It's about a half hour from here. I have a map and—"

"That's fine. Thank you. Can I just get the address and I'll punch it into my phone? Actually, I'd better take that map too." An exhausted Ozzie returned to his rental car and sat staring at the bright neon hotel sign in the parking lot. His telephone's battery light flashed red.

"Seriously? Crap. Can't I get a break here?" he screamed as he looked skyward and slammed his hands up and down on the steering wheel. Then he stopped and took four deep breaths. His temples stopped pulsating and he turned on the ignition.

He pulled out and headed south on the I-95. Tomorrow, he would be meeting with Riley Sawyer and the Detroit coaching staff about the danger their golden boy was in.

* * *

"He's gone where?" gasped a distraught Danielle Wright to the night captain at New York's 40th Precinct station house.

"Listen, lady, I said too much already, so that's it. He's gone to Miami. And I'm only telling you that because you said you had an appointment booked with him, even though there's nothing in his calendar to support that. So, I have to say good evening now, okay?"

"Yeah, sure," nodded the Free Press reporter grudgingly.

One of the best tactics for an investigative journalist was the pop-in visit. Catch people off guard and fire questions when they were unprepared and could not escape your inquisition. But, it appeared this time it had been a poor strategy. Ozzie was gone—to Florida no less.

She laid her small bag at her feet and sat down on a hard wooden bench in the public waiting room and began searching various phone apps. Detroit Red Wings schedule. Next game was against the Florida Panthers in Miami. Could this just be a coincidence? People from New York vacationed in Miami all the time. It had been weeks since she talked to Ozzie and over that time all the indicators and her professional instincts told her the Riley Sawyer story was bigger and more extreme than Wings' management had offered up to the media.

She clicked on the telephone icon and, in a minute, a groggy David was answering her call. "H-h-hello?"

"Hi, honey. How's it goin'?"

"Seriously? What are you doing, Danielle? Its 4:30 in the

morning here and pretty close to that in Detroit, so what's up?"

"Nothing, I just missed you and couldn't sleep, so I thought I'd call. Anything exciting happening?"

"No. We're in bed. It's the night before a game. I'm supposed to be sleeping."

"Who are you rooming with?" She continued.

"Sawyer and a few others. Really, I've got to go back to sleep or I'll be up all night."

"Sawyer, he's not your regular roomie."

"Why does everything with you turn into an interrogation?"

"Just asking. It seems odd though."

"It's not odd. They put me, Sawyer, Hilts and Abramov in a suite together. We missed out on the bedrooms. We just have to sleep—now, really."

"I heard you guys have more security these days. Is that true?"

"Boy, you are nosey and I'm not answering. I'm hanging up now. You need to go to bed, okay, dear. I need to sleep."

"Oh fine, you big wuss. I'll see you when you get back."

"Thanks Danielle, I'll call you after the game. Sorry I'm such a grouch."

"Don't worry about it. Have a good game. Sleep tight." She hung up.

So the Red Wings had doubled up roommates and they had more security. That little tidbit had leaked out during a late morning presser at the arena, prompting Danielle to board the next direct flight to New York to confront Ozzie Stark with her growing theory that Riley Sawyer was in imminent danger of something. She wanted the truth of what had happened in New York or she was going to pen a hypothetical story about a cover up by the NYPD and the Detroit Red Wings that was putting the life of one of its marquis young players at risk. Now, no Ozzie. He's headed to Miami at the exact same time the Red Wings arrive for a game and had increased their security.

She looked at her watch. 5:38 AM, New York time. She quickly went into her travel app to see when the next flight to Miami left New York and was thrilled when she saw a 7:55 AM direct hop, and with a cheap last-minute fare no less, arriving at Miami International Airport at 10:45 AM. That would give her lots of time to find out what the hell was going on with Ozzie and, if her intuition was right, she would find him and the Detroit Red Wings at the same place, where she could confront them both.

This might turn out even better than her original plan.

* * *

One. Two. Andriy delivered solid blows to the heavy metal door at precisely 2 AM. It opened a crack.

"What the fuck you want?"

"Marco told me to meet him here. So I'm here. Where the fuck is he?"

"Up yours, man, there's no Marco here—get lost!"

"Hey, I drove over to meet Marco and if you don't open this fucking door and get him, I'll blow a hole in you the size of my fist. I'm not fucking around."

"Ooowee, Nik was right, you're intense," laughed a smiling Marco as he opened the door and pulled Andriy into the darkness.

In a heartbeat, Andriy slammed Marco's head into the wall and held a serrated army blade to the terrified man's jugular.

"Are you fucking crazy, you stupid shit. You think I'm playing games here? Nik said you were his guy, but I think you're a fucking idiot and I think I should kill you right now."

"Hey, whoa, soldier, I'm your guy. Easy. Just wanted to test your mettle a bit."

"Next time you test my mettle I'll use it to cut your tongue out and shove it up your ass. Are we clear?"

"Got it! Got it!"

Andriy moved the blade away from Marco's throat and shoved it back into his belt.

"So, what's the plan, Mr. Fucking Serious," Marco spat in disgust.

"Nothing." Andriy turned and walked back toward the door.

"Hey, I'm all in and I'm Nik's guy and your guy. Sorry things got off wrong. Just needed to check you out."

Andriy turned back towards the heavy-set Jew. "Don't ever fuck around with me. Ever. Is that clear?"

"Got it. So, what's on your mind?"

"I need to get some heavy duty guns and stun grenades into

the club for a job tomorrow night. Target's a hockey player. You need to manage the crowd in the area a bit and make sure I have access to the players and specifically a guy named Riley Sawyer. He's the target. Here's his picture."

"Timings good. We've had some bad gang shit around town lately. If you want it to look good, I'll give you a couple of spics to bag too and then we both win. Your mark just gets caught in the crossfire."

"That works. Now, show me where you'll put them. And, how I get out after all the fun."

"Oh, I've got the perfect spot. A virtual shooting gallery. Big thumping music and strobes. You could shoot fifty people before anyone even knew bullets were flying. Maybe scream Allah Akbar or something to really fuck with people's minds. Since Orlando, that's on everyone's radar."

"Let's just go with the gang thing. Don't need the Fed's on this or worse, Homeland Security."

Chapter 33

The mood in the dressing room was relaxed and upbeat. Winning had a way of doing that. Players got in a groove. They began to relax and let their instincts take over. They believed in themselves and from that belief a wellspring of success usually flowed.

Riley was certainly feeling it—to the extent he was able to go a few hours enjoying his blessed life as a hockey player before crashing again psychologically into the fear that was always in the back of his mind, an anchor on his thoughts and, at times, his legs.

This morning however was not that time. Riley was up. Stone was pumped. And everyone else on the Red Wings were anxious to destroy the hapless Florida Panthers in about ten hours. As the team sped around the Florida Ice Den, the Panthers official practice facility in Coral Springs, it seemed as though their blades barely touched the glistening ice surface. Passes were crisp. Drills executed to perfection, and every shot was a glorious expression of a team that was on point and ready to explode offensively.

"Okay, Stone, Sawyer, Hilton—three-on-three's with Dreger, Bassen and Abramov. No hitting, just from centre in and make sure you get a shot. No shot, you give me 25 ice-ups." Larry Davies directed the players at the morning skate.

Blades flashed and pucks whizzed from stick to stick, a shot and then around the boards. One goal. Two goals. Then a third, on a blistering shot by Sawyer into the top corner.

"Sawyer, coach needs you in the trainer's room, double time." Buzz Lanyard motioned to Riley as the line returned to centre ice.

Riley glanced at David and shrugged. "Hopefully, they're moving me to a better line."

Hilts, catching the comment laughed and tapped Sawyer on the shin pads. "You look great, superstar, and trust me, I never thought I'd say that."

Riley began the short walk down the hallway and into a makeshift trainer's room. "Ahhh fuck," he moaned as he moved through the open door that was quickly closed by Detroit's security chief—Eddie Watkins.

Standing with Coach McCroy was Riley's worst nightmare. The bulldog-faced, slightly balding detective from New York.

"So, Riley, I guess you guys know each other so we'll skip introductions and pleasantries. Mr. Stark needs to talk to you."

"What do you want, Stark, and what the fuck are you doing here?" sneered the noticeably agitated player.

"I think your life is in real danger right now and as much as I think you're a pompous little shit, well, I don't want you to get killed and I do want to catch, or kill, and I'm not picky on which one, a really bad fucking dude named Alexi Tsarnov, the guy you likely saw kill that lawyer during your little adventure in New York."

"But I told you—"

"Stop fucking with me," Ozzie responded angrily. "Don't you get it? You're putting your life and the lives of every player on this team in peril with your bullshit 'I don't remember' story. I know what you saw and so do you. So, if you won't give it to me for your own good, do it for your teammates. Or do it for this organization. But do it! These crazy, sadistic kooks will blow your plane right out of the sky if they have too. They've got spies on every team. They're so far beyond what you think that you need to come clean with me—now." Ozzie slammed his fist down on the training table, his face red from a high-octane cocktail of poor sleep, adrenaline and rage. The room was silent.

"He's right, kid," said Watkins calmly. "You have to talk, let us know everything you saw. For everybody's safety. This has likely got a bit more dangerous now that we know who's involved. We can't afford to hope this problem simply goes away. That's not going to happen."

Riley slumped down on the training table and laid his head on his arm. "I see that miserable, twisted face all the time. It comes back to me dozens of times a day and gets clearer each time. Every excruciating wrinkle, scar and expression. Cruel and murderous. I just want him to disappear from my memory. I want that night to go away so I can get on with my life. It literally haunts me. I can't sleep. I can barely eat. My stomach hurts all the time. If it wasn't for the guys on this team I think I would have cracked up by now."

Ozzie reached in his bag and pulled out a large black and white photo. "Is this the guy you saw kill Denman? Oh, by the way, the guy you saw get chopped, his name was Mike Denman. He was a scumbag mob lawyer, who likely would have got killed anyway, someday—but it just happened to be while you were watching. So you and him are linked now, like it or not—forever."

Riley looked up from his arm and nodded yes.

"Do you have any doubt this is the guy?"

"No. That's him. I see him constantly—everywhere—in everything. He scares the shit out of me."

Ozzie nodded with a satisfied look on his face. "Okay, now we're making some progress. Coach, Mr. Watkins—it's time we catch or kill this son-of-a-bitch and any of his sleazy associates to save your player here and maybe this whole team."

* * *

Danielle exited the aircraft's gangway and headed immediately for the car rental hub located 15 minutes from the main terminal. It was almost 1:00 PM by the time she finalized her rental, found the car and pulled out of the parking lot on her way to the Panther's arena in Sunrise to try and catch the pre-game skate, if indeed they were having one. Doing things on the fly and without proper planning always made outcomes a little risky. If she could just get there while the team was on the ice, she was quite sure she would find Ozzie Stark in the same general area. Then she could get to the truth.

Florida's I-75 freeway was the most direct route from the airport to Sunrise. Unfortunately, today it was a parking lot. *I wonder how my dear David is doing*, she thought as her car inched down the clogged interstate. Far, far in the distance she could see the blue and red flashing lights of numerous Florida Highway Patrol cruisers.

"...And, if you're one of those poor folks sitting on the I-75, I hope you have a lot of gas, cause you ain't going anywhere," yelled an irritating announcer's voice from Danielle's radio. "There's a huge, seven-car pile-up at off-ramp 256, so you might as well just sit back and listen to some tunes with me, Cajun Charlie Chicken, Florida's country cousin."

Country music? She thought. I wish David was here.

***

"So, we're going to have extra security everywhere around the team's dressing room tonight. Nobody gets near the Wings without us checking and double-checking credentials."

Ozzie was surrounded by members of the Sunrise County Police Department, two organized crime task force detectives, four FBI agents and a half dozen Red Wings security officials.

"What makes you think something's going on here?" asked a task force official.

Ozzie laid out what he knew. "We got a report from a New York informant that a big-hitter for Odessa bought an airline ticket to Miami and some wiretaps caught a couple of conversations with Miami crime family affiliates. Plus, the timing and location make sense. It's far from New York, completely off the radar. And, it's before the truth has come out about the hockey player being involved. Also, it's away from Detroit, so the players can be more easily tracked, stalked and manipulated than when they're at home. Finally, I've just got this gut feeling something's going down."

"But how do we possibly watch these guys 24/7 on and off the ice? They're almost impossible to protect. They're at the rink, meeting fans in public places and for sure they'll all want to be out at night."

"Pretty sure that's what Odessa is counting on," came Ozzie's dark retort. "Jocks are creatures of habit. They come to town. Do the same bars, restaurants, girls every time. They're predictable. Makes finding them and potentially harming them that much easier. So, what's the hockey crowd's favourite hangout?"

"Pearlman's, without question," noted a Red Wing official. "A few guys have already asked me about making arrangements to get them in after the game, because we got another day off here."

"Then, there's a good bet that's where the action takes place. Though it's pretty tough to tell how or where the players will be the most exposed. Would it be possible to put an undercover with the team as a stand-in for Sawyer? Same size, build and as close to the look as we can get? He'd use his name and mingle with the guys at the club. We'll try and draw out the hitter if this is his plan."

"Why not just bring the whole fucking team straight back to the hotel and lock them down?" Watkins responded to Ozzie's seemingly outrageous plan.

"Because I could be wrong and, secondly, if you change the players' routine that much it will signal to Odessa that we know what's going on and that could be much worse for your organization. We're dealing with savages here. They're motivated. They want just one guy: Sawyer. So, they'll be somewhat careful not to make waves too much and try to take him as under the radar as possible. So, let's offer him up, at least in their eyes, and we run a whole lot less risk of anything happening to anyone else. My fear is, if they think we're on to them and Sawyer is talking, they'll be forced to do something much less focused and likely in more of a panicked way which could be far worse for everyone. That might sound crazy to you, but it's not. They don't care who or how many get killed. They need to get rid of a witness. We'll need lots of undercovers at the club tonight, especially around and mixed in with the team. Sawyer will be the only one going back to the hotel and hopefully no one is the wiser. He'll be safer there with a private security detail around him. Guys, honestly, I hope I'm wrong. I really, really hope I'm wrong, but I can't shake this feeling."

* * *

Marco carried a black duffle bag with a weight belt cinched around it through Pearlman's bustling kitchen during its hectic pre-lunch prep period.

"You better get to the gym, you fat bastard," came catcalls from behind the glowing grills as twin doors swung closed and he entered a dark deserted club compound.

He moved quickly through the silent space toward some bathrooms at the club's north end. An aged and bent Hispanic cleaner slowly moved his stainless steel polisher back and forth over the room's glistening concrete floors as he prepared them for another evening of lust and debauchery.

Rumour had it a couple of NHL teams were coming later that evening and the Oakland Raiders were also in town and primed for a bit of partying prior to a Sunday game with the Dolphins. It was going to be one very crazy night at Pearlman's.

* * *

"Okay, guys, this is a big one. We need a complete effort and no passengers. These guys may not have the best record, but they've got a great goaltender and some major-league firepower on their first line and power play. So, get focused, play for each other and protect each other out there."

Coach McCroy seemed a bit more emotional tonight, David thought. His pre-game rant was more about the need to watch out for one another and be good teammates than game strategy or line match-ups. Whatever, it didn't matter to him; he just needed to get focused and play well. He leaned over to Hilts and Sawyer. "Hey, let's make some big noise out there tonight. I feel great. Are you guys with me?"

"You bet, little man," said Hilts, fist bumping the much smaller Stone.

"Me too," grunted Riley. "Just send me the biscuit and I'll put it in the basket."

The linemates groaned at the ever-so-lame cliché as the players streamed out of the room and down the tunnel toward the ice. Into the darkness they jumped, awaiting the home team, the fireworks celebration and rock music that would explode upon the Panther's arrival.

* * *

Ozzie sat anxiously beside the visitor's bench and tried to look into the cavernous crowd for anything suspicious. The glint of a gun muzzle. A hurtling shape. Someone that did not belong. A loud explosion made his heart leap and he jumped out of his chair, only to realize the home team had arrived on the ice with their regular pre-game celebrations. *Man, I don't need this shit anymore,* he thought.

Both teams buzzed around the rink to finish their warm-up. The starting line-ups gathered along the blue lines for the anthem and finally it was game time. Three intense hours of stress for every security person in the building and the dozens watching from various command posts throughout the city.

* * *

The seat off concourse B, 42 rows up and 7 in from the aisle was vacant. A young girl and her grizzled boyfriend were dutifully waving an oversized Panthers flag and screaming at the top of their lungs as an unassuming European-looking man slid in behind them and slumped into his seat.

He didn't look like much of a hockey fan, but who could tell anymore? Everyone just sort of blended in.

* * *

The action began and before the game was two minutes old Florida's young rookie, Oscar Kletko, had given the home side a one to nothing lead.

McCroy grimaced as his team struggled to gain any play in the opposing end. "Stone, you guys go. Big pressure in the offensive zone, okay? We need that goal back. They don't give up a lot of chances, so pressure all the time, even behind the net."

Stone, Hilton and Sawyer jumped over the boards and headed to the face-off dot adjacent the Panther's goal. David stared at his opponent, whom he recognized from hours of game film. He felt he could win the draw cleanly. Straight back. He turned and motioned at Sawyer to move over behind him while Hilts drifted in to join the brief discussion.

"If I get this to you, fire it low," David instructed Riley. "Hilts, you crash the front straight off and try to power one in. I can take this guy. It'll come back fast so be ready."

"Just get me the biscuit and—"

"Yeah, yeah, got it Saw." David grinned as he turned and went back into his face-off stance.

The puck sailed through David's legs in perfect alignment with Riley's blade. Like a cobra strike his carbon stick hit the fast moving disc with perfect timing and sent a low screamer along the ice and right into the far corner of the net. The clock ticked off two seconds. Hilts didn't even get a chance to move, nor did he have to. Game tied.

"Oh, are we gonna have fun tonight," laughed David, turning to congratulate his teammate.

"Just get me the biscuit." Riley smiled as Hilts gave him a face wash with his glove and the three skated back to centre ice.

* * *

Danielle, jumped up from her chair to celebrate Detroit's goal. She had finally made it to the rink extremely late due to the car crash and then a flat tire. Her day had been a nightmare and she was almost comatose from being up for 23 hours straight and travelling through three major airports during that time.

As she had not been assigned proper press credentials, she had to wait until her boss contacted the Panthers' press administrator to clear her for the game. He had also demanded to know what the hell she was doing at the Red Wings-Panthers game while reminding her that she had pulled basketball detail for the week. Now, here she was, perched high above the ice in a mostly deserted press box with a pair of high-powered binoculars, scanning the crowd for Ozzie Stark. And then the goal had happened.

"That was so awesome," she silently whispered to herself. "C'mon David, get another one."

"Huh?" said a writer sitting beside her from the Miami Herald. "Were you talking to me?"

"Uh, no. Just really liked that goal. Detroit press and a big fan." She pointed to her credentials.

"Yeah, sure," responded the disinterested reporter, dipping his french fries into a large dollop of ketchup.

Danielle continued to scan the crowd. Down by the visiting team bench. Over. Up. Down. Nothing.

"Where are you, Detective Stark? I know you're here. There's no way in hell you flew to Miami for a holiday," she quietly murmured to herself.

Then, in the corner of the hallway by the Detroit bench, a balding head popped around the corner for an instant and Danielle grinned broadly.

"Got you!"

* * *

"Not seeing anything, Ranger," came the static voices of imbedded undercover officers spread throughout the stadium. "All clear for now, sir."

"Keep looking," grunted Ozzie. "My radars going crazy here. Have you got anything from facial recognition yet?"

The Florida crime lab was running real time video through their national and international databases for New York's top mob hitters to see if anything popped. So far, nothing. But, it was early in the game.

* * *

Andriy smirked at the young couple's distressed reaction to the Detroit goal. He wondered what they would think if he told them the goal scorer would be dead before they got home tonight. That would probably make them feel better. He chuckled in a macabre manner.

The assassin then lifted a pair of micro-binoculars to his eyes and stared at the face of Riley Sawyer, soaking in every detail. You never knew what issues might arise in this line of work, so he had to commit every characteristic of the young man to memory, just in case the light was low, he turned and ran, or whatever other unplanned circumstance may occur. Killing was a very exact science and he considered himself a master of the discipline. But, even the best laid plans came with wrinkles one did not foresee, so a professional always understood his target and tried to imagine every conceivable negative situation that could happen and how he would deal with it, if it did.

After studying Sawyer for an extended time, something else caught the Russian's experienced eye. There seemed to be an inordinate number of uniformed police in the building, particularly around the access points to seating sections. A team of security guys also seemed to be milling around the player's entry to their bench and the access tunnel that led back to where he assumed the dressing rooms were.

It was obvious security officials and local police were in a heightened state of preparedness and were expecting some type of action in the arena. Andriy grinned knowingly and pulled his brand new, black, Panthers ball cap a little further down his forehead and continued staring down at the game. Looked like he would not be going for popcorn or beer during the first or second intermissions like he had planned.

* * *

"Hey, Stark, we might have something from facial," came a voice through his ear piece. "It looks like we have a positive ID on a Russian dude from the Odessa gang in New York. A bad motherfucker named Andriy Korpikosky. He's one of Tsarnov's right-hand men. He showed up on some airport footage three days ago. Came off a connecting flight through Chicago, so he slipped through our regular screening programs because the departure destination was wrong."

"OK, that's good. Now, is he at this game? Where are we on the arena security footage from the entry gates?"

"So far, nothing. But seriously, almost everyone is wearing a Panthers or Red Wing cap. Tough to get a good look at people, especially guys. It's like finding a needle in a haystack, but we'll keep trying."

"Doesn't matter. Run that pic through all the security footage. He's got to be here. Also, get copies of his image to every cop and security guy in the arena and with both teams. At least we know who it might be," Stark ordered.

"10/4, Detective. On it."

Okay, so his instincts were likely correct. Something was going to go down. But what? How? Could he shoot him from the crowd? That seemed like a stretch, plus there were so many uniforms and undercovers here. The guy could likely not make it work from the crowd. When the players left or came onto the ice? Lots of commotion and close contact. Kind of a Lee Harvey Oswald thing where Ruby came out of the crowd and shot him point blank in the heart. But, he'd never get away and that was not a good plan for a high-ranking lieutenant with a bright mob future. He'd been picked for this job because he could get away. What about around the dressing room? No, too much security. Poison in a water bottle? Hmm, Russians love poisonings. It was the assassination method de jour in Moscow with the KGB types, but in America, the thugs liked it mono–a–mono. Likely a shooting.

That really only left after the game - transportation or the parking lot, or at a club. It had to be the club. That was the perfect place. Dark. Busy. Anonymous. Everyone was posing and had their guard down. No, it would be at the club. That's why he came to town early, to scope the place out and set it up for an execution.

Ozzie turned quickly toward the dressing room so he could see what security was doing between periods and after the game. They were going to need a body double for Sawyer to go to the club. A cop with a bulletproof vest and a whole lot of good luck.

"Well, what a surprise to see you here, Mr. Stark," screamed Danielle over the noise of the crowd as she stared angrily into his mortified eyes.

Ozzie pulled up abruptly and bumped into the beautiful reporter unintentionally.

"Let me guess, thought you'd catch an out-of-market game while you were on holidays in Miami? Hmm?"

"What the fuck are you doing here?" Ozzie spat, as he stepped around her.

"First rule of being a lawyer, Detective, don't ask a question you don't know the answer to."

Ozzie stopped and stared at her. "What the fuck does that mean? You're not a lawyer."

"No, but I know what's going on here and you lied to me and now I'm going to break the biggest story about Sawyer, murder, an NYPD cover-up and the Red Wings' complicity in endangering the life of a veritable child by not dealing with it."

"I don't know what you think you know, but you're way off base. I just happened to be in town and I got to know some security guys with the team. Wanted to see how the little prince was doing."

"Listen, you asshole, I've written my story and I'm sending it to Detroit tonight. Seeing you here confirms what I know and so let's go this route. Would you like to comment on the allegations of a murder-cover-up involving Riley Sawyer and the Detroit Red Wings, Detective Stark? This is on the record Ozzie, so don't fuck with me. I know what's going on. Any comment, Detective?" Danielle held up her iPhone to Ozzie's mouth and stared coldly into his face, her head cocked knowingly to the right and lips pressed perfectly tight. Her story might be a bluff, but she was raising the heat on Ozzie to try and force him to give up some more details.

Ozzie grabbed the reporter's arm and walked her into an empty maintenance room further down the player's tunnel. "You need to get the fuck out of here!" Ozzie stated bluntly. "Riley is in to something pretty deep and I think he could be a target of the Russian mob. The only advantage we have is they likely don't think we know, since no one in Detroit or New York other than me has been investigating this and the story is pretty much dead. You bring it up again with those details and you might as well kill him yourself. Maybe the whole fucking team. Now, I need you to get back on whatever plane you came in on, and let me find the motherfucker that flew here from New York three days ago, through Chicago, to kill Sawyer—likely tonight. Is that clear enough for you? Once I get the killer or stop this thing, I'll give you the exclusive story with all the salacious details your half-wit readers crave. But, you gotta get out of here. You are a big complication right now that this situation can't deal with."

"Yeah, no can do," responded Danielle. "I was sent here to cover the Wings and I'll damn well cover the Wings. But, I will take you up on that story offer and I'll do whatever you tell me to do to protect the team, players and myself. So, what is it?"

Ozzie frowned and exhaled deeply. "Get out of here! Don't talk to anybody. Go to your hotel and wait for me to call you. If nothing happens, we'll meet tomorrow morning for coffee and I'll tell you what I know. Everything. Then we'll be even."

"Deal. Can I call David tonight? Tell him I'm in town?"

"What? No, of course not." Ozzie shook his head in frustration at the reporter's lack of comprehension. "I need everything as boring and routine as possible and guys sneaking out to meet up with girls would only add to my stress and maybe put other people at risk. This is deadly serious, Danielle. These are really brutal people. They kill for business and pleasure—anyone—a whole team if they have too."

The gravity of Stark's voice seemed to finally make an impression on Danielle and she nodded her head cooperatively. "Okay. Coffee tomorrow at 11 AM if nothing happens." She pointed at Ozzie's eyes with two fingers.

"Yeah, you got my word on that." Ozzie turned and left the room, rubbing his head with both hands.

* * *

Danielle turned and went back to the press box. She would

go back to her hotel after the game and simply file her story. She would talk to David much later. Of course she had only been guessing at most of the facts in her imaginary cover-up story but the magnitude of concern in Ozzie's voice let her know she had not been that far from the truth and, in fact, may be pretty darn close to accurate. The Russian mob? That was very bad indeed.

Chapter 34

"OK, fellas, good game out there," began McCroy. "A big win at a good time. We needed that. You all played great. You played for each other and that's usually when good things happen. Don't get too crazy tonight if you're going out. I know there's no curfew and tomorrow we are hanging around town, but we don't need a repeat of New York and I really want us to get on a roll. So, stay focused on hockey and let all the other stuff go."

Ozzie listened to the coach patiently, knowing tonight was likely going to be very crazy indeed. Maybe even deadly. As GM Hellan strolled around the corner, Stark intercepted him. "Sir, you need to come and talk with me, now."

The two men went over to a meeting room, away from the main dressing room doors, and began a very animated discussion. Within minutes, Stark and Hellan were joined by Eddie Watkins, the Red Wing's senior security official and a few plain-clothes detectives from Miami's organized crime division.

Ozzie began the discussion. "So, it sounds like a heavyweight wise guy from the Odessa crime family flew into town three days ago. We think he's here to go after Sawyer because of what happened in New York. They've likely pieced together what the kid saw and that he can identify their boss as Mike Denman's murderer and who knows what else. This is a massive threat to their organization and makes Riley a dangerous loose end that needs to be, well, eliminated. At worst, he could bring down their whole operation and, at best, maybe the distraction of Alexi's arrest and trial would just weaken the organization enough so that other crime syndicates could move on their turf. Neither option is good for Odessa. Regardless, Sawyer is in a very bad place right now. About the only thing I know is we might be able to use this intel to draw them out and if we can take the assassin down, then we can tie him to Tsarnov and make a major move against the whole group. And, in the process, get Sawyer his life back. Otherwise, he'll be looking over his shoulder forever and eventually they will get him."

"Oh shit! We need to lock the team down immediately. Get everyone back to the hotel and we're flying out of here tomorrow morning," responded Hellan desperately.

"With all due respect, sir, as I discussed with your security team, that's the worst thing you could do. If Odessa suspects we know too much about Sawyer, it significantly elevates the threat level and maybe pushes them to do something far more extreme and more people get hurt—or killed. Right now, they're focused on Sawyer. They don't want any further complications or scrutiny than getting rid of the immediate threat. We need to keep it contained to that and not escalate the severity of the situation higher."

"Oh my God," moaned the GM. "This can't be happening."

"Sir, believe me, this threat is real. It happened in Russia. An entire hockey team was wiped out in Minsk. Airplane sabotaged and blown out of the sky due to mob retaliation. There were two ex-NHL guys on that plane and a coach. These syndicates run multi-billion dollar enterprises and, for them, life and death is inconsequential. So, we need to play along and be ready to respond when they make a move—which could be tonight. I've spoken with Sunrise PD detectives and they're going to give us a stand-in for Sawyer to go out with the guys tonight, just like always. If anything happens, he's armed and trained to draw out the perps and take them down with the help of a large undercover force. We don't know how many hitters there are—likely only one or two. The only logical place for this kind of assassination would be the nightclub—Pearlman's. They would try to make it look like a random gang or drug beef that caught up a few people like Sawyer as collateral damage."

"What? You think we're sending players into harm's way for some guy to take shots at them? No way. We shut down everything," Hellan shrieked, his face turning crimson at the absurd plan devised by Ozzie and his own security team. "Eddie, you don't agree with this nonsense do you?"

The team security lead nodded his head. "Dave, with all due respect, our boys are in as much danger right now walking across the street as they will be in this nightclub, given the circumstances. This plan gives us control. It's not as crazy as it sounds."

Ozzie, seeing submission in Hellan's face responded quickly while momentum for the plan appeared to be growing. "Mr. Hellan, tell your team we'll be imbedding guys with them, even tell them what we're doing, but do not change your routine here too dramatically or things could get very dangerous."

Dave looked over at McCroy, who stood silently staring at the floor, dumbstruck by the thought of what he would have to tell his players.

"I'm not sure I can even allow this without Mr. Layton's approval. These are his guys. It's his team," responded the overwhelmed GM. What are the legal and financial ramifications to the team if something goes wrong? The lawsuits. Everything. I can't do this."

"Sir, you don't have an option anymore," Stark shot back, taking special note to emphasize his next point dramatically. "A major crime organization sent a hit man down here to do something, and he will do something—soon. This may be our only and best shot to turn the tables on them and stop everything in its tracks while his plan is still small and concentrated. Please, we know what we're doing. We have to deal with this while it's at this stage or the risk quotient goes way up."

"Detective! I've got over 140 million dollars-worth of hockey players sitting 60 feet away and you want me to send them into a shooting gallery. That's knowing what you're doing?" Hellan glared at the New York detective.

Silence for a few minutes. No one spoke. But it was becoming clear Ozzie's plan was taking hold. Finally, Hellan spoke again. "I'll go call Mr. Layton. Mike, talk to the team with Eddie. Each guy is free to do what he wants and they don't have to go out tonight. Make that abundantly clear. Everybody pray this works."

"We're all in this with you, Dave, don't forget that. I'll talk to the guys now," stated McCroy as he turned to leave. "God help us when the media gets hold of this story."

* * *

McCroy, followed by the burly security chief, went back to the dressing room and asked the media for a few minutes of private time with his players. The few writers travelling with the team were a bit taken aback at the suddenness of their banishment—especially after a 7–2 win—but it had happened before, so was not that big a deal, though it certainly seemed a departure from the contented, caring coach they had listened to just minutes before.

"Gather 'round, guys," he began, eyes faced downward to the

floor. "We need to have a very important talk and I want you to do whatever you think is best for you this evening."

The boisterous banter that had reverberated around the dressing room minutes earlier took on a more sober tone with the coach's first comments and then died out into complete silence.

* * *

Bzzzzz. Bzzzzzz.

Valeri Voyov felt the vibrations and heard the muted buzzing of his cell phone as he sat listening to the incredible story being divulged to the players for the first time. He wanted to just sit and listen. He did not want to see the message and certainly not the messenger. But, it would not stop. Finally, he reached in his pocket and stared at the screen in horror.

UNKNOWN: Ava says hi, and wants to know what you guys are doing later tonight? Big win. Good for you. Are you going to a club? Which one? She is anxious of course because she worries so much about you and I know you are worried about her, as you should be. So many bad things happening in Russia these days."

Voyov felt a wave of revulsion sweep over him and a chill moved through his body. What should he do? What could he do? He decided not to answer the text. Maybe if he just ignored it, he could say he had not received it.

Bzzzzz. Bzzzzz.

Valeri could not help but read the message. He knew he had no choice.

UNKNOWN: My good friend Anya is heading to your family's house in Russia right now with a present for your mom and dad. They will both be taken care of soon. So, I wanted to let her know what you were doing tonight so she could tell Ava before she leaves. You should really tell your mom what you are doing. It will make her feel so much better.

Valeri slowly tapped the keys on his screen.

VALERI: We are going to club. Pearlman's. Everyone going.
Bzzzzz.
UNKNOWN: You sure everyone going?
VALERI: One guy, Sawyer back to hotel. Not feel good.
Bzzzzz.

UNKNOWN: Have nice night, be careful, Florida is crazy what with all the terrorists, gangs and shit. Your mom very happy to hear you having fun and doing well. Enjoy night.

"Hey what's up? You're not listening, man," whispered Eric Richards, Valeri's linemate.

"Yeah, yeah, just texting my mom to let her know how the game was and that I'm okay. She worries a lot. I have to text her after every game."

"Now that's being a good son," smirked Richards.

"You don't know the half of it, Eric," Valeri stated in a quiet tone as he stared toward McCroy with a forlorn look on his face. What had he just done?

* * *

The lights, loud music, energy and chaos of Miami's hottest nightclub on a Saturday night was exhilarating. Porsches, Rolls, Bentleys and Benzes quietly rolled by the unassuming front entry, dropping off their high-value cargo of sports and entertainment celebrities, business men, high rollers and drug lords, complemented by an endless array of beautiful women in evening garb that left little to the imagination. It was the biblical equivalent of Sodom and Gomorrah, and also the hottest place to party in south Florida.

Three black limos pulled up to the valet station and, with a boisterous outburst, Hilton and David piled out of the huge car at the back of the procession, accompanied by six other teammates. Their first glimpse of the club, with its flashing pink neon rippling across a Mediterranean-style flat-roofed building, was followed by ear to ear grins. Other limos followed delivering their player payload to the Red Wings' muster point, along with some management and security personnel.

"Boy, this is gonna be fun," Hilts howled with delight.

"Okay, everybody, we go to the back door and they already have a place for us. Stay together and keep your wits about you," came a stern reminder from Security Chief, Eddie Watkins. "Do not wander from our assigned area and there's no going into backrooms with girls or card games in private dens or anything else. We stay close together tonight."

The excited players nodded and followed their security chief past a long line of regulars waiting at the main entry and a larger group of no-hopers behind them who would likely never get in.

The Red Wings were quickly processed and ID's examined by the club concierge and then they were escorted into a seductively lit VIP area of the club by four hostesses with world-class supermodel credentials, accentuated by minimalist club uniforms.

"Wow, if those are the hostesses, I can't wait to see the main attractions," squealed Hilts, clenching his fists and eyes in blissful glee.

David nodded, but was a lot more interested in everything going on around them including throngs of writhing bodies, crazy glow sticks and lots of special effects. He also noted the two closest emergency exits, barely visible from the location where they would be sitting. That might be important information later in the evening.

"Okay, guys, this is Pearlman's most exclusive VIP club section and our Floor Manager, Marco saved it especially for you. You have an open tab on him and everyone here is at your service, if ya know what I mean," instructed a statuesque brunette with a southern Georgia accent. "We just love hockey players here, so I'm sure the girls are gonna be extra friendly tonight. Enjoy everything Pearlman's has to offer. If you wanna gamble, let me or any of the girls know and we'll take care of everything. Tonight boys, is all about you."

"This place is awesome," yelled Hilts into David's ear.

"Jesus, Hilts, settle down. There could be a guy in here looking to take one of us out and you think it's awesome? Seriously?"

"C'mon, Stone, get your head out of your ass. You honestly think some bogey-man is gonna jump out of the crowd and take a shot at a professional hockey team surrounded by security? This is all fucking crazy. That cop. The big lecture. I'm basically in heaven and if you think I'm letting some overblown snow job overshadow my soon-to-be-overgrown blow job…well that just ain't gonna happen. Bring on the girls and the booze."

"You really are impossible." David shook his head.

"Hey, gorgeous. Can I get you something?"

"Yeah, how about a cab back to my hotel," David stammered as he turned and looked into the face of a lovely blonde hostess who had sidled up beside him.

"No, no, no," she cooed innocently, placing a slender finger on his lips. "I'm here to make this a night you'll never forget. So, what can I do for you?"

Her hands floated over David's face and down the side of his neck. Then, she slowly moved the agitated hockey player toward a massive cushioned lounge chair and perched herself on his lap while angling the top of her head up under his chin.

* * *

Danielle was finishing her game story at a quiet food court in the arena's main concourse. It had been a great game for Detroit, an easy 7–2 win.

The speed with which Sawyer and Stone moved the puck in the Panther's zone was remarkably efficient. Like two acrobats, they whizzed through space and time in perfect synchronization, culminating in breathtaking feats that defied reality. Add in Darcy Hilton's more down-to-earth crashing and banging of everything that moved in the corners and along the boards, and you had the emergence of a bona-fide NHL line that accounted for three goals and five assists between them.

She slowly read her last line and then moved in to edit some text. It had been almost three hours since the game ended and the arena was completely empty. She wished she could call David and let him know she was in town, but Ozzie had been adamant that she should not interfere with the team right now. She felt scared but was not really sure why. Was it that David was in danger? The team? Her? Or, was it just knowing you didn't have a clue what could happen and when? She began rereading her story one last time before sending it in when the sound of large metal doors crashing in the concourse caught her attention.

What or who was that? She glimpsed down the concourse and saw two men leaving with a well-dressed young man she believed was Riley Sawyer. But wasn't Riley out with the team? Why was he alone in a dark arena leaving long after the game? And, where was he going? Who were those men? Police? Where was Ozzie?

He lied to me, she thought.

"That sleazy, New York hustler lied to me," she whispered

angrily under her breath.

Something was going on and he did not want to tell me, so he made up a story about the club and a shooter and now something else was up and he just wanted me out of the way. Well, not so fast asshole, she thought.

Danielle jumped up and quickly exited the arena through a set of side doors from where she could watch the trio. They walked, virtually arm-in-arm, toward a black Cadillac SUV parked in the visiting team stalls. As Riley climbed in, the two men stood outside and looked carefully into the darkness for hints of anything out of the ordinary, hands mounted on their hips. They were obviously a professional security detail, given their actions and the vehicle they were driving.

Well, one thing for sure, they were certainly taking extra precautions, she thought. Maybe I'll just tag along and see where they go. Likely heading to the club, but why so late?

She flagged down one of the cabs still sitting outside the arena and asked him to follow the black SUV as it headed past them and left the parking lot. The cab did a hard right turn and followed the slow-moving vehicle down Ford Road.

"Should I phone David? No, I better not." Danielle questioned herself in the darkness. *I've really got to stop talking to myself,* she thought as she looked up and noticed the cabbie staring at her in his rear view mirror. She smiled back at him. "Sorry, I've got a lot on my mind tonight. Just rambling, you can ignore me."

The dark SUV maneuvered in and out of traffic, eventually turning up Hanson Drive to the Excelsior Hotel. It disappeared through a large, steel garage door. The cabbie pulled over into the carriageway in front of the hotel, but far enough away to not elicit a scathing rebuke from the night Bell Captain.

"Okay, lady, that's as far as I can go. $23.57, please. And, I prefer cash. You can have it for $20 if you pay cash."

"Yeah, no problem. Here's $25. Thanks for the ride."

Danielle jumped out of the cab. Riley had just gone back to the hotel. No club? No teammates? It seemed like odd behaviour when Ozzie had told her everyone would be doing everything just the same as always. Nothing would be changing. Yet this was clearly a change. Danielle was getting madder by the minute as she thought about Ozzie's manipulation of the truth.

Fine, she thought. *I can't talk to David. Maybe I'll go straight to the source and see if he has anything to say. He's alone anyway and everyone else is at the club, so why not see what Sawyer has to say about the incredible events in New York.*

* * *

"Listen, sweetheart, I don't get off until 2 AM, so I can't pick you up until at least 2:30 AM," moaned a dishevelled bellman in the employee locker room. "No, I can't take off early. We're so busy and, let's face it, I can't afford to lose this job. We've got some pro hockey team here and its Saturday. For sure, they'll fire my ass if I leave."

As Chris Toller tried to appease his new girlfriend about the timing of their late night rendezvous, Andriy moved past him to the back of the room, bumping him as he went. The young man dropped the phone from his ear.

"Hey, big man, easy. How about a little respect? Sheesh." He put the phone back to his ear and began chatting again.

Andriy quietly strode through the change room, checking the shower area, locker room and toilets to ensure no one else was around. When he was completely sure they were alone, he locked the only access door and headed back to the area where Chris's telephone call was still in rapid-fire conversation. He waited.

"Okay, 2:45 AM, baby. I'll pick you up outside the house. I don't want your old man goin all crazy on me. So come out to the street, then we're off to my place for a night of hot lovin'. Alright, love you too. See you later, sweet thing."

A wide smile full of beautiful white teeth gave away the happiness and excitement Chris was feeling about his plans for later. "This is gonna be great." He clicked the button on his cell phone and turned toward the locker room's front door. He was stunned to see Andriy, and the long-barreled pistol in his hand. "Hey! What the—"

A muffled spit and a red dot in the young man's forehead would be the reality of his night. A life snuffed out brutally just for being in the wrong place at the wrong time. As Toller's body fell to the floor, Andriy leaped like a panther and stuffed his lifeless corpse into a full-sized locker, carefully removing his ID card, key ring, hotel access card and the top of his uniform before any blood spilled that far. A generic combination lock was affixed to the locker and its tungsten alloy finish ensured it would be a very long time until anyone had the notion or the tools to open its metal door.

Andriy had already purchased identical black pants to the ones staff wore, but he needed the rest of the uniform to blend in. While this one may not have been a perfect fit, it was serviceable and would pass unnoticed for the late night shift. He unlocked the door. The great thing about 1:22 AM at a hotel is that only a skeleton staff is around and no one really comes into the locker room until shift change at 6 AM. This would give him lots of time.

Andriy took out a small scalpel and cut around the picture of the dead youth on the hotel ID card, replacing it with his own black and white picture, just like every other staff member. He took out a pocket-sized laminator and quickly patched the photo almost flawlessly. The first part of his plan had gone smoothly. No loose ends, unless you counted a soon-to-be-very-distraught girlfriend that was not going out tonight. Oh well, her dad would be happy.

Andriy straightened his uniform and stuffed two small concussion grenades in the deep pockets of his pants, a pistol in his back belt and another holstered by his armpit with a silencer. Time to go and service one very special guest.

* * *

David was finding the noise and chaos of the club to be a bit much this evening. Knowing that his friend and teammate might be in danger certainly took a lot of the fun out of the evening, evidenced by the fact he had spurned some fairly aggressive advances from not only scantily clad dancers, but an actual Sports Illustrated swimsuit model with a penchant for hockey players.

David screamed, trying to elevate his voice above the pulsating synthesized club music. "Hilts, I think I'm gonna call it a night. This just isn't working for me. I'm tired and I just feel weird knowing there are cops around and maybe a mob guy and, well, who knows? It's all too strange. I'm gonna head back to the hotel and call Danielle."

"Are you nuts, Stone? I feel like James Bond here. Bad guys. Broads. Booze. And, at any moment, maybe there's a chance for me to be the hero. Stick around. Grow a pair."

"Hilts—you're an idiot. I hope they miss the fake Sawyer and shoot you. See you in the morning."

Hilton laughed and buried his head deep in the breasts of a table dancer that was currently at his beck and call. He then pulled out his face and buried it again while she laughed and writhed away on top of him.

David took a quick look at the rest of his preoccupied teammates and headed for the club entrance and a limousine back to the hotel. *God, it's only 1:15 AM,* he thought as he attempted to find the team driver who was supposed to be sitting in the front foyer. *I guess I really am a wimp.*

* * *

"Hi there. I was asked to come by Riley Sawyer's room tonight," Danielle gushed, flashing her long legs and flicking her blond hair at the night desk attendant. "But, I don't know what room he's in. Could you give me his room number, please? I'd really appreciate it."

"Uh, sorry, ma'am, but we're not allowed to give out any room or guest information to anyone and we have a special notice to be especially careful about giving out Red Wing player information. I'm very sorry."

"Oh no, you don't understand, I'm a reporter with the Detroit Free Press and I have a post-game interview to do with him. It's all been set up. I just did not get his room number and my cell phone is dead or I'd call him."

With that, Danielle pulled out her press credentials, which were completely legitimate, and created a compelling case for the young desk attendant to deal with.

He was growing more stressed by the minute, given the tenacity of the reporter and his desire to help her out. "Listen, I'd love to help, but when we get these special notices, it could mean my job. I really can't give you that number. What I could do is check with my manager and maybe call the room and have Mr. Sawyer call the front desk and give you the room number himself. Would that work?"

"Sure," beamed a happy Danielle. "What the heck? Let's see how that goes." Her sentiments were real because she figured Riley would have no issue with a little company right now and would maybe even talk to her. They knew each other pretty well and, other than it was very late, there was nothing unusual about her trying to get a story.

"Great. Just wait a minute while I call the room and see if he's there. I did not see any of them come in," mused the obliging attendant as he leaned over to dial the room.

Within a minute he was handing the telephone over to Danielle.

"Hello," she said.

"Danielle? What the hell are you doing here at 1 AM in the morning—in Miami? I didn't see you with any of the press guys."

"No," she stammered. "Well, it's a little embarrassing, but I asked my boss if I could come down and maybe spend a few days with you guys and well, see David for a bit. You guys have been on the road for a long time. Is he up there?"

"Seriously?" laughed Riley. "You came to hang with Stone? C'mon, that is so not you. What's going on? You're digging for something, and trust me, I'm not talking. Not here. Not now. No way. Good night."

"Riley, I'm serious. I just wanted to quietly watch you guys play tonight and not be a reporter for once. Try out this whole hockey fan thing. Might give me a new perspective and help my writing in the future. Had to pay my own airfare to boot."

"Wow, that's great. Anyway, David's not here, he's at Pearlman's with the rest of the team, or most of them, anyway."

"And you're a choir boy and just came home to go to bed?" questioned Danielle.

"Here we go," moaned Riley. "I'm taking the fifth. My right to remain silent on the grounds whatever I say will most certainly come back to bite me in the ass."

"Well, now you're way off base. That's legalese. I'm a reporter and, quite frankly, I don't care why you're not at the club—though it is odd. Anyway, can I come up or not? Stop being a weirdo."

"Sure. We're in suite P114. The P is for penthouse."

"OOOOOOH, that's so very impressive. I thought it was for punk—obnoxious punk at that," laughed Danielle. "See you in a minute."

"We've got some security posted so don't get freaked out and I'll let them know you're coming."

Danielle returned the telephone to the attendant. "Thank you, my friend," she said. "Everything is perfect and you still have your job. I guess that's a win-win all the way around."

With that, she turned from the reception desk and walked toward a bank of gold-encrusted elevators and up to suite P114.

* * *

Andriy walked through the grand foyer of the Excelsior Hotel and, for a moment, was very impressed by how beautiful it was, with its magnificent lighting and chandeliers glowing. His goal now, however, was to get the room number for one Riley Sawyer. He knew that was going to be difficult, but he had two options: see if there was anything moving through food services or try and get it from the reception computers.

He walked into the kitchen, which was virtually deserted except for a disinterested-looking cook or busboy or something sitting by a table, thumbing through People magazine.

"Uh, excuse me, I just started and was told room services were booked through here. A guy from the professional hockey team flagged me down in the hall and asked if I could get him some champagne—you know, for him and a friend. A really good-looking friend." Andriy raised his eyebrows up and the two men laughed at the obvious inference of the comment.

"Sorry, man, I just cook. But Miranda is the room service concierge; she can help you out." With that, he pointed to a small room down the hall. "By the way, you really should talk to them about that jacket—not exactly a great fit, if ya know what I mean. Day manager would kill you if he saw that."

"Yeah, it's a bit tight but it's the one they gave me. Thanks for your help." Andriy moved quickly down the corridor toward a small office where Miranda was sitting and staring at her computer screen. She was playing solitaire. He quietly approached the door and knocked gently so as not to startle her.

"Yes," came a shrill response. "Come in."

Andriy opened the door and peered in like a subservient immigrant working at his first job in a strange country. "Good evening Miss Miranda. I am new here and a special guest-a Mr. Sawyer-asked me to order him a bottle of champagne, for him and his lady friend. I said I was not sure if I could, but he was very insistent and so I said I would try. Can you make the order for him and I can take it up?"

"Oh, those high-maintenance, fucking hockey players. Probably got some hooker up there. Well, I don't have their room numbers here and the pro team's numbers are restricted to the front desk. Let me call reception and see what it is—give me a minute—uh, what's your name?"

"Arlo, my name is Arlo Paschuk." He flashed the doctored ID card at her from 15 feet away, knowing there was no way she could see anything but maybe his picture. She nodded. "I will just wait outside while you call." Andriy stepped back outside the door.

After a few minutes on the telephone, she turned and looked at Andriy through the large window. Andriy's eyes squinted. Would he have to kill this lady and abort his mission? This seemed to be taking an exceptionally long time. He slowly slid his hand around to the back of his belt and gripped the pistol stock. He glanced over his shoulder almost imperceptibly to where the other kitchen attendant had been sitting. The area was empty now. Andriy's heart raced for the first time since he had started his mission. He did not want to kill this woman and, worse, he had nowhere to put her body. He might have to go in a different direction.

Then, as his heart rate spiked, Miranda smiled and waved at him to come back in.

Andriy moved slowly, staying in his immigrant character and opened the door a crack. "Yes, Miss Miranda," he stammered, careful to keep his eyes looking downward.

"Okay, so they said we are not supposed to do this, but, yeah, they'll make up a bottle and ice bucket for you in the lounge and you can pick it up there and take it upstairs. By the way, they were really impressed that you are going the extra mile for our guests. Way to go, suck-up. Make it harder for the rest of us." Miranda laughed and shooed him away.

"But, Miss, where am I taking this?"

"Oh, right. He's in P114. That's the Penthouse level. You need card access to get up there. Have you ever been to the penthouses before?"

"Uh, I don't think so."

"Well, your ID card has a magnetic strip and, if you're authorized, it will take you there once you slide it through the card reader in the elevator. If you're not authorized, they may need someone else to take it up. Good luck."

Andriy nodded and backed out again. "Thank you. I will check my card."

"Most of them work, so yours should too," Miranda concluded.

Great, thought Andriy. *Now I have to go and test this stupid card. Of course that floor would be secured.* How could he have not thought about that? He hoped his key card would work.

* * *

David was standing alone outside the club waiting for a limousine to take him back to the hotel. He wondered how Riley was handling all of this security stuff back at their room. *I should really call Danielle when I get back to the hotel,* he thought. *I sure do miss her. God, we've been on the road for a long time.*

The limo driver walked up to David. "Sorry, mate, just had to visit the loo. I'll go get the car and we'll be on our way. Just be a minute."

"Thanks," said David wearily. He could hardly wait to get back to the hotel.

Chapter 35

Darcy walked over to the undercover detective standing in as Riley Sawyer. He slung his giant arm around the guy's shoulder, causing him to recoil in shock and then clench his jaw in anger. "So, you're supposed to be the great Riley Sawyer," Hilts deadpanned, in his best Frank Columbo impersonation, unaware of his terrible judgement under the circumstances.

"Easy, friend. I don't cope well with surprises when I'm working. Normally, I would have busted your face for a move like that."

"Then you're definitely not Sawyer—he's a pussy. Big name and little game, if you know what I mean. Do you really think someone would take a shot at him—here?"

"Listen, buddy, I gotta pay attention to what's going on around us, so why don't you just head back to the girls. They seem to really like you and I'm working. I don't mean any disrespect. But this is deadly serious stuff for me—us."

"Yeah, I get it. I just wish something would happen already if it's going too. I'm getting kind of bored."

The girly pop tune ended and on came the dance-crazy song, Timber, a sure-fire, country-pop hybrid that always got the sexiest girls dancing and the men reaching into their pockets for more $20s. Hilts was no exception and, with the new tune, he started shimmying back toward his table and his gorgeous date, who seemed absolutely lost without him—as in losing money without him in his chair. She waved and Hilts began swinging his hips as he moved back to sit down.

At first, it was hard to tell if the staccato pops that filled the room were part of the techno soundtrack booming from the audio system but, within seconds, a multitude of screams let Hilts know he'd better hit the floor. Gunfire erupted from the right side of the room and the wall, the one behind his chair, started to fill with bullet holes.

Oh fuck, he thought as he dived down on the floor with his dancer friend shrieking at the top of her lungs. He began crawling toward a booth where another teammate had already taken cover.

* * *

Damian Dirk, Miami Metro's imbedded double for Riley Sawyer, pulled out his standard issue, Glock 22 and tried to locate the source of the shots from behind some staging. But, in the darkness punctuated by wild strobe lights and dry ice haze, it was almost impossible. Then a barrel flash. He felt the burn of a round striking the outside of his arm and dived back down behind a table. Crashing almost immediately beside him was Ozzie Stark, pistol drawn and ready for action.

"Stay down!" Ozzie barked breathlessly. "They think you're Sawyer!"

The shots seemed to be moving away from them, which seemed wrong for the situation, but that was good, thought Ozzie. It meant the shooters were moving. But, how many were there? It felt like two.

Ozzie jumped up and raced toward the gunshots that were still hailing down from the opposite end of the room. He tripped over cowering players and half-naked girls and then suddenly slipped in a blood pool. Unless latino gangsters had taken over the hockey world, the body didn't belong to a Red Wing. He kept moving.

Then, for an instant, he saw the shooters as a white spot light lit up their brazen attack, illuminating them and their weaponry for a split second. Ozzie instinctively fired at the moving torsos, hitting one in the side. The shooting subsided for a moment and then a final machine gun burst high and across the room ended the deadly assault. Ozzie waited, but all he heard were the wails and pandemonium in the club.

The shooters had likely run out of the building. There must have been a rear exit by their position. Ozzie jumped over the remaining tables and scurried toward the darkened area where he had last seen the would-be assassins. Dirk was right behind him. Police, security and EMT's had filled the club and were rushing people out through its front entry toward cover and waiting ambulances.

Ozzie saw a half-opened service door and wondered how safe it would be to exit into the night. Were they waiting for him? It could be a death sentence. What the hell, his assassins were getting away. "I'm going out!" he screamed at Damian. "Get back-up and then follow me."

He jumped and rolled through the back door and when he did he could see in the night two men running awkwardly down the narrow alley. He started firing at the shadows, hoping to at least take one out. In the dull light he thought he saw one fall. The other turned and fired and then ran the opposite direction down another side-street.

Ozzie leaped back to his feet and assuming a full combat position began running at full speed toward the prone body. But, as he got closer, he noticed the perp on the ground was moving so he slowed down and moved toward a dumpster just as a torrent of gunshots rose from the pavement spraying the narrow street.

"Shit." He waited and when the shots slowed he ducked out and fired again.

The form on the ground was dragging itself deeper into the darkness. He could just make out a silhouetted shape. Ozzie aimed his gun and fired three shots precisely at the darkest part of the mass. It went limp. With that, he stalked the final 30 yards, feeling confident whomever it was had been successfully neutralized.

The assassination did not seem right to him. He knew the second guy was gone; they'd likely never find him. But, why had they not split up? Very odd. And the shots at his fake Sawyer had been far too random for a professional hit team.

Soon, he was standing over the body of a 25 or 26-year-old male with a dark balaclava and an automatic machine pistol. Definitely high-end, military-grade ordinance. He was dead to be sure. Multiple bullet holes in his torso and one in the head. Stark reached down and pulled off his face mask. The guy looked Mediterranean, but more like a gang kid, not a professional hitman.

"What the fuck?" he muttered to himself, confused.

Damian and four other uniforms were sprinting down the dark alley, screaming at the person standing with the gun to get on his knees.

"Hey, guys, it's me," Ozzie yelled as he raised his hands. Still Stark stared at the body, trying to process who this was. He could not believe this was what it seemed.

"Who's the shooter, Ozzie?" Damian asked trying to catch his breath.

"Well, he's definitely one of our shooters, but him nor his

accomplice shot, acted or tried to escape like a pro. That was perhaps the worst targeted hit ever. Who got shot inside?"

"I don't know. We left, but I'll radio the team lead."

Ozzie bent down and moved up the sleeves on the kid's arm. They were etched with tattoos of gang affiliations.

This guy was an actor. A decoy ordered to shoot up the club and then run. This was not a professional. If it had been, the attack would have been more controlled and focused directly on the fake Sawyer.

The real assassin, was he still out there? Ozzie began to get a sick feeling in his stomach. He turned and stared up at Damian. "So, how many and who were they?"

"Looks like three gang bangers. Bad dudes for sure. One's dead, the others are serious, but likely not going to die. Doesn't appear to be anyone else. Looks like a gang beef."

"No way, man. It's a set up. The real crime's about to take place somewhere else. They wanted us tied up here. Oh fuck—the hotel. He's going to hit the hotel." Ozzie started running back toward the club, screaming over his shoulder, "Get SWAT to the Excelsior Hotel fast and get me a car!"

Chapter 36

David paid the cab and double-skipped the stairs toward the main hotel entry.

"Good evening, sir. Heard you guys had a great game tonight," a pleasant doorman beamed as he doffed his cap and pulled open the large glass door for his high-profile guest.

"Yeah, it was a good one for us, thanks." David reached into his pocket and handed the man a fiver as he strode through the door and headed to the elevators. He pushed the button.

Come on, he thought. He was so stressed and tired and really just needed some sleep to feel like himself again. He looked down at his watch; it read 2:37 AM. At that moment the doors opened and a young couple bolted out, almost knocking him over.

"Hey, sorry dude. I might have had a bit too much to—"

"Save it, pal," David shot back and pressed the close button on the doors.

Oh, I'm going to sleep so good tonight, he thought. It appeared all the hype over the mobsters and hit men had been a bust. "Nothing to see here, folks," he whispered to himself as the doors opened again and he walked down the hall toward his suite. The one he shared with Riley Sawyer that now appeared to have a guard out front.

"Hey," David nodded at the barrel-chested security officer standing by his door.

The mountain of a man subtly nodded back and grinned at David. "You might want to check before you bust in there, man. Some pretty blonde piece just showed up. Just giving you a heads up."

"Huh," replied David. Surely Sawyer hadn't ordered a hooker. Not in their suite. And not while everyone was out trying to save his sorry ass. Not even he could be that dense, could he? David swung the door open and his eyes widened in shock. "Danielle. What are you doing here?"

Sitting on the large luxurious sofa was a second security officer, a sprawled out Riley Sawyer and a rather cozy-looking Danielle with a very large glass of red Chardonnay.

"David!" she screamed. "Surprise! I'm being a fan."

"Yeah, I can see that, but what are you doing in our room? With Riley."

"Whoa, cowboy. We're just talking—off the record—right? She told me she came here to see you, though for the life of me, I can't understand why."

Danielle jumped up and ran towards David, who was slowly closing the door behind him.

"I wanted to see what it was like to just be a fan and watch one of your games, so here I am. Oh, and I was supposed to cover the game too, but that was easy. You guys played awesome. I was going to ask Riley some questions but he said, 'No way—I'm not talking to you about anything.' So we've just been sitting here having a little party of our own with a few drinks and waiting for you to get home. How was the club? Lots of pretty ladies, I imagine," she whispered in his ear as she hugged her beau.

"Well, it was very loud and pretty boring, actually. Hilts is in heaven, of course—thinks he's James Bond or something, and the place is full of cops and then—nothing. Not a thing happened. Just really boring, so I came back. I'm tired anyway and just wanted to get to bed."

"Ooh, that sounds great," smiled Danielle as she began nibbling his ear.

The security guy and Riley couldn't help but grin at the slightly inebriated reporter draped all over David. They even looked a bit envious.

"So, what have you heard about the team, my dear," David began, "given that you travelled a few thousand miles to get here. Riley what does she know?"

"Oh, lighten up, I already talked to Stark and got the general down low on the big bad mobster chasing Riley. Looks like his gut feeling was a bit off. So don't worry, there's no secrets here among us friends. I'm not here to spill the beans on your little misadventure—yet. But, I do have dibs on whatever does happen. That's my deal with Stark, so I really don't even need you guys to comment anymore. Eventually, it will be my byline under this story. Woohoo!"

"Thank God. Actually, we have an off-day tomorrow, so maybe the timing of your fan trip is pretty darn good," grinned

David as he strengthened his grasp of the beautiful reporter. "But, before we have too much to drink, why don't we just calmly go to a room. Hilt's can sleep out here tonight. Riley you don't mind, do you?"

"No way, bro. Good on you."

"And, Mr. Security guy, you're okay too, right?" Danielle nodded.

"Yes, ma'am. I'm just fine."

"Okay then. I think we'll exit stage right," smiled David as he and Danielle, in full embrace, awkwardly stumbled through the foyer and past the couch.

* * *

The elevator doors opened and a tall, muscular hotel server with a bright new Red Wing jersey slung over his arm slowly pushed his cart and a crisp bottle of champagne on ice toward room P114.

He moved slowly, with his head mostly down but at times he would steal glances of the very empty hallways around him. He could see the large security guard down the hall ahead of him. He did not want to startle the behemoth – not yet anyway.

The agent noticed the server moving toward his position but didn't really think much of it. He appeared tired and was likely just sick of waiting on the decadent desires of wealthy idiots at these ungodly hours. Yet, the agent maintained a steady bead on the approaching cart and moved his hand toward his holstered hip pistol.

What was that he had on his arm? It appeared to be a Red Wings jersey. Seriously? This hack was going to try and score an autograph when he made his delivery. Well, you had to admire his chutzpah.

* * *

The ring of the security agent's telephone broke David and Danielle's tender, if somewhat awkward, reunion as everyone stopped in mid-sentence to see what was up.

"Yes? No, we're fine here. Nothing happening. Everything's quiet. One of the other guys just got home and he has a friend with him, so things are actually kind of funny. But I'll tell Jason to be extra vigilant outside." The agent spoke to the others. "Okay, you guys, there was a shooting at the nightclub. May have just been some gang stuff, but we really don't know. Stark thinks it could be a decoy for something bigger here at the hotel. So, you guys need to just stay calm until our reinforcements get here. I'm going to tell Jason outside to be on alert.

* * *

The server slowly looked up at the security man from about ten feet away with a big smile on his face. Jason stepped from his position and put up his arm. "Not so fast, man. What you got there?"

"Uhhh, Mr. Sawyer asked for some champagne to be delivered to him. I'm just bringing it up. And maybe I could get him to sign my jersey, no?"

The guard stared at the big man hunched over the cart. Something seemed off. Just then the door swung open and the second security officer stepped into the hall.

"There's been a shooting at the club, so we have to lock down—"

Automatic gunfire blasted from under the jersey, striking Jason in the head and killing him instantly.

Three other bullets hit the second agent in his bulletproof vest, leg and arm as he ducked behind his dead or dying associate. He reached for his gun but the withering blast from the machine pistol kept cutting into his appendages. He pushed the dead body towards the gunman and fell back into the room, slamming the door behind him. He was covered in blood.

"You guys get to cover. Call the desk. Call the cops. There's a killer outside. He shot Jason. Call 911. Now!" The injured agent screamed in terror as he fumbled for his gun to prepare for a limited counter-attack.

The stunned hockey players froze at the surreal situation and then all three turned and ran towards the furthest bedroom. There were phones in each room. Riley had his cell phone but the sheer terror he was dealing with made it impossible to hit the numbers as they awkwardly moved toward their hideaway.

"Riley, Danielle, quick, get into Abramov's room. It's the biggest and closest to the hallway. Move," David directed.

The two quickly changed direction and veered left into the room, past its heavy wooden door. Behind them they could hear loud banging and crashing on the main entry door as the bulky assassin tried to gain entry to finish his mission. Rapid gunshots sounded and then a thud came as the hit man crashed through the door with a military-like maneuver and fired two rounds into the flailing security agent lying on the ground.

As David quietly closed the bedroom door, there were two muzzle flashes from an elongated machine pistol and the final shriek of life from the agent. Riley, Danielle and David were now in for the fight of their life, quite literally.

* * *

Andriy's focus had been on dispatching the security detail first, which meant he had not seen where his primary prey had fled to in the oversized penthouse suite. The cavernous room had a multitude of doors and time was of the essence. He was pretty sure security would be up within two to three minutes and then he would be trapped. He had to move quickly.

He lumbered across the floor toward the doors that were closest to the sitting area and lunged at the first, crashing it to the floor. He burst in, commando style, and came up gun aimed and ready to kill whatever was in front of him. Nothing but silence. No sign of anyone. He clicked on the light and then ran to the suite's private bathroom and pushed open the door. Again, nothing.

"Shit," he mumbled to himself. He was wasting valuable time. He had to find Sawyer quickly.

* * *

David and Riley began pushing a massive double bed up against the door and looked for a way to jam it to increase the difficulty of it being breached. Danielle was praying quietly to herself and whispering in desperation to a hotel operator what was going on, begging them to hurry with security.

"So, you're telling me some guy busted into your room and is trying to kill you? With what?"

"Seriously, who cares? Get armed security up here now. He's

killed two people already and we're next so get them up here—now!"

"Ok, I'll see what I can do. Mercy me."

"Please, for the love of God, get someone up here."

David secured a sturdy couch behind the bed, which was wedged between the door and a load-bearing wall. It would not hold forever but it would certainly make entering the room through the door much more difficult. It may buy them enough time until help arrived. Next they needed a plan to fight back.

David grinned as he noticed four hockey sticks leaning against the doors of Abramov's walk-in closet. Pavel was one of those guys who never let his game sticks out of his sight. He was very superstitious about the tools of his trade and liked to work on them constantly, filing each to just the right blade width and tip shape. And, sure enough, there they were. He would often shoot paper wads into a garbage can and practice stick-handling moves in the dark to get a bit of extra touch before he went to bed at night. Now those sticks might truly become weapons of war and perhaps their only chance of salvation.

"Riley, grab a stick. Our only chance if he breaks through the door is to take out his eyes or break his shooting arm with the biggest match-penalty slash of your life. I sure wish Hilts was here right now. This is more his specialty. So, I don't know which one of us might get the shot but we need to make it count—swing hard and head high. Aim for the eyes. Try to blind him."

"What? How do I do that?"

"C'mon, you idiot, swing the blade tip first and aim for his eyes. The sheer pain will stun him for a second and maybe we can get another head or arm shot to disable him. We've got to stay away from that gun though. He looked big and he's probably used to pain, but we don't really have any other plan. Now shut up and be ready. Danielle, get down behind that couch. I don't think he wants to kill you."

At that moment, large chunks of door began splitting off and flying through the room as everyone hit the floor. The assassin had finally made his way to their room and he was about to come in—ready or not.

* * *

Andriy stood six feet away and blasted the heavy door with gun fire to weaken it and then took a run at it to finish the job. He hit the bullet-riddled, oak mass with such force that the whole building seemed to shake for an instant. His body recoiled from the massive blow, hurled backwards as the solid metal bed frame and couch wedge inside the room made the massive door's facia as solid as concrete. He grimaced at the pain in his shoulder. It was likely separated. He had not expected that and the shock shook his confidence momentarily.

Somewhat dazed, he thought, *Who the hell is in there? It should just be Sawyer. What the hell's behind that door?*

His attack time was approaching 90 seconds and he likely had only another two minutes, tops, before security and police flooded the suite. At that point, it would be a shoot-out and almost certain mission failure.

For the first time, Andriy considered that he may actually die trying to take out this little puke. But, no problem, that was his job. He was a good, no make that a great, soldier. He would not let Alexi down.

He began firing away again until the whole top third of the door was blown away, from which he could see the huge metal frame that stood between him and access to his prey. He emptied his clip into the frame, but it didn't weaken very much if at all. It appeared he would have to climb over the wreckage in front of him.

* * *

As, the firing subsided for a minute, David popped his head up from behind a chair

"Riley," he whispered, "look at me."

Sawyer's head popped up instantly, hockey stick clutched tightly in his hands and his eyes as wide as poker chips. "What?"

"Get ready. He can't move the blockade so he's got to bust though the clutter. That's going to be tough. Get ready to swing with all your might. He doesn't know what's waiting for him. Also, stay back from the door frame until you see him start to come through. He could shoot around it to kill anyone standing by his entry point.

Remember, you go for his eyes. Those are the easiest. I'll swing for the arms or the gun. Swing hard, buddy. It could be the difference between life and death."

Riley crawled back from the door frame and, in the dark silence, they waited and waited for what felt like an eternity. Then another burst of gunfire. A hail of bullets ripped more of the door apart and cut lines around its frame. Both players pulled way back and waited for the inevitable assault.

Danielle was sobbing and rushed over to David's side of the room. Just as she moved, a small metal canister flew over her head and exploded behind the couch where she had been. It was a concussion grenade and it portended the invasion that was about to take place. Fortunately, the grenade had hit and rolled to the back of the room, far from the front door, and settled behind a large, heavy, ornate lounge chair. The blast momentarily stunned everyone and their eardrums were pierced in pain, but other than a manageable bit of shock and disorientation there were no other real ramifications from the blast. The chair had taken the worst of that.

David prepared for battle and readied his weapon. The first thing through the doorway was the arm and machine pistol, spraying bullets everywhere around the room, but again focused toward the back, not on either side of the door.

The assassin's greatest miscalculation had been where his target would be. He must have thought Sawyer would be cowering at the rear of the room where the deck was. That was human nature; get as far away from the danger as possible. He had not expected to face any kind of physical obstacles upon entering the suite or in making the kill.

David swung his hockey stick straight down as hard as he could on the wrist of the shooter. He knew exactly where to land the blow to shatter the bone and disable the arm. It was the vulnerable area just above the thumb, where the protruding bone, joint and ligaments all converged. Any Saskatchewan hockey player worth his salt knew a few things about how to best hobble an opponent with a great wrist shot. There was a loud crack as the assassin's hand went limp and the gunfire stopped. The heavy machine pistol fell harmlessly to the floor behind the bed frame as a massive shriek of pain and then howls of Russian obscenities raged from the outside room.

* * *

Andriy could not believe the excruciating pain from his now destroyed wrist, and it was on his primary shooting hand. He fumbled to pull the other gun from the backside of his pants but it had been positioned for his shooting hand and was now out of reach. His blood boiled and the rage seethed. He was not about to be out-fought by some teenage punk.

He was finally able to clumsily reach around and extricate his other handgun from his back holster. He reset himself for attack and moved toward the bed frame, running at top speed to hit the hole with power like a fullback would do. He hit just above the frame and felt his shoulder give a bit more. The same shoulder that he had injured in his earlier assault. He winced in pain but felt the massive blockade of oak and metal give way. If he just pushed a bit harder it would break and he would be in.

He raised the gun in his non-shooting hand and looked through the frame to see where his target was. The pain in his wrist and shoulder was searing and tears flooded from his eyes in a natural response to his body being under such stress. But, he had to see who and what was in the room—even through the darkness and wisps of smoke from his concussion grenade.

* * *

Riley froze momentarily as the giant Russian's head popped through the door opening and the bedframe as he peered into the darkness. It was one of them. His tormentors. One of the murderous faces that had haunted him for months since that night in a New York alley. Fear gripped him for an instant and then pure anger and uncontrollable rage flooded through him like a mighty river and a massive shot of adrenaline surged like electricity into his arms.

"You son of a bitch!" Riley screamed as he swung the blade of his stick with all the force he could muster and landed a direct blow into the right eye of his attacker. "Take that cock sucker."

Riley felt a sudden rush of power and jubilation as he heard the anguished howl of pain and shrieking from his nemesis. He saw a stream of blood burst from the area in and around the assassin's eye.

At that same moment, David crashed his stick into the back of the killer's head, further incapacitating him. Then he took a swing at the other eye but missed as the killer, perhaps sensing an unexpected counter-attack from more than one person, covered his face and fired off shots indiscriminately.

With his head down, David grabbed the assassin and slammed his head into the sharp edge of the bedframe, knocking him into semi-consciousness while his other gun fell into the debris and disappeared from sight.

The injured assailant roiled in agony with his broken wrist and ravaged eyeball. He instinctively pulled into a shell as Riley crashed the hockey stick back into his head again, this time just above the ear.

"Danielle, Riley, quick! Let's get out of here! Follow me!" David grabbed Danielle's hand and guided her through the hole the killer had cleared in the bedframe and, with Riley in hot pursuit, the three bolted across the suite towards the main entry where the two dead security officers lay.

* * *

Andriy wiped the streaming blood and ocular fluid from his haemorrhaging eyeball and tried to regain some sense of consciousness quickly.

"I've got to kill this guy—this little bastard—this garbage," he wailed as a way of letting himself know he could still go on.

From his one functional though bleeding eye, he could see a glimmer of his weapon on the floor. He had to get it and then shoot them in the hall. He had to run. He tried to get up, but when he pushed up with his dominant hand, a flood of unbearable pain shot through his body from the shattered wrist and he almost passed out. Again, he refocused. He limped to stand and pushed away some debris to grab the pistol, costing him more precious seconds. Then he turned and began stumbling as fast as possible towards the main door.

He knew they had to run through that entry point and if he moved quickly enough he could get Riley in the hallway. Then he could use the back stairwell for his escape. As he moved across the room, he could see the last blurry person heading out of the suite and, if he was lucky, it would be Sawyer. Right now, he really didn't care who it was; somebody was going to die.

* * *

David and Danielle were first into the hallway, hurdling one body and bouncing off the opposite wall, then turning towards the main elevators.

Riley was sick as he looked down at the lifeless bodies by the door, but the rumbling behind him and the glimpse he caught of the killer rising from the rubble of the bedroom area let him know he was not out of danger. He burst through the suite's doorway and then, without looking, tripped over Jason's motionless corpse. The force of his fall threw him sideways and his head crashed heavily into a decorative marble table holding a Grecian vase that was positioned in the hall. The velocity of the blow left him dazed and bleeding, but he still had the sense to know he had to get up. In the distance, he could hear David shouting instructions as the hallway spun around him.

"Riley, get up! C'mon! We need to go. God, please c'mon. Danielle, get out of here! Just go!"

Riley tried to get up but the pain in his head throbbed and he could not focus his eyes. He tried desperately to stand and then stumbled again over the dead body. The best he could manage was to start crawling as fast as he could down the hall, but he was moving so slowly. He tried again in vain to get to his feet.

"Oh God, help us," moaned David as he began running back toward his injured friend. "Riley, get up. Can you hear me? We need to go." David bent over his injured friend and hoisted him to his feet.

As he pulled Riley along about 20 feet, an ominous dark figure emerged from the penthouse and, behind the streams of blood that covered his face, there came a large, crooked smile. He was unsteady and wavering, but there was no mistaking the large silencer and the semi-automatic machine pistol he was holding.

"Bonus time," said the killer as he focused on the two young men trying to get away. "Die, you little bastards," he yelled as he tried to steady the pistol, using the forearm of his shooting hand as an arc for the weapon.

Riley stared at the barrel of the gun and suddenly a sense of calm came over him. He was about to die, but at least he'd fought back. He had faced one of the murderous bastards that had tormented him for so long and while he had not won—he had given him one hell of a fight. Hopefully, he would not kill his friends. "David, run! Get out of here." Riley looked at the assassin. "Go ahead, you lousy motherfucker and kill me. You win." He closed his eyes, fell to his knees and waited for the pain.

Spits of bullets sprayed the walls around him, but they seemed far away or higher up. The powerful kick of the heavy machine pistol in the killer's off hand, combined with his significant visual impairment, made aiming and holding the gun steady extremely difficult, and shooting straight was therefore impossible. The killer slumped against the doorway in an attempt to correct his bead on Riley and prepared to fire again.

David screamed, "No, Riley! No!"

A single, loud crack pierced the hallway. A different sound than the rapid fire bursts of the machine pistol. A red dot simultaneously appeared in the forehead of the big Russian and grew quickly as the killer slumped to his knees and then dropped, dead, face first onto the hallway floor.

The crouching figure of Ozzie Stark appeared in the shadows at the opposite end of the hall by the stairwell. A second insurance shot rang out and pierced the lifeless heap. And finally, silence.

David froze. "Oh no. Another killer? Please don't be another killer."

"Police. Don't you move a muscle or you're dead."

"Stark, it's me, Sawyer. Stone's with me; don't shoot him. For God's sake don't shoot him," Riley begged deliriously, looking up from the floor.

David's arms shot into the air as sounds of sirens echoed outside and stampeding SWAT officers converged from every direction. Maybe, just maybe, this terrible ordeal was now over.

Riley placed his hand on the wall and tried to pull himself to his feet.

Ozzie rushed over, kicked at the dead Russian to see if there was a response, and then helped the young man up. "Kid, you may have just saved yourself and a whole lot of other good people here tonight. Nice job. You alright?"

"No. No, Ozzie, I'm not alright. I'm just so exhausted and my head is killing me. I can't see very well and I'm just so tired of being scared all the time. I just want everything to be over now, you know? Just make this all be over."

"Yeah, I know, kid. And I think maybe you can relax a bit now. Man, you two really did a number on this guy."

* * *

Ozzie stared at the carnage of the two dead security men. Brave souls that had given their life to protect another. It was their job.

What a fucked up world we live in, Ozzie thought, shaking his head as he stepped across one of the corpses towards David, still standing in shock, his hands raised in the air. "Ozzie Stark, NYPD. You can put your hands down now," the detective chuckled as he reached his hand out to Stone.

Stone took the hand and shook it. "Thanks. Thanks for saving us."

"You know, you should have kept running. You just about gave him another notch on his belt trying to save Sawyer. That was a stupid move."

"I couldn't leave him, sir. I couldn't leave Riley. We were so close to being in the clear. I just couldn't let it end there, not like that. What would you have done?"

"Probably the same idiotic thing. But, you two bozos are both just dumb lucky. And tomorrow you're going to be the biggest news on the planet. Like I said, what a fucked up world we live in."

Danielle quickly ran around the corner of the hall, a terrified look on her face, followed by a phalanx of uniformed police officers and EMT's.

"And, of course, you would be here." Ozzie said, shaking his head as Danielle stopped just short of him. "Is this story big enough for you?" he smirked as he looked into Danielle's red, swollen eyes.

From behind the tears and terror, Danielle smiled weakly but did not speak. She just reached out to Ozzie and hugged him.

"What, no questions?" Ozzie choked up. "I'm glad you're safe. You're certifiably nuts, but I may have just got to like you a bit over the past few months."

Danielle pulled back and stared at the exhausted-looking detective, sort of the way a sister and older brother come together after a family tragedy. "Thank you, Stark. Thank you for being here. Thank you for not giving up on this. Thank you for being, well, a really great cop. Just thank you."

"Yeah, whatever, go over and see how that mutt of a boyfriend of yours is doing, and the superstar. Those two louts are lucky to still be around. I'll tell ya, they've got an army of angels watching over them. All in all, they had a pretty good day. We all did."

Danielle moved over and pushed herself into David's arms and then reached out and pulled Riley into a group hug. Around the trio, scores of law enforcement agents, emergency workers and firemen were moving up and down the hallway, clearing areas and setting up perimeters.

Ozzie pulled out his cell phone and called his New York precinct. "Get me the Captain, please." For the first time, Ozzie noticed his heart was still pounding and beads of sweat were pouring down his forehead. It was a humid night in Miami, but certainly not hot enough to soak his clothes and brow like this. *This is what real fear feels and looks like*, he thought to himself.

The captain came on the line.

"Hey, Captain, it's Stark. We got the shooter down here. Looks like Odessa's top gun and he's dead. You need to go and get that pig, Tsarnov, fast, before he finds out the kid's still alive and goes into the wind. Trust me, we can build a case from here. I've got the hitter's phone, and it's full of text and phone messages. Tsarnov's filthy hands are all over this assassination attempt and I think the kid, with the help and resources he's going to have around him, will be happy to testify and put him away. Then we'll rip down the rest of his crew and operations. I'm guessing he's waiting by the phone right now for a call from this piece of trash, so get him quick. Every second counts."

"That's great, Oz. Are you okay?"

"Always okay, boss. Tired, sweaty and underpaid, but always okay."

"I'll get SWAT and the organized crime team on Tsarnov as soon as I get a warrant. Should be within the half hour. Great job, Ozzie. Be safe and get home. We kind of miss your surly puss around here and Fergus is developing a detachment disorder."

"Thanks boss. I'll be home Monday." With that, Stark clicked the button and a quick flash disconnected him.

"Looks like you guys were busy."

Ozzie turned and saw Damian Dirk approaching him, clutching a few evidence bags and his side arm.

"Probably a little more action than any of us needed." The New York detective smiled back weakly before stretching his hand toward the Florida cop. "Certainly for those two. By the way, great job at the club, Detective. Without you, this piece of shit might have offed our boy tonight. Glad I got here when I did and that wouldn't have been possible without your help. I appreciate it. You saved lives tonight."

"Thanks, Oz. I'll look you up if I ever get to New York."

"Yeah, you make sure to do that. And look after that arm."

The two shook hands and Damian quickly moved past Ozzie toward the dead assassin to begin analyzing and bagging the mountains of evidence strewn across the floor, in the suite and down the hall.

"Jesus, this guy's a mess. You two did this to him?" Damian chided David and Riley, finding it hard to believe two amateurs could inflict so much physical damage on a trained paramilitary assassin. "I'm glad I don't have to face you guys on the ice." The Miami detective laughed as he reached for a number of shell casings strewn randomly around the assassin's body.

Ozzie picked up a chair, sat down and exhaled a deep breath. When he looked up, Danielle was walking toward him again.

"You look so tired," she quipped as she wiped away some sweat from his cheek.

Ozzie chuckled. "Looks like you, missy, are going to have the story of the century. And, that's good. You deserve it. You're very good at what you do and when people like us try to put you in your place, don't ever let them. Because we're always hiding something—always."

"I know. And, I knew you were. But I never thought it was this. I had no idea. This is a little too real for me. I think I'll stick to sports reporting. Anyway, I just wanted to say thank you again from David, Riley and me for everything. Especially tonight."

"My pleasure, Miss Wright."

"Anything you'd like to add for my story?"

"Yeah, I'll never watch another Detroit hockey game again. Rangers all the way, baby."

Danielle smiled softly. "Got it, and I'll quote that word for word. Goodbye, Ozzie."

Ozzie watched as Riley, David and Danielle were escorted by Red Wings team security and some EMT's toward the elevators. Except for a quick shoulder glance and subtle nod, nothing more transpired between the crusty New York detective and Riley Sawyer.

Ozzie calmly holstered his service revolver, turned and moved toward the stairwell. The same unappreciated exit that had allowed him to get the drop on Andriy would now serve as his low profile escape from the chaos engulfing the Excelsior Hotel.

"Time to get some sleep," he whispered as he pulled up his jacket collar and almost imperceptibly strode past the legion of police cars, flashing lights and reporters that had descended on the building. He would meet with local police in the morning and then head home to help in the interrogation of Alexi Tsarnov. Or so he hoped.

Chapter 37

"Sawyer turns and gets open in the slot, quick feed from Stone. He shoots, he scores," came the enthusiastic play-by-play of the colour man for NBC's Game of the Week telecast. "Sawyer, an incredible move in front of the net, and it's another goal, giving him three on the night. This guy is on fire. This is the player Detroit expected when they made him the first overall pick this year."

"Yes, it is," stated another game analyst in the booth. "And, throw in the incredible season David Stone is having and the emergence of Darcy Hilton as a legitimate power forward and you have the makings of a play-off line-up for years to come."

High in the press box, furiously hammering away on her laptop keyboard, Danielle was putting the finishing touches on her game story. She could hardly wait to finish the column so she could get home and pack for her first trip to Saskatchewan with David over the Christmas holidays.

". . . After the traumatic events in Miami, where the lives of Riley Sawyer and David Stone nearly vanished like a poorly executed two-on-one, Detroit has apparently found a new wind beneath their Red Wings in the form of said Sawyer, Stone and Hilton. It's a spirit that's lifting them to unimagined heights from just a few weeks ago.

The bond of comradery and commitment to each other that was forged through that terrible night has brought this team together in a way rarely seen in professional sports. They're not playing any longer for the fame or the money or maybe even the Stanley Cup—they're playing for each other. A band of brothers brought together by an organization to achieve a dream, but galvanized to greatness by a threat to one of their own. This is truly what great sport is all about."

With the final words of her article complete, she reviewed the passage again with satisfaction and hit send.

* * *

"Hey, Ozzie. Sawyer just got his third to bury the Rangers,

that little prick."

Ozzie, sitting at his worn desk, surrounded by those stale green walls, just shook his head and stared at the mounds of paperwork in front of him. "Good for you, kid. Good for you."

About the Author
Jim Malner

Jim is a new author focused on writing dynamic action adventure novels using professional sports as the setting for his heroes' dramatic adventures.

A professional advertising copywriter, with over 30 years of experience in the competitive world of communications, Jim brings his unique humour, writing style and love of sports and intrigue novels together in one heart-pounding, edge-of-your-seat literary journey for his readers.

Jim's greatest wish is that you enjoy this novel, let your mind escape for a few hours into a great story with great characters, and when it's over feel satisfied you experienced a truly unique adventure.

Made in the USA
Middletown, DE
16 June 2019